S0-AWF-445

THE TRIALS OF APOLLO

◄ 1 ►

THE HIDDEN ORACLE

Also by Rick Riordan

Percy Jackson and the Olympians
Book One: *The Lightning Thief*
Book Two: *The Sea of Monsters*
Book Three: *The Titan's Curse*
Book Four: *The Battle of the Labyrinth*
Book Five: *The Last Olympian*
The Demigod Files
The Lightning Thief: The Graphic Novel
The Sea of Monsters: The Graphic Novel
The Titan's Curse: The Graphic Novel
The Battle of the Labyrinth: The Graphic Novel
The Last Olympian: The Graphic Novel
Percy Jackson's Greek Gods
Percy Jackson's Greek Heroes

The Kane Chronicles
Book One: *The Red Pyramid*
Book Two: *The Throne of Fire*
Book Three: *The Serpent's Shadow*
The Red Pyramid: The Graphic Novel
The Throne of Fire: The Graphic Novel
The Serpent's Shadow: The Graphic Novel

The Heroes of Olympus
Book One: *The Lost Hero*
Book Two: *The Son of Neptune*
Book Three: *The Mark of Athena*
Book Four: *The House of Hades*
Book Five: *The Blood of Olympus*
The Demigod Diaries
The Lost Hero: The Graphic Novel
The Son of Neptune: The Graphic Novel
Demigods & Magicians

Magnus Chase and the Gods of Asgard
Book One: *The Sword of Summer*
Book Two: *The Hammer of Thor*
Book Three: *The Ship of the Dead*

The Trials of Apollo
Book One: *The Hidden Oracle*
Book Two: *The Dark Prophecy*
Book Three: *The Burning Maze*
Book Four: *The Tyrant's Tomb*

Riordan, Rick, author.
Hidden oracle

2016
33305249307012
gi   02/05/21

RDAN

THE TRIALS OF
APOLLO

◄ 1 ►

THE HIDDEN ORACLE

𝕯𝖎𝖘𝖓𝖊𝖞 • HYPERION
Los Angeles   New York

If you purchased this book without a cover, you should be aware that this book is stolen property. It was reported as "unsold and destroyed" to the publisher, and neither the author nor the publisher has received any payment for this "stripped" book.

Copyright © 2016 by Rick Riordan

All rights reserved. Published by Disney • Hyperion, an imprint of Disney Book Group. No part of this book may be reproduced or transmitted in any form or by any means, electronic or mechanical, including photocopying, recording, or by any information storage and retrieval system, without written permission from the publisher. For information address Disney • Hyperion, 125 West End Avenue, New York, New York 10023.

First Hardcover Edition, May 2016
First Paperback Edition, October 2017

"Percy Jackson and the Singer of Apollo" was first published in a short story anthology, *Guys Read: Other Worlds*, edited by Jon Scieszka, published by HarperCollins in September 2013

Map illustration by Kayley LeFavier

SUSTAINABLE FORESTRY INITIATIVE

Certified Chain of Custody
Promoting Sustainable Forestry

www.sfiprogram.org
SFI-01054

The SFI label applies to the text stock

10 9 8
FAC-025438-19354
Printed in the United States of America

This book is set in Danton, Gauthier FY/Fontspring; Goudy, Goudy Oldstyle, Sabon/Monotype

Library of Congress Control Number for Hardcover Edition: 2015045235
ISBN 978-1-4847-4641-7

Visit www.DisneyBooks.com

To the Muse Calliope
This is long overdue. Please don't hurt me.

1

Hoodlums punch my face
I would smite them if I could
Mortality blows

MY NAME IS APOLLO. I used to be a god.

In my four thousand six hundred and twelve years, I have done many things. I inflicted a plague on the Greeks who besieged Troy. I blessed Babe Ruth with three home runs in game four of the 1926 World Series. I visited my wrath upon Britney Spears at the 2007 MTV Video Music Awards.

But in all my immortal life, I never before crash-landed in a Dumpster.

I'm not even sure how it happened.

I simply woke up falling. Skyscrapers spiraled in and out of view. Flames streamed off my body. I tried to fly. I tried to change into a cloud or teleport across the world or do a hundred other things that should have been easy for me, but I just kept falling. I plunged into a narrow canyon between two buildings and *BAM!*

Is anything sadder than the sound of a god hitting a pile of garbage bags?

I lay groaning and aching in the open Dumpster. My nostrils burned with the stench of rancid bologna and used diapers. My ribs felt broken, though that shouldn't have been possible.

My mind stewed in confusion, but one memory floated to the surface—the voice of my father, Zeus: *YOUR FAULT. YOUR PUNISHMENT.*

I realized what had happened to me. And I sobbed in despair.

Even for a god of poetry such as myself, it is difficult to describe how I felt. How could you—a mere mortal—possibly understand? Imagine being stripped of your clothes, then blasted with a fire hose in front of a laughing crowd. Imagine the ice-cold water filling your mouth and lungs, the pressure bruising your skin, turning your joints to putty. Imagine feeling helpless, ashamed, completely vulnerable—publicly and brutally stripped of everything that makes you *you*. My humiliation was worse than that.

YOUR FAULT, Zeus's voice rang in my head.

"No!" I cried miserably. "No, it wasn't! Please!"

Nobody answered. On either side of me, rusty fire escapes zigzagged up brick walls. Above, the winter sky was gray and unforgiving.

I tried to remember the details of my sentencing. Had my father told me how long this punishment would last? What was I supposed to do to regain his favor?

My memory was too fuzzy. I could barely recall what Zeus looked like, much less why he'd decided to toss me to earth. There'd been a war with the giants, I thought. The gods had been caught off guard, embarrassed, almost defeated.

The only thing I knew for certain: my punishment was

unfair. Zeus needed someone to blame, so of course he'd picked the handsomest, most talented, most popular god in the pantheon: me.

I lay in the garbage, staring at the label inside the Dumpster lid: FOR PICK-UP, CALL 1-555-STENCHY.

Zeus will reconsider, I told myself. *He's just trying to scare me. Any moment, he will yank me back to Olympus and let me off with a warning.*

"Yes . . ." My voice sounded hollow and desperate. "Yes, that's it."

I tried to move. I wanted to be on my feet when Zeus came to apologize. My ribs throbbed. My stomach clenched. I clawed the rim of the Dumpster and managed to drag myself over the side. I toppled out and landed on my shoulder, which made a cracking sound against the asphalt.

"*Araggeeddeee*," I whimpered through the pain. "Stand up. Stand up."

Getting to my feet was not easy. My head spun. I almost passed out from the effort. I stood in a dead-end alley. About fifty feet away, the only exit opened onto a street with grimy storefronts for a bail bondsman's office and a pawnshop. I was somewhere on the west side of Manhattan, I guessed, or perhaps Crown Heights, in Brooklyn. Zeus must have been really angry with me.

I inspected my new body. I appeared to be a teenaged Caucasian male, clad in sneakers, blue jeans, and a green polo shirt. How utterly *drab*. I felt sick, weak, and so, so human.

I will never understand how you mortals tolerate it. You live your entire life trapped in a sack of meat, unable to enjoy simple pleasures like changing into a hummingbird or dissolving into pure light.

And now, heavens help me, I was one of you—just another meat sack.

I fumbled through my pants pockets, hoping I still had the keys to my sun chariot. No such luck. I found a cheap nylon wallet containing a hundred dollars in American currency—lunch money for my first day as a mortal, perhaps—along with a New York State junior driver's license featuring a photo of a dorky, curly-haired teen who could not possibly be me, with the name *Lester Papadopoulos*. The cruelty of Zeus knew no bounds!

I peered into the Dumpster, hoping my bow, quiver, and lyre might have fallen to earth with me. I would have settled for my harmonica. There was nothing.

I took a deep breath. *Cheer up*, I told myself. *I must have retained some of my godly abilities. Matters could be worse.*

A raspy voice called, "Hey, Cade, take a look at this loser."

Blocking the alley's exit were two young men: one squat and platinum blond, the other tall and redheaded. Both wore oversize hoodies and baggy pants. Serpentine tattoo designs covered their necks. All they were missing were the words I'M A THUG printed in large letters across their foreheads.

The redhead zeroed in on the wallet in my hand. "Now, be nice, Mikey. This guy looks friendly enough." He grinned and pulled a hunting knife from his belt. "In fact, I bet he wants to give us all his money."

———

I blame my disorientation for what happened next.

I knew my immortality had been stripped away, but I still considered myself the mighty Apollo! One cannot change one's way of thinking as easily as one might, say, turn into a snow leopard.

Also, on previous occasions when Zeus had punished me by making me mortal (yes, it had happened twice before), I had retained massive strength and at least some of my godly powers. I assumed the same would be true now.

I was *not* going to allow two young mortal ruffians to take Lester Papadopoulos's wallet.

I stood up straight, hoping Cade and Mikey would be intimidated by my regal bearing and divine beauty. (Surely those qualities could not be taken from me, no matter what my driver's license photo looked like.) I ignored the warm Dumpster juice trickling down my neck.

"I am Apollo," I announced. "You mortals have three choices: offer me tribute, flee, or be destroyed."

I wanted my words to echo through the alley, shake the towers of New York, and cause the skies to rain smoking ruin. None of that happened. On the word *destroyed*, my voice squeaked.

The redhead Cade grinned even wider. I thought how amusing it would be if I could make the snake tattoos around his neck come alive and strangle him to death.

"What do you think, Mikey?" he asked his friend. "Should we give this guy tribute?"

Mikey scowled. With his bristly blond hair, his cruel small eyes, and his thick frame, he reminded me of the monstrous sow that terrorized the village of Crommyon back in the good old days.

"Not feeling the tribute, Cade." His voice sounded like he'd been eating lit cigarettes. "What were the other options?"

"Fleeing?" said Cade.

"Nah," said Mikey.

"Being destroyed?"

Mikey snorted. "How about we destroy *him* instead?"

Cade flipped his knife and caught it by the handle. "I can live with that. After you."

I slipped the wallet into my back pocket. I raised my fists. I did not like the idea of flattening mortals into flesh waffles, but I was sure I could do it. Even in my weakened state, I would be far stronger than any human.

"I warned you," I said. "My powers are far beyond your comprehension."

Mikey cracked his knuckles. "Uh-huh."

He lumbered forward.

As soon as he was in range, I struck. I put all my wrath into that punch. It should have been enough to vaporize Mikey and leave a thug-shaped impression on the asphalt.

Instead he ducked, which I found quite annoying.

I stumbled forward. I have to say that when Prometheus fashioned you humans out of clay he did a shoddy job. Mortal legs are clumsy. I tried to compensate, drawing upon my boundless reserves of agility, but Mikey kicked me in the back. I fell on my divine face.

My nostrils inflated like air bags. My ears popped. The

taste of copper filled my mouth. I rolled over, groaning, and found the two blurry thugs staring down at me.

"Mikey," said Cade, "are you comprehending this guy's power?"

"Nah," said Mikey. "I'm not comprehending it."

"Fools!" I croaked. "I will destroy you!"

"Yeah, sure." Cade tossed away his knife. "But first I think we'll stomp you."

Cade raised his boot over my face, and the world went black.

2

A girl from nowhere
Completes my embarrassment
Stupid bananas

I HAD NOT BEEN STOMPED so badly since my guitar contest against Chuck Berry in 1957.

As Cade and Mikey kicked me, I curled into a ball, trying to protect my ribs and head. The pain was intolerable. I retched and shuddered. I blacked out and came to, my vision swimming with red splotches. When my attackers got tired of kicking me, they hit me over the head with a bag of garbage, which burst and covered me in coffee grounds and moldy fruit peels.

At last they stepped away, breathing heavily. Rough hands patted me down and took my wallet.

"Lookee here," said Cade. "Some cash and an ID for . . . Lester Papadopoulos."

Mikey laughed. "*Lester?* That's even worse than Apollo."

I touched my nose, which felt roughly the size and texture of a water-bed mattress. My fingers came away glistening red.

"Blood," I muttered. "That's not possible."

"It's very possible, Lester." Cade crouched next to me. "And there might be more blood in your near future. You want to explain why you don't have a credit card? Or a phone? I'd hate to think I did all that stomping for just a hundred bucks."

I stared at the blood on my fingertips. I was a god. I did not *have* blood. Even when I'd been turned mortal before, golden ichor still ran through my veins. I had never before been so . . . *converted*. It must be a mistake. A trick. Something.

I tried to sit up.

My hand hit a banana peel and I fell again. My attackers howled in delight.

"I love this guy!" Mikey said.

"Yeah, but the boss told us he'd be loaded," Cade complained.

"Boss . . ." I muttered. "Boss?"

"That's right, Lester." Cade flicked a finger against the side of my head. "'Go to that alley,' the boss told us. 'Easy score.' He said we should rough you up, take whatever you had. But this"—he waved the cash under my nose—"this isn't much of a payday."

Despite my predicament, I felt a surge of hopefulness. If these thugs had been sent here to find me, their "boss" must be a god. No mortal could have known I would fall to earth at this spot. Perhaps Cade and Mikey were not human either. Perhaps they were cleverly disguised monsters or spirits. At least that would explain why they had beaten me so easily.

"Who—who is your boss?" I struggled to my feet, coffee grounds dribbling from my shoulders. My dizziness made me feel as if I were flying too close to the fumes of primordial

Chaos, but I refused to be humbled. "Did Zeus send you? Or perhaps Ares? I demand an audience!"

Mikey and Cade looked at each other as if to say, *Can you believe this guy?*

Cade picked up his knife. "You don't take a hint, do you, Lester?"

Mikey pulled off his belt—a length of bike chain—and wrapped it around his fist.

I decided to sing them into submission. They may have resisted my fists, but no mortal could resist my golden voice. I was trying to decide between "You Send Me" and an original composition, "I'm Your Poetry God, Baby," when a voice yelled, "HEY!"

The hooligans turned. Above us, on the second-story fire escape landing, stood a girl of about twelve. "Leave him alone," she ordered.

My first thought was that Artemis had come to my aid. My sister often appeared as a twelve-year-old girl for reasons I'd never fully understood. But something told me this was not she.

The girl on the fire escape did not exactly inspire fear. She was small and pudgy, with dark hair chopped in a messy pageboy style and black cat-eye glasses with rhinestones glittering in the corners. Despite the cold, she wore no coat. Her outfit looked like it had been picked by a kindergartener—red sneakers, yellow tights, and a green tank dress. Perhaps she was on her way to a costume party dressed as a traffic light.

Still . . . there was something fierce in her expression.

She had the same obstinate scowl my old girlfriend Cyrene used to get whenever she wrestled lions.

Mikey and Cade did not seem impressed.

"Get lost, kid," Mikey told her.

The girl stamped her foot, causing the fire escape to shudder. "My alley. My rules!" Her bossy nasal voice made her sound like she was chiding a playmate in a game of make-believe. "Whatever that loser has is mine, including his money!"

"Why is everyone calling me a loser?" I asked weakly. The comment seemed unfair, even if I was beat-up and covered in garbage; but no one paid me any attention.

Cade glared at the girl. The red from his hair seemed to be seeping into his face. "You've got to be kidding me. Beat it, you brat!" He picked up a rotten apple and threw it.

The girl didn't flinch. The fruit landed at her feet and rolled harmlessly to a stop.

"You want to play with food?" The girl wiped her nose. "Okay."

I didn't see her kick the apple, but it came flying back with deadly accuracy and hit Cade in the nose. He collapsed on his rump.

Mikey snarled. He marched toward the fire escape ladder, but a banana peel seemed to slither directly into his path. He slipped and fell hard. "OWWW!"

I backed away from the fallen thugs. I wondered if I should make a run for it, but I could barely hobble. I also did not want to be assaulted with old fruit.

The girl climbed over the railing. She dropped to the

ground with surprising nimbleness and grabbed a sack of garbage from the Dumpster.

"Stop!" Cade did a sort of scuttling crab walk to get away from the girl. "Let's talk about this!"

Mikey groaned and rolled onto his back.

The girl pouted. Her lips were chapped. She had wispy black fuzz at the corners of her mouth.

"I don't like you guys," she said. "You should go."

"Yeah!" Cade said. "Sure! Just . . ."

He reached for the money scattered among the coffee grounds.

The girl swung her garbage bag. In mid arc the plastic exploded, disgorging an impossible number of rotten bananas. They knocked Cade flat. Mikey was plastered with so many peels he looked like he was being attacked by carnivorous starfish.

"Leave my alley," the girl said. "Now."

In the Dumpster, more trash bags burst like popcorn kernels, showering Cade and Mikey with radishes, potato peelings, and other compost material. Miraculously, none of it got on me. Despite their injuries, the two thugs scrambled to their feet and ran away, screaming.

I turned toward my pint-size savior. I was no stranger to dangerous women. My sister could rain down arrows of death. My stepmother, Hera, regularly drove mortals mad so that they would hack each other to pieces. But this garbage-wielding twelve-year-old made me nervous.

"Thank you," I ventured.

The girl crossed her arms. On her middle fingers she wore matching gold rings with crescent signets. Her eyes glinted darkly like a crow's. (I can make that comparison because I invented crows.)

"Don't thank me," she said. "You're still in my alley."

She walked a full circle around me, scrutinizing my appearance as if I were a prize cow. (I can also make that comparison, because I used to collect prize cows.)

"You're the god Apollo?" She sounded less than awe-struck. She also didn't seem fazed by the idea of gods walking among mortals.

"You were listening, then?"

She nodded. "You don't look like a god."

"I'm not at my best," I admitted. "My father, Zeus, has exiled me from Olympus. And who are you?"

She smelled faintly of apple pie, which was surprising, since she looked so grubby. Part of me wanted to find a fresh towel, clean her face, and give her money for a hot meal. Part of me wanted to fend her off with a chair in case she decided to bite me. She reminded me of the strays my sister was always adopting: dogs, panthers, homeless maidens, small dragons.

"Name is Meg," she said.

"Short for Megara? Or Margaret?"

"Margaret. But don't ever call me Margaret."

"And are you a demigod, Meg?"

She pushed up her glasses. "Why would you think that?"

Again she didn't seem surprised by the question. I sensed she had heard the term *demigod* before.

"Well," I said, "you obviously have some power. You chased off those hooligans with rotten fruit. Perhaps you have banana-kinesis? Or you can control garbage? I once knew a Roman goddess, Cloacina, who presided over the city's sewer system. Perhaps you're related . . . ?"

Meg pouted. I got the impression I might have said something wrong, though I couldn't imagine what.

"I think I'll just take your money," Meg said. "Go on. Get out of here."

"No, wait!" Desperation crept into my voice. "Please, I—I may need a bit of assistance."

I felt ridiculous, of course. Me—the god of prophecy, plague, archery, healing, music, and several other things I couldn't remember at the moment—asking a colorfully dressed street urchin for help. But I had no one else. If this child chose to take my money and kick me into the cruel winter streets, I didn't think I could stop her.

"Say I believe you . . ." Meg's voice took on a singsong tone, as if she were about to announce the rules of the game: *I'll be the princess, and you'll be the scullery maid.* "Say I decide to help. What then?"

Good question, I thought. "We . . . we are in Manhattan?"

"Mm-hmm." She twirled and did a playful skip-kick. "Hell's Kitchen."

It seemed wrong for a child to say *Hell's Kitchen.* Then again, it seemed wrong for a child to live in an alley and have garbage fights with thugs.

I considered walking to the Empire State Building. That was the modern gateway to Mount Olympus, but I doubted the guards would let me up to the secret six hundredth floor. Zeus would not make it so easy.

Perhaps I could find my old friend Chiron the centaur. He had a training camp on Long Island. He could offer me shelter and guidance. But that would be a dangerous journey. A defenseless god makes for a juicy target. Any monster along the way would cheerfully disembowel me. Jealous spirits and minor gods might also welcome the opportunity. Then there was Cade and Mikey's mysterious "boss." I had no idea who he was, or whether he had other, worse minions to send against me.

Even if I made it to Long Island, my new mortal eyes might not be able to *find* Chiron's camp in its magically camouflaged valley. I needed a guide to get me there—someone experienced and close by. . . .

"I have an idea." I stood as straight as my injuries allowed. It wasn't easy to look confident with a bloody nose and coffee grounds dripping off my clothes. "I know someone who might help. He lives on the Upper East Side. Take me to him, and I shall reward you."

Meg made a sound between a sneeze and a laugh. "Reward me with what?" She danced around, plucking twenty-dollar bills from the trash. "I'm already taking all your money."

"Hey!"

She tossed me my wallet, now empty except for Lester Papadopoulos's junior driver's license.

Meg sang, "I've got your money, I've got your money."

I stifled a growl. "Listen, child, I won't be mortal forever. Someday I will become a god again. Then I will reward those who helped me—and punish those who didn't."

She put her hands on her hips. "How do *you* know what will happen? Have you ever been mortal before?"

"Yes, actually. Twice! Both times, my punishment only lasted a few years at most!"

"Oh, yeah? And how did you get back to being all goddy or whatever?"

"*Goddy* is not a word," I pointed out, though my poetic sensibilities were already thinking of ways I might use it. "Usually Zeus requires me to work as a slave for some important demigod. This fellow uptown I mentioned, for instance. He'd be perfect! I do whatever tasks my new master requires for a few years. As long as I behave, I am allowed back to Olympus. Right now I just have to recover my strength and figure out—"

"How do you know for sure which demigod?"

I blinked. "What?"

"Which demigod you're supposed to serve, dummy."

"I . . . uh. Well, it's usually obvious. I just sort of run into them. That's why I want to get to the Upper East Side. My new master will claim my service and—"

"I'm Meg McCaffrey!" Meg blew me a raspberry. "And I claim your service!"

Overhead, thunder rumbled in the gray sky. The sound echoed through the city canyons like divine laughter.

Whatever was left of my pride turned to ice water and trickled into my socks. "I walked right into that, didn't I?"

"Yep!" Meg bounced up and down in her red sneakers. "We're going to have fun!"

With great difficulty, I resisted the urge to weep. "Are you sure you're not Artemis in disguise?"

"I'm that other thing," Meg said, counting my money. "The thing you said before. A demigod."

"How do you know?"

"Just do." She gave me a smug smile. "And now I have a sidekick god named Lester!"

I raised my face to the heavens. "Please, Father, I get the point. Please, I can't do this!"

Zeus did not answer. He was probably too busy recording my humiliation to share on Snapchat.

"Cheer up," Meg told me. "Who's that guy you wanted to see—the guy on the Upper East Side?"

"Another demigod," I said. "He knows the way to a camp where I might find shelter, guidance, food—"

"Food?" Meg's ears perked up almost as much as the points on her glasses. "*Good* food?"

"Well, normally I just eat ambrosia, but, yes, I suppose."

"Then that's my first order! We're going to find this guy to take us to the camp place!"

I sighed miserably. It was going to be a very long servitude.

"As you wish," I said. "Let's find Percy Jackson."

3

Used to be goddy
Now uptown feeling shoddy
Bah, haiku don't rhyme

AS WE TRUDGED up Madison Avenue, my mind swirled with questions: Why hadn't Zeus given me a winter coat? Why did Percy Jackson live so far uptown? Why did pedestrians keep staring at me?

I wondered if my divine radiance was starting to return. Perhaps the New Yorkers were awed by my obvious power and unearthly good looks.

Meg McCaffrey set me straight.

"You smell," she said. "You look like you've just been mugged."

"I *have* just been mugged. Also enslaved by a small child."

"It's not slavery." She chewed off a piece of her thumb cuticle and spit it out. "It's more like mutual cooperation."

"Mutual in the sense that you give orders and I am forced to cooperate?"

"Yep." She stopped in front of a storefront window. "See? You look gross."

My reflection stared back at me, except it was *not* my

reflection. It couldn't be. The face was the same as on Lester Papadopoulos's ID.

I looked about sixteen. My medium-length hair was dark and curly—a style I had rocked in Athenian times, and again in the 1970s. My eyes were blue. My face was pleasing enough in a dorkish way, but it was marred by a swollen eggplant-colored nose, which had dripped a gruesome mustache of blood down my upper lip. Even worse, my cheeks were covered with some sort of rash that looked suspiciously like . . . My heart climbed into my throat.

"Horrors!" I cried. "Is that— Is that *acne?*"

Immortal gods do not *get* acne. It is one of our inalienable rights. Yet I leaned closer to the glass and saw that my skin was indeed a scarred landscape of whiteheads and pustules.

I balled my fists and wailed to the cruel sky, "Zeus, what have I done to deserve this?"

Meg tugged at my sleeve. "You're going to get yourself arrested."

"What does it matter? I have been made a teenager, and not even one with perfect skin! I bet I don't even have . . ." With a cold sense of dread, I lifted my shirt. My midriff was covered with a floral pattern of bruises from my fall into the Dumpster and my subsequent kicking. But even worse, I had *flab.*

"Oh, no, no, no." I staggered around the sidewalk, hoping the flab would not follow me. "Where are my eight-pack abs? I *always* have eight-pack abs. I *never* have love handles. Never in four thousand years!"

Meg made another snorting laugh. "Sheesh, crybaby, you're fine."

"I'm fat!"

"You're average. Average people don't have eight-pack abs. C'mon."

I wanted to protest that I was not average *nor* a person, but with growing despair, I realized the term now fit me perfectly.

On the other side of the storefront window, a security guard's face loomed, scowling at me. I allowed Meg to pull me farther down the street.

She skipped along, occasionally stopping to pick up a coin or swing herself around a streetlamp. The child seemed unfazed by the cold weather, the dangerous journey ahead, and the fact that I was suffering from acne.

"How are you so calm?" I demanded. "You are a demigod, walking with a god, on your way to a camp to meet others of your kind. Doesn't any of that surprise you?"

"Eh." She folded one of my twenty-dollar bills into a paper airplane. "I've seen a bunch of weird stuff."

I was tempted to ask what could be weirder than the morning we had just had. I decided I might not be able to stand the stress of knowing. "Where are you from?"

"I told you. The alley."

"No, but . . . your parents? Family? Friends?"

A ripple of discomfort passed over her face. She returned her attention to her twenty-dollar airplane. "Not important."

My highly advanced people-reading skills told me she was hiding something, but that was not unusual for demigods. For children blessed with an immortal parent, they were strangely sensitive about their backgrounds. "And you've never heard of Camp Half-Blood? Or Camp Jupiter?"

"Nuh-uh." She tested the airplane's point on her fingertip. "How much farther to Perry's house?"

"Percy's. I'm not sure. A few more blocks . . . I think."

That seemed to satisfy Meg. She hopscotched ahead, throwing the cash airplane and retrieving it. She cartwheeled through the intersection at East Seventy-Second Street—her clothes a flurry of traffic-light colors so bright I worried the drivers might get confused and run her down. Fortunately, New York drivers were used to swerving around oblivious pedestrians.

I decided Meg must be a feral demigod. They were rare but not unheard of. Without any support network, without being discovered by other demigods or taken in for proper training, she had still managed to survive. But her luck would not last. Monsters usually began hunting down and killing young heroes around the time they turned thirteen, when their true powers began to manifest. Meg did not have long. She needed to be brought to Camp Half-Blood as much as I did. She was fortunate to have met me.

(I know that last statement seems obvious. *Everyone* who meets me is fortunate, but you take my meaning.)

Had I been my usual omniscient self, I could have gleaned Meg's destiny. I could have looked into her soul and seen all I needed to know about her godly parentage, her powers, her motives and secrets.

Now I was blind to such things. I could only be sure she was a demigod because she had successfully claimed my service. Zeus had affirmed her right with a clap of thunder. I felt the binding upon me like a shroud of tightly wrapped banana peels. Whoever Meg McCaffrey was, however she had happened to find me, our fates were now intertwined.

It was almost as embarrassing as the acne.

We turned east on Eighty-Second Street.

By the time we reached Second Avenue, the neighborhood started to look familiar—rows of apartment buildings, hardware shops, convenience stores, and Indian restaurants. I knew that Percy Jackson lived around here somewhere, but my trips across the sky in the sun chariot had given me something of a Google Earth orientation. I wasn't used to traveling at street level.

Also, in this mortal form, my flawless memory had become . . . flawed. Mortal fears and needs clouded my thoughts. I wanted to eat. I wanted to use the restroom. My body hurt. My clothes stank. I felt as if my brain had been stuffed with wet cotton. Honestly, how do you humans stand it?

After a few more blocks, a mixture of sleet and rain began to fall. Meg tried to catch the precipitation on her tongue, which I thought a very ineffective way to get a drink—and of dirty water, no less. I shivered and concentrated on happy thoughts: the Bahamas, the Nine Muses in perfect harmony, the many horrible punishments I would visit on Cade and Mikey when I became a god again.

I still wondered about their boss, and how he had known where I would fall to earth. No mortal could've had that knowledge. In fact, the more I thought about it, I didn't see how even a god (other than myself) could have foreseen the future so accurately. After all, I had been the god of prophecy, master of the Oracle of Delphi, distributor of the highest quality sneak previews of destiny for millennia.

Of course, I had no shortage of enemies. One of the natural consequences of being so awesome is that I attracted envy from all quarters. But I could only think of one adversary who might be able to tell the future. And if *he* came looking for me in my weakened state . . .

I tamped down that thought. I had enough to worry about. No point scaring myself to death with what-ifs.

We began searching side streets, checking names on apartment mailboxes and intercom panels. The Upper East Side had a surprising number of Jacksons. I found that annoying.

After several failed attempts, we turned a corner and there—parked under a crape myrtle—sat an older model blue Prius. Its hood bore the unmistakable dents of pegasus hooves. (How was I sure? I know my hoof marks. Also, normal horses do not gallop over Toyotas. Pegasi often do.)

"Aha," I told Meg. "We're getting close."

Half a block down, I recognized the building: a five-story brick row house with rusty air conditioner units sagging from the windows. *"Voilà!"* I cried.

At the front steps, Meg stopped as if she'd run into an invisible barrier. She stared back toward Second Avenue, her dark eyes turbulent.

"What's wrong?" I asked.

"Thought I saw them again."

"Them?" I followed her gaze but saw nothing unusual. "The thugs from the alley?"

"No. Couple of . . ." She waggled her fingers. "Shiny blobs. Saw them back on Park Avenue."

My pulse increased from an andante tempo to a lively allegretto. "Shiny blobs? Why didn't you say anything?"

She tapped the temples of her glasses. "I've seen a lot of weird stuff. Told you that. Mostly, things don't bother me, but . . ."

"But if they are following us," I said, "that would be bad."

I scanned the street again. I saw nothing amiss, but I didn't doubt Meg had seen shiny blobs. Many spirits could appear that way. My own father, Zeus, once took the form of a shiny blob to woo a mortal woman. (Why the mortal woman found that attractive, I have no idea.)

"We should get inside," I said. "Percy Jackson will help us."

Still, Meg held back. She had shown no fear while pelting muggers with garbage in a blind alley, but now she seemed to be having second thoughts about ringing a doorbell. It occurred to me she might have met demigods before. Perhaps those meetings had not gone well.

"Meg," I said, "I realize some demigods are not good. I could tell you stories of all the ones I've had to kill or transform into herbs—"

"Herbs?"

"But Percy Jackson has always been reliable. You have nothing to fear. Besides, he likes me. I taught him everything he knows."

She frowned. "You did?"

I found her innocence somewhat charming. So many obvious things she did not know. "Of course. Now let's go up."

I rang the buzzer. A few moments later, the garbled voice of a woman answered, "Yes?"

"Hello," I said. "This is Apollo."

Static.

"The *god* Apollo," I said, thinking perhaps I should be more specific. "Is Percy home?"

More static, followed by two voices in muted conversation. The front door buzzed. I pushed it open. Just before I stepped inside, I caught a flash of movement in the corner of my eye. I peered down the sidewalk but again saw nothing.

Perhaps it had been a reflection. Or a whirl of sleet. Or perhaps it had been a shiny blob. My scalp tingled with apprehension.

"What?" Meg asked.

"Probably nothing." I forced a cheerful tone. I did not want Meg bolting off when we were so close to reaching safety. We were bound together now. I would have to follow her if she ordered me to, and I did not fancy living in the alley with her forever. "Let's go up. We can't keep our hosts waiting."

After all I had done for Percy Jackson, I expected delight upon my arrival. A tearful welcome, a few burnt offerings, and a small festival in my honor would not have been inappropriate.

Instead, the young man swung open the apartment door and said, "Why?"

As usual, I was struck by his resemblance to his father, Poseidon. He had the same sea-green eyes, the same dark tousled hair, the same handsome features that could shift from humor to anger so easily. However, Percy Jackson did not favor his father's chosen garb of beach shorts and Hawaiian shirts. He was dressed in ragged jeans and a blue hoodie with the words AHS SWIM TEAM stitched across the front.

Meg inched back into the hallway, hiding behind me.

I tried for a smile. "Percy Jackson, my blessings upon you! I am in need of assistance."

Percy's eyes darted from me to Meg. "Who's your friend?"

"This is Meg McCaffrey," I said, "a demigod who must be taken to Camp Half-Blood. She rescued me from street thugs."

"Rescued . . ." Percy scanned my battered face. "You mean the 'beat-up teenager' look isn't just a disguise? Dude, what happened to you?"

"I may have mentioned the street thugs."

"But you're a god."

"About that . . . I *was* a god."

Percy blinked. *"Was?"*

"Also," I said, "I'm fairly certain we're being followed by malicious spirits."

If I didn't know how much Percy Jackson adored me, I would have sworn he was about to punch me in my already-broken nose.

He sighed. "Maybe you two should come inside."

4

Casa de Jackson
No gold-plated throne for guests
Seriously, dude?

ANOTHER THING I have never understood: How can you mortals live in such tiny places? Where is your pride? Your sense of style?

The Jackson apartment had no grand throne room, no colonnades, no terraces or banquet halls or even a thermal bath. It had a tiny living room with an attached kitchen and a single hallway leading to what I assumed were the bedrooms. The place was on the fifth floor, and while I wasn't so picky as to expect an elevator, I did find it odd there was no landing deck for flying chariots. What did they do when guests from the sky wanted to visit?

Standing behind the kitchen counter, making a smoothie, was a strikingly attractive mortal woman of about forty. Her long brown hair had a few gray streaks, but her bright eyes, quick smile, and festive tie-dyed sundress made her look younger.

As we entered, she turned off the blender and stepped out from behind the counter.

"Sacred Sibyl!" I cried. "Madam, there is something wrong with your midsection!"

The woman stopped, mystified, and looked down at her hugely swollen belly. "Well, I'm seven months pregnant."

I wanted to cry for her. Carrying such a weight didn't seem natural. My sister, Artemis, had experience with midwifery, but I had always found it one area of the healing arts best left to others. "How can you bear it?" I asked. "My mother, Leto, suffered through a long pregnancy, but only because Hera cursed her. Are you cursed?"

Percy stepped to my side. "Um, Apollo? She's not cursed. And can you not mention Hera?"

"You poor woman." I shook my head. "A goddess would never allow herself to be so encumbered. She would give birth as soon as she felt like it."

"That must be nice," the woman agreed.

Percy Jackson coughed. "So anyway. Mom, this is Apollo and his friend Meg. Guys, this is my mom."

The Mother of Jackson smiled and shook our hands. "Call me Sally."

Her eyes narrowed as she studied my busted nose. "Dear, that looks painful. What happened?"

I attempted to explain, but I choked on my words. I, the silver-tongued god of poetry, could not bring myself to describe my fall from grace to this kind woman.

I understood why Poseidon had been so smitten with her. Sally Jackson possessed just the right combination of compassion, strength, and beauty. She was one of those rare mortal women who could connect spiritually with a god as an equal—to be neither terrified of us nor greedy for what we can offer, but to provide us with true companionship.

If I had still been an immortal, I might have flirted

with her myself. But I was now a sixteen-year-old boy. My mortal form was working its way upon my state of mind. I saw Sally Jackson as a mom—a fact that both consternated and embarrassed me. I thought about how long it had been since I had called my own mother. I should probably take her to lunch when I got back to Olympus.

"I tell you what." Sally patted my shoulder. "Percy can help you get bandaged and cleaned up."

"I can?" asked Percy.

Sally gave him the slightest motherly eyebrow raise. "There's a first-aid kit in your bathroom, sweetheart. Apollo can take a shower, then wear your extra clothes. You two are about the same size."

"That," Percy said, "is truly depressing."

Sally cupped her hand under Meg's chin. Thankfully, Meg did not bite her. Sally's expression remained gentle and reassuring, but I could see the worry in her eyes. No doubt she was thinking, *Who dressed this poor girl like a traffic light?*

"I have some clothes that might fit you, dear," Sally said. "Pre-pregnancy clothes, of course. Let's get you cleaned up. Then we'll get you something to eat."

"I like food," Meg muttered.

Sally laughed. "Well, we have that in common. Percy, you take Apollo. We'll meet you back here in a while."

In short order, I was showered, bandaged, and dressed in Jacksonesque hand-me-downs. Percy left me alone in the bathroom to take care of all this myself, for which I was grateful. He offered me some ambrosia and nectar—food and drink of the gods—to heal my wounds, but I was not sure it would be safe to consume in my mortal state. I didn't want to self-combust, so I stuck with mortal first-aid supplies.

When I was done, I stared at my battered face in the bathroom mirror. Perhaps teenage angst had permeated the clothes, because I felt more like a sulky high schooler than ever. I thought how unfair it was that I was being punished, how lame my father was, how no one else in the history of time had ever experienced problems like mine.

Of course, all that was empirically true. No exaggeration was required.

At least my wounds seemed to be healing at a faster rate than a normal mortal's. The swelling in my nose had subsided. My ribs still ached, but I no longer felt as if someone were knitting a sweater inside my chest with hot needles.

Accelerated healing was the *least* Zeus could do for me. I was a god of medicinal arts, after all. Zeus probably just wanted me to get well quickly so I could endure more pain, but I was grateful nonetheless.

I wondered if I should start a small fire in Percy Jackson's sink, perhaps burn some bandages in thanks, but I decided that might strain the Jacksons' hospitality.

I examined the black T-shirt Percy had given me. Emblazoned on the front was Led Zeppelin's logo for their record label: winged Icarus falling from the sky. I had no problem with Led Zeppelin. I had inspired all their best songs. But I had a sneaking suspicion that Percy had given me this shirt as a joke—the fall from the sky. Yes, ha-ha. I didn't need to be a god of poetry to spot the metaphor. I decided not to comment on it. I wouldn't give him the satisfaction.

I took a deep breath. Then I did my usual motivational speech in the mirror: "You are gorgeous and people love you!"

I went out to face the world.

Percy was sitting on his bed, staring at the trail of blood droplets I had made across his carpet.

"Sorry about that," I said.

Percy spread his hands. "Actually, I was thinking about the last time I had a nosebleed."

"Oh . . ."

The memory came back to me, though hazy and incomplete. Athens. The Acropolis. We gods had battled side by side with Percy Jackson and his comrades. We defeated an army of giants, but a drop of Percy's blood hit the earth and awakened the Earth Mother Gaea, who had not been in a good mood.

That's when Zeus turned on me. He'd accused me of starting the whole thing, just because Gaea had duped one of my progeny, a boy named Octavian, into plunging the Roman and Greek demigod camps into a civil war that almost destroyed human civilization. I ask you: How was that my fault?

Regardless, Zeus had held *me* responsible for Octavian's delusions of grandeur. Zeus seemed to consider egotism a trait the boy had inherited from me. Which is ridiculous. I am much too self-aware to be egotistical.

"What happened to you, man?" Percy's voice stirred me from my reverie. "The war ended in August. It's January."

"It is?" I suppose the wintry weather should have been a clue, but I hadn't given it much thought.

"Last I saw you," Percy said, "Zeus was chewing you out at the Acropolis. Then *bam*—he vaporized you. Nobody's seen or heard from you for six months."

I tried to recall, but my memories of godhood were getting fuzzier rather than clearer. What had happened in the last six months? Had I been in some kind of stasis? Had Zeus taken that long to decide what to do with me? Perhaps there was a reason he'd waited until this moment to hurl me to earth.

Father's voice still rang in my ears: *Your fault. Your punishment.* My shame felt fresh and raw, as if the conversation had just happened, but I could not be sure.

After being alive for so many millennia, I had trouble keeping track of time even in the best of circumstances. I would hear a song on Spotify and think, Oh, that's new! Then I'd realize it was Mozart's Piano Concerto no. 20 in D Minor from two hundred years ago. Or I'd wonder why Herodotus the historian wasn't in my contacts list. Then I'd remember Herodotus didn't have a smartphone, because he had been dead since the Iron Age.

It's very irritating how quickly you mortals die.

"I—I don't know where I've been," I admitted. "I have some memory gaps."

Percy winced. "I hate memory gaps. Last year I lost an entire semester thanks to Hera."

"Ah, yes." I couldn't quite remember what Percy Jackson was talking about. During the war with Gaea, I had been focused mostly on my own fabulous exploits. But I suppose he and his friends had undergone a few minor hardships.

"Well, never fear," I said. "There are always new opportunities to win fame! That's why I've come to you for help!"

He gave me that confusing expression again: as if he wanted to kick me, when I was sure he must be struggling to contain his gratitude.

"Look, man—"

"Would you please refrain from calling me *man?*" I asked. "It is a painful reminder that I am a man."

"Okay . . . Apollo, I'm fine with driving you and Meg to camp if that's what you want. I never turn away a demigod who needs help—"

"Wonderful! Do you have something besides the Prius? A Maserati, perhaps? I'd settle for a Lamborghini."

"*But,*" Percy continued, "I can't get involved in another Big Prophecy or whatever. I've made promises."

I stared at him, not quite comprehending. "Promises?"

Percy laced his fingers. They were long and nimble. He would have made an excellent musician. "I lost most of my junior year because of the war with Gaea. I've spent this entire fall playing catch-up with my classes. If I want to go to college with Annabeth next fall, I have to stay out of trouble and get my diploma."

"Annabeth." I tried to place the name. "She's the blond scary one?"

"That's her. I promised her *specifically* that I wouldn't get myself killed while she's gone."

"Gone?"

Percy waved vaguely toward the north. "She's in Boston for a few weeks. Some family emergency. The point is—"

"You're saying you cannot offer me your undivided service to restore me to my throne?"

"Um . . . yeah." He pointed at the bedroom doorway. "Besides, my mom's pregnant. I'm going to have a baby sister. I'd like to be around to get to know her."

"Well, I understand that. I remember when Artemis was born—"

"Aren't you twins?"

"I've always regarded her as my little sister."

Percy's mouth twitched. "Anyway, my mom's got that going on, and her first novel is going to be published this spring as well, so I'd like to stay alive long enough to—"

"Wonderful!" I said. "Remind her to burn the proper sacrifices. Calliope is quite touchy when novelists forget to thank her."

"Okay. But what I'm saying . . . I can't go off on another world-stomping quest. I can't do that to my family."

Percy glanced toward his window. On the sill was a potted plant with delicate silver leaves—possibly moonlace. "I've already given my mom enough heart attacks for one lifetime. She's just about forgiven me for disappearing last year, but I swore to her and Paul that I wouldn't do anything like that again."

"Paul?"

"My stepdad. He's at a teacher in-service today. He's a good guy."

"I see." In truth, I didn't see. I wanted to get back to talking about my problems. I was impatient with Percy for turning the conversation to himself. Sadly, I have found this sort of self-centeredness common among demigods.

"You *do* understand that I must find a way to return to Olympus," I said. "This will probably involve many harrowing trials with a high chance of death. Can you turn down such glory?"

"Yeah, I'm pretty sure I can. Sorry."

I pursed my lips. It always disappointed me when mortals put themselves first and failed to see the big picture—the importance of putting *me* first—but I had to remind myself that this young man had helped me out on many previous occasions. He had earned my goodwill.

"I understand," I said with incredible generosity. "You will at least escort us to Camp Half-Blood?"

"That I can do." Percy reached into his hoodie pocket and pulled out a ballpoint pen. For a moment I thought he wanted my autograph. I can't tell you how often that happens. Then I remembered the pen was the disguised form of his sword, Riptide.

He smiled, and some of that old demigod mischief twinkled in his eyes. "Let's see if Meg's ready for a field trip."

5

Seven-layer dip
Chocolate chip cookies in blue
I love this woman

SALLY JACKSON was a witch to rival Circe. She had transformed Meg from a street urchin into a shockingly pretty young girl. Meg's dark pageboy hair was glossy and brushed. Her round face was scrubbed clean of grime. Her cat-eye glasses had been polished so the rhinestones sparkled. She had evidently insisted on keeping her old red sneakers, but she wore new black leggings and a knee-length frock of shifting green hues.

Mrs. Jackson had figured out how to keep Meg's old look but tweak it to be more complementary. Meg now had an elfish springtime aura that reminded me very much of a dryad. In fact . . .

A sudden wave of emotion overwhelmed me. I choked back a sob.

Meg pouted. "Do I look that bad?"

"No, no," I managed. "It's just . . ."

I wanted to say: *You remind me of someone*. But I didn't dare open that line of conversation. Only two mortals *ever* had broken my heart. Even after so many centuries, I couldn't think of her, couldn't say her name without falling into despair.

Don't misunderstand me. I felt no attraction to Meg. I was sixteen (or four thousand plus, depending on how you looked at it). She was a very young twelve. But the way she appeared now, Meg McCaffrey might have been the daughter of my former love . . . if my former love had lived long enough to have children.

It was too painful. I looked away.

"Well," Sally Jackson said with forced cheerfulness, "how about I make some lunch while you three . . . talk."

She gave Percy a worried glance, then headed to the kitchen, her hands protectively over her pregnant belly.

Meg sat on the edge of the sofa. "Percy, your mom is so normal."

"Thanks, I guess." He picked up a stack of test preparation manuals from the coffee table and chucked them aside.

"I see you like to study," I said. "Well done."

Percy snorted. "I *hate* to study. I've been guaranteed admission with a full scholarship to New Rome University, but they're still requiring me to pass all my high school courses and score well on the SAT. Can you believe that? Not to mention I have to pass the DSTOMP."

"The what?" Meg asked.

"An exam for Roman demigods," I told her. "The Demigod Standard Test of Mad Powers."

Percy frowned. "That's what it stands for?"

"I should know. I wrote the music and poetry analysis sections."

"I will never forgive you for that," Percy said.

Meg swung her feet. "So you're really a demigod? Like me?"

"Afraid so." Percy sank into the armchair, leaving me to take the sofa next to Meg. "My dad is the godly one—Poseidon. What about your parents?"

Meg's legs went still. She studied her chewed cuticles, the matching crescent rings glinting on her middle fingers. "Never knew them . . . much."

Percy hesitated. "Foster home? Stepparents?"

I thought of a certain plant, the *Mimosa pudica*, which the god Pan created. As soon as its leaves are touched, the plant closes up defensively. Meg seemed to be playing mimosa, folding inward under Percy's questions.

Percy raised his hands. "Sorry. Didn't mean to pry." He gave me an inquisitive look. "So how did you guys meet?"

I told him the story. I may have exaggerated my brave defense against Cade and Mikey—just for narrative effect, you understand.

As I finished, Sally Jackson returned. She set down a bowl of tortilla chips and a casserole dish filled with elaborate dip in multicolored strata, like sedimentary rock.

"I'll be back with the sandwiches," she said. "But I had some leftover seven-layer dip."

"Yum." Percy dug in with a tortilla chip. "She's kinda famous for this, guys."

Sally ruffled his hair. "There's guacamole, sour cream, refried beans, salsa—"

"Seven layers?" I looked up in wonder. "You knew seven is my sacred number? You invented this for *me*?"

Sally wiped her hands on her apron. "Well, actually, I can't take credit—"

"You are too modest!" I tried some of the dip. It tasted almost as good as ambrosia nachos. "You will have immortal fame for this, Sally Jackson!"

"That's sweet." She pointed to the kitchen. "I'll be right back."

Soon we were plowing through turkey sandwiches, chips and dip, and banana smoothies. Meg ate like a chipmunk, shoving more food in her mouth than she could possibly chew. My belly was full. I had never been so happy. I had a strange desire to fire up an Xbox and play *Call of Duty*.

"Percy," I said, "your mom is awesome."

"I know, right?" He finished his smoothie. "So back to your story . . . you have to be Meg's servant now? You guys barely know each other."

"*Barely* is generous," I said. "Nevertheless, yes. My fate is now linked with young McCaffrey."

"We are *cooperating*," Meg said. She seemed to savor that word.

From his pocket, Percy fished his ballpoint pen. He tapped it thoughtfully against his knee. "And this whole turning-into-a-mortal thing . . . you've done it twice before?"

"Not by choice," I assured him. "The first time, we had a little rebellion in Olympus. We tried to overthrow Zeus."

Percy winced. "I'm guessing that didn't go well."

"I got most of the blame, naturally. Oh, and your father, Poseidon. We were both cast down to earth as mortals, forced to serve Laomedon, the king of Troy. He was a harsh master. He even refused to pay us for our work!"

Meg nearly choked on her sandwich. "I have to pay you?"

I had a terrifying image of Meg McCaffrey trying to pay me in bottle caps, marbles, and pieces of colored string.

"Never fear," I told her. "I won't be presenting you with a bill. But as I was saying, the second time I became mortal, Zeus got mad because I killed some of his Cyclopes."

Percy frowned. "Dude, not cool. My brother is a Cyclops."

"These were wicked Cyclopes! They made the lightning bolt that killed one of my sons!"

Meg bounced on the arm of the sofa. "Percy's brother is a Cyclops? That's crazy!"

I took a deep breath, trying to find my happy place. "At any rate, I was bound to Admetus, the king of Thessaly. He was a kind master. I liked him so much, I made all his cows have twin calves."

"Can I have baby cows?" Meg asked.

"Well, Meg," I said, "first you would have to have some mommy cows. You see—"

"Guys," Percy interrupted. "So, just to recap, you have to be Meg's servant for . . . ?"

"Some unknown amount of time," I said. "Probably a year. Possibly more."

"And during that time—"

"I will undoubtedly face many trials and hardships."

"Like getting me my cows," Meg said.

I gritted my teeth. "What those trials will be, I do not yet know. But if I suffer through them and prove I am worthy, Zeus will forgive me and allow me to become a god again."

Percy did not look convinced—probably because I did not sound convincing. I *had* to believe my mortal punishment was temporary, as it had been the last two times. Yet Zeus had created a strict rule for baseball and prison sentences: *Three strikes, you're out.* I could only hope this would not apply to me.

"I need time to get my bearings," I said. "Once we get to Camp Half-Blood, I can consult with Chiron. I can figure out which of my godly powers remain with me in this mortal form."

"If any," Percy said.

"Let's think positive."

Percy sat back in his armchair. "Any idea what kind of spirits are following you?"

"Shiny blobs," Meg said. "They were shiny and sort of . . . blobby."

Percy nodded gravely. "Those are the worst kind."

"It hardly matters," I said. "Whatever they are, we have to flee. Once we reach camp, the magical borders will protect me."

"And me?" Meg asked.

"Oh, yes. You, too."

Percy frowned. "Apollo, if you're really mortal, like, one hundred percent mortal, can you even get *in* to Camp Half-Blood?"

The seven-layer dip began to churn in my stomach. "Please don't say that. Of course I'll get in. I *have* to."

"But you could get hurt in battle now . . ." Percy mused. "Then again, maybe monsters would ignore you because you're not important?"

"Stop!" My hands trembled. Being a mortal was traumatic enough. The thought of being barred from camp, of being *unimportant* . . . No. That simply could not be.

"I'm sure I've retained some powers," I said. "I'm still gorgeous, for instance, if I could just get rid of this acne and lose some flab. I must have other abilities!"

Percy turned to Meg. "What about you? I hear you throw a mean garbage bag. Any other skills we should know about? Summoning lightning? Making toilets explode?"

Meg smiled hesitantly. "That's not a power."

"Sure it is," Percy said. "Some of the best demigods have gotten their start by blowing up toilets."

Meg giggled.

I did not like the way she was grinning at Percy. I didn't want the girl to develop a crush. We might never get out of here. As much as I enjoyed Sally Jackson's cooking—the divine smell of baking cookies was even now wafting from the kitchen—I needed to make haste to camp.

"Ahem." I rubbed my hands. "How soon can we leave?"

Percy glanced at the wall clock. "Right now, I guess. If you're being followed, I'd rather have monsters on our trail than sniffing around the apartment."

"Good man," I said.

Percy gestured with distaste at his test manuals. "I just have to be back tonight. Got a lot of studying. The first two times I took the SAT—ugh. If it wasn't for Annabeth helping me out—"

"Who's that?" Meg asked.

"My girlfriend."

Meg frowned. I was glad there were no garbage bags nearby for her to throw.

"So take a break!" I urged. "Your brain will be refreshed after an easy drive to Long Island."

"Huh," Percy said. "There's a lazy kind of logic to that. Okay. Let's do it."

He rose just as Sally Jackson walked in with a plate of fresh-baked chocolate chip cookies. For some reason, the cookies were blue, but they smelled heavenly—and I should know. I'm from heaven.

"Mom, don't freak," Percy said.

Sally sighed. "I hate it when you say that."

"I'm just going to take these two to camp. That's all. I'll be right back."

"I think I've heard that before."

"I *promise*."

Sally looked at me, then Meg. Her expression softened, her innate kindness perhaps overweighing her concern. "All right. Be careful. It was lovely meeting you both. Please try not to die."

Percy kissed her on the cheek. He reached for the cookies, but she moved the plate away.

"Oh, no," she said. "Apollo and Meg can have one, but I'm keeping the rest hostage until you're back safely. And hurry, dear. It would be a shame if Paul ate them all when he gets home."

Percy's expression turned grim. He faced us. "You hear that, guys? A batch of cookies is depending on me. If you get me killed on the way to camp, I am going be ticked off."

6

Aquaman driving
Couldn't possibly be worse
Oh, wait, now it is

MUCH TO MY DISAPPOINTMENT, the Jacksons did not have a spare bow or quiver to lend me.

"I suck at archery," Percy explained.

"Yes, but *I* don't," I said. "This is why you should always plan for *my* needs."

Sally lent Meg and me some proper winter fleece jackets, however. Mine was blue, with the word BLOFIS written inside the neckline. Perhaps that was an arcane ward against evil spirits. Hecate would have known. Sorcery really wasn't my thing.

Once we reached the Prius, Meg called shotgun, which was yet another example of my unfair existence. Gods do not ride in the back. I again suggested following them in a Maserati or a Lamborghini, but Percy admitted he had neither. The Prius was the only car his family owned.

I mean . . . wow. Just *wow*.

Sitting in the backseat, I quickly became carsick. I was used to driving my sun chariot across the sky, where every lane was the fast lane. I was not used to the Long Island

Expressway. Believe me, even at midday in the middle of January, there is nothing *express* about your expressways.

Percy braked and lurched forward. I sorely wished I could launch a fireball in front of us and melt cars to make way for our clearly more important journey.

"Doesn't your Prius have flamethrowers?" I demanded. "Lasers? At least some Hephaestian bumper blades? What sort of cheap economy vehicle is this?"

Percy glanced in the rearview mirror. "You have rides like that on Mount Olympus?"

"We don't have traffic jams," I said. "That, I can promise you."

Meg tugged at her crescent moon rings. Again I wondered if she had some connection to Artemis. The moon was my sister's symbol. Perhaps Artemis had sent Meg to look after me?

Yet that didn't seem right. Artemis had trouble sharing anything with me—demigods, arrows, nations, birthday parties. It's a twin thing. Also, Meg McCaffrey did not strike me as one of my sister's followers. Meg had another sort of aura . . . one I would have been able to recognize easily if I were a god. But, no. I had to rely on mortal intuition, which was like trying to pick up sewing needles while wearing oven mitts.

Meg turned and gazed out the rear windshield, probably checking for any shiny blobs pursuing us. "At least we're not being—"

"Don't say it," Percy warned.

Meg huffed. "You don't know what I was going to—"

"You were going to say, 'At least we're not being followed,'" Percy said. "That'll jinx us. Immediately we'll notice that we *are* being followed. Then we'll end up in a big battle that totals my family car and probably destroys the whole freeway. Then we'll have to run all the way to camp."

Meg's eyes widened. "You can tell the future?"

"Don't need to." Percy changed lanes to one that was crawling slightly less slowly. "I've just done this a lot. Besides"—he shot me an accusing look—"nobody can tell the future anymore. The Oracle isn't working."

"What Oracle?" Meg asked.

Neither of us answered. For a moment, I was too stunned to speak. And believe me, I have to be *very* stunned for that to happen.

"It *still* isn't working?" I said in a small voice.

"You didn't know?" Percy asked. "I mean, sure, you've been out of it for six months, but this happened on your watch."

That was unjust. I had been busy hiding from Zeus's wrath at the time, which was a perfectly legitimate excuse. How was I to know that Gaea would take advantage of the chaos of war and raise my oldest, greatest enemy from the depths of Tartarus so he could take possession of his old lair in the cave of Delphi and cut off the source of my prophetic power?

Oh, yes, I hear you critics out there: *You're the god of prophecy, Apollo. How could you* not *know that would happen?*

The next sound you hear will be me blowing you a giant Meg-McCaffrey-quality raspberry.

I swallowed back the taste of fear and seven-layer dip. "I just . . . I assumed—I hoped this would be taken care of by now."

"You mean by demigods," Percy said, "going on a big quest to reclaim the Oracle of Delphi?"

"Exactly!" I knew Percy would understand. "I suppose Chiron just forgot. I'll remind him when we get to camp, and he can dispatch some of you talented fodder—I mean heroes—"

"Well, here's the thing," Percy said. "To go on a quest, we need a prophecy, right? Those are the rules. If there's no Oracle, there *are* no prophecies, so we're stuck in a—"

"A Catch-88." I sighed.

Meg threw a piece of lint at me. "It's a Catch-22."

"No," I explained patiently. "This is a Catch-88, which is four times as bad."

I felt as if I were floating in a warm bath and someone had pulled out the stopper. The water swirled around me, tugging me downward. Soon I would be left shivering and exposed, or else I would be sucked down the drain into the sewers of hopelessness. (Don't laugh. That's a perfectly fine metaphor. Also, when you're a god, you can get sucked down a drain quite easily—if you're caught off guard and relaxed, and you happen to change form at the wrong moment. Once I woke up in a sewage treatment facility in Biloxi, but that's another story.)

I was beginning to see what was in store for me during my mortal sojourn. The Oracle was held by hostile forces. My adversary lay coiled and waiting, growing stronger every day on the magical fumes of the Delphic caverns. And I was a weak mortal bound to an untrained demigod who threw garbage and chewed her cuticles.

No. Zeus could not *possibly* expect me to fix this. Not in my present condition.

And yet . . . *someone* had sent those thugs to intercept me in the alley. Someone had known where I would land.

Nobody can tell the future anymore, Percy had said.

But that wasn't quite true.

"Hey, you two." Meg hit us both with pieces of lint. Where was she finding this lint?

I realized I'd been ignoring her. It had felt good while it lasted.

"Yes, sorry, Meg," I said. "You see, the Oracle of Delphi is an ancient—"

"I don't care about that," she said. "There are three shiny blobs now."

"What?" Percy asked.

She pointed behind us. "Look."

Weaving through the traffic, closing in on us rapidly, were three glittery, vaguely humanoid apparitions—like billowing plumes from smoke grenades touched by King Midas.

"Just once I'd like an easy commute," Percy grumbled. "Everybody, hold on. We're going cross-country."

Percy's definition of *cross-country* was different from mine.

I envisioned crossing an actual countryside. Instead, Percy shot down the nearest exit ramp, wove across the parking lot of a shopping mall, then blasted through the drive-through of a Mexican restaurant without even ordering anything. We swerved into an industrial area of dilapidated warehouses, the smoking apparitions still closing in behind us.

My knuckles turned white on my seat belt's shoulder strap. "Is your plan to avoid a fight by dying in a traffic accident?" I demanded.

"Ha-ha." Percy yanked the wheel to the right. We sped north, the warehouses giving way to a hodgepodge of apartment buildings and abandoned strip malls. "I'm getting us to the beach. I fight better near water."

"Because Poseidon?" Meg asked, steadying herself against the door handle.

"Yep," Percy agreed. "That pretty much describes my entire life: *Because Poseidon.*"

Meg bounced up and down with excitement, which seemed pointless to me, since we were already bouncing quite a lot.

"You're gonna be like Aquaman?" she asked. "Get the fish to fight for you?"

"Thanks," Percy said. "I haven't heard enough Aquaman jokes for one lifetime."

"I wasn't joking!" Meg protested.

I glanced out the rear window. The three glittering plumes were still gaining. One of them passed through a middle-aged man crossing the street. The mortal pedestrian instantly collapsed.

"Ah, I know these spirits!" I cried. "They are . . . um . . ." My brain clouded over.

"What?" Percy demanded. "They are what?"

"I've forgotten! I *hate* being mortal! Four thousand years

of knowledge, the secrets of the universe, a sea of wisdom—lost, because I can't contain it all in this teacup of a head!"

"Hold on!" Percy flew through a railroad crossing and the Prius went airborne. Meg yelped as her head hit the ceiling. Then she began giggling uncontrollably.

The landscape opened into actual countryside—fallow fields, dormant vineyards, orchards of bare fruit trees.

"Just another mile or so to the beach," Percy said. "Plus we're almost to the western edge of camp. We can do it. We can do it."

Actually, we couldn't. One of the shiny smoke clouds pulled a dirty trick, pluming from the pavement directly in front of us.

Instinctively, Percy swerved.

The Prius went off the road, straight through a barbed wire fence and into an orchard. Percy managed to avoid hitting any of the trees, but the car skidded in the icy mud and wedged itself between two trunks. Miraculously, the air bags did not deploy.

Percy popped his seat belt. "You guys okay?"

Meg shoved against her passenger-side door. "Won't open. Get me out of here!"

Percy tried his own door. It was firmly jammed against the side of a peach tree.

"Back here," I said. "Climb over!"

I kicked my door open and staggered out, my legs feeling like worn shock absorbers.

The three smoky figures had stopped at the edge of the orchard. Now they advanced slowly, taking on solid shapes.

They grew arms and legs. Their faces formed eyes and wide, hungry mouths.

I knew instinctively that I had dealt with these spirits before. I couldn't remember what they were, but I had dispelled them many times, swatting them into oblivion with no more effort than I would a swarm of gnats.

Unfortunately, I wasn't a god now. I was a panicky sixteen-year-old. My palms sweated. My teeth chattered. My only coherent thought was: *YIKES!*

Percy and Meg struggled to get out of the Prius. They needed time, which meant I had to run interference.

"STOP!" I bellowed at the spirits. "I am the god Apollo!"

To my pleasant surprise, the three spirits stopped. They hovered in place about forty feet away.

I heard Meg grunt as she tumbled out of the backseat. Percy scrambled after her.

I advanced toward the spirits, the frosty mud crunching under my shoes. My breath steamed in the cold air. I raised my hand in an ancient three-fingered gesture for warding off evil.

"Leave us or be destroyed!" I told the spirits. "BLOFIS!"

The smoky shapes trembled. My hopes lifted. I waited for them to dissipate or flee in terror.

Instead, they solidified into ghoulish corpses with yellow eyes. Their clothes were tattered rags, their limbs covered with gaping wounds and running sores.

"Oh, dear." My Adam's apple dropped into my chest like a billiard ball. "I remember now."

Percy and Meg stepped to either side of me. With a

metallic *shink*, Percy's pen grew into a blade of glowing Celestial bronze.

"Remember what?" he asked. "How to kill these things?"

"No," I said. "I remember what they are: *nosoi*, plague spirits. Also . . . they can't be killed."

7

Tag with plague spirits
You're it, and you're infectious
Have fun with that, LOL

"NOSOI?" PERCY PLANTED HIS FEET in a fighting stance. "You know, I keep thinking, *I have now killed every single thing in Greek mythology.* But the list never seems to end."

"You haven't killed me yet," I noted.

"Don't tempt me."

The three nosoi shuffled forward. Their cadaverous mouths gaped. Their tongues lolled. Their eyes glistened with a film of yellow mucus.

"These creatures are *not* myths," I said. "Of course, most things in those old myths are not myths. Except for that story about how I flayed the satyr Marsyas alive. That was a total lie."

Percy glanced at me. "You did *what?*"

"Guys." Meg picked up a dead tree branch. "Could we talk about that later?"

The middle plague spirit spoke. "Apollooooo . . ." His voice gurgled like a seal with bronchitis. "We have coooome to—"

"Let me stop you right there." I crossed my arms and feigned arrogant indifference. (Difficult for me, but I managed.) "You've come to take your revenge on me, eh?" I looked at my demigod friends. "You see, nosoi are the spirits of disease. Once *I* was born, spreading illnesses became part of *my* job. I use plague arrows to strike down naughty populations with smallpox, athlete's foot, that sort of thing."

"Gross," Meg said.

"Somebody's got to do it!" I said. "Better a god, regulated by the Council of Olympus and with the proper health permits, than a horde of uncontrolled spirits like *these*."

The spirit on the left gurgled. "We're trying to have a mooooment here. Stop interrupting! We wish to be free, uncontrooooolled—"

"Yes, I know. You'll destroy me. Then you'll spread every known malady across the world. You've been wanting to do that ever since Pandora let you out of that jar. But you can't. I will strike you down!"

Perhaps you are wondering how I could act so confident and calm. In fact, I was terrified. My sixteen-year-old mortal instincts were screaming, RUN! My knees were knocking together, and my right eye had developed a nasty twitch. But the secret to dealing with plague spirits was to keep talking so as to appear in charge and unafraid. I trusted that this would allow my demigod companions time to come up with a clever plan to save me. I certainly *hoped* Meg and Percy were working on such a plan.

The spirit on the right bared his rotten teeth. "What will you strike us down with? Where is your booooow?"

"It appears to be missing," I agreed. "But is it really? What if it's cleverly hidden under this Led Zeppelin T-shirt, and I am about to whip it out and shoot you all?"

The nosoi shuffled nervously.

"Yooou lie," said the one in the middle.

Percy cleared his throat. "Um, hey, Apollo . . ."

Finally! I thought.

"I know what you're going to say," I told him. "You and Meg have come up with a clever plan to hold off these spirits while I run away to camp. I hate to see you sacrifice yourselves, but—"

"That's not what I was going to say." Percy raised his blade. "I was going to ask what happens if I just slice and dice these mouth-breathers with Celestial bronze."

The middle spirit chortled, his yellow eyes gleaming. "A sword is such a small weapon. It does not have the pooooetry of a good epidemic."

"Stop right there!" I said. "You can't claim both my plagues *and* my poetry!"

"You are right," said the spirit. "Enough wooooords."

The three corpses shambled forward. I thrust out my arms, hoping to blast them to dust. Nothing happened.

"This is insufferable!" I complained. "How do demigods do it without an auto-win power?"

Meg jabbed her tree branch into the nearest spirit's chest. The branch stuck. Glittering smoke began swirling down the length of the wood.

"Let go!" I warned. "Don't let the nosoi touch you!"

Meg released the branch and scampered away.

Meanwhile, Percy Jackson charged into battle. He swung his sword, dodging the spirits' attempts to snare him, but his efforts were futile. Whenever his blade connected with the nosoi, their bodies simply dissolved into glittery mist, then resolidified.

A spirit lunged to grab him. From the ground, Meg scooped up a frozen black peach and threw it with such force it embedded itself in the spirit's forehead, knocking him down.

"We gotta run," Meg decided.

"Yeah." Percy backtracked toward us. "I like that idea."

I knew running would not help. If it were possible to run from disease spirits, the medieval Europeans would've put on their track shoes and escaped the Black Death. (And FYI, the Black Death was *not* my fault. I took one century off to lie around the beach in Cabo, and came back and found that the nosoi had gotten loose and a third of the continent was dead. *Gods*, I was so irritated.)

But I was too terrified to argue. Meg and Percy sprinted off through the orchard, and I followed.

Percy pointed to a line of hills about a mile ahead. "That's the western border of camp. If we can just get there . . ."

We passed an irrigation tank on a tractor-trailer. With a casual flick of his hand, Percy caused the side of the tank to rupture. A wall of water crashed into the three nosoi behind us.

"That was good." Meg grinned, skipping along in her new green dress. "We're going to make it!"

No, I thought, we're not.

My chest ached. Each breath was a ragged wheeze. I resented that these two demigods could carry on a conversation while running for their lives while I, the immortal Apollo, was reduced to gasping like a catfish.

"We can't—" I gulped. "They'll just—"

Before I could finish, three glittering pillars of smoke plumed from the ground in front of us. Two of the nosoi solidified into cadavers—one with a peach for a third eye, the other with a tree branch sticking out of his chest.

The third spirit . . . Well, Percy didn't see it in time. He ran straight into the plume of smoke.

"Don't breathe!" I warned him.

Percy's eyes bugged out as if to say, *Seriously?* He fell to his knees, clawing at his throat. As a son of Poseidon, he could probably breathe underwater, but holding one's breath for an indeterminate amount of time was a different matter altogether.

Meg picked up another withered peach from the field, but it would offer her little defense against the forces of darkness.

I tried to figure out how to help Percy—because I am all about helping—but the branch-impaled nosos charged at me. I turned and fled, running face-first into a tree. I'd like to tell you that was part of my plan, but even I, with all my poetic skill, cannot put a positive spin on it.

I found myself flat on my back, spots dancing in my eyes, the cadaverous visage of the plague spirit looming over me.

"Which fatal illness shall I use to kill the great Apolloooo?" the spirit gurgled. "Anthrax? Perhaps eboooola . . ."

"Hangnails," I suggested, trying to squirm away from my tormentor. "I live in fear of hangnails."

"I have the answer!" the spirit cried, rudely ignoring me. "Let's try this!"

He dissolved into smoke and settled over me like a glittering blanket.

8

Peaches in combat
I am hanging it up now
My brain exploded

I WILL NOT SAY my life passed before my eyes.

I wish it had. That would've taken several months, giving me time to figure out an escape plan.

Instead, my regrets passed before my eyes. Despite being a gloriously perfect being, I do have a few regrets. I remembered that day at Abbey Road Studios, when my envy led me to set rancor in the hearts of John and Paul and break up the Beatles. I remembered Achilles falling on the plains of Troy, cut down by an unworthy archer because of my wrath.

I saw Hyacinthus, his bronze shoulders and dark ringlets gleaming in the sunlight. Standing on the sideline of the discus field, he gave me a brilliant smile. *Even you can't throw that far,* he teased.

Watch me, I said. I threw the discus, then stared in horror as a gust of wind made it veer, inexplicably, toward Hyacinthus's handsome face.

And of course I saw *her*—the other love of my life—her fair skin transforming into bark, her hair sprouting green leaves, her eyes hardening into rivulets of sap.

Those memories brought back so much pain, you might think I would welcome the glittering plague mist descending over me.

Yet my new mortal self rebelled. I was too young to die! I hadn't even had my first kiss! (Yes, my godly catalogue of exes was filled with more beautiful people than a Kardashian party guest list, but none of that seemed real to me.)

If I'm being totally honest, I have to confess something else: all gods fear death, even when we are *not* encased in mortal forms.

That may seem silly. We are immortal. But as you've seen, immortality can be taken away. (In my case, *three stinking times*.)

Gods know about fading. They know about being forgotten over the centuries. The idea of ceasing to exist altogether terrifies us. In fact . . . well, Zeus would not like me sharing this information—and if you tell anyone I will deny I ever said it—but the truth is we gods are a little in awe of you mortals. You spend your whole lives knowing you will die. No matter how many friends and relatives you have, your puny existence will quickly be forgotten. How do you cope with it? Why are you not running around constantly screaming and pulling your hair out? Your bravery, I must admit, is quite admirable.

Now where was I?

Right. I was dying.

I rolled around in the mud, holding my breath. I tried to brush off the disease cloud, but it was not as easy as swatting a fly or an uppity mortal.

I caught a glimpse of Meg, playing a deadly game of tag

with the third nosos, trying to keep a peach tree between herself and the spirit. She yelled something to me, but her voice seemed tinny and far away.

Somewhere to my left, the ground shook. A miniature geyser erupted from the field. Percy crawled toward it desperately. He thrust his face in the water, washing away the smoke.

My eyesight began to dim.

Percy struggled to his feet. He ripped out the source of the geyser—an irrigation pipe—and turned the water on me.

Normally I do not like being doused. Every time I go camping with Artemis, she likes to wake me up with a bucket of ice-cold water. But in this case, I didn't mind.

The water disrupted the smoke, allowing me to roll away and gasp for air. Nearby, our two gaseous enemies re-formed as dripping wet corpses, their yellow eyes glowing with annoyance.

Meg yelled again. This time I understood her words. "GET DOWN!"

I found this inconsiderate, since I'd only just gotten up. All around the orchard, the frozen blackened remnants of the harvest were beginning to levitate.

Believe me, in four thousand years I have seen some strange things. I have seen the dreaming face of Ouranos etched in stars across the heavens, and the full fury of Typhon as he raged across the earth. I've seen men turn into snakes, ants turn into men, and otherwise rational people dance the macarena.

But never before had I seen an uprising of frozen fruit.

Percy and I hit the ground as peaches shot around

the orchard, ricocheting off trees like eight balls, ripping through the nosoi's cadaverous bodies. If I had been standing up, I would have been killed, but Meg simply stood there, unfazed and unhurt, as frozen dead fruit zinged around her.

All three nosoi collapsed, riddled with holes. Every piece of fruit dropped to the ground.

Percy looked up, his eyes red and puffy. "Whah jus happened?"

He sounded congested, which meant he hadn't completely escaped the effects of the plague cloud, but at least he wasn't dead. That was generally a good sign.

"I don't know," I admitted. "Meg, is it safe?"

She was staring in amazement at the carnage of fruit, mangled corpses, and broken tree limbs. "I—I'm not sure."

"How'd you do thah?" Percy snuffled.

Meg looked horrified. "I didn't! I just knew it would happen."

One of the cadavers began to stir. It got up, wobbling on its heavily perforated legs.

"But you *did* doooo it," the spirit growled. "Yooou are strong, child."

The other two corpses rose.

"Not strong enough," said the second nosos. "We will finish you now."

The third spirit bared his rotten teeth. "Your guardian would be sooooo disappointed."

Guardian? Perhaps the spirit meant me. When in doubt, I usually assumed the conversation was about me.

Meg looked as if she'd been punched in the gut. Her

face paled. Her arms trembled. She stamped her foot and yelled, "NO!"

More peaches swirled into the air. This time the fruit blurred together in a fructose dust devil, until standing in front of Meg was a creature like a pudgy human toddler wearing only a linen diaper. Protruding from his back were wings made of leafy branches. His babyish face might have been cute except for the glowing green eyes and pointy fangs. The creature snarled and snapped at the air.

"Oh, no." Percy shook his head. "I hate these things."

The three nosoi also did not look pleased. They edged away from the snarling baby.

"Wh-what is it?" Meg asked.

I stared at her in disbelief. She had to be the cause of this fruit-based strangeness, but she looked as shocked as we were. Unfortunately, if Meg didn't know how she had summoned this creature, she would not know how to make it go away, and like Percy Jackson, I was no fan of *karpoi*.

"It's a grain spirit," I said, trying to keep the panic out of my voice. "I've never seen a peach karpos before, but if it's as vicious as other types . . ."

I was about to say, *we're doomed*, but that seemed both obvious and depressing.

The peach baby turned toward the nosoi. For a moment, I feared he would make some hellish alliance—an axis of evil between illnesses and fruits.

The middle corpse, the one with the peach in his forehead, inched backward. "Do not interfere," he warned the karpos. "We will not allooow—"

The peach baby launched himself at the nosos and bit his head off.

That is not a figure of speech. The karpos's fanged mouth unhinged, expanding to an unbelievable circumference, then closed around the cadaver's head, and chomped it off in one bite.

Oh, dear . . . I hope you weren't eating dinner as you read that.

In a matter of seconds, the nosos had been torn to shreds and devoured.

Understandably, the other two nosoi retreated, but the karpos crouched and sprang. He landed on the second corpse and proceeded to rip it into plague-flavored Cream of Wheat.

The last spirit dissolved into glittering smoke and tried to fly away, but the peach baby spread his leafy wings and launched himself in pursuit. He opened his mouth and inhaled the sickness, snapping and swallowing until every wisp of smoke was gone.

He landed in front of Meg and belched. His green eyes gleamed. He did not appear even slightly sick, which I suppose wasn't surprising, since human diseases don't infect fruit trees. Instead, even after eating three whole nosoi, the little fellow looked hungry.

He howled and beat his small chest. "Peaches!"

Slowly, Percy raised his sword. His nose was still red and runny, and his face was puffy. "Meg, don move," he snuffled. "I'm gonna—"

"No!" she said. "Don't hurt him."

She put her hand tentatively on the creature's curly head. "You saved us," she told the karpos. "Thank you."

I started mentally preparing a list of herbal remedies for regenerating severed limbs, but to my surprise, the peach baby did not bite off Meg's hand. Instead he hugged Meg's leg and glared at us as if daring us to approach.

"Peaches," he growled.

"He likes you," Percy noted. "Um . . . why?"

"I don't know," Meg said. "Honestly, I didn't summon him!"

I was certain Meg *had* summoned him, intentionally or unintentionally. I also had some ideas now about her godly parentage, and some questions about this "guardian" that the spirits had mentioned, but I decided it would be better to interrogate her when she did not have a snarling carnivorous toddler wrapped around her leg.

"Well, whatever the case," I said, "we owe the karpos our lives. This brings to mind an expression I coined ages ago: *A peach a day keeps the plague spirits away!*"

Percy sneezed. "I thought it was apples and doctors."

The karpos hissed.

"Or peaches," Percy said. "Peaches work too."

"Peaches," agreed the karpos.

Percy wiped his nose. "Not criticizing, but why is he grooting?"

Meg frowned. "Grooting?"

"Yeah, like thah character in the movie . . . only saying one thing over and over."

"I'm afraid I haven't seen that movie," I said. "But this

karpos does seem to have a very . . . targeted vocabulary."

"Maybe Peaches is his name." Meg stroked the karpos's curly brown hair, which elicited a demonic purring from the creature's throat. "That's what I'll call him."

"Whoa, you are not adopting thah—" Percy sneezed with such force, another irrigation pipe exploded behind him, sending up a row of tiny geysers. "Ugh. Sick."

"You're lucky," I said. "Your trick with the water diluted the spirit's power. Instead of getting a deadly illness, you got a head cold."

"I hate head colds." His green irises looked like they were sinking in a sea of bloodshot. "Neither of you got sick?"

Meg shook her head.

"I have an excellent constitution," I said. "No doubt that's what saved me."

"And the fact thah I hosed the smoke off of you," Percy said.

"Well, yes."

Percy stared at me as if waiting for something. After an awkward moment, it occurred to me that if he was a god and I was a worshipper, he might expect gratitude.

"Ah . . . thank you," I said.

He nodded. "No problem."

I relaxed a little. If he had demanded a sacrifice, like a white bull or a fatted calf, I'm not sure what I would've done.

"Can we go now?" Meg asked.

"An excellent idea," I said. "Though I'm afraid Percy is in no condition—"

"I can drive you the rest of the way," he said. "If we can get my car out from between those trees. . . ." He glanced in that direction and his expression turned even more miserable. "Aw, Hades no. . . ."

A police cruiser was pulling over on the side of the road. I imagined the officers' eyes tracing the tire ruts in the mud, which led to the plowed-down fence and continued to the blue Toyota Prius wedged between two peach trees. The cruiser's roof lights flashed on.

"Great," Percy muttered. "If they tow the Prius, I'm dead. My mom and Paul *need* thah car."

"Go talk to the officers," I said. "You won't be any use to us anyway in your current state."

"Yeah, we'll be fine," Meg said. "You said the camp is right over those hills?"

"Right, but . . ." Percy scowled, probably trying to think straight through the effects of his cold. "Most people enter camp from the east, where Half-Blood Hill is. The western border is wilder—hills and woods, all heavily enchanted. If you're not careful, you can get lost. . . ." He sneezed again. "I'm still not even sure Apollo can get *in* if he's fully mortal."

"I'll get in." I tried to exude confidence. I had no alternative. If I was unable to enter Camp Half-Blood . . . No. I'd already been attacked twice on my first day as a mortal. There was no plan B that would keep me alive.

The police car's doors opened.

"Go," I urged Percy. "We'll find our way through the woods. You explain to the police that you're sick and you lost control of the car. They'll go easy on you."

Percy laughed. "Yeah. Cops love me almost as much as teachers do." He glanced at Meg. "You sure you're okay with the baby fruit demon?"

Peaches growled.

"All good," Meg promised. "Go home. Rest. Get lots of fluids."

Percy's mouth twitched. "You're telling a son of Poseidon to get lots of fluids? Okay, just try to survive until the weekend, will you? I'll come to camp and check on you guys if I can. Be careful and—CHOOOO!"

Muttering unhappily, he touched the cap of his pen to his sword, turning it back into a simple ballpoint. A wise precaution before approaching law enforcement. He trudged down the hill, sneezing and sniffling.

"Officer?" he called. "Sorry, I'm up here. Can you tell me where Manhattan is?"

Meg turned to me. "Ready?"

I was soaking wet and shivering. I was having the worst day in the history of days. I was stuck with a scary girl and an even scarier peach baby. I was by no means ready for anything. But I also desperately wanted to reach camp. I might find some friendly faces there—perhaps even jubilant worshippers who would bring me peeled grapes, Oreos, and other holy offerings.

"Sure," I said. "Let's go."

Peaches the karpos grunted. He gestured for us to follow, then scampered toward the hills. Maybe he knew the way. Maybe he just wanted to lead us to a grisly death.

Meg skipped after him, swinging from tree branches and cartwheeling through the mud as the mood took her.

You might've thought we'd just finished a nice picnic rather than a battle with plague-ridden cadavers.

I turned my face to the sky. "Are you sure, Zeus? It's not too late to tell me this was an elaborate prank and recall me to Olympus. I've learned my lesson. I promise."

The gray winter clouds did not respond. With a sigh, I jogged after Meg and her homicidal new minion.

9

A walk through the woods

Voices driving me bonkers

I hate spaghetti

I SIGHED WITH RELIEF. "This should be easy."

Granted, I'd said the same thing before I fought Poseidon in hand-to-hand combat, and that had *not* turned out to be easy. Nevertheless, our path into Camp Half-Blood looked straightforward enough. For starters, I was pleased I could *see* the camp, since it was normally shielded from mortal eyes. This boded well for me getting in.

From where we stood at the top of a hill, the entire valley spread out below us: roughly three square miles of woods, meadows, and strawberry fields bordered by Long Island Sound to the north and rolling hills on the other three sides. Just below us, a dense forest of evergreens covered the western third of the vale.

Beyond that, the buildings of Camp Half-Blood gleamed in the wintry light: the amphitheater, the sword-fighting stadium, the open-air dining pavilion with its white marble columns. A trireme floated in the canoe lake. Twenty cabins lined the central green where the communal hearth fire glowed cheerfully.

At the edge of the strawberry fields stood the Big House:

a four-story Victorian painted sky blue with white trim. My friend Chiron would be inside, probably having tea by the fireplace. I would find sanctuary at last.

My gaze rose to the far end of the valley. There, on the tallest hill, the Athena Parthenos shone in all its gold-and-alabaster glory. Once, the massive statue had graced the Parthenon in Greece. Now it presided over Camp Half-Blood, protecting the valley from intruders. Even from here I could feel its power, like the subsonic thrum of a mighty engine. Old Gray Eyes was on the lookout for threats, being her usual vigilant, no-fun, all-business self.

Personally, I would have installed a more interesting statue—of myself, for instance. Still, the panorama of Camp Half-Blood was an impressive sight. My mood always improved when I saw the place—a small reminder of the good old days when mortals knew how to build temples and do proper burnt sacrifices. Ah, everything was better in ancient Greece! Well, except for a few small improvements modern humans had made—the Internet, chocolate croissants, life expectancy.

Meg's mouth hung open. "How come I've never heard about this place? Do you need tickets?"

I chuckled. I always enjoyed the chance to enlighten a clueless mortal. "You see, Meg, magical borders camouflage the valley. From the outside, most humans would spy nothing here except boring farmland. If they approached, they would get turned around and find themselves wandering out again. Believe me, I tried to get a pizza delivered to camp once. It was quite annoying."

"You ordered a pizza?"

"Never mind," I said. "As for tickets . . . it's true the camp doesn't let in just anybody, but you're in luck. I know the management."

Peaches growled. He sniffed the ground, then chomped a mouthful of dirt and spit it out.

"He doesn't like the taste of this place," Meg said.

"Yes, well . . ." I frowned at the karpos. "Perhaps we can find him some potting soil or fertilizer when we arrive. I'll convince the demigods to let him in, but it would be helpful if he doesn't bite their heads off—at least not right away."

Peaches muttered something about peaches.

"Something doesn't feel right." Meg bit her nails. "Those woods . . . Percy said they were wild and enchanted and stuff."

I, too, felt as if something was amiss, but I chalked this up to my general dislike of forests. For reasons I'd rather not go into, I find them . . . uncomfortable places. Nevertheless, with our goal in sight, my usual optimism was returning.

"Don't worry," I assured Meg. "You're traveling with a god!"

"Ex-god."

"I wish you wouldn't keep harping on that. Anyway, the campers are very friendly. They'll welcome us with tears of joy. And wait until you see the orientation video!"

"The what?"

"I directed it myself! Now, come along. The woods can't be that bad."

———

The woods were that bad.

As soon as we entered their shadows, the trees seemed to crowd us. Trunks closed ranks, blocking old paths and opening new ones. Roots writhed across the forest floor, making an obstacle course of bumps, knots, and loops. It was like trying to walk across a giant bowl of spaghetti.

The thought of spaghetti made me hungry. It had only been a few hours since Sally Jackson's seven-layer dip and sandwiches, but my mortal stomach was already clenching and squelching for food. The sounds were quite annoying, especially while walking through dark scary woods. Even the karpos Peaches was starting to smell good to me, giving me visions of cobbler and ice cream.

As I said earlier, I was generally not a fan of the woods. I tried to convince myself that the trees were not watching me, scowling and whispering among themselves. They were just trees. Even if they had dryad spirits, those dryads couldn't possibly hold me responsible for what had happened thousands of years ago on a different continent.

Why not? I asked myself. *You still hold yourself responsible.*

I told myself to stuff a sock in it.

We hiked for hours . . . much longer than it should have taken to reach the Big House. Normally I could navigate by the sun—which shouldn't be a surprise, since I spent millennia driving it across the sky—but under the canopy of trees, the light was diffuse, the shadows confusing.

After we passed the same boulder for the third time, I stopped and admitted the obvious. "I have no idea where we are."

Meg plopped herself down onto a fallen log. In the green light, she looked more like a dryad than ever, though tree spirits do not often wear red sneakers and hand-me-down fleece jackets.

"Don't you have any wilderness skills?" she asked. "Reading moss on the sides of trees? Following tracks?"

"That's more my sister's thing," I said.

"Maybe Peaches can help." Meg turned to her karpos. "Hey, can you find us a way out of the woods?"

For the past few miles, the karpos had been muttering nervously, cutting his eyes from side to side. Now he sniffed the air, his nostrils quivering. He tilted his head.

His face flushed bright green. He emitted a distressed bark, then dissolved in a swirl of leaves.

Meg shot to her feet. "Where'd he go?"

I scanned the woods. I suspected Peaches had done the intelligent thing. He'd sensed danger approaching and abandoned us. I didn't want to suggest that to Meg, though. She'd already become quite fond of the karpos. (Ridiculous, getting attached to a small dangerous creature. Then again, we gods got attached to humans, so I had no room to criticize.)

"Perhaps he went scouting," I suggested. "Perhaps we should—"

APOLLO.

The voice reverberated in my head, as if someone had installed Bose speakers behind my eyes. It was not the voice of my conscience. My conscience was not female, and it was not that loud. Yet something about the woman's tone was eerily familiar.

"What's wrong?" Meg asked.

The air turned sickly sweet. The trees loomed over me like trigger hairs of a Venus flytrap.

A bead of sweat trickled down the side of my face.

"We can't stay here," I said. "Attend me, mortal."

"Excuse me?" Meg said.

"Uh, I mean come on!"

We ran, stumbling over tree roots, fleeing blindly through a maze of branches and boulders. We reached a clear stream over a bed of gravel. I barely slowed down. I waded in, sinking shin-deep into the ice-cold water.

The voice spoke again: *FIND ME*.

This time it was so loud, it stabbed through my forehead like a railroad spike. I stumbled, falling to my knees.

"Hey!" Meg gripped my arm. "Get up!"

"You didn't hear that?"

"Hear what?"

THE FALL OF THE SUN, the voice boomed. *THE FINAL VERSE*.

I collapsed face-first into the stream.

"Apollo!" Meg rolled me over, her voice tight with alarm. "Come on! I can't carry you!"

Yet she tried. She dragged me across the river, scolding me and cursing until, with her help, I managed to crawl to shore.

I lay on my back, staring wildly at the forest canopy. My soaked clothes were so cold they burned. My body trembled like an open E string on an electric bass.

Meg tugged off my wet winter coat. Her own coat was much too small for me, but she draped the warm dry fleece over my shoulders. "Keep yourself together," she ordered. "Don't go crazy on me."

My own laughter sounded brittle. "But I—I heard—"

THE FIRES WILL CONSUME ME. MAKE HASTE!

The voice splintered into a chorus of angry whispers. Shadows grew longer and darker. Steam rose from my clothes, smelling like the volcanic fumes of Delphi.

Part of me wanted to curl into a ball and die. Part of me wanted to get up and run wildly after the voices—to find their source—but I suspected that if I tried, my sanity would be lost forever.

Meg was saying something. She shook my shoulders. She put her face nose-to-nose with mine so my own derelict reflection stared back at me from the lenses of her cat-eye glasses. She slapped me, *hard*, and I managed to decipher her words: "GET UP!"

Somehow I did. Then I doubled over and retched.

I hadn't vomited in centuries. I'd forgotten how unpleasant it was.

The next thing I knew, we were staggering along, Meg bearing most of my weight. The voices whispered and argued, tearing off little pieces of my mind and carrying them away into the forest. Soon I wouldn't have much left.

There was no point. I might as well wander off into the forest and go insane. The idea struck me as funny. I began to giggle.

Meg forced me to keep walking. I couldn't understand her words, but her tone was insistent and stubborn, with just enough anger to outweigh her own terror.

In my fractured mental state, I thought the trees were

parting for us, grudgingly opening a path straight out of the woods. I saw a bonfire in the distance, and the open meadows of Camp Half-Blood.

It occurred to me that Meg was talking to the trees, telling them to get out of the way. The idea was ridiculous, and at the moment it seemed hilarious. Judging from the steam billowing from my clothes, I guessed I was running a fever of about a hundred and six.

I was laughing hysterically as we stumbled out of the forest, straight toward the campfire where a dozen teenagers sat making s'mores. When they saw us, they rose. In their jeans and winter coats, with assorted weapons at their sides, they were the dourest bunch of marshmallow roasters I had ever seen.

I grinned. "Oh, hi! I'm Apollo!"

My eyes rolled up in my head, and I passed out.

10

My bus is in flames
My son is older than me
Please, Zeus, make it stop

I DREAMED I WAS DRIVING the sun chariot across the sky. I had the top down in Maserati mode. I was cruising along, honking at jet planes to get out of my way, enjoying the smell of cold stratosphere, and bopping to my favorite jam: Alabama Shakes' "Rise to the Sun."

I was thinking about transforming the Spyder into a Google self-driving car. I wanted to get out my lute and play a scorching solo that would make Brittany Howard proud.

Then a woman appeared in my passenger seat. "You've got to hurry, man."

I almost jumped out of the sun.

My guest was dressed like a Libyan queen of old. (I should know. I dated a few of them.) Her gown swirled with red, black, and gold floral designs. Her long dark hair was crowned with a tiara that looked like a curved miniature ladder—two gold rails lined with rungs of silver. Her face was mature but stately, the way a benevolent queen should look.

So definitely not Hera, then. Besides, Hera would never smile at me so kindly. Also . . . this woman wore a large metal peace symbol around her neck, which did not seem like Hera's style.

Still, I felt I should know her. Despite the elder-hippie vibe, she was so attractive that I assumed we must be related.

"Who are you?" I asked.

Her eyes flashed a dangerous shade of gold, like a feline predator's. "Follow the voices."

A lump swelled in my throat. I tried to think straight, but my brain felt like it had been recently run through a Vitamix. "I heard you in the woods. . . . Were you—were you speaking a prophecy?"

"Find the gates." She grabbed my wrist. "You've gotta find them first, you dig?"

"But—"

The woman burst into flames. I pulled back my singed wrist and grabbed the wheel as the sun chariot plunged into a nosedive. The Maserati morphed into a school bus—a mode I only used when I had to transport a large number of people. Smoke filled the cabin.

Somewhere behind me, a nasal voice said, "By all means, find the gates."

I glanced in the rearview mirror. Through the smoke, I saw a portly man in a mauve suit. He lounged across the backseat, where the troublemakers normally sat. Hermes was fond of that seat—but this man was not Hermes.

He had a weak jawline, an overlarge nose, and a beard that wrapped around his double chin like a helmet strap. His hair was curly and dark like mine, except not as fashionably tousled or luxuriant. His lip curled as if he smelled something unpleasant. Perhaps it was the burning seats of the bus.

"Who are you?" I yelled, desperately trying to pull the chariot out of its dive. "Why are you on my bus?"

The man smiled, which made his face even uglier. "My own forefather does not recognize me? I'm hurt!"

I tried to place him. My cursed mortal brain was too small, too inflexible. It had jettisoned four thousand years of memories like so much ballast.

"I—I don't," I said. "I'm sorry."

The man laughed as flames licked at his purple sleeves. "You're not sorry *yet*, but you will be. Find me the gates. Lead me to the Oracle. I'll enjoy burning it down!"

Fire consumed me as the sun chariot careened toward the earth. I gripped the wheel and stared in horror as a massive bronze face loomed outside the windshield. It was the face of the man in purple, fashioned from an expanse of metal larger than my bus. As we hurtled toward it, the features shifted and became my own.

Then I woke, shivering and sweating.

"Easy." Someone's hand rested on my shoulder. "Don't try to sit up."

Naturally I tried to sit up.

My bedside attendant was a young man about my age— my *mortal* age—with shaggy blond hair and blue eyes. He wore doctor's scrubs with an open ski jacket, the words OKEMO MOUNTAIN stitched on the pocket. His face had a skier's tan. I felt I should know him. (I'd been having that sensation a lot since my fall from Olympus.)

I was lying in a cot in the middle of a cabin. On either

side, bunk beds lined the walls. Rough cedar beams ribbed the ceiling. The white plaster walls were bare except for a few hooks for coats and weapons.

It could have been a modest abode in almost any age—ancient Athens, medieval France, the farmlands of Iowa. It smelled of clean linen and dried sage. The only decorations were some flowerpots on the windowsill, where cheerful yellow blooms were thriving despite the cold weather outside.

"Those flowers . . ." My voice was hoarse, as if I'd inhaled the smoke from my dream. "Those are from Delos, my sacred island."

"Yep," said the young man. "They only grow in and around Cabin Seven—*your* cabin. Do you know who I am?"

I studied his face. The calmness of his eyes, the smile resting easily on his lips, the way his hair curled around his ears . . . I had a vague memory of a woman, an alt-country singer named Naomi Solace, whom I'd met in Austin. I blushed thinking about her even now. To my teenaged self, our romance felt like something that I'd watched in a movie a long ago time—a movie my parents wouldn't have allowed me to see.

But this boy was definitely Naomi's son.

Which meant he was *my* son too.

Which felt very, very strange.

"You're Will Solace," I said. "My, ah . . . erm—"

"Yeah," Will agreed. "It's awkward."

My frontal lobe did a one-eighty inside my skull. I listed sideways.

"Whoa, there." Will steadied me. "I tried to heal you, but honestly, I don't understand what's wrong. You've got blood, not ichor. You're recovering quickly from your injuries, but your vital signs are completely human."

"Don't remind me."

"Yeah, well . . ." He put his hand on my forehead and frowned in concentration. His fingers trembled slightly. "I didn't *know* any of that until I tried to give you nectar. Your lips started steaming. I almost killed you."

"Ah . . ." I ran my tongue across my bottom lip, which felt heavy and numb. I wondered if that explained my dream about smoke and fire. I hoped so. "I guess Meg forgot to tell you about my condition."

"I guess she did." Will took my wrist and checked my pulse. "You seem to be about my age, fifteen or so. Your heart rate is back to normal. Ribs are mending. Nose is swollen, but not broken."

"And I have acne," I lamented. "And flab."

Will tilted his head. "You're mortal, and *that's* what you're worried about?"

"You're right. I'm powerless. Weaker even than you puny demigods!"

"Gee, thanks. . . ."

I got the feeling that he almost said *Dad* but managed to stop himself.

It was difficult to think of this young man as my son. He was so poised, so unassuming, so free of acne. He also didn't appear to be awestruck in my presence. In fact, the corner of his mouth had started twitching.

"Are—are you amused?" I demanded.

Will shrugged. "Well, it's either find this funny or freak out. My dad, the god Apollo, is a fifteen-year-old—"

"*Sixteen*," I corrected. "Let's go with sixteen."

"A sixteen-year-old mortal, lying in a cot in my cabin, and with all my healing arts—which I got from *you*—I still can't figure out how to fix you."

"There is no fixing this," I said miserably. "I am cast out of Olympus. My fate is tied to a girl named Meg. It could not be worse!"

Will laughed, which I thought took a great deal of gall. "Meg seems cool. She's already poked Connor Stoll in the eyes and kicked Sherman Yang in the crotch."

"She did *what?*"

"She'll get along just fine here. She's waiting for you outside—along with most of the campers." Will's smile faded. "Just so you're prepared, they're asking a lot of questions. Everybody is wondering if your arrival, your *mortal* situation, has anything to do with what's been going on at camp."

I frowned. "What has been going on at camp?"

The cabin door opened. Two more demigods stepped inside. One was a tall boy of about thirteen, his skin burnished bronze and his cornrows woven like DNA helixes. In his black wool peacoat and black jeans, he looked as if he'd stepped from the deck of an eighteenth-century whaling vessel. The other newcomer was a younger girl in olive camouflage. She had a full quiver on her shoulder, and her short ginger hair was dyed with a shock of bright green, which seemed to defeat the point of wearing camouflage.

I smiled, delighted that I actually remembered their names.

"Austin," I said. "And Kayla, isn't it?"

Rather than falling to their knees and blubbering gratefully, they gave each other a nervous glance.

"So it's really you," Kayla said.

Austin frowned. "Meg told us you were beaten up by a couple of thugs. She said you had no powers and you went hysterical out in the woods."

My mouth tasted like burnt school bus upholstery. "Meg talks too much."

"But you're mortal?" Kayla asked. "As in completely mortal? Does that mean I'm going to lose my archery skills? I can't even qualify for the Olympics until I'm sixteen!"

"And if I lose my music . . ." Austin shook his head. "No, man, that's wrong. My last video got, like, five hundred thousand views in a week. What am I supposed to do?"

It warmed my heart that my children had the right priorities: their skills, their images, their views on YouTube. Say what you will about gods being absentee parents; our children inherit many of our finest personality traits.

"My problems should not affect you," I promised. "If Zeus went around retroactively yanking my divine power out of all my descendants, half the medical schools in the country would be empty. The Rock and Roll Hall of Fame would disappear. The Tarot-card reading industry would collapse overnight!"

Austin's shoulders relaxed. "That's a relief."

"So if you die while you're mortal," Kayla said, "we won't disappear?"

"Guys," Will interrupted, "why don't you run to the Big House and tell Chiron that our . . . our *patient* is conscious. I'll bring him along in a minute. And, uh, see if you can disperse the crowd outside, okay? I don't want everybody rushing Apollo at once."

Kayla and Austin nodded sagely. As my children, they no doubt understood the importance of controlling the paparazzi.

As soon as they were gone, Will gave me an apologetic smile. "They're in shock. We all are. It'll take some time to get used to . . . whatever this is."

"You do not seem shocked," I said.

Will laughed under his breath. "I'm terrified. But one thing you learn as head counselor: you have to keep it together for everyone else. Let's get you on your feet."

It was not easy. I fell twice. My head spun, and my eyes felt as if they were being microwaved in their sockets. Recent dreams continued to churn in my brain like river silt, muddying my thoughts—the woman with the crown and the peace symbol, the man in the purple suit. *Lead me to the Oracle. I'll enjoy burning it down!*

The cabin began to feel stifling. I was anxious to get some fresh air.

One thing my sister, Artemis, and I agree on: every worthwhile pursuit is better outdoors than indoors. Music is best played under the dome of heaven. Poetry should be shared in the *agora*. Archery is definitely easier outside, as I can attest after that one time I tried target practice in my father's throne room. And driving the sun . . . well, that's not really an indoor sport either.

Leaning on Will for support, I stepped outside. Kayla and Austin had succeeded in shooing the crowd away. The only one waiting for me—oh, joy and happiness—was my young overlord, Meg, who had apparently now gained fame at camp as Crotchkicker McCaffrey.

She still wore Sally Jackson's hand-me-down green dress, though it was a bit dirtier now. Her leggings were ripped and torn. On her bicep, a line of butterfly bandages closed a nasty cut she must have gotten in the woods.

She took one look at me, scrunched up her face, and stuck out her tongue. "You look *yuck*."

"And you, Meg," I said, "are as charming as ever."

She adjusted her glasses until they were just crooked enough to be annoying. "Thought you were going to die."

"Glad to disappoint you."

"Nah." She shrugged. "You still owe me a year of service. We're bound, whether you like it or not!"

I sighed. It was ever so wonderful to be back in Meg's company.

"I suppose I should thank you. . . ." I had a hazy memory of my delirium in the forest, Meg carrying me along, the trees seeming to part before us. "How did you get us out of the woods?"

Her expression turned guarded. "Dunno. Luck." She jabbed a thumb at Will Solace. "From what he's been telling me, it's a good thing we got out before nightfall."

"Why?"

Will started to answer, then apparently thought better of it. "I should let Chiron explain. Come on."

I rarely visited Camp Half-Blood in winter. The last time had been three years ago, when a girl named Thalia Grace crash-landed my bus in the canoe lake.

I expected the camp to be sparsely populated. I knew

most demigods only came for the summer, leaving a small core of year-rounders during the school term—those who for various reasons found camp the only safe place they could live.

Still, I was struck by how few demigods I saw. If Cabin Seven was any indication, each god's cabin could hold beds for about twenty campers. That meant a maximum capacity of four hundred demigods—enough for several phalanxes or one really amazing yacht party.

Yet, as we walked across camp, I saw no more than a dozen people. In the fading light of sunset, a lone girl was scaling the climbing wall as lava flowed down either side. At the lake, a crew of three checked the rigging on the trireme.

Some campers had found reasons to be outside just so they could gawk at me. Over by the hearth, one young man sat polishing his shield, watching me in its reflective surface. Another fellow glared at me as he spliced barbed wire outside the Ares cabin. From the awkward way he walked, I assumed he was Sherman Yang of the recently kicked crotch.

In the doorway of the Hermes cabin, two girls giggled and whispered as I passed. Normally this sort of attention wouldn't have fazed me. My magnetism was understandably irresistible. But now my face burned. Me—the manly paragon of romance—reduced to a gawky, inexperienced boy!

I would have screamed at the heavens for this unfairness, but that would've been super-embarrassing.

We made our way through the fallow strawberry fields. Up on Half-Blood Hill, the Golden Fleece glinted in the lowest branch of a tall pine tree. Whiffs of steam rose from the head of Peleus, the guardian dragon coiled around the base of the trunk. Next to the tree, the Athena Parthenos looked angry red in the sunset. Or perhaps she just wasn't happy to see me. (Athena had never gotten over our little tiff during the Trojan War.)

Halfway down the hillside, I spotted the Oracle's cave, its entrance shrouded by thick burgundy curtains. The torches on either side stood unlit—usually a sign that my prophetess, Rachel Dare, was not in residence. I wasn't sure whether to be disappointed or relieved.

Even when she was not channeling prophecies, Rachel was a wise young lady. I had hoped to consult her about my problems. On the other hand, since her prophetic power had apparently stopped working (which I suppose in some *small* part was my fault), I wasn't sure Rachel would want to see me. She would expect explanations from her Main Man, and while I had invented *mansplaining* and was its foremost practitioner, I had no answers to give her.

The dream of the flaming bus stayed with me: the groovy crowned woman urging me to find the gates, the ugly mauve-suited man threatening to burn the Oracle.

Well . . . the cave was right there. I wasn't sure why the woman in the crown was having such trouble finding it, or why the ugly man would be so intent on burning its "gates," which amounted to nothing more than purple curtains.

Unless the dream was referring to something other than the Oracle of Delphi. . . .

I rubbed my throbbing temples. I kept reaching for memories that weren't there, trying to plunge into my vast lake of knowledge only to find it had been reduced to a kiddie pool. You simply can't do much with a kiddie pool brain.

On the porch of the Big House, a dark-haired young man was waiting for us. He wore faded black trousers, a Ramones T-shirt (bonus points for musical taste), and a black leather bomber jacket. At his side hung a Stygian iron sword.

"I remember you," I said. "Is it Nicholas, son of Hades?"

"Nico di Angelo." He studied me, his eyes sharp and colorless, like broken glass. "So it's true. You're completely mortal. There's an aura of death around you—a thick possibility of death."

Meg snorted. "Sounds like a weather forecast."

I did not find this amusing. Being face-to-face with a son of Hades, I recalled the many mortals I had sent to the Underworld with my plague arrows. It had always seemed like good clean fun—meting out richly deserved punishments for wicked deeds. Now, I began to understand the terror in my victims' eyes. I did not want an aura of death hanging over me. I definitely did not want to stand in judgment before Nico di Angelo's father.

Will put his hand on Nico's shoulder. "Nico, we need to have another talk about your people skills."

"Hey, I'm just stating the obvious. If this *is* Apollo, and he dies, we're all in trouble."

Will turned to me. "I apologize for my boyfriend."

Nico rolled his eyes. "Could you not—"

"Would you prefer *special guy?*" Will asked. "Or *significant other?*"

"Significant *annoyance*, in your case," Nico grumbled.

"Oh, I'll get you for that."

Meg wiped her dripping nose. "You guys fight a lot. I thought we were going to see a centaur."

"And here I am." The screen door opened. Chiron trotted out, ducking his head to avoid the doorframe.

From the waist up, he looked every bit the professor he often pretended to be in the mortal world. His brown wool jacket had patches on the elbows. His plaid dress shirt did not quite match his green tie. His beard was neatly trimmed, but his hair would have failed the tidiness inspection required for a proper rat's nest.

From the waist down, he was a white stallion.

My old friend smiled, though his eyes were stormy and distracted. "Apollo, it's good you are here. We need to talk about the disappearances."

11

Check your spam folder
The prophecies might be there
No? Well, I'm stumped. Bye

MEG GAWKED. "He—he really *is* a centaur."

"Well spotted," I said. "I suppose the lower body of a horse is what gave him away?"

She punched me in the arm.

"Chiron," I said, "this is Meg McCaffrey, my new master and wellspring of aggravation. You were saying something about disappearances?"

Chiron's tail flicked. His hooves clopped on the planks of the porch.

He was immortal, yet his visible age seemed to vary from century to century. I did not remember his whiskers ever being so gray, or the lines around his eyes so pronounced. Whatever was happening at camp must not have been helping his stress levels.

"Welcome, Meg." Chiron tried for a friendly tone, which I thought quite heroic, seeing as . . . well, *Meg*. "I understand you showed great bravery in the woods. You brought Apollo here despite many dangers. I'm glad to have you at Camp Half-Blood."

"Thanks," said Meg. "You're really tall. Don't you hit your head on light fixtures?"

Chiron chuckled. "Sometimes. If I want to be closer to human size, I have a magical wheelchair that allows me to compact my lower half into . . . Actually, that's not important now."

"Disappearances," I prompted. "What has disappeared?"

"Not *what*, but *who*," Chiron said. "Let's talk inside. Will, Nico, could you please tell the other campers we'll gather for dinner in one hour? I'll give everyone an update, then. In the meantime, no one should roam the camp alone. Use the buddy system."

"Understood." Will looked at Nico. "Will you be my buddy?"

"You are a dork," Nico announced.

The two of them strolled off bickering.

At this point, you may be wondering how I felt seeing my son with Nico di Angelo. I'll admit I did not understand Will's attraction to a child of Hades, but if the dark foreboding type was what made Will happy . . .

Oh. Perhaps some of you are wondering how I felt seeing him with a boyfriend rather than a girlfriend. If that's the case, *please*. We gods are not hung up about such things. I myself have had . . . let's see, thirty-three mortal girlfriends and eleven mortal boyfriends? I've lost count. My two greatest loves were, of course, Daphne and Hyacinthus, but when you're a god as popular as I am—

Hold on. Did I just tell you who I liked? I did, didn't I? Gods of Olympus, forget I mentioned their names! I am so embarrassed. Please don't say anything. In this mortal life, I've never been in love with *anyone*!

I am so confused.

Chiron led us into the living room, where comfy leather couches made a V facing the stone fireplace. Above the mantel, a stuffed leopard head was snoring contentedly.

"Is it alive?" Meg asked.

"Quite." Chiron trotted over to his wheelchair. "That's Seymour. If we speak quietly, we should be able to avoid waking him."

Meg immediately began exploring the living room. Knowing her, she was searching for small objects to throw at the leopard to wake him up.

Chiron settled into his wheelchair. He placed his rear legs into the false compartment of the seat, then backed up, magically compacting his equine hindquarters until he looked like a man sitting down. To complete the illusion, hinged front panels swung closed, giving him fake human legs. Normally those legs were fitted with slacks and loafers to augment his "professor" disguise, but today it seemed Chiron was going for a different look.

"That's new," I said.

Chiron glanced down at his shapely female mannequin legs, dressed in fishnet stockings and red sequined high heels. He sighed heavily. "I see the Hermes cabin have been watching *Rocky Horror Picture Show* again. I will have to have a chat with them."

Rocky Horror Picture Show brought back fond memories. I used to cosplay as Rocky at the midnight showings, because, naturally, the character's perfect physique was based on my own.

"Let me guess," I said. "Connor and Travis Stoll are the pranksters?"

From a nearby basket, Chiron grabbed a flannel blanket and spread it over his fake legs, though the ruby shoes still peeked out at the bottom. "Actually, Travis went off to college last autumn, which has mellowed Connor quite a bit."

Meg looked over from the old *Pac-Man* arcade game. "I poked that guy Connor in the eyes."

Chiron winced. "That's nice, dear. . . . At any rate, we have Julia Feingold and Alice Miyazawa now. They have taken up pranking duty. You'll meet them soon enough."

I recalled the girls who had been giggling at me from the Hermes cabin doorway. I felt myself blushing all over again.

Chiron gestured toward the couches. "Please sit."

Meg moved on from *Pac-Man* (having given the game twenty seconds of her time) and began literally climbing the wall. Dormant grapevines festooned the dining area—no doubt the work of my old friend Dionysus. Meg scaled one of the thicker trunks, trying to reach the Gorgon-hair chandelier.

"Ah, Meg," I said, "perhaps you should watch the orientation film while Chiron and I talk?"

"I know plenty," she said. "I talked to the campers while you were passed out. 'Safe place for modern demigods.' Blah, blah, blah."

"Oh, but the film is very good," I urged. "I shot it on a

tight budget in the 1950s, but some of the camera work was revolutionary. You should really—"

The grapevine peeled away from the wall. Meg crashed to the floor. She popped up completely unscathed, then spotted a platter of cookies on the sideboard. "Are those free?"

"Yes, child," Chiron said. "Bring the tea as well, would you?"

So we were stuck with Meg, who draped her legs over the couch's armrest, chomped on cookies, and threw crumbs at Seymour's snoring head whenever Chiron wasn't looking.

Chiron poured me a cup of Darjeeling. "I'm sorry Mr. D is not here to welcome you."

"Mr. Dee?" Meg asked.

"Dionysus," I explained. "The god of wine. Also the director of this camp."

Chiron handed me my tea. "After the battle with Gaea, I thought Mr. D might return to camp, but he never did. I hope he's all right."

The old centaur looked at me expectantly, but I had nothing to share. The last six months were a complete void; I had no idea what the other Olympians might be up to.

"I don't know anything," I admitted. I hadn't said those words very often in the last four millennia. They tasted bad. I sipped my tea, but that was no less bitter. "I'm a bit behind on the news. I was hoping you could fill me in."

Chiron did a poor job hiding his disappointment. "I see. . . ."

I realized he had been hoping for help and guidance—the

exact same things I needed from *him*. As a god, I was used to lesser beings relying on me—praying for this and pleading for that. But now that I was mortal, being relied upon was a little terrifying.

"So what is your crisis?" I asked. "You have the same look Cassandra had in Troy, or Jim Bowie at the Alamo—as if you're under siege."

Chiron did not dispute the comparison. He cupped his hands around his tea.

"You know that during the war with Gaea, the Oracle of Delphi stopped receiving prophecies. In fact, all known methods of divining the future suddenly failed."

"Because the original cave of Delphi was retaken," I said with a sigh, trying not to feel picked on.

Meg bounced a chocolate chip off Seymour the leopard's nose. "Oracle of Delphi. Percy mentioned that."

"Percy Jackson?" Chiron sat up. "Percy was with you?"

"For a time." I recounted our battle in the peach orchard and Percy's return to New York. "He said he would drive out this weekend if he could."

Chiron looked disheartened, as if my company alone wasn't good enough. Can you imagine?

"At any rate," he continued, "we hoped that once the war was over, the Oracle might start working again. When it did not . . . Rachel became concerned."

"Who's Rachel?" Meg asked.

"Rachel Dare," I said. "The Oracle."

"Thought the Oracle was a place."

"It is."

"Then Rachel is a place, and she stopped working?"

Had I still been a god, I would have turned her into a blue-belly lizard and released her into the wilderness never to be seen again. The thought soothed me.

"The original Delphi was a place in Greece," I told her. "A cavern filled with volcanic fumes, where people would come to receive guidance from my priestess, the Pythia."

"*Pythia.*" Meg giggled. "That's a funny word."

"Yes. Ha-ha. So the Oracle is both a place and a person. When the Greek gods relocated to America back in . . . what was it, Chiron, 1860?"

Chiron seesawed his hand. "More or less."

"I brought the Oracle here to continue speaking prophecies on my behalf. The power has passed down from priestess to priestess over the years. Rachel Dare is the present Oracle."

From the cookie platter, Meg plucked the only Oreo, which I had been hoping to have myself. "Mm-kay. Is it too late to watch that movie?"

"Yes," I snapped. "Now, the way I gained possession of the Oracle of Delphi in the first place was by killing this monster called Python who lived in the depths of the cavern."

"A python like the snake," Meg said.

"Yes and no. The snake species is named after Python the monster, who is also rather snaky, but who is much bigger and scarier and devours small girls who talk too much. At any rate, last August, while I was . . . indisposed, my ancient foe Python was released from Tartarus. He reclaimed the cave of Delphi. That's why the Oracle stopped working."

"But if the Oracle is in America now, why does it matter if some snake monster takes over its old cave?"

That was about the longest sentence I had yet heard her speak. She'd probably done it just to spite me.

"It's too much to explain," I said. "You'll just have to—"

"Meg." Chiron gave her one of his heroically tolerant smiles. "The original site of the Oracle is like the deepest taproot of a tree. The branches and leaves of prophecy may extend across the world, and Rachel Dare may be our loftiest branch, but if the taproot is strangled, the whole tree is endangered. With Python back in residence at his old lair, the spirit of the Oracle has been completely blocked."

"Oh." Meg made a face at me. "Why didn't you just say so?"

Before I could strangle her like the annoying taproot she was, Chiron refilled my teacup.

"The larger problem," he said, "is that we have no other source of prophecies."

"Who cares?" Meg asked. "So you don't know the future. Nobody knows the future."

"*Who cares?!*" I shouted. "Meg McCaffrey, prophecies are the catalysts for every important event—every quest or battle, disaster or miracle, birth or death. Prophecies don't simply foretell the future. They shape it! They *allow* the future to happen."

"I don't get it."

Chiron cleared his throat. "Imagine prophecies are flower seeds. With the right seeds, you can grow any garden you desire. Without seeds, no growth is possible."

"Oh." Meg nodded. "That would suck."

I found it strange that Meg, a street urchin and Dumpster warrior, would relate so well to garden metaphors, but Chiron was an excellent teacher. He had picked up on something about the girl . . . an impression that had been lurking in the back of my mind as well. I hoped I was wrong about what it meant, but with my luck, I would be right. I usually was.

"So where is Rachel Dare?" I asked. "Perhaps if I spoke with her . . . ?"

Chiron set down his tea. "Rachel planned to visit us during her winter vacation, but she never did. It might not mean anything. . . ."

I leaned forward. It was not unheard of for Rachel Dare to be late. She was artistic, unpredictable, impulsive, and rule-averse—all qualities I dearly admired. But it wasn't like her not to show up at all.

"Or?" I asked.

"Or it might be part of the larger problem," Chiron said. "Prophecies are not the only things that have failed. Travel and communication have become difficult in the last few months. We haven't heard from our friends at Camp Jupiter in weeks. No new demigods have arrived. Satyrs aren't reporting from the field. Iris messages no longer work."

"Iris what?" Meg asked.

"Two-way visions," I said. "A form of communication overseen by the rainbow goddess. Iris has always been flighty. . . ."

"Except that normal human communications are also on the fritz," Chiron said. "Of course, phones have always been dangerous for demigods—"

"Yeah, they attract monsters," Meg agreed. "I haven't used a phone in *forever*."

"A wise move," Chiron said. "But recently our phones have stopped working altogether. Mobile, landline, Internet . . . it doesn't seem to matter. Even the archaic form of communication known as *e-mail* is strangely unreliable. The messages simply don't arrive."

"Did you look in the junk folder?" I offered.

"I fear the problem is more complicated," Chiron said. "We have no communication with the outside world. We are alone and understaffed. You are the first newcomers in almost two months."

I frowned. "Percy Jackson mentioned nothing of this."

"I doubt Percy is even aware," Chiron said. "He's been busy with school. Winter is normally our quietest time. For a while, I was able to convince myself that the communication failures were nothing but an inconvenient happenstance. Then the disappearances started."

In the fireplace, a log slipped from the andiron. I may or may not have jumped in my seat.

"The disappearances, yes." I wiped drops of tea from my pants and tried to ignore Meg's snickering. "Tell me about those."

"Three in the last month," Chiron said. "First it was Cecil Markowitz from the Hermes cabin. One morning his bunk was simply empty. He didn't say anything about wanting to leave. No one saw him go. And in the past few weeks, no one has seen or heard from him."

"Children of Hermes do tend to sneak around," I offered.

"At first, that's what we thought," said Chiron. "But a

week later, Ellis Wakefield disappeared from the Ares cabin. Same story: empty bunk, no signs that he had either left on his own *or* was . . . ah, taken. Ellis was an impetuous young man. It was conceivable he might have charged off on some ill-advised adventure, but it made me uneasy. Then this morning we realized a third camper had vanished: Miranda Gardiner, head of the Demeter cabin. That was the worst news of all."

Meg swung her feet off the armrest. "Why is that the worst?"

"Miranda is one of our senior counselors," Chiron said. "She would never leave on her own without notice. She is too smart to be tricked away from camp, and too powerful to be forced. Yet something happened to her . . . something I can't explain."

The old centaur faced me. "Something is very wrong, Apollo. These problems may not be as alarming as the rise of Kronos or the awakening of Gaea, but in a way I find them even more unsettling, because I have never seen anything like this before."

I recalled my dream of the burning sun bus. I thought of the voices I'd heard in the woods, urging me to wander off and find their source.

"These demigods . . ." I said. "Before they disappeared, did they act unusual in any way? Did they report . . . hearing things?"

Chiron raised an eyebrow. "Not that I am aware of. Why?"

I was reluctant to say more. I didn't want to cause a panic without knowing what we were facing. When mortals panic, it can be an ugly scene, especially if they expect *me* to fix the problem.

Also, I will admit I felt a bit impatient. We had not yet addressed the most important issues—*mine*.

"It seems to me," I said, "that our first priority is to bend all the camp's resources to helping me regain my divine state. Then I can assist you with these other problems."

Chiron stroked his beard. "But what if the problems are connected, my friend? What if the only way to restore you to Olympus is by reclaiming the Oracle of Delphi, thus freeing the power of prophecy? What if Delphi is the key to it all?"

I had forgotten about Chiron's tendency to lay out obvious and logical conclusions that I tried to avoid thinking about. It was an infuriating habit.

"In my present state, that's impossible." I pointed at Meg. "Right now, my job is to serve this demigod, probably for a year. After I've done whatever tasks she assigns me, Zeus will judge that my sentence has been served, and I can once again become a god."

Meg pulled apart a Fig Newton. "I could order you to go to this Delphi place."

"No!" My voice cracked in midshriek. "You should assign me *easy* tasks—like starting a rock band, or just hanging out. Yes, hanging out is good."

Meg looked unconvinced. "Hanging out isn't a task."

"It is if you do it right. Camp Half-Blood can protect me while I hang out. After my year of servitude is up, I'll become a god. *Then* we can talk about how to restore Delphi."

Preferably, I thought, by ordering some demigods to undertake the quest for me.

"Apollo," Chiron said, "if demigods keep disappearing, we may not have a year. We may not have the strength to protect you. And, forgive me, but Delphi *is* your responsibility."

I tossed up my hands. "I wasn't the one who opened the Doors of Death and let Python out! Blame Gaea! Blame Zeus for his bad judgment! When the giants started to wake, I drew up a very clear *Twenty-Point Plan of Action to Protect Apollo and Also You Other Gods,* but he didn't even read it!"

Meg tossed half of her cookie at Seymour's head. "I still think it's your fault. Hey, look! He's awake!"

She said this as if the leopard had decided to wake up on his own rather than being beaned in the eye with a Fig Newton.

"*RARR,*" Seymour complained.

Chiron wheeled his chair back from the table. "My dear, in that jar on the mantel, you'll find some Snausages. Why don't you feed him dinner? Apollo and I will wait on the porch."

We left Meg happily making three-point shots into Seymour's mouth with the treats.

Once Chiron and I reached the porch, he turned his wheelchair to face me. "She's an interesting demigod."

"*Interesting* is such a nonjudgmental term."

"She really summoned a karpos?"

"Well . . . the spirit appeared when she was in trouble. Whether she consciously summoned it, I don't know. She named him Peaches."

Chiron scratched his beard. "I have not seen a demigod with the power to summon grain spirits in a very long time. You know what it means?"

My feet began to quake. "I have my suspicions. I'm trying to stay positive."

"She guided you out of the woods," Chiron noted. "Without her—"

"Yes," I said. "Don't remind me."

It occurred to me that I'd seen that keen look in Chiron's eyes before—when he'd assessed Achilles's sword technique and Ajax's skill with a spear. It was the look of a seasoned coach scouting new talent. I'd never dreamed the centaur would look at *me* that way, as if I had something to prove to him, as if my mettle were untested. I felt so . . . so *objectified*.

"Tell me," Chiron said, "what did you hear in the woods?"

I silently cursed my big mouth. I should not have asked whether the missing demigods had heard anything strange.

I decided it was fruitless to hold back now. Chiron was more perceptive than your average horse-man. I told him what I'd experienced in the forest, and afterward in my dream.

His hands curled into his lap blanket. The bottom of it rose higher above his red sequined pumps. He looked about as worried as it is possible for a man to look while wearing fishnet stockings.

"We will have to warn the campers to stay away from the forest," he decided. "I do not understand what is happening, but I still maintain it *must* be connected to Delphi, and your present . . . ah, situation. The Oracle must be liberated from the monster Python. We must find a way."

I translated that easily enough: *I* must find a way.

Chiron must have read my desolate expression.

"Come, come, old friend," he said. "You have done it before. Perhaps you are not a god now, but the first time you killed Python it was no challenge at all! Hundreds of storybooks have praised the way you easily slew your enemy."

"Yes," I muttered. "Hundreds of storybooks."

I recalled some of those stories: I had killed Python without breaking a sweat. I flew to the mouth of the cave, called him out, unleashed an arrow, and *BOOM!*—one dead giant snake monster. I became Lord of Delphi, and we all lived happily ever after.

How did storytellers get the idea that I vanquished Python so quickly?

All right . . . possibly it's because I told them so. Still, the truth was rather different. For centuries after our battle, I had bad dreams about my old foe.

Now I was almost grateful for my imperfect memory. I could not recollect all of the nightmarish details of my fight with Python, but I *did* know he had been no pushover. I had needed all my godly strength, my divine powers, and the world's most deadly bow.

What chance would I have as a sixteen-year-old mortal with acne, hand-me-down clothes, and the nom de guerre Lester Papadopoulos? I was not going to charge off to Greece and get myself killed, thank you very much, especially not without my sun chariot or the ability to teleport. I'm sorry; gods do *not* fly commercial.

I tried to figure out how to explain this to Chiron in a calm, diplomatic way that did not involve stomping my feet or screaming. I was saved from the effort by the sound of a conch horn in the distance.

"That means dinner." The centaur forced a smile. "We will talk more later, eh? For now, let's celebrate your arrival."

12

Ode to a hot dog
With bug juice and tater chips
I got nothing, man

I WAS NOT IN THE MOOD TO CELEBRATE.

Especially sitting at a picnic table eating mortal food. With mortals.

The dining pavilion was pleasant enough. Even in winter, the camp's magical borders shielded us from the worst of the elements. Sitting outdoors in the warmth of the torches and braziers, I felt only slightly chilly. Long Island Sound glittered in the light of the moon. (Hello, Artemis. Don't bother to say hi.) On Half-Blood Hill, the Athena Parthenos glowed like the world's largest nightlight. Even the woods did not seem so creepy with the pine trees blanketed in soft silvery fog.

My dinner, however, was less than poetic. It consisted of hot dogs, potato chips, and a red liquid I was told was bug juice. I did not know why humans consumed bug juice, or from which type of bug it had been extracted, but it was the tastiest part of the meal, which was disconcerting.

I sat at the Apollo table with my children Austin, Kayla, and Will, plus Nico di Angelo. I could see no difference between my table and any of the other gods' tables. Mine should have been shinier and more elegant. It should have played music or recited poetry upon command. Instead it was just a slab of stone with benches on either side. I found the seating uncomfortable, though my offspring didn't seem to mind.

Austin and Kayla peppered me with questions about Olympus, the war with Gaea, and what it felt like to be a god and then a human. I knew they did not mean to be rude. As my children, they were inherently inclined to the utmost grace. However, their questions were painful reminders of my fallen status.

Besides, as the hours passed, I remembered less and less about my divine life. It was alarming how fast my cosmically perfect neurons had deteriorated. Once, each memory had been like a high-definition audio file. Now those recordings were on wax cylinders. And believe me, I remember wax cylinders. They did not last long in the sun chariot.

Will and Nico sat shoulder to shoulder, bantering good-naturedly. They were so cute together it made me feel desolate. It jogged my memories of those few short golden months I'd shared with Hyacinthus before the jealousy, before the horrible accident . . .

"Nico," I said at last, "shouldn't you be sitting at the Hades table?"

He shrugged. "Technically, yes. But if I sit alone at my table, strange things happen. Cracks open in the floor. Zombies crawl out and start roaming around. It's a mood disorder. I can't control it. That's what I told Chiron."

"And is it true?" I asked.

Nico smiled thinly. "I have a note from my doctor."

Will raised his hand. "I'm his doctor."

"Chiron decided it wasn't worth arguing about," Nico said. "As long as I sit at a table with other people, like . . . oh, these guys for instance . . . the zombies stay away. Everybody's happier."

Will nodded serenely. "It's the strangest thing. Not that Nico would ever misuse his powers to get what he wants."

"Of course not," Nico agreed.

I glanced across the dining pavilion. As per camp tradition, Meg had been placed with the children of Hermes, since her godly parentage had not yet been determined. Meg didn't seem to mind. She was busy re-creating the Coney Island Hot Dog Eating Contest all by herself. The other two girls, Julia and Alice, watched her with a mixture of fascination and horror.

Across the table from her sat an older skinny boy with curly brown hair—Connor Stoll, I deduced, though I'd never been able to tell him apart from his older brother, Travis. Despite the darkness, Connor wore sunglasses, no doubt to protect his eyes from a repeat poking. I also noted that he wisely kept his hands away from Meg's mouth.

In the entire pavilion, I counted nineteen campers. Most sat alone at their respective tables—Sherman Yang for Ares; a girl I did not know for Aphrodite; another girl for Demeter. At the Nike table, two dark-haired young ladies who were obviously twins conversed over a war map. Chiron himself, again in full centaur form, stood at the head table, sipping his bug juice as he chatted with two satyrs, but their mood was subdued. The goat-men kept glancing at me, then eating their silverware, as satyrs tend to do when nervous. Half a dozen gorgeous dryads moved between the tables, offering food and drink, but I was so preoccupied I couldn't fully appreciate their beauty. Even more tragic: I felt too embarrassed to flirt with them. What was *wrong* with me?

I studied the campers, hoping to spot some potential servants . . . I mean new friends. Gods always like to keep a few strong veteran demigods handy to throw into battle, send on dangerous quests, or pick the lint off our togas. Unfortunately, no one at dinner jumped out at me as a likely minion. I longed for a bigger pool of talent.

"Where are the . . . others?" I asked Will.

I wanted to say *the A-List*, but I thought that might be taken the wrong way.

Will took a bite of his pizza. "Were you looking for somebody in particular?"

"What about the ones who went on that quest with the boat?"

Will and Nico exchanged a look that might have meant, *Here we go*. I suppose they got asked a lot about the seven legendary demigods who had fought side by side with the gods against Gaea's giants. It pained me that I had not gotten to see those heroes again. After any major battle, I liked to get a group photo—along with exclusive rights to compose epic ballads about their exploits.

"Well," Nico started, "you saw Percy. He and Annabeth

are spending their senior year in New York. Hazel and Frank are at Camp Jupiter doing the Twelfth Legion thing."

"Ah, yes." I tried to bring up a clear mental picture of Camp Jupiter, the Roman enclave near Berkeley, California, but the details were hazy. I could only remember my conversations with Octavian, the way he'd turned my head with his flattery and promises. That stupid boy . . . it was his fault I was here.

A voice whispered in the back of my mind. This time I thought it might be my conscience: *Who was the stupid boy? It wasn't Octavian.*

"Shut up," I murmured.

"What?" Nico asked.

"Nothing. Continue."

"Jason and Piper are spending the school year in Los Angeles with Piper's dad. They took Coach Hedge, Mellie, and Little Chuck with them."

"Uh-huh." I did not know those last three names, so I decided they probably weren't important. "And the seventh hero . . . Leo Valdez?"

Nico raised his eyebrows. "You remember his name?"

"Of course! He invented the Valdezinator. Oh, what a musical instrument! I barely had time to master its major scales before Zeus zapped me at the Parthenon. If anyone could help me, it would be Leo Valdez."

Nico's expression tightened with annoyance. "Well, Leo isn't here. He died. Then he came back to life. And if I see him again, I'll kill him."

Will elbowed him. "No, you won't." He turned to me.

"During the fight with Gaea, Leo and his bronze dragon, Festus, disappeared in a midair fiery explosion."

I shivered. After so many centuries driving the sun chariot, the term *midair fiery explosion* did not sit well with me.

I tried to remember the last time I'd seen Leo Valdez on Delos, when he'd traded the Valdezinator for information. . . .

"He was looking for the physician's cure," I recalled, "the way to bring someone back from the dead. I suppose he planned all along to sacrifice himself?"

"Yep," Will said. "He got rid of Gaea in the explosion, but we all assumed he died too."

"Because he *did*," Nico said.

"Then, a few days later," Will continued, "this scroll came fluttering into camp on the wind. . . ."

"I still have it." Nico rummaged through the pockets of his bomber jacket. "I look at it whenever I want to get angry."

He produced a thick parchment scroll. As soon as he spread it on the table, a flickering hologram appeared above the surface: Leo Valdez, looking impish as usual with his dark wispy hair, his mischievous grin, and his diminutive stature. (Of course, the hologram was only three inches tall, but even in real life Leo was not much more imposing.) His jeans, blue work shirt, and tool belt were speckled with machine oil.

"Hey, guys!" Leo spread his arms for a hug. "Sorry to leave you like that. Bad news: I died. Good news: I got better! I had to go rescue Calypso. We're both fine now. We're taking Festus to—" The image guttered like a flame in a strong breeze, disrupting Leo's voice. "Back as soon as—" Static. "Cook tacos when—" More static. "¡Vaya con queso! Love ya!" The image winked out.

"That's all we got," Nico complained. "And that was in August. We have no idea what he was planning, where he is now, or whether he's still safe. Jason and Piper spent most of September looking for him until Chiron finally insisted they go start their school year."

"Well," I said, "it sounds like Leo was planning to cook tacos. Perhaps that took longer than he anticipated. And *vaya con queso* . . . I believe he is admonishing us to go *with cheese*, which is always sound advice."

This did not seem to reassure Nico.

"I don't like being in the dark," he muttered.

An odd complaint for a child of Hades, but I understood what he meant. I, too, was curious to know the fate of Leo Valdez. Once upon a time, I could have divined his whereabouts as easily as you might check a Facebook timeline, but now I could only stare at the sky and wonder when a small impish demigod might appear with a bronze dragon and a plate of tacos.

And if Calypso was involved . . . that complicated things. The sorceress and I had a rocky history, but even *I* had to admit she was beguiling. If she'd captured Leo's heart, it was entirely possible he had gotten sidetracked. Odysseus spent seven years with her before returning home.

Whatever the case, it seemed unlikely that Valdez would be back in time to help me. My quest to master the Valdezinator's arpeggios would have to wait.

Kayla and Austin had been very quiet, following our

conversation with wonder and amazement. (My words have that effect on people.)

Now Kayla scooted toward me. "What did you guys talk about in the Big House? Chiron told you about the disappearances . . . ?"

"Yes." I tried to avoid looking in the direction of the woods. "We discussed the situation."

"And?" Austin spread his fingers on the table. "What's going on?"

I didn't want to talk about it. I didn't want them to see my fear.

I wished my head would stop pounding. On Olympus, headaches were so much easier to cure. Hephaestus simply split one's skull open and extracted whatever newborn god or goddess happened to be banging around in there. In the mortal world, my options were more limited.

"I need time to think about it," I said. "Perhaps in the morning I'll have some of my godly powers back."

Austin leaned forward. In the torchlight, his cornrows seemed to twist into new DNA patterns. "Is that how it works? Your strength comes back over time?"

"I—I think so." I tried to remember my years of servitude with Admetus and Laomedon, but I could barely conjure their names and faces. My contracting memory terrified me. It made each moment of the present balloon in size and importance, reminding me that time for mortals was limited.

"I have to get stronger," I decided. "I *must*."

Kayla squeezed my hand. Her archer's fingers were rough

and calloused. "It's okay, Apollo . . . Dad. We'll help you."

Austin nodded. "Kayla's right. We're in this together. If anybody gives you trouble, Kayla will shoot them. Then I'll curse them so bad they'll be speaking in rhyming couplets for weeks."

My eyes watered. Not so long ago—like this morning, for instance—the idea of these young demigods being able to help me would have struck me as ridiculous. Now their kindness moved me more than a hundred sacrificial bulls. I couldn't recall the last time someone had cared about me enough to curse my enemies with rhyming couplets.

"Thank you," I managed.

I could not add *my children*. It didn't seem right. These demigods were my protectors and my family, but for the present I could not think of myself as their father. A father should do more—a father should give more to his children than he takes. I have to admit that this was a novel idea for me. It made me feel even worse than before.

"Hey . . ." Will patted my shoulder. "It's not so bad. At least with everybody being on high alert, we might not have to do Harley's obstacle course tomorrow."

Kayla muttered an ancient Greek curse. If I had been a *proper* godly father, I would have washed her mouth out with olive oil.

"I forgot all about that," she said. "They'll *have* to cancel it, won't they?"

I frowned. "What obstacle course? Chiron mentioned nothing about this."

I wanted to object that my entire day had been an

obstacle course. Surely they couldn't expect me to do their camp activities as well. Before I could say as much, one of the satyrs blew a conch horn at the head table.

Chiron raised his arms for attention.

"Campers!" His voice filled the pavilion. He could be quite impressive when he wanted to be. "I have a few announcements, including news about tomorrow's three-legged death race!"

13

Three-legged death race

Five terrible syllables

Oh, gods. Please not Meg

IT WAS ALL HARLEY'S FAULT.

After addressing the disappearance of Miranda Gardiner—"As a precautionary measure, please stay away from the woods until we know more"—Chiron called forward the young son of Hephaestus to explain how the three-legged death race would work. It quickly became apparent that Harley had masterminded the whole project. And, really, the idea was so horrifying, it could only have sprung from the mind of an eight-year-old boy.

I confess I lost track of the specifics after he explained the exploding chain-saw Frisbees.

"And they'll be like, ZOOM!" He bounced up and down with excitement. "And then BUZZ! And POW!" He pantomimed all sorts of chaos with his hands. "You have to be really quick or you'll die, and it's awesome!"

The other campers grumbled and shifted on their benches.

Chiron raised his hand for silence. "Now, I know there were problems last time," he said, "but fortunately our healers in the Apollo cabin were able to reattach Paolo's arms."

At a table in back, a muscular teen boy rose and began ranting in what I thought was Portuguese. He wore a white tank top over his dark chest, and I could see faint white scars around the tops of his biceps. Cursing rapidly, he pointed at Harley, the Apollo cabin, and pretty much everyone else.

"Ah, thank you, Paolo," Chiron said, clearly baffled. "I'm glad you are feeling better."

Austin leaned toward me and whispered, "Paolo understands English okay, but he only speaks Portuguese. At least, that's what he claims. None of us can understand a word he says."

I didn't understand Portuguese either. Athena had been lecturing us for years about how Mount Olympus might migrate to Brazil someday, and we should all be prepared for the possibility. She'd even bought the gods Berlitz Portuguese DVDs for Saturnalia presents, but what does Athena know?

"Paolo seems agitated," I noted.

Will shrugged. "He's lucky he's a fast healer—son of Hebe, goddess of youth, and all that."

"You're staring," Nico noted.

"I am not," Will said. "I am merely assessing how well Paolo's arms are functioning after surgery."

"Hmph."

Paolo finally sat down. Chiron went through a long list of other injuries they had experienced during the first three-legged death race, all of which he hoped to avoid this time: second-degree burns, burst eardrums, a pulled groin, and two cases of chronic Irish step dancing.

The lone demigod at the Athena table raised his hand.

"Chiron, just going to throw this out there. . . . We've had three campers disappear. Is it really wise to be running a dangerous obstacle course?"

Chiron gave him a pained smile. "An excellent question, Malcolm, but this course will not take you into the woods, which we believe is the most hazardous area. The satyrs, dryads, and I will continue to investigate the disappearances. We will not rest until our missing campers are found. In the meantime, however, this three-legged race can foster important team-building skills. It also expands our understanding of the Labyrinth."

The word smacked me in the face like Ares's body odor. I turned to Austin. "The Labyrinth? As in *Daedalus's* Labyrinth?"

Austin nodded, his fingers worrying the ceramic camp beads around his neck. I had a sudden memory of his mother, Latricia—the way she used to fiddle with her cowry necklace when she lectured at Oberlin. Even *I* learned things from Latricia Lake's music theory class, though I had found her distractingly beautiful.

"During the war with Gaea," Austin said, "the maze reopened. We've been trying to map it ever since."

"That's impossible," I said. "Also insane. The Labyrinth is a malevolent sentient creation! It can't be mapped or trusted."

As usual, I could only draw on random bits and pieces of my memories, but I was fairly certain I spoke the truth. I remembered Daedalus. Back in the old days, the king of Crete had ordered him to build a maze to contain the monstrous Minotaur. But, oh no, a simple maze wasn't *good* enough for a brilliant inventor like Daedalus. He had to make his Labyrinth self-aware and self-expanding. Over the centuries, it had honeycombed under the planet's surface like an invasive root system.

Stupid brilliant inventors.

"It's different now," Austin told me. "Since Daedalus died . . . I don't know. It's hard to describe. Doesn't feel so evil. Not quite as deadly."

"Oh, that's hugely reassuring. So of course you decided to do three-legged races through it."

Will coughed. "The other thing, Dad . . . Nobody wants to disappoint Harley."

I glanced at the head table. Chiron was still holding forth about the virtues of team building while Harley bounced up and down. I could see why the other campers might adopt the boy as their unofficial mascot. He was a cute little pip-squeak, even if he was scarily buff for an eight-year-old. His grin was infectious. His enthusiasm seemed to lift the mood of the entire group. Still, I recognized the mad gleam in his eyes. It was the same look his father, Hephaestus, got whenever he invented some automaton that would later go berserk and start destroying cities.

"Also keep in mind," Chiron was saying, "that none of the unfortunate disappearances has been linked to the Labyrinth. Remain with your partner and you should be safe . . . at least, as safe as one can be in a three-legged death race."

"Yeah," Harley said. "Nobody has even *died* yet." He sounded disappointed, as if he wanted us to try harder.

"In the face of a crisis," Chiron said, "it's important to

stick to our regular activities. We must stay alert and in top condition. Our missing campers would expect no less from us. Now, as to the teams for the race, you will be allowed to choose your partner—"

There followed a sort of piranha attack of campers lunging toward each other to grab their preferred teammate. Before I could contemplate my options, Meg McCaffrey pointed at me from across the pavilion, her expression exactly like Uncle Sam's in the recruitment poster.

Of course, I thought. Why should my luck improve now?

Chiron struck his hoof against the floor. "All right, everyone, settle down! The race will be tomorrow afternoon. Thank you, Harley, for your hard work on the . . . um, various lethal surprises in store."

"BLAM!" Harley ran back to the Hephaestus table to join his older sister, Nyssa.

"This brings us to our other news," Chiron said. "As you may have heard, two special newcomers joined us today. First, please welcome the god Apollo!"

Normally this was my cue to stand up, spread my arms, and grin as radiant light shone around me. The adoring crowd would applaud and toss flowers and chocolate bonbons at my feet.

This time I received no applause—just nervous looks. I had a strange, uncharacteristic impulse to slide lower in my seat and pull my coat over my head. I restrained myself through heroic effort.

Chiron struggled to maintain his smile. "Now, I know this is unusual," he said, "but gods *do* become mortal from time to time. You should not be overly alarmed. Apollo's presence among us could be a good omen, a chance for us to . . ." He seemed to lose track of his own argument. "Ah . . . do something good. I'm sure the best course of action will become clear in time. For now, please make Apollo feel at home. Treat him as you would any other new camper."

At the Hermes table, Connor Stoll raised his hand. "Does that mean the Ares cabin should stick Apollo's head in a toilet?"

At the Ares table, Sherman Yang snorted. "We don't do that to everyone, Connor. Just the newbies who deserve it."

Sherman glanced at Meg, who was obliviously finishing her last hot dog. The wispy black whiskers at the sides of her mouth were now frosted with mustard.

Connor Stoll grinned back at Sherman—a conspiratorial look if ever I saw one. That's when I noticed the open backpack at Connor's feet. Peeking from the top was something that looked like a net.

The implication sank in: two boys whom Meg had humiliated, preparing for payback. I didn't have to be Nemesis to understand the allure of revenge. Still . . . I felt an odd desire to warn Meg.

I tried to catch her eye, but she remained focused on her dinner.

"Thank you, Sherman," Chiron continued. "It's good to know you won't be giving the god of archery a swirly. As for the rest of you, we will keep you posted on our guest's situation. I'm sending two of our finest satyrs, Millard and Herbert"—he gestured to the satyrs on his left—"to hand-deliver a message to Rachel Dare in New York. With any luck, she will be able to join us soon and help determine how we can best assist Apollo."

There was some grumbling about this. I caught the words *Oracle* and *prophecies*. At a nearby table, a girl muttered to herself in Italian: *The blind leading the blind*.

I glared at her, but the young lady was quite beautiful. She was perhaps two years older than I (mortally speaking), with dark pixie hair and devastatingly fierce almond eyes. I may have blushed.

I turned back to my tablemates. "Um . . . yes, satyrs. Why not send that other satyr, the friend of Percy's?"

"Grover?" Nico asked. "He's in California. The whole Council of Cloven Elders is out there, meeting about the drought."

"Oh." My spirits fell. I remembered Grover as being quite resourceful, but if he was dealing with California's natural disasters, he was unlikely to be back anytime in the next decade.

"Finally," Chiron said, "we welcome a new demigod to camp—Meg McCaffrey!"

She wiped her mouth and stood.

Next to her, Alice Miyazawa said, "Stand up, Meg."

Julia Feingold laughed.

At the Ares table, Sherman Yang rose. "Now *this* one—this one deserves a special welcome. What do you think, Connor?"

Connor reached into his backpack. "I think maybe the canoe lake."

I started to say, "Meg—"

Then all Hades broke loose.

Sherman Yang strode toward Meg. Connor Stoll pulled out a golden net and threw it over her head. Meg yelped and tried to squirm free, while some of the campers chanted, "Dunk—her! Dunk—her!" Chiron did his best to shout them down: "Now, demigods, wait a moment!"

A guttural howl interrupted the proceedings. From the top of the colonnade, a blur of chubby flesh, leafy wings, and linen diaper hurtled downward and landed on Sherman Yang's back, knocking him face-first into the stone floor. Peaches the karpos stood and wailed, beating his chest. His eyes glowed green with anger. He launched himself at Connor Stoll, locked his plump legs around the demigod's neck, and began pulling out Connor's hair with his claws.

"Get it off!" Connor wailed, thrashing blindly around the pavilion. "Get it off!"

Slowly the other demigods overcame their shock. Several drew swords.

"C'è un karpos!" yelled the Italian girl.

"Kill it!" said Alice Miyazawa.

"No!" I cried.

Normally such a command from me would've initiated a prison lockdown situation, with all the mortals dropping to their bellies to await my further orders. Alas, now I was a mere mortal with a squeaky adolescent voice.

I watched in horror as my own daughter Kayla nocked an arrow in her bow.

"Peaches, get off him!" Meg screamed. She untangled herself from the net, threw it down, then ran toward Connor.

The karpos hopped off Connor's neck. He landed at

Meg's feet, baring his fangs and hissing at the other camp-ers who had formed a loose semicircle with weapons drawn.

"Meg, get out of the way," said Nico di Angelo. "That thing is dangerous."

"No!" Meg's voice was shrill. "Don't kill him!"

Sherman Yang rolled over, groaning. His face looked worse than it probably was—a gash on the forehead can produce a shocking amount of blood—but the sight steeled the resolve of the other campers. Kayla drew her bow. Julia Feingold unsheathed a dagger.

"Wait!" I pleaded.

What happened next, a lesser mind could never have processed.

Julia charged. Kayla shot her arrow.

Meg thrust out her hands and faint gold light flashed between her fingers. Suddenly young McCaffrey was hold-ing two swords—each a curved blade in the old Thracian style, *siccae* made from Imperial gold. I had not seen such weapons since the fall of the Rome. They seemed to have appeared from nowhere, but my long experience with magic items told me they must have been summoned from the crescent rings Meg always wore.

Both her blades whirled. Meg simultaneously sliced Kayla's arrow out of the air and disarmed Julia, sending her dagger skittering across the floor.

"What the Hades?" Connor demanded. His hair had been pulled out in chunks so he looked like an abused doll. "Who *is* this kid?"

Peaches crouched at Meg's side, snarling, as Meg fended off the confused and enraged demigods with her two swords.

My vision must have been better than the average mortal's, because I saw the glowing sign first—a light shining above Meg's head.

When I recognized the symbol, my heart turned to lead. I hated what I saw, but I thought I should point it out. "Look."

The others seemed confused. Then the glow became brighter: a holographic golden sickle with a few sheaves of wheat, rotating just above Meg McCaffrey.

A boy in the crowd gasped. "She's a communist!"

A girl who'd been sitting at Cabin Four's table gave him a disgusted sneer. "No, Damien, that's my *mom's* symbol." Her face went slack as the truth sank in. "Uh, which means . . . it's *her* mom's symbol."

My head spun. I did not want this knowledge. I did not want to serve a demigod with Meg's parentage. But now I understood the crescents on Meg's rings. They were not moons; they were sickle blades. As the only Olympian present, I felt I should make her title official.

"My friend is no longer unclaimed," I announced.

The other demigods knelt in respect, some more reluctantly than others.

"Ladies and gentlemen," I said, my voice as bitter as Chiron's tea, "please give it up for Meg McCaffrey, daughter of Demeter."

14

You've got to be kid—
Well, crud, what just happened there?
I ran out of syl—

NO ONE KNEW WHAT TO MAKE OF MEG.

I couldn't blame them.

The girl made even less sense to me now that I knew who her mother was.

I'd had my suspicions, yes, but I'd hoped to be proven wrong. Being right so much of the time was a terrible burden.

Why would I dread a child of Demeter?

Good question.

Over the past day, I had been doing my best to piece together my remembrances of the goddess. Once Demeter had been my favorite aunt. That first generation of gods could be a stuffy bunch (I'm looking at you, Hera, Hades, Dad), but Demeter had always been a kind and loving presence—except when she was destroying mankind through pestilence and famine, but everyone has their bad days.

Then I made the mistake of dating one of her daughters. I think her name was Chrysothemis, but you'll have to excuse me if I'm wrong. Even when I was a god, I had trouble remembering the names of all my exes. The young woman sang a harvest song at one of my Delphic festivals. Her voice was so beautiful, I fell in love. True, I fell in love with each year's winner and the runners-up, but what can I say? I'm a sucker for a melodious voice.

Demeter did not approve. Ever since her daughter Persephone had been kidnapped by Hades, she'd been a little touchy about her children dating gods.

At any rate, she and I had words. We reduced a few mountains to rubble. We laid waste to a few city-states. You know how family arguments can get. Finally we settled into an uneasy truce, but since then I'd made a point to steer clear of Demeter's children.

Now here I was—a servant to Meg McCaffrey, the most ragamuffin daughter of Demeter ever to swing a sickle.

I wondered who Meg's father had been to attract the attention of the goddess. Demeter rarely fell in love with mortals. Meg was unusually powerful, too. Most children of Demeter could do little more than make crops grow and keep bacterial fungi at bay. Dual-wielding golden blades and summoning karpoi—that was top-shelf stuff.

All of this went through my mind as Chiron dispersed the crowd, urging everyone to put away their weapons. Since head counselor Miranda Gardiner was missing, Chiron asked Billie Ng, the only other camper from Demeter, to escort Meg to Cabin Four. The two girls made a quick retreat, Peaches bouncing along excitedly behind them. Meg shot me a worried look.

Not sure what else to do, I gave her two thumbs-up. "See you tomorrow!"

She seemed less than encouraged as she disappeared in the darkness.

Will Solace tended to Sherman Yang's head injuries. Kayla and Austin stood over Connor, debating the need for a hair graft. This left me alone to make my way back to the Me cabin.

I lay on my sick cot in the middle of the room and stared at the ceiling beams. I thought again about what a depressingly simple, utterly mortal place this was. How did my children stand it? Why did they not keep a blazing altar, and decorate the walls with hammered gold reliefs celebrating my glory?

When I heard Will and the others coming back, I closed my eyes and pretended to be asleep. I could not face their questions or kindnesses, their attempts to make me feel at home when I clearly did not belong.

As they came in the door, they got quiet.

"Is he okay?" whispered Kayla.

Austin said, "Would you be, if you were him?"

A moment of silence.

"Try to get some sleep, guys," Will advised.

"This is crazy weird," Kayla said. "He looks so . . . human."

"We'll watch out for him," Austin said. "We're all he's got now."

I held back a sob. I couldn't bear their concern. Not being able to reassure them, or even disagree with them, made me feel very small.

A blanket was draped over me.

Will said, "Sleep well, Apollo."

Perhaps it was his persuasive voice, or the fact that I was more exhausted than I had been in centuries. Immediately, I drifted into unconsciousness.

Thank the remaining eleven Olympians, I had no dreams.

I woke in the morning feeling strangely refreshed. My chest no longer hurt. My nose no longer felt like a water balloon attached to my face. With the help of my offspring (*cabin mates*—I will call them cabin mates), I managed to master the arcane mysteries of the shower, the toilet, and the sink. The toothbrush was a shock. The last time I was mortal, there had been no such thing. And under-arm deodorant—what a ghastly idea that I should need enchanted salve to keep my armpits from producing stench!

When I was done with my morning ablutions and dressed in clean clothes from the camp store—sneakers, jeans, an orange Camp Half-Blood T-shirt, and a comfy winter coat of flannel wool—I felt almost optimistic. Perhaps I could survive this human experience.

I perked up even more when I discovered bacon.

Oh, gods—bacon! I promised myself that once I achieved immortality again, I would assemble the Nine Muses and together we would create an ode, a hymnal to the power of bacon, which would move the heavens to tears and cause rapture across the universe.

Bacon is good.

Yes—that may be the title of the song: "Bacon Is Good."

Seating for breakfast was less formal than dinner. We filled our trays at a buffet line and were allowed to sit wherever we wished. I found this delightful. (Oh, what a sad commentary on my new mortal mind that I, who once dictated the course of nations, should get excited about open seating.) I took my tray and found Meg, who was sitting by herself on the edge of the pavilion's retaining wall, dangling her feet over the side and watching the waves at the beach.

"How are you?" I asked.

Meg nibbled on a waffle. "Yeah. Great."

"You are a powerful demigod, daughter of Demeter."

"Mm-hm."

If I could trust my understanding of human responses, Meg did not seem thrilled.

"Your cabin mate, Billie . . . Is she nice?"

"Sure. All good."

"And Peaches?"

She looked at me sideways. "Disappeared overnight. Guess he only shows up when I'm in danger."

"Well, that's an appropriate time for him to show up."

"Ap-pro-pri-ate." Meg touched a waffle square for each syllable. "Sherman Yang had to get seven stitches."

I glanced over at Sherman, who sat at a safe distance across the pavilion, glaring daggers at Meg. A nasty red zigzag ran down the side of his face.

"I wouldn't worry," I told Meg. "Ares's children like scars. Besides, Sherman wears the Frankenstein look rather well."

The corner of her mouth twitched, but her gaze remained far away. "Our cabin has a grass floor—like, *green* grass. There's a huge oak tree in the middle, holding up the ceiling."

"Is that bad?"

"I have allergies."

"Ah . . ." I tried to imagine the tree in her cabin. Once upon a time, Demeter had had a sacred grove of oaks. I remembered she'd gotten quite angry when a mortal prince tried to cut it down.

A sacred grove . . .

Suddenly the bacon in my stomach expanded, wrapping around my organs.

Meg gripped my arm. Her voice was a distant buzz. I only heard the last, most important word: "—Apollo?"

I stirred. "What?"

"You blanked out." She scowled. "I said your name six times."

"You did?"

"Yeah. Where did you go?"

I could not explain. I felt as if I'd been standing on the deck of a ship when an enormous, dark, and dangerous shape passed beneath the hull—a shape almost discernible, then simply gone.

"I—I don't know. Something about trees. . . ."

"Trees," Meg said.

"It's probably nothing."

It *wasn't* nothing. I couldn't shake the image from my dreams: the crowned woman urging me to find the gates. That woman wasn't Demeter—at least, I didn't think so. But the idea of sacred trees stirred a memory within me . . . something very old, even by *my* standards.

I didn't want to talk about this with Meg, not until I'd had time to reflect. She had enough to worry about. Besides, after last night, my new young master made me more apprehensive than ever.

I glanced at the rings on her middle fingers. "So yesterday . . . those swords. And don't do that thing."

Meg's eyebrows furrowed. "What thing?"

"That thing where you shut down and refuse to talk. Your face turns to cement."

She gave me a furious pout. "It does not. I've got swords. I fight with them. So what?"

"So it might have been nice to know that earlier, when we were in combat with plague spirits."

"You said it yourself: those spirits couldn't be killed."

"You're sidestepping." I knew this because it was a tactic I had mastered centuries ago. "The style you fight in, with two curved blades, is the style of a *dimachaerus*, a gladiator from the late Roman Empire. Even back then, it was rare— possibly the most difficult fighting style to master, and one of the most deadly."

Meg shrugged. It was an eloquent shrug, but it did not offer much in the way of explanation.

"Your swords are Imperial gold," I said. "That would indicate *Roman* training, and mark you as a good prospect for Camp Jupiter. Yet your mother is Demeter, the goddess in her Greek form, not Ceres."

"How do you know?"

"Aside from the fact that I was a god? Demeter claimed you here at Camp Half-Blood. That was no accident. Also, her older Greek form is much more powerful. You, Meg, are powerful."

Her expression turned so guarded I expected Peaches to hurtle from the sky and start pulling out chunks of my hair.

"I never met my mom," she said. "I didn't know who she was."

"Then where did you get the swords? Your father?"

Meg tore her waffle into tiny pieces. "No. . . . My stepdad raised me. He gave me these rings."

"Your stepfather. Your stepfather gave you rings that turn into Imperial golden swords. What sort of man—"

"A good man," she snapped.

I noted the steel in Meg's voice and let the subject rest. I sensed a great tragedy in her past. Also, I feared that if I pressed my questions, I might find those golden blades at my neck.

"I'm sorry," I said.

"Mm-hm." Meg tossed a piece of waffle into the air. Out of nowhere, one of the camp's cleaning harpies swooped down like a two-hundred-pound kamikaze chicken, snatched up the food, and flew away.

Meg continued as if nothing had happened. "Let's just get through today. We've got the race after lunch."

A shiver ran down my neck. The last thing I wanted was to be strapped to Meg McCaffrey in the Labyrinth, but I managed to avoid screaming.

"Don't worry about the race," I said. "I have a plan for how to win it."

She raised an eyebrow. "Yeah?"

"Or rather, I *will* have a plan by this afternoon. All I need is a little time—"

Behind us, the conch horn blew.

"Morning boot camp!" Sherman Yang bellowed. "Let's go, you special snowflakes! I want you all in tears by lunchtime!"

15

Practice makes perfect
Ha, ha, ha, I don't think so
Ignore my sobbing

I WISHED I HAD A DOCTOR'S NOTE. I wanted to be excused from PE.

Honestly, I will never understand you mortals. You try to maintain good physical shape with push-ups, sit-ups, five-mile runs, obstacle courses, and other hard work that involves sweating. All the while, you know it is a losing battle. Eventually your weak, limited-use bodies will deteriorate and fail, giving you wrinkles, sagging parts, and old-person breath.

It's horrific! If I want to change shape, or age, or gender, or species, I simply wish it to happen and—*ka-bam!*—I am a young, large, female three-toed sloth. No amount of push-ups will accomplish that. I simply don't see the logic in your constant struggles. Exercise is nothing more than a depressing reminder that one is not a god.

By the end of Sherman Yang's boot camp, I was gasping and drenched in sweat. My muscles felt like quivering columns of gelatinous dessert.

I did *not* feel like a special snowflake (though my

mother, Leto, always assured me I was one), and I was sorely tempted to accuse Sherman of not treating me as such.

I grumbled about this to Will. I asked where the old head counselor of Ares had gone. Clarisse La Rue I could at least charm with my dazzling smile. Alas, Will reported she was attending the University of Arizona. Oh, why does college have to happen to perfectly good people?

After the torture, I staggered back to my cabin and took another shower.

Showers are good. Perhaps not as good as bacon, but good.

My second morning session was painful for a different reason. I was assigned to music lessons in the amphitheater with a satyr named Woodrow.

Woodrow seemed nervous to have me join his little class. Perhaps he had heard the legend about my skinning the satyr Marsyas alive after he challenged me to a music contest. (As I said, the flaying part was *totally* untrue, but rumors do have amazing staying power, especially when I may have been guilty of spreading them.)

Using his panpipe, Woodrow reviewed the minor scales. Austin had no problem with these, even though he was challenging himself by playing the violin, which was not his instrument. Valentina Diaz, a daughter of Aphrodite, did her best to throttle a clarinet, producing sounds like a basset hound whimpering in a thunderstorm. Damien White, son of Nemesis, lived up to his namesake by wreaking vengeance on an acoustic guitar. He played with such force that he broke the D string.

"You killed it!" said Chiara Benvenuti. She was the pretty Italian girl I'd noticed the night before—a child of Tyche, goddess of good fortune. "I needed to use that guitar!"

"Shut up, Lucky," Damien muttered. "In the *real* world, accidents happen. Strings snap sometimes."

Chiara unleashed some rapid-fire Italian that I decided not to translate.

"May I?" I reached for the guitar.

Damien reluctantly handed it over. I leaned toward the guitar case by Woodrow's feet. The satyr leaped several inches into the air.

Austin laughed. "Relax, Woodrow. He's just getting another string."

I'll admit I found the satyr's reaction gratifying. If I could still scare satyrs, perhaps there was hope for me reclaiming some of my former glory. From here I could work my way up to scaring farm animals, then demigods, monsters, and minor deities.

In a matter of seconds, I had replaced the string. It felt good to do something so familiar and simple. I adjusted the pitch, but stopped when I realized Valentina was sobbing.

"That was so beautiful!" She wiped a tear from her cheek. "What was that song?"

I blinked. "It's called tuning."

"Yeah, Valentina, control yourself," Damien chided, though his eyes were red. "It wasn't *that* beautiful."

"No." Chiara sniffled. "It wasn't."

Only Austin seemed unaffected. His eyes shone with what looked like pride, though I didn't understand why he would feel that way.

I played a C minor scale. The B string was flat. It's *always* the B string. Three thousand years since I invented the guitar (during a wild party with the Hittites—long story), and I still couldn't figure out how to make a B string that stays in tune.

I ran through the other scales, delighted that I still remembered them.

"Now this is a Lydian progression," I said. "It starts on the fourth of the major scale. They say it's called Lydian after the old kingdom of Lydia, but actually, I named it for an old girlfriend of mine, Lydia. She was the fourth woman I dated that year, so . . ."

I looked up mid-arpeggio. Damien and Chiara were weeping in each other's arms, hitting each other weakly and cursing, "I hate you. I hate you."

Valentina lay on the amphitheater bench, silently shaking. Woodrow was pulling apart his panpipes.

"I'm worthless!" he sobbed. "Worthless!"

Even Austin had a tear in his eye. He gave me a thumbs-up.

I was thrilled that some of my old skill remained intact, but I imagined Chiron would be annoyed if I drove the entire music class into major depression.

I pulled the D string slightly sharp—a trick I used to use to keep my adoring fans from exploding in rapture at my concerts. (And I mean literally exploding. Some of those gigs at the Fillmore in the 1960s . . . well, I'll spare you the gruesome details.)

I strummed a chord that was intentionally out of tune. To me it sounded awful, but the campers stirred from their misery. They sat up, wiped their tears, and watched in fascination as I played a simple one-four-five progression.

"Yeah, man." Austin brought his violin to his chin and began to improvise. His resin bow danced across the strings. He and I locked eyes, and for a moment we were more than family. We became part of the music, communicating on a level only gods and musicians will ever understand.

Woodrow broke the spell.

"That's amazing," the satyr sobbed. "You two should be teaching the class. What was I thinking? Please don't flay me!"

"My dear satyr," I said, "I would never—"

Suddenly, my fingers spasmed. I dropped the guitar in surprise. The instrument tumbled down the stone steps of the amphitheater, clanging and *sproinging*.

Austin lowered his bow. "You okay?"

"I . . . yes, of course."

But I was not okay. For a few moments, I had experienced the bliss of my formerly easy talent. Yet, clearly, my new mortal fingers were not up to the task. My hand muscles were sore. Red lines dug into my finger pads where I had touched the fret board. I had overextended myself in other ways, too. My lungs felt shriveled, drained of oxygen, even though I had done no singing.

"I'm . . . tired," I said, dismayed.

"Well, yeah." Valentina nodded. "The way you were playing was *unreal*!"

"It's okay, Apollo," Austin said. "You'll get stronger. When demigods use their powers, especially at first, they get tired quickly."

"But I'm not . . ."

I couldn't finish the sentence. I wasn't a demigod. I wasn't a god. I wasn't even myself. How could I ever play music again, knowing that I was a flawed instrument? Each note would bring me nothing but pain and exhaustion. My B string would *never* be in tune.

My misery must have shown on my face.

Damien White balled his fists. "Don't you worry, Apollo. It's not your fault. I'll make that stupid guitar pay for this!"

I didn't try to stop him as he marched down the stairs. Part of me took perverse satisfaction in the way he stomped the guitar until it was reduced to kindling and wires.

Chiara huffed. "*Idiota!* Now I'll never get my turn!"

Woodrow winced. "Well, um . . . thanks, everyone! Good class!"

Archery was an even bigger travesty.

If I ever become a god again (no, not if; *when, when*), my first act will be to wipe the memories of everyone who saw me embarrass myself in that class. I hit one bull's-eye. *One*. The grouping on my other shots was abysmal. Two arrows actually hit *outside* the black ring at a mere one hundred yards. I threw down my bow and wept with shame.

Kayla was our class instructor, but her patience and kindness only made me feel worse. She scooped up my bow and offered it back to me.

"Apollo," she said, "those shots were fantastic. A little more practice and—"

"I'm the god of archery!" I wailed. "I don't practice!"

Next to me, the daughters of Nike snickered.

They had the insufferably appropriate names Holly and Laurel Victor. They reminded me of the gorgeous, ferociously athletic African nymphs Athena used to hang out with at Lake Tritonis.

"Hey, ex-god," Holly said, nocking an arrow, "practice is the only way to improve." She scored a seven on the red ring, but she did not seem at all discouraged.

"For *you*, maybe," I said. "You're a mortal!"

Her sister, Laurel, snorted. "So are you now. Suck it up. Winners don't complain." She shot her arrow, which landed next to her sister's but just inside the red ring. "That's why I'm better than Holly. She's always complaining."

"Yeah, right," Holly growled. "The only thing I complain about is how lame *you* are."

"Oh, yeah?" said Laurel. "Let's go. Right now. Best two out of three shots. The loser scrubs the toilets for a month."

"You're on!"

Just like that, they forgot about me. They definitely would've made excellent Tritonian nymphs.

Kayla took me by the arm and led me downrange. "Those two, I swear. We made them Nike co-counselors so they'd compete with each other. If we hadn't, they would've taken over the camp by now and proclaimed a dictatorship."

I suppose she was trying to cheer me up, but I was not consoled.

I stared at my fingers, now blistered from archery as well as sore from guitar. Impossible. Agonizing.

"I can't do this, Kayla," I muttered. "I'm too old to be sixteen again!"

Kayla cupped her hand over mine. Beneath the green

shock of her hair, she had a ginger complexion—like cream painted over copper, the auburn sheen peeking through in the freckles of her face and arms. She reminded me very much of her father, the Canadian archery coach Darren Knowles.

I mean her *other* father. And, yes, of course it's possible for a demigod child to spring from such a relationship. Why not? Zeus gave birth to Dionysus out of his own thigh. Athena once had a child who was created from a handkerchief. Why should such things surprise you? We gods are capable of infinite marvels.

Kayla took a deep breath, as if preparing for an important shot. "You can do it, Dad. You're already good. *Very* good. You've just got to adjust your expectations. Be patient; be brave. You'll get better."

I was tempted to laugh. How could I get used to being merely *good*? Why would I strain myself to get better when before I had been *divine*?

"No," I said bitterly. "No, it is too painful. I swear upon the River Styx—until I am a god again, I will not use a bow or a musical instrument!"

Go ahead and chide me. I know it was a foolish oath, spoken in a moment of misery and self-pity. And it was binding. An oath sworn on the River Styx can have terrible consequences if broken.

But I didn't care. Zeus had cursed me with mortality. I was not going to pretend that everything was normal. I would not be Apollo until I was *really* Apollo. For now, I was just a stupid young man named Lester Papadopoulos. Maybe I would waste my time on skills I didn't care about—like sword fighting or badminton—but I would *not* sully the memory of my once-perfect music and archery.

Kayla stared at me in horror. "Dad, you don't mean it."

"I do!"

"Take it back! You can't . . ." She glanced over my shoulder. "What is he doing?"

I followed her gaze.

Sherman Yang was walking slowly, trancelike, into the woods.

It would have been foolhardy to run after him, straight into the most dangerous part of camp.

So that's exactly what Kayla and I did.

We almost didn't make it. As soon as we reached the tree line, the forest darkened. The temperature dropped. The horizon stretched out as if bent through a magnifying glass.

A woman whispered in my ear. This time I knew the voice well. It had never stopped haunting me. *You did this to me. Come. Chase me again.*

Fear rolled through my stomach.

I imagined the branches turning to arms; the leaves undulated like green hands.

Daphne, I thought.

Even after so many centuries, the guilt was overwhelming. I could not look at a tree without thinking of her. Forests made me nervous. The life force of each tree seemed to bear down on me with righteous hatred, accusing me of so many crimes. . . . I wanted to fall to my knees. I wanted to beg forgiveness. But this was not the time.

I couldn't allow the woods to confuse me again. I would not let anyone else fall into its trap.

Kayla didn't seem affected. I grabbed her hand to make sure we stayed together. We only had to go a few steps, but it felt like a boot camp run before we reached Sherman Yang.

"Sherman." I grabbed his arm.

He tried to shake me off. Fortunately, he was sluggish and dazed, or I would have ended up with scars of my own. Kayla helped me turn him around.

His eyes twitched as if he were in some sort of half-conscious REM sleep. "No. Ellis. Got to find him. Miranda. My girl."

I glanced at Kayla for explanation.

"Ellis is from the Ares cabin," she said. "He's one of the missing."

"Yes, but Miranda, his girl?"

"Sherman and she started dating about a week ago."

"Ah."

Sherman struggled to free himself. "Find her."

"Miranda is right over here, my friend," I lied. "We'll take you there."

He stopped fighting. His eyes rolled until only the whites were visible. "Over . . . here?"

"Yes."

"Ellis?"

"Yes, it's me," I said. "I'm Ellis."

"I love you, man," Sherman sobbed.

Still, it took all our strength to lead him out of the trees. I was reminded of the time Hephaestus and I had to wrestle the god Hypnos back to bed after he sleepwalked into Artemis's private chambers on Mount Olympus. It's a wonder any of us escaped without silver arrows pincushioning our posteriors.

We led Sherman to the archery range. Between one step and the next, he blinked his eyes and became his normal self. He noticed our hands on his arms and shook us off.

"What is this?" he demanded.

"You were walking into the woods," I said.

He gave us his drill sergeant glower. "No, I wasn't."

Kayla reached for him, then obviously thought better about it. Archery would be difficult with broken fingers. "Sherman, you were in some kind of trance. You were muttering about Ellis and Miranda."

Along Sherman's cheek, his zigzag scar darkened to bronze. "I don't remember that."

"Although you didn't mention the other missing camper," I added helpfully. "Cecil?"

"Why would I mention Cecil?" Sherman growled. "I can't stand the guy. And why should I believe you?"

"The woods had you," I said. "The trees were pulling you in."

Sherman studied the forest, but the trees looked normal again. The lengthening shadows and swaying green hands were gone.

"Look," Sherman said, "I have a head injury, thanks to your annoying friend Meg. If I was acting strange, *that's* why."

Kayla frowned. "But—"

"Enough!" Sherman snapped. "If either of you mention this, I'll make you eat your quivers. I don't need people questioning my self-control. Besides, I've got the race to think about."

He brushed past us.

"Sherman," I called.

He turned, his fists clenched.

"The last thing you remember," I said, "before you found yourself with us . . . what were you thinking about?"

For a microsecond, the dazed look passed across his face again. "About Miranda and Ellis . . . like you said. I was thinking . . . I wanted to know where they were."

"You were asking a question, then." A blanket of dread settled over me. "You wanted information."

"I . . ."

At the dining pavilion, the conch horn blew.

Sherman's expression hardened. "Doesn't matter. Drop it. We've got lunch now. Then I'm going to destroy you all in the three-legged death race."

As threats went, I had heard worse, but Sherman made it sound intimidating enough. He marched off toward the pavilion.

Kayla turned to me. "What just happened?"

"I think I understand now," I said. "I know why those campers went missing."

16

Tied to McCaffrey
We might end up in Lima
Harley is evil

NOTE TO SELF: trying to reveal important information just before a three-legged death race is not a good idea.

No one would listen to me.

Despite last night's grumbling and complaining, the campers were now buzzing with excitement. They spent their lunch hour frantically cleaning weapons, lacing armor straps, and whispering among one another to form secret alliances. Many tried to convince Harley, the course architect, to share hints about the best strategies.

Harley loved the attention. By the end of lunch, his table was piled high with offerings (read: bribes)—chocolate bars, peanut butter cups, gummy bears, and Hot Wheels. Harley would have made an excellent god. He took the gifts, mumbled a few pleasantries, but told his worshippers nothing helpful.

I tried to speak with Chiron about the dangers of the woods, but he was so frantic with last-minute race preparations that I almost got trampled just standing near him. He trotted nervously around the pavilion with a team of satyr and dryad referees in tow, comparing maps and issuing orders.

"The teams will be almost impossible to track," he murmured, his face buried in a Labyrinth schematic. "And we don't have any coverage in grid D."

"But, Chiron," I said, "if I could just—"

"The test group this morning ended up in Peru," he told the satyrs. "We can't have that happen again."

"About the woods," I said.

"Yes, I'm sorry, Apollo. I understand you are concerned—"

"The woods are actually speaking," I said. "You remember the old—"

A dryad ran up to Chiron with her dress billowing smoke. "The flares are exploding!"

"Ye gods!" Chiron said. "Those were for emergencies!"

He galloped over my feet, followed by his mob of assistants.

And so it went. When one is a god, the world hangs on your every word. When one is sixteen . . . not so much.

I tried to talk to Harley, hoping he might postpone the race, but the boy brushed me off with a simple "Nah."

As was so often the case with Hephaestus's children, Harley was tinkering with some mechanical device, moving the springs and gears around. I didn't really care what it was, but I asked Harley about it, hoping to win the boy's goodwill.

"It's a beacon," he said, adjusting a knob. "For lost people."

"You mean the teams in the Labyrinth?"

"No. You guys are on your own. This is for Leo."

"Leo Valdez."

Harley squinted at the device. "Sometimes, if you can't find your way back, a beacon can help. Just got to find the right frequency."

"And . . . how long have you been working on this?"

"Since he disappeared. Now I gotta concentrate. Can't stop the race." He turned his back on me and walked off.

I stared after him in amazement. For six months, the boy had been working on a beacon to help his missing brother Leo. I wondered if anyone would work so hard to bring me back home to Olympus. I very much doubted it.

I stood forlornly in a corner of the pavilion and ate a sandwich. I watched the sun wane in the winter sky and I thought about my chariot, my poor horses stuck in their stables with no one to take them out for a ride.

Of course, even without my help, other forces would keep the cosmos chugging along. Many different belief systems powered the revolution of the planets and stars. Wolves would still chase Sol across the sky. Ra would continue his daily journey in his sun barque. Tonatiuh would keep running on his surplus blood from human sacrifices back in the Aztec days. And that other thing—science—would still generate gravity and quantum physics and whatever.

Nevertheless, I felt like I wasn't doing my part, standing around waiting for a three-legged race.

Even Kayla and Austin were too distracted to talk with me. Kayla had told Austin about our experience rescuing

Sherman Yang from the woods, but Austin was more inter-ested in swabbing out his saxophone.

"We can tell Chiron at dinner," he mumbled with a reed in his mouth. "Nobody's going to listen until the race is over, and we'll be staying out of the woods anyway. Besides, if I can play the right tune in the Labyrinth . . ." He got a gleam in his eyes. "Ooh. Come here, Kayla. I have an idea."

He steered her away and left me alone again.

I understood Austin's enthusiasm, of course. His sax-ophone skills were so formidable, I was certain he would become the foremost jazz instrumentalist of his genera-tion, and if you think it's easy to get half a million views on YouTube playing jazz saxophone, think again. Still, his musical career was not going to happen if the force in the woods destroyed us all.

As a last resort (a *very* last resort), I sought out Meg McCaffrey.

I spotted her at one of the braziers, talking with Julia Feingold and Alice Miyazawa. Or rather, the Hermes girls were talking while Meg devoured a cheeseburger. I marveled that Demeter—the queen of grains, fruits, and vegetables—could have a daughter who was such an unre-pentant carnivore.

Then again, Persephone was the same way. You'll hear stories about the goddess of springtime being all sweetness and daffodils and nibbling on pomegranate seeds, but I'm telling you, that girl was frightening when she attacked a mound of pork spareribs.

I strode over to Meg's side. The Hermes girls stepped

back as if I were a snake handler. I found this reaction pleasing.

"Hello," I said. "What are we talking about?"

Meg wiped her mouth on the back of her hand. "These two wanna know our plans for the race."

"I'm sure they do." I plucked a small magnetic listening device from Meg's coat sleeve and tossed it back to Alice.

Alice smiled sheepishly. "Can't blame us for trying."

"No, of course not," I said. "In the same spirit, I hope you won't mind what I did to your shoes. Have a good race!"

The girls shuffled off nervously, checking the soles of their sneakers.

Meg looked at me with something resembling respect. "What did you do to them?"

"Nothing," I said. "Half the trick to being a god is knowing how to bluff."

She snorted. "So what's our top secret plan? Wait. Let me guess. You don't have one."

"You're learning. Honestly, I meant to come up with one, but I got sidetracked. We have a problem."

"Sure do." From her coat pocket, she pulled two loops of bronze, like resistance bands of braided metal. "You've seen these? They wrap around our legs. Once they're on, they *stay* on until the race is over. No way to get them off. I *hate* restraints."

"I agree." I was tempted to add *especially when I am tied to a small child named Meg*, but my natural diplomacy won out. "However, I was referring to a different problem."

I told her about the incident during archery, when Sherman had almost been lured into the forest.

Meg removed her cat-eye glasses. Without the lenses, her dark irises looked softer and warmer, like tiny plots of planting soil. "You think something in the woods is calling to people?"

"I think something in the woods is *answering* people. In ancient times, there was an Oracle—"

"Yeah, you told me. Delphi."

"No. Another Oracle, even older than Delphi. It involved trees. An entire grove of talking trees."

"Talking trees." Meg's mouth twitched. "What was that Oracle called?"

"I—I can't remember." I ground my teeth. "I *should* know. I should be able to tell you instantly! But the information . . . It's almost as if it is eluding me on purpose."

"That happens sometimes," Meg said. "You'll think of it."

"But it *never* happens to me! Stupid human brain! At any rate, I believe this grove is somewhere in those woods. I don't know how or why. The whispering voices, though . . . they are from this hidden Oracle. The sacred trees are trying to speak prophecies, reaching out to those with burning questions, luring them in."

Meg put her glasses back on. "You know that sounds crazy, right?"

I steadied my breathing. I had to remind myself that I was no longer a god. I had to put up with insults from mortals without being able to blast them to ashes.

"Just be on guard," I said.

"But the race doesn't even go through the woods."

"Nevertheless . . . we are not safe. If you can summon your friend Peaches, I would welcome his company."

"I told you, he sort of pops up when he feels like it. I can't—"

Chiron blew a hunting horn so loudly my vision doubled. Another pledge to myself: once I became a god again, I would descend upon this camp and take away all their horns.

"Demigods!" said the centaur. "Tie your legs together and follow me to your starting positions!"

We gathered in a meadow about a hundred yards from the Big House. Making it *that* far without a single life-threatening incident was a minor miracle. With my left leg bound to Meg's right, I felt the way I used to in Leto's womb just before my sister and I were born. And, yes, I remember that quite well. Artemis was always shoving me aside, elbowing me in the ribs and generally being a womb hog.

I said a silent prayer that if I got through this race alive, I would sacrifice a bull to myself and possibly even build myself a new temple. I am a sucker for bulls and temples.

The satyrs directed us to spread out across the meadow.

"Where is the starting line?" Holly Victor demanded, shoving her shoulder ahead of her sister's. "I want to be the closest."

"*I* want to be closest," Laurel corrected. "You can be *second* closest."

"Not to worry!" Woodrow the satyr sounded very worried. "We'll explain everything in a moment. As soon as I, um, know what to explain."

Will Solace sighed. He was, of course, tied to Nico. He

propped his elbow on Nico's shoulder as if the son of Hades were a convenient shelf. "I miss Grover. He used to organize things like this so well."

"I'd settle for Coach Hedge." Nico pushed Will's arm off. "Besides, don't talk about Grover too loudly. Juniper's right over there."

He pointed to one of the dryads—a pretty girl dressed in pale green.

"Grover's girlfriend," Will explained to me. "She misses him. A lot."

"Okay, everybody!" Woodrow shouted. "Spread out a little bit more, please! We want you to have plenty of room so, you know, if you die, you won't take down all the other teams too!"

Will sighed. "I am *so* excited."

He and Nico loped off. Julia and Alice from the Hermes cabin checked their shoes one more time, then glared at me. Connor Stoll was paired with Paolo Montes, the Brazilian son of Hebe, and neither of them seemed happy about it.

Perhaps Connor looked glum because his mangled scalp was covered in so much medicinal salve his head looked like it had been coughed up by a cat. Or perhaps he just missed his brother Travis.

As soon as Artemis and I were born, we couldn't *wait* to get some distance between us. We staked out our own territories and that was that. But I would've given anything to see her just then. I was sure Zeus had threatened her with severe punishment if she tried to help me during my time as a mortal, but she could have at least sent me a care package from Olympus—a decent toga, some magical acne cream, and maybe a dozen cranberry ambrosia scones from the Scylla Cafe. They made *excellent* scones.

I scanned the other teams. Kayla and Austin were bound together, looking like a deadly pair of street performers with her bow and his saxophone. Chiara, the cute girl from Tyche, was stuck with her nemesis, Damien White, son of . . . well, Nemesis. Billie Ng from Demeter was leg-tied with Valentina Diaz, who was hastily checking her makeup in the reflective surface of Billie's silver coat. Valentina didn't seem to notice that two twigs were sprouting from her hair like tiny deer antlers.

I decided the biggest threat would be Malcolm Pace. You can never be too careful with children of Athena. Surprisingly, though, he'd paired himself with Sherman Yang. That didn't seem like a natural partnership, unless Malcolm had some sort of plan. Those Athena children *always* had a plan. It rarely included letting me win.

The only demigods not participating were Harley and Nyssa, who had set up the course.

Once the satyrs judged we had all spread out sufficiently and our leg bindings had been double-checked, Harley clapped for our attention.

"Okay!" He bounced up and down eagerly, reminding me of the Roman children who used to cheer for executions at the Colosseum. "Here's the deal. Each team has to find three golden apples, then get back to this meadow alive."

Grumbling broke out among the demigods.

"Golden apples," I said. "I *hate* golden apples. They bring nothing but trouble."

Meg shrugged. "I like apples."

I remembered the rotten one she'd used to break Cade's nose in the alley. I wondered if perhaps she could use golden apples with the same deadly skill. Perhaps we stood a chance after all.

Laurel Victor raised her hand. "You mean the first team back wins?"

"*Any* team that gets back alive wins!" Harley said.

"That's ridiculous!" Holly said. "There can only be one winner. First team back wins!"

Harley shrugged. "Have it your way. My only rules are stay alive, and don't kill each other."

"*O quê?*" Paolo started complaining so loudly in Portuguese that Connor had to cover his left ear.

"Now, now!" Chiron called. His saddlebags were overflowing with extra first-aid kits and emergency flares. "We won't need any *help* making this a dangerous challenge. Let's have a good clean three-legged death race. And another thing, campers, given the problems our test group had this morning, please repeat after me: *Do not end up in Peru.*"

"Do not end up in Peru," everyone chanted.

Sherman Yang cracked his knuckles. "So where *is* the starting line?"

"There is no starting line," Harley said with glee. "You're all starting from right where you are."

The campers looked around in confusion. Suddenly the

meadow shook. Dark lines etched across the grass, forming a giant green checkerboard.

"Have fun!" Harley squealed.

The ground opened beneath our feet, and we fell into the Labyrinth.

17

Bowling balls of death
Rolling toward my enemies
I'll trade you problems

AT LEAST WE DID NOT LAND IN PERU.

My feet hit stone, jarring my ankles. We stumbled against a wall, but Meg provided me with a convenient cushion.

We found ourselves in a dark tunnel braced with oaken beams. The hole we'd fallen through was gone, replaced by an earthen ceiling. I saw no sign of the other teams, but from somewhere above I could vaguely hear Harley chanting, "Go! Go! Go!"

"When I get my powers back," I said, "I will turn Harley into a constellation called the Ankle Biter. At least constellations are silent."

Meg pointed down the corridor. "Look."

As my eyes adjusted, I realized the tunnel's dim light emanated from a glowing piece of fruit about thirty yards away.

"A golden apple," I said.

Meg lurched forward, pulling me with her.

"Wait!" I said. "There might be traps!"

As if to illustrate my point, Connor and Paolo emerged

from the darkness at the other end of the corridor. Paolo scooped up the golden apple and shouted, *"BRASIL!"*

Connor grinned at us. "Too slow, suckers!"

The ceiling opened above them, showering them with iron orbs the size of cantaloupes.

Connor yelped, "Run!"

He and Paolo executed an awkward one-eighty and hobbled away, hotly pursued by a rolling herd of cannon-balls with sparking fuses.

The sounds quickly faded. Without the glowing apple, we were left in total darkness.

"Great." Meg's voice echoed. "Now what?"

"I suggest we go the other direction."

That was easier said than done. Being blind seemed to bother Meg more than it did me. Thanks to my mor-tal body, I already felt crippled and deprived of my senses. Besides, I often relied on more than sight. Music required keen hearing. Archery required a sensitive touch and the ability to feel the direction of the wind. (Okay, sight was also helpful, but you get the idea.)

We shuffled ahead, our arms extended in front of us. I listened for suspicious clicks, snaps, or creaks that might indicate an incoming flock of explosions, but I suspected that if I *did* hear any warning signs, it would be too late.

Eventually Meg and I learned to walk with our bound legs in synchronicity. It wasn't easy. I had a flawless sense of rhythm. Meg was always a quarter beat slow or fast, which kept us veering left or right and running into walls.

We lumbered along for what might have been minutes or days. In the Labyrinth, time was deceptive.

I remembered what Austin had told me about the Labyrinth feeling different since the death of its creator. I was beginning to understand what he meant. The air seemed fresher, as if the maze hadn't been chewing up quite so many bodies. The walls didn't radiate the same malignant heat. As far as I could tell, they weren't oozing blood or slime, either, which was a definite improvement. In the old days, you couldn't take a step inside Daedalus's Labyrinth without sensing its all-consuming desire: *I will destroy your mind and your body.* Now the atmosphere was sleepier, the message not quite as virulent: *Hey, if you die in here, that's cool.*

"I never liked Daedalus," I muttered. "That old rascal didn't know when to stop. He always had to have the latest tech, the most recent updates. I *told* him not to make his maze self-aware. 'A.I. will destroy us, man,' I said. But noooo. He *had* to give the Labyrinth a malevolent consciousness."

"I don't know what you're talking about," Meg said. "But maybe you shouldn't bad-mouth the maze while we're inside it."

Once, I stopped when I heard the sound of Austin's saxophone. It was faint, echoing through so many corridors I couldn't pinpoint where it was coming from. Then it was gone. I hoped he and Kayla had found their three apples and escaped safely.

Finally, Meg and I reached a Y in the corridor. I could tell this from the flow of the air and the temperature differential against my face.

"Why'd we stop?" Meg asked.

"Shh." I listened intently.

From the right-hand corridor came a faint whining sound like a table saw. The left-hand corridor was quiet, but it exuded a faint odor that was unpleasantly familiar . . . not sulfur, exactly, but a vaporous mix of minerals from deep in the earth.

"I don't hear anything," Meg complained.

"A sawing noise to the right," I told her. "To the left, a bad smell."

"I choose the bad smell."

"Of course you do."

Meg blew me one of her trademark raspberries, then hobbled to the left, pulling me along with her.

The bronze bands around my leg began to chafe. I could feel Meg's pulse through her femoral artery, messing up my rhythm. Whenever I get nervous (which doesn't happen often), I like to hum a song to calm myself—usually Ravel's *Boléro* or the ancient Greek "Song of Seikilos." But with Meg's pulse throwing me off, the only tune I could conjure was the "Chicken Dance." That was not soothing.

We edged forward. The smell of volcanic fumes intensified. My pulse lost its perfect rhythm. My heart knocked against my chest with every *cluck, cluck, cluck, cluck* of the "Chicken Dance." I feared I knew where we were. I told myself it wasn't possible. We couldn't have walked halfway around the world. But this was the Labyrinth. Down here, distance was meaningless. The maze knew how to exploit its victims' weaknesses. Worse: it had a vicious sense of humor.

"I see light!" Meg said.

She was right. The absolute darkness had changed to

murky gray. Up ahead, the tunnel ended, joining with a narrow, lengthwise cavern like a volcanic vent. It looked as if a colossal claw had slashed across the corridor and left a wound in the earth. I had seen creatures with claws that big down in Tartarus. I did not fancy seeing them again.

"We should turn around," I said.

"That's stupid," Meg said. "Don't you see the golden glow? There's an apple in there."

All I saw were swirling plumes of ash and gas. "The glow could be lava," I said. "Or radiation. Or eyes. Glowing eyes are *never* good."

"It's an apple," Meg insisted. "I can smell apple."

"Oh, *now* you develop keen senses?"

Meg forged onward, giving me little choice but to go with. For a small girl, she was quite good at throwing her weight around. At the end of the tunnel, we found ourselves on a narrow ledge. The cliff wall opposite was only ten feet away, but the crevasse seemed to plunge downward forever. Perhaps a hundred feet above us, the jagged vent opened into a bigger chamber.

A painfully large ice cube seemed to be working its way down my throat. I had never seen this place from below, but I knew exactly where we were. We stood at the *omphalus*—the navel of the ancient world.

"You're shaking," Meg said.

I tried to cover her mouth with my hand, but she promptly bit it.

"Don't touch me," she snarled.

"*Please* be quiet."

"Why?"

"Because right above us—" My voice cracked. "Delphi. The chamber of the Oracle."

Meg's nose quivered like a rabbit's. "That's impossible."

"No, it's not," I whispered. "And if this is Delphi, that means . . ."

From overhead came a hiss so loud, it sounded as if the entire ocean had hit a frying pan and evaporated into a massive steam cloud. The ledge shook. Pebbles rained down. Above, a monstrous body slid across the crevasse, completely covering the opening. The smell of molting snakeskin seared my nostrils.

"Python." My voice was now an octave higher than Meg's. "He is here."

18

The Beast is calling
Tell him I'm not here. Let's hide
Where? In garbage. Natch

HAD I EVER BEEN SO TERRIFIED?

Perhaps when Typhon raged across the earth, scattering the gods before him. Perhaps when Gaea unleashed her giants to tear down Olympus. Or perhaps when I accidentally saw Ares naked in the gymnasium. That had been enough to turn my hair white for a century.

But I had been a god all of those times. Now I was a weak, tiny mortal cowering in the darkness. I could only pray my old enemy would not sense my presence. For once in my long glorious life, I wanted to be invisible.

Oh, why had the Labyrinth brought me here?

As soon as I thought this, I chided myself: Of *course* it would bring me where I least wanted to be. Austin had been wrong about the maze. It was still evil, designed to kill. It was just a little subtler about its homicides now.

Meg seemed oblivious to our danger. Even with an immortal monster a hundred feet above us, she had the nerve to stay on task. She elbowed me and pointed to a tiny ledge on the opposite wall, where a golden apple glowed cheerfully.

Had Harley *placed* it there? I couldn't imagine. More likely the boy had simply rolled golden apples down various corridors, trusting that they would find the most dangerous spots to roost. I was really starting to dislike that boy.

Meg whispered, "Easy jump."

I gave her a look that under different circumstances would've incinerated her. "Too dangerous."

"Apple," she hissed.

"Monster!" I hissed back.

"One."

"No!"

"Two."

"No!"

"Three." She jumped.

Which meant that I also jumped. We made the ledge, though our heels sent a spray of rubble into the chasm. Only my natural coordination and grace saved us from toppling backward to our deaths. Meg snatched up the apple.

Above us, the monster rumbled, "Who approaches?"

His voice . . . Gods above, I remembered that voice— deep and gruff, as if he breathed xenon rather than air. For all I knew, he did. Python could certainly *produce* his share of unhealthy gasses.

The monster shifted his weight. More gravel spilled into the crevasse.

I stood absolutely still, pressed against the cold face of the rock. My eardrums pulsed with every beat of my heart. I wished I could stop Meg from breathing. I wished I could stop the rhinestones on her eyeglasses from glittering.

Python had heard us. I prayed to all the gods that the monster would decide the noise was nothing. All he had to do was breathe down into the crevasse and he would kill us. There was no escaping his poisonous belch—not from this distance, not for a mortal.

Then, from the cavern above, came another voice, smaller and much closer to human. "Hello, my reptilian friend."

I nearly wept with relief. I had no idea who this newcomer was, or why he had been so foolish as to announce his presence to Python, but I always appreciated it when humans sacrificed themselves to save me. Common courtesy was not dead after all!

Python's harsh laugh shook my teeth. "Well, I was wondering if you would make the trip, Monsieur Beast."

"Don't call me that," the man snapped. "And the commute was quite easy now that the Labyrinth is back in service."

"I'm so pleased." Python's tone was dry as basalt.

I couldn't tell much about the man's voice, muffled as it was by several tons of reptile flesh, but he sounded calmer and more in control than I would have been talking to Python. I had heard the term *Beast* used to describe someone before, but as usual, my mortal brainpower failed me.

If only I'd been able to retain just the *important* information! Instead, I could tell you what I had for dessert the first time I dined with King Minos. (Spice cake.) I could tell you what color *chitons* the sons of Niobe were wearing when I slew them. (A very unflattering shade of orange.)

But I couldn't remember something as basic as whether this Beast was a wrestler, a movie star, or a politician. Possibly all three?

Next to me, in the glow of the apple, Meg seemed to have turned to bronze. Her eyes were wide with fear. A little late for that, but at least she was quiet. If I didn't know better, I might have thought the man's voice terrified her more than the monster's.

"So, Python," the man continued, "any prophetic words to share with me?"

"In time . . . my lord."

The last words were spoken with amusement, but I'm not sure anyone else would've recognized it. Aside from myself, few had been on the receiving end of Python's sarcasm and lived to tell the tale.

"I need more than your assurances," the man said. "Before we proceed, we must have *all* the Oracles under our control."

All the Oracles. Those words almost sent me off the cliff, but somehow I retained my balance.

"In time," Python said, "as we agreed. We have come this far by biding our time, yes? You did not reveal your hand when the Titans stormed New York. I did not march to war with Gaea's giants. We both realized the time for victory was not yet right. You must remain patient for a while longer."

"Don't lecture me, snake. While you slumbered, I built an empire. I have spent centuries—"

"Yes, yes." The monster exhaled, causing a tremor along

the cliff face. "And if you ever want your empire to come out of the shadows, you need to deliver on *your* side of the bargain first. When will you destroy Apollo?"

I stifled a yelp. I should not have been surprised that they were talking about me. For millennia, I had assumed that *everyone* talked about me all the time. I was so interesting they simply couldn't help it. But this business about destroying me—I didn't like that.

Meg looked more terrified than I'd ever seen her. I wanted to think she was worried for my sake, but I had a feeling she was equally concerned about herself. Again, those mixed-up demigod priorities.

The man stepped closer to the chasm. His voice became clearer and louder. "Don't worry about Apollo. He is exactly where I need him to be. He will serve our purpose, and once he is no longer useful . . ."

He did not bother finishing the statement. I was afraid it did not end with *we will give him a nice present and send him on his way.* With a chill, I recognized the voice from my dream. It was the nasal sneer of the man in the purple suit. I also had a feeling I'd heard him sing before, years and years ago, but that didn't make sense. . . . Why would I suffer through a concert given by an ugly purple-suited man who called himself the Beast? I was not even a *fan* of death metal polka!

Python shifted his bulk, showering us with more rubble. "And how exactly will you convince him to serve our purpose?"

The Beast chuckled. "I have well-placed help within

the camp who will steer Apollo toward us. Also, I have upped the stakes. Apollo will have no choice. He and the girl will open the gates."

A whiff of Python vapor floated across my nose—enough to make me dizzy, hopefully not enough to kill me.

"I trust you are right," said the monster. "Your judgment in the past has been . . . questionable. I wonder if you have chosen the right tools for this job. Have you learned from your past mistakes?"

The man snarled so deeply I could almost believe he was turning into a beast. I'd seen that happen enough times. Next to me, Meg whimpered.

"Listen here, you overgrown reptile," the man said, "my only mistake was not burning my enemies fast enough, often enough. I assure you, I am stronger than ever. My organization is everywhere. My colleagues stand ready. When we control all four Oracles, we will control fate itself!"

"And what a glorious day that will be." Python's voice was jagged with contempt. "But beforehand, you must destroy the *fifth* Oracle, yes? That is the only one I *cannot* control. You must set flame to the grove of—"

"Dodona," I said.

The word leaped unbidden from my mouth and echoed through the chasm. Of all the stupid times to retrieve a piece of information, of all the stupid times to say it aloud . . . oh, the body of Lester Papadopoulos was a terrible place to live.

Above us, the conversation stopped.

Meg hissed at me, "You idiot."

The Beast said, "What was that sound?"

Rather than answer, *Oh, that's just us*, we did something

even more foolish. One of us, Meg or me—personally, I blame her—must have slipped on a pebble. We toppled off the ledge and fell into the sulfurous clouds below.

SQUISH.

The Labyrinth most definitely had a sense of humor. Instead of allowing us to smash into a rock floor and die, the maze dropped us into a mound of wet, full garbage bags.

If you're keeping score, that was the *second* time since becoming mortal that I had crash-landed in garbage, which was two times more than any god should endure.

We tumbled down the pile in a frenzy of three-legged flailing. We landed at the bottom, covered with muck, but, miraculously, still alive.

Meg sat up, glazed in a layer of coffee grounds.

I pulled a banana peel off my head and flicked it aside. "Is there some reason you keep landing us in trash heaps?"

"Me? You're the one who lost his balance!" Meg wiped her face without much luck. In her other hand, she clutched the golden apple with trembling fingers.

"Are you all right?" I asked.

"Fine," she snapped.

Clearly that was not true. She looked as if she'd just gone through Hades's haunted house. (Pro tip: DO NOT.) Her face was pallid. She had bit her lip so hard, her teeth were pink with blood. I also detected the faint smell of urine, meaning one of us had gotten scared enough to lose bladder control, and I was seventy-five percent sure it wasn't me.

"That man upstairs," I said. "You recognized his voice?"

"Shut up. That's an order!"

I attempted to reply. To my consternation, I found that I couldn't. My voice had heeded Meg's command all on its own, which did not bode well. I decided to file away my questions about the Beast for later.

I scanned our surroundings. Garbage chutes lined the walls on all four sides of the dismal little basement. As I watched, another bag of refuse slid down the right-hand chute and hit the pile. The smell was so strong, it could have burned paint off the walls, if the gray cinder blocks had been painted. Still, it was better than smelling the fumes of Python. The only visible exit was a metal door marked with a biohazard sign.

"Where are we?" Meg asked.

I glared at her, waiting.

"You can talk now," she added.

"This is going to shock you," I said, "but it appears we are in a garbage room."

"But where?"

"Could be anywhere. The Labyrinth intersects with subterranean places all around the world."

"Like Delphi." Meg glowered at me as if our little Greek excursion had been my fault and not . . . well, only indirectly my fault.

"That was unexpected," I agreed. "We need to speak with Chiron."

"What is Dodona?"

"I—I'll explain it all later." I didn't want Meg to shut me up again. I also didn't want to talk about Dodona while trapped in the Labyrinth. My skin was crawling, and I didn't think it was just because I was covered in sticky soda syrup. "First, we need to get out of here."

Meg glanced behind me. "Well, it wasn't a total waste." She reached into the garbage and pulled out a second piece of glowing fruit. "Only one more apple to go."

"Perfect." The last thing I cared about was finishing Harley's ridiculous race, but at least it would get Meg moving. "Now, why don't we see what fabulous biohazards await us behind that door?"

19

They have gone missing?
No, no, no, no, no, no, no
No, et cetera

THE ONLY BIOHAZARDS we encountered were vegan cupcakes.

After navigating several torchlit corridors, we burst into a crowded modern bakery that, according to the menu board, had the dubious name THE LEVEL TEN VEGAN. Our garbage/volcanic gas stench quickly dispersed the customers, driving most toward the exit, and causing many non-dairy gluten-free baked goods to be trampled. We ducked behind the counter, charged through the kitchen doors, and found ourselves in a subterranean amphitheater that looked centuries old.

Tiers of stone seats ringed a sandy pit about the right size for a gladiator fight. Hanging from the ceiling were dozens of thick iron chains. I wondered what ghastly spectacles might have been staged here, but we didn't stay very long.

We limped out the opposite side, back into the Labyrinth's twisting corridors.

By this point, we had perfected the art of three-legged

running. Whenever I started to tire, I imagined Python behind us, spewing poisonous gas.

At last we turned a corner, and Meg shouted, "There!"

In the middle of the corridor sat a third golden apple.

This time I was too exhausted to care about traps. We loped forward until Meg scooped up the fruit.

In front of us, the ceiling lowered, forming a ramp. Fresh air filled my lungs. We climbed to the top, but instead of feeling elated, my insides turned as cold as the garbage juice on my skin. We were back in the woods.

"Not here," I muttered. "Gods, no."

Meg hopped us in a full circle. "Maybe it's a different forest."

But it wasn't. I could feel the resentful stare of the trees, the horizon stretching out in all directions. Voices began to whisper, waking to our presence.

"Hurry," I said.

As if on cue, the bands around our legs sprang loose. We ran.

Even with her arms full of apples, Meg was faster. She veered between trees, zigzagging left and right as if following a course only she could see. My legs ached and my chest burned, but I didn't dare fall behind.

Up ahead, flickering points of light resolved into torches. At last we burst out of the woods, right into a crowd of campers and satyrs.

Chiron galloped over. "Thank the gods!"

"You're welcome," I gasped, mostly out of habit. "Chiron . . . we have to talk."

In the torchlight, the centaur's face seemed carved from shadow. "Yes, we do, my friend. But first, I fear one more team is still missing . . . your children, Kayla and Austin."

Chiron forced us to take showers and change clothes. Otherwise I would have plunged straight back into the woods.

By the time I was done, Kayla and Austin still had not returned.

Chiron had sent search parties of dryads into the forest, on the assumption that they would be safe in their home territory, but he adamantly refused to let demigods join the hunt.

"We cannot risk anyone else," he said. "Kayla, Austin, and—and the other missing . . . They would not want that."

Five campers had now disappeared. I harbored no illusions that Kayla and Austin would return on their own. The Beast's words still echoed in my ears: *I have upped the stakes. Apollo will have no choice.*

Somehow he had targeted my children. He was inviting me to look for them, and to find the gates of this hidden Oracle. There was still so much I did not understand—how the ancient grove of Dodona had relocated here, what sort of "gates" it might have, why the Beast thought I could open them, and how he'd snared Austin and Kayla. But there was one thing I did know: the Beast was right. I had no choice. I had to find my children . . . my *friends*.

I would have ignored Chiron's warning and run into the forest except for Will's panicked shout: "Apollo, I need you!"

At the far end of the field, he had set up an impromptu hospital where half a dozen campers lay injured on stretchers. He was frantically tending to Paolo Montes while Nico held down the screaming patient.

I ran to Will's side and winced at what I saw.

Paolo had managed to get one of his legs sawed off.

"I got it reattached," Will told me, his voice shaky with exhaustion. His scrubs were speckled with blood. "I need somebody to keep him stable."

I pointed to the woods. "But—"

"I know!" Will snapped. "Don't you think I want to be out there searching too? We're shorthanded for healers. There's some salve and nectar in that pack. Go!"

I was stunned by his tone. I realized he was just as concerned about Kayla and Austin as I was. The only difference: Will knew his duty. He had to heal the injured first. And he needed my help.

"Y-yes," I said. "Yes, of course."

I grabbed the supply pack and took charge of Paolo, who had conveniently passed out from the pain.

Will changed his surgical gloves and glared at the woods. "We *will* find them. We *have* to."

Nico di Angelo gave him a canteen. "Drink. Right now, this is where you need to be."

I could tell the son of Hades was angry too. Around his feet, the grass steamed and withered.

Will sighed. "You're right. But that doesn't make me feel better. I have to set Valentina's broken arm now. You want to assist?"

"Sounds gruesome," Nico said. "Let's go."

I tended to Paolo Montes until I was sure he was out of danger, then asked two satyrs to carry his stretcher to the Hebe cabin.

I did what I could to nurse the others. Chiara had a mild concussion. Billie Ng had come down with a case of Irish step dancing. Holly and Laurel needed pieces of shrapnel removed from their backs, thanks to a close encounter with an exploding chain-saw Frisbee.

The Victor twins had placed in first, predictably, but they also demanded to know which of them had the *most* pieces of shrapnel extracted, so they could have bragging rights. I told them to be quiet or I would never allow them to wear laurel wreaths again. (As the guy who held the patent on laurel wreaths, that was my prerogative.)

I found my mortal healing skills were passable. Will Solace far outshone me, but that didn't bother me as much as my failures with archery and music had. I suppose I was used to being second in healing. My son Asclepius had become the god of medicine by the time he was fifteen, and I couldn't have been happier for him. It left me time for my other interests. Besides, it's every god's dream to have a child who grows up to be a doctor.

As I was washing up from the shrapnel extraction, Harley shuffled over, fiddling with his beacon device. His eyes were puffy from crying.

"It's my fault," he muttered. "I got them lost. I . . . I'm sorry."

He was shaking. I realized the little boy was terrified of what I might do.

For the past two days, I had yearned to cause fear in mortals again. My stomach had boiled with resentment and bitterness. I wanted someone to blame for my predicament, for the disappearances, for my own powerlessness to fix things.

Looking at Harley, my anger evaporated. I felt hollow, silly, ashamed of myself. Yes, me, Apollo . . . ashamed. Truly, it was an event so unprecedented, it should have ripped apart the cosmos.

"It's all right," I told him.

He sniffled. "The racecourse went into the woods. It shouldn't have done that. They got lost and . . . and—"

"Harley"—I placed my hands over his—"may I see your beacon?"

He blinked the tears away. I guess he was afraid I might smash his gadget, but he let me take it.

"I'm not an inventor," I said, turning the gears as gently as possible. "I don't have your father's skills. But I *do* know music. I believe automatons prefer a frequency of E at 329.6 hertz. It resonates best with Celestial bronze. If you adjust your signal—"

"Festus might hear it?" Harley's eyes widened. "Really?"

"I don't know," I admitted. "Just as you could not have known what the Labyrinth would do today. But that doesn't mean we should stop trying. Never stop inventing, son of Hephaestus."

I gave him back his beacon. For a count of three, Harley stared at me in disbelief. Then he hugged me so hard he nearly rebroke my ribs, and he dashed away.

I tended to the last of the injured while the harpies

cleaned the area, picking up bandages, torn clothing, and damaged weapons. They gathered the golden apples in a basket and promised to bake us some lovely glowing apple turnovers for breakfast.

At Chiron's urging, the remaining campers dispersed back to their cabins. He promised them we would determine what to do in the morning, but I had no intention of waiting.

As soon as we were alone, I turned to Chiron and Meg.

"I'm going after Kayla and Austin," I told them. "You can join me or not."

Chiron's expression tightened. "My friend, you're exhausted and unprepared. Go back to your cabin. It will serve no purpose—"

"No." I waved him off, as I once might have done when I was a god. The gesture probably looked petulant coming from a sixteen-year-old nobody, but I didn't care. "I have to do this."

The centaur lowered his head. "I should have listened to you before the race. You tried to warn me. What—what did you discover?"

The question stopped my momentum like a seat belt.

After rescuing Sherman Yang, after listening to Python in the Labyrinth, I had felt certain I knew the answers. I had remembered the name *Dodona*, the stories about talking trees . . .

Now my mind was once again a bowl of fuzzy mortal soup. I couldn't recall what I'd been so excited about, or what I had intended to do about it.

Perhaps exhaustion and stress had taken their toll. Or

maybe Zeus was manipulating my brain—allowing me tantalizing glimpses of the truth, then snatching them away, turning my aha! moments into huh? moments.

I howled in frustration. "I don't remember!"

Meg and Chiron exchanged nervous glances.

"You're not going," Meg told me firmly.

"*What?* You can't—"

"That's an order," she said. "No going into the woods until I say so."

The command sent a shudder from the base of my skull to my heels.

I dug my fingernails into my palms. "Meg McCaffrey, if my children die because you wouldn't let me—"

"Like Chiron said, you'd just get yourself killed. We'll wait for daylight."

I thought how satisfying it would be to drop Meg from the sun chariot at high noon. Then again, some small rational part of me realized she might be right. I was in no condition to launch a one-man rescue operation. That just made me angrier.

Chiron's tail swished from side to side. "Well, then . . . I will see you both in the morning. We *will* find a solution. I promise you that."

He gave me one last look, as if worried I might start running in circles and baying at the moon. Then he trotted back toward the Big House.

I scowled at Meg. "I'm staying out here tonight, in case Kayla and Austin come back. Unless you want to forbid me from doing that, *too.*"

She only shrugged. Even her *shrugs* were annoying.

I stormed off to the Me cabin and grabbed a few supplies: a flashlight, two blankets, a canteen of water. As an after-thought, I took a few books from Will Solace's bookshelf. No surprise, he kept reference materials about me to share with new campers. I thought perhaps the books might help jog my memories. Failing that, they'd make good tinder for a fire.

When I returned to the edge of the woods, Meg was still there.

I hadn't expected her to keep vigil with me. Being Meg, she had apparently decided it would be the best way to irri-tate me.

She sat next to me on my blanket and began eating a golden apple, which she had hidden in her coat. Win-ter mist drifted through the trees. The night breeze rippled through the grass, making patterns like waves.

Under different circumstances, I might have written a poem about it. In my present state of mind, I could only have managed a funeral dirge, and I did not want to think about death.

I tried to stay mad at Meg, but I couldn't manage it. I supposed she'd had my best interests at heart . . . or at least, she wasn't ready to see her new godly servant get himself killed.

She didn't try to console me. She asked me no ques-tions. She amused herself by picking up small rocks and tossing them into the woods. That, I didn't mind. I happily would've given her a catapult if I had one.

As the night wore on, I read about myself in Will's books.

Normally this would have been a happy task. I am, after all, a fascinating subject. This time, however, I gained no satisfaction from my glorious exploits. They all seemed like exaggerations, lies, and . . . well, myths. Unfortunately, I found a chapter about Oracles. Those few pages stirred my memory, confirming my worst suspicions.

I was too angry to be terrified. I stared at the woods and dared the whispering voices to disturb me. I thought, *Come on, then. Take me, too.* The trees remained silent. Kayla and Austin did not return.

Toward dawn, it started to snow. Only then did Meg speak. "We should go inside."

"And abandon them?"

"Don't be stupid." Snow salted the hood of her winter coat. Her face was hidden except for the tip of her nose and the glint of rhinestones on her glasses. "You'll freeze out here."

I noticed she didn't complain about the cold herself. I wondered if she even felt uncomfortable, or if the power of Demeter kept her safe through the winter like a leafless tree or a dormant seed in the earth.

"They were my children." It hurt me to use the past tense, but Kayla and Austin felt irretrievably lost. "I should've done more to protect them. I should have anticipated that my enemies would target them to hurt me."

Meg chucked another rock at the trees. "You've had a lot of children. You take the blame every time one of them gets in trouble?"

The answer was no. Over the millennia, I had barely managed to remember my children's names. If I sent them an occasional birthday card or a magic flute, I felt really good about myself. Sometimes I wouldn't realize one of them had died until decades later. During the French Revolution, I got worried about my boy Louis XIV, the Sun King, then went down to check on him and found out he had died seventy-five years earlier.

Now, though, I had a mortal conscience. My sense of guilt seemed to have expanded as my life span contracted. I couldn't explain that to Meg. She would never understand. She'd probably just throw a rock at me.

"It's my fault Python retook Delphi," I said. "If I had killed him the moment he reappeared, while I was still a god, he would never have become so powerful. He would never have made an alliance with this . . . this *Beast*."

Meg lowered her face.

"You know him," I guessed. "In the Labyrinth, when you heard the Beast's voice, you were terrified."

I was worried she might order me to shut up again. Instead, she silently traced the crescents on her gold rings.

"Meg, he wants to *destroy* me," I said. "Somehow, he's behind these disappearances. The more we understand about this man—"

"He lives in New York."

I waited. It was difficult to glean much information from the top of Meg's hood.

"All right," I said. "That narrows it down to eight and a half million people. What else?"

Meg picked at the calluses on her fingers. "If you're a demigod on the streets, you hear about the Beast. He takes people like me."

A snowflake melted on the back of my neck. "Takes people . . . why?"

"To train," Meg said. "To use like . . . servants, soldiers. I don't know."

"And you've met him."

"Please don't ask me—"

"Meg."

"He killed my dad."

Her words were quiet, but they hit me harder than a rock in the face. "Meg, I—I'm sorry. How . . . ?"

"I refused to work for him," she said. "My dad tried to . . ." She closed her fists. "I was really small. I hardly remember it. I got away. Otherwise, the Beast would've killed me, too. My stepdad took me in. He was good to me. You asked why he trained me to fight? Why he gave me the rings? He wanted me to be safe, to be able to protect myself."

"From the Beast."

Her hood dipped. "Being a good demigod, training hard . . . that's the only way to keep the Beast away. Now you know."

In fact, I had more questions than ever, but I sensed that Meg was in no mood for further sharing. I remembered her expression as we stood on that ledge under the chamber of Delphi—her look of absolute terror when she recognized the Beast's voice. Not all monsters were three-ton reptiles with poisonous breath. Many wore human faces.

I peered into the woods. Somewhere in there, five demigods were being used as bait, including two of my children. The Beast wanted me to search for them, and I would. But I would *not* let him use me.

I have well-placed help within the camp, the Beast had said. That bothered me.

I knew from experience that any demigod could be turned against Olympus. I had been at the banquet table when Tantalus tried to poison the gods by feeding us his chopped-up son in a stew. I'd watched as King Mithridates sided with the Persians and massacred every Roman in Anatolia. I'd witnessed Queen Clytemnestra turn homicidal, killing her husband Agamemnon just because he made one little human sacrifice to me. Demigods are an unpredictable bunch.

I glanced at Meg. I wondered if she could be lying to me—if she was some sort of spy. It seemed unlikely. She was too contrary, impetuous, and annoying to be an effective mole. Besides, she was technically my master. She could order me to do almost any task and I would have to obey. If she was out to destroy me, I was already as good as dead.

Perhaps Damien White . . . a son of Nemesis was a natural choice for backstabbing duty. Or Connor Stoll, Alice, or Julia . . . a child of Hermes had recently betrayed the gods by working for Kronos. They might do so again. Maybe that pretty Chiara, daughter of Tyche, was in league with the Beast. Children of luck were natural gamblers. The truth was, I had no idea.

The sky turned from black to gray. I became aware of a distant *thump, thump, thump*—a quick, relentless pulse that got louder and louder. At first, I feared it might be the blood in my head. Could human brains explode from too many worrisome thoughts? Then I realized the noise was mechanical, coming from the west. It was the distinctly modern sound of rotor blades cutting the air.

Meg lifted her head. "Is that a helicopter?"

I got to my feet.

The machine appeared—a dark red Bell 412 cutting north along the coastline. (Riding the skies as often as I do, I know my flying machines.) Painted on the helicopter's side was a bright green logo with the letters D.E.

Despite my misery, a small bit of hope kindled inside me. The satyrs Millard and Herbert must have succeeded in delivering their message.

"That," I told Meg, "is Rachel Elizabeth Dare. Let's go see what the Oracle of Delphi has to say."

20

Don't paint over gods
If you're redecorating
That's, like, common sense

RACHEL ELIZABETH DARE was one of my favorite mortals. As soon as she'd become the Oracle two summers ago, she'd brought new vigor and excitement to the job.

Of course, the previous Oracle had been a withered corpse, so perhaps the bar was low. Regardless, I was elated as the Dare Enterprises helicopter descended just beyond the eastern hills, outside the camp's boundary. I wondered what Rachel had told her father—a fabulously wealthy real estate magnate—to convince him she needed to borrow a helicopter. I knew Rachel could be quite convincing.

I jogged across the valley with Meg in tow. I could already imagine the way Rachel would look as she came over the summit: her frizzy red hair, her vivacious smile, her paint-spattered blouse, and jeans covered with doodles. I needed her humor, wisdom, and resilience. The Oracle would cheer us all up. Most importantly, she would cheer *me* up.

I was not prepared for the reality. (Which again, was a stunning surprise. Normally, reality prepares itself for *me*.)

Rachel met us on the hill near the entrance to her cave. Only later would I realize Chiron's two satyr messengers were not with her, and I would wonder what had happened to them.

Miss Dare looked thinner and older—less like a high school girl and more like a young farmer's wife from ancient times, weathered from hard work and gaunt from shortage of food. Her red hair had lost its vibrancy. It framed her face in a curtain of dark copper. Her freckles had faded to watermarks. Her green eyes did not sparkle. And she was wearing a dress—a white cotton frock with a white shawl, and a patina-green jacket. Rachel *never* wore dresses.

"Rachel?" I didn't trust myself to say any more. She was not the same person.

Then I remembered that I wasn't either.

She studied my new mortal form. Her shoulders slumped. "So it's true."

From below us came the voices of other campers. No doubt woken by the sound of the helicopter, they were emerging from their cabins and gathering at the base of the hill. None tried to climb toward us, though. Perhaps they sensed that all was not right.

The helicopter rose from behind Half-Blood Hill. It veered toward Long Island Sound, passing so close to the Athena Parthenos that I thought its landing skids might clip the goddess's winged helmet.

I turned to Meg. "Would you tell the others that Rachel needs some space? Fetch Chiron. He should come up. The rest should wait."

It wasn't like Meg to take orders from me. I half expected her to kick me. Instead, she glanced nervously at Rachel, turned, and trudged down the hill.

"A friend of yours?" Rachel asked.

"Long story."

"Yes," she said. "I have a story like that, too."

"Shall we talk in your cave?"

Rachel pursed her lips. "You won't like it. But yes, that's probably the safest place."

The cave was not as cozy as I remembered.

The sofas were overturned. The coffee table had a broken leg. The floor was strewn with easels and canvases. Even Rachel's tripod stool, the throne of prophecy itself, lay on its side on a pile of paint-splattered drop cloths.

Most disturbing was the state of the walls. Ever since taking up residence, Rachel had been painting them, like her cave-dwelling ancestors of old. She had spent hours on elaborate murals of events from the past, images from the future she'd seen in prophecies, favorite quotes from books and music, and abstract designs so good they would have given M. C. Escher vertigo. The art made the cave feel like a mixture of art studio, psychedelic hangout, and graffiti-covered highway underpass. I loved it.

But most of the images had been blotted out with a sloppy coat of white paint. Nearby, a roller was stuck in an encrusted tray. Clearly Rachel had defaced her own work months ago and hadn't been back since.

She waved listlessly at the wreckage. "I got frustrated."

"Your art . . ." I gaped at the field of white. "There was a lovely portrait of me—right there."

I get offended whenever art is damaged, especially if that art features me.

Rachel looked ashamed. "I—I thought a blank canvas might help me think." Her tone made it obvious that the whitewashing had accomplished nothing. I could have told her as much.

The two of us did our best to clean up. We hauled the sofas back into place to form a sitting area. Rachel left the tripod stool where it lay.

A few minutes later, Meg returned. Chiron followed in full centaur form, ducking his head to fit through the entrance. They found us sitting at the wobbly coffee table like civilized cave people, sharing lukewarm Arizona tea and stale crackers from the Oracle's larder.

"Rachel." Chiron sighed with relief. "Where are Millard and Herbert?"

She bowed her head. "They arrived at my house badly wounded. They . . . they didn't make it."

Perhaps it was the morning light behind him, but I fancied I could see new gray whiskers growing in Chiron's beard. The centaur trotted over and lowered himself to the ground, folding his legs underneath himself. Meg joined me on the couch.

Rachel leaned forward and steepled her fingers, as she did when she spoke a prophecy. I half hoped the spirit of Delphi would possess her, but there was no smoke, no hissing, no raspy voice of divine possession. It was a bit disappointing.

"You first," she told us. "Tell me what's been going on here."

We brought her up to speed on the disappearances and my misadventures with Meg. I explained about the three-legged race and our side trip to Delphi.

Chiron blanched. "I did not know this. You went to Delphi?"

Rachel stared at me in disbelief. "*The* Delphi. You saw Python and you . . ."

I got the feeling she wanted to say *and you didn't kill him?* But she restrained herself.

I felt like standing with my face against the wall. Perhaps Rachel could blot me out with white paint. Disappearing would've been less painful than facing my failures.

"At present," I said, "I cannot defeat Python. I am much too weak. And . . . well, the Catch-88."

Chiron sipped his Arizona tea. "Apollo means that we cannot send a quest without a prophecy, and we cannot get a prophecy without an Oracle."

Rachel stared at her overturned tripod stool. "And this man . . . the Beast. What do you know about him?"

"Not much." I explained what I had seen in my dream, and what Meg and I had overheard in the Labyrinth. "The Beast apparently has a reputation for snatching up young demigods in New York. Meg says . . ." I faltered when I saw her expression, clearly cautioning me to stay away from her personal history. "Um, she's had some experience with the Beast."

Chiron raised his brows. "Can you tell us anything that might help, dear?"

Meg sank into the sofa's cushions. "I've crossed paths with him. He's—he's scary. The memory is blurry."

"Blurry," Chiron repeated.

Meg became very interested in the cracker crumbs on her dress.

Rachel gave me a quizzical look. I shook my head, trying my best to impart a warning: *Trauma. Don't ask. Might get attacked by a peach baby.*

Rachel seemed to get the message. "That's all right, Meg," she said. "I have some information that may help."

She fished her phone from her coat pocket. "Don't touch this. You guys have probably figured it out, but phones are going even more haywire than usual around demigods. I'm not technically one of you, and even *I* can't place calls. I was able to take a couple of pictures, though." She turned the screen toward us. "Chiron, you recognize this place?"

The nighttime shot showed the upper floors of a glass residential tower. Judging from the background, it was somewhere in downtown Manhattan.

"That is the building you described last summer," Chiron said, "where you parleyed with the Romans."

"Yeah," Rachel said. "Something didn't feel right about that place. I got to thinking . . . how did the Romans take over such prime Manhattan real estate on such short notice? Who owns it? I tried to contact Reyna, to see if she could tell me anything, but—"

"Communication problems?" Chiron guessed.

"Exactly. I even sent physical mail to Camp Jupiter's drop box in Berkeley. No response. So I asked my dad's real estate lawyers to do some digging."

Meg peeked over the top of her glasses. "Your dad has lawyers? And a helicopter?"

"Several helicopters." Rachel sighed. "He's annoying. Anyway, that building is owned by a shell corporation, which is owned by another shell corporation, blah, blah, blah. The mother company is something called Triumvirate Holdings."

I felt a trickle like white paint rolling down my back. "*Triumvirate* . . ."

Meg made a sour face. "What does that mean?"

"A triumvirate is a ruling council of three," I said. "At least, that's what it meant in ancient Rome."

"Which is interesting," Rachel said, "because of this next shot." She tapped her screen. The new photo zoomed in on the building's penthouse terrace, where three shadowy figures stood talking together—men in business suits, illuminated only by the light from inside the apartment. I couldn't see their faces.

"These are the owners of Triumvirate Holdings," Rachel said. "Just getting this *one* picture wasn't easy." She blew a frizzy strand of hair out of her face. "I've spent the last two months investigating them, and I don't even know their names. I don't know where they live or where they came from. But I can tell you they own so much property and have so much money, they make my dad's company look like a kid's lemonade stand."

I stared at the picture of the three shadowy figures. I could almost imagine that the one on the left was the Beast. His slouching posture and the over-large shape of his head reminded me of the man in purple from my dream.

"The Beast said that his organization was everywhere," I recalled. "He mentioned he had colleagues."

Chiron's tail flicked, sending a paintbrush skidding across the cave floor. "Adult demigods? I can't imagine they would be Greek, but perhaps Roman? If they helped Octavian with his war—"

"Oh, they helped," Rachel said. "I found a paper trail—not much, but you remember those siege weapons Octavian built to destroy Camp Half-Blood?"

"No," said Meg.

I would have ignored her, but Rachel was a more generous soul.

She smiled patiently. "Sorry, Meg. You seem so at home here, I forgot you were new. Basically, the Roman demigods attacked this camp with giant catapulty things called onagers. It was all a big misunderstanding. Anyway, the weapons were paid for by Triumvirate Holdings."

Chiron frowned. "That is not good."

"I found something even more disturbing," Rachel continued. "You remember before that, during the Titan War, Luke Castellan mentioned he had backers in the mortal world? They had enough money to buy a cruise ship, helicopters, weapons. They even hired mortal mercenaries."

"Don't remember that, either," Meg said.

I rolled my eyes. "Meg, we can't stop and explain every major war to you! Luke Castellan was a child of Hermes. He betrayed this camp and allied himself with the Titans. They attacked New York. Big battle. I saved the day. Et cetera."

Chiron coughed. "At any rate, I do remember Luke

claiming that he had lots of supporters. We never found out exactly who they were."

"Now we know," Rachel said. "That cruise ship, the *Princess Andromeda*, was property of Triumvirate Holdings."

A cold sense of unease gripped me. I felt I should know something about this, but my mortal brain was betraying me again. I was more certain than ever that Zeus was toying with me, keeping my vision and memory limited. I remembered some assurances Octavian had given me, though—how easy it would be to win his little war, to raise new temples to me, how much support he had.

Rachel's phone screen went dark—much like my brain— but the grainy photo remained burned into my retinas.

"These men . . ." I picked up an empty tube of burnt sienna paint. "I'm afraid they are not modern demigods."

Rachel frowned. "You think they're ancient demigods who came through the Doors of Death—like Medea, or Midas? The thing is, Triumvirate Holdings has been around since way before Gaea started to wake. Decades, at least."

"Centuries," I said. "The Beast said that he'd been building his empire for centuries."

The cave became so silent, I imagined the hiss of Python, the soft exhale of fumes from deep in the earth. I wished we had some background music to drown it out . . . jazz or classical. I would have settled for death metal polka.

Rachel shook her head. "Then who—?"

"I don't know," I admitted. "But the Beast . . . in my dream, he called me his forefather. He assumed I would recognize him. And if my godly memory was intact, I think

I would. His demeanor, his accent, his facial structure—I have met him before, just not in modern times."

Meg had grown very quiet. I got the distinct impression she was trying to disappear into the couch cushions. Normally, this would not have bothered me, but after our experience in the Labyrinth, I felt guilty every time I mentioned the Beast. My pesky mortal conscience must have been acting up.

"The name Triumvirate . . ." I tapped my forehead, trying to shake loose information that was no longer there. "The last triumvirate I dealt with included Lepidus, Marc Antony, and my son, the *original* Octavian. A triumvirate is a very Roman concept . . . like patriotism, skullduggery, and assassination."

Chiron stroked his beard. "You think these men are ancient Romans? How is that possible? Hades is quite good at tracking down escaped spirits from the Underworld. He would not allow three men from ancient times to run amok in the modern world for centuries."

"Again, I do not know." Saying this so often offended my divine sensibilities. I decided that when I returned to Olympus, I would have to gargle the bad taste out of my mouth with Tabasco-flavored nectar. "But it seems these men have been plotting against us for a very long time. They funded Luke Castellan's war. They supplied aid to Camp Jupiter when the Romans attacked Camp Half-Blood. And despite those two wars, the Triumvirate is still out there— still plotting. What if this company is the root cause of . . . well, everything?"

Chiron looked at me as if I were digging his grave. "That is a very troubling thought. Could three men be so powerful?"

I spread my hands. "You've lived long enough to know, my friend. Gods, monsters, Titans . . . these are always dangerous. But the greatest threat to demigods has always been other demigods. Whoever this Triumvirate is, we must stop them before they take control of the Oracles."

Rachel sat up straight. "Excuse me? Oracles plural?"

"Ah . . . didn't I tell you about them when I was a god?"

Her eyes regained some of their dark green intensity. I feared she was envisioning ways she might inflict pain upon me with her art supplies.

"No," she said levelly, "you did not tell me about them."

"Oh . . . well, my mortal memory has been faulty, you see. I had to read some books in order to—"

"Oracles," she repeated. "Plural."

I took a deep breath. I wanted to assure her that those other Oracles didn't mean a thing to me! Rachel was special! Unfortunately, I doubted she was in a place where she could hear that right now. I decided it was best to speak plainly.

"In ancient times," I said, "there were many Oracles. Of course Delphi was the most famous, but there were four others of comparable power."

Chiron shook his head. "But those were destroyed ages ago."

"So I thought," I agreed. "Now I am not so sure. I believe Triumvirate Holdings wants to control *all* the ancient Oracles. And I believe the most ancient Oracle of all, the Grove of Dodona, is right here at Camp Half-Blood."

21

Up in my business
Always burning Oracles
Romans gonna hate

I WAS A DRAMATIC GOD.

I thought my last statement was a great line. I expected gasps, perhaps some organ music in the background. Maybe the lights would go out just before I could say more. Moments later, I would be found dead with a knife in my back. That would be exciting!

Wait. I'm mortal. Murder would kill me. Never mind.

At any rate, none of that happened. My three companions just stared at me.

"Four other Oracles," Rachel said. "You mean you have four other Pythias—"

"No, my dear. There is only one Pythia—*you*. Delphi is absolutely unique."

Rachel still looked like she wanted to jam a number ten bristle paintbrush up my nose. "So these other four *non-unique* Oracles . . ."

"Well, one was the Sybil of Cumae." I wiped the sweat off my palms. (Why did mortal palms sweat?) "You know, she wrote the Sibylline Books—those prophecies that Ella the harpy memorized."

Meg looked back and forth between us. "A harpy . . . like those chicken ladies who clean up after lunch?"

Chiron smiled. "Ella is a very special harpy, Meg. Years ago, she somehow came across a copy of the prophetic books, which we thought were burned before the Fall of Rome. Right now, our friends at Camp Jupiter are trying to reconstruct them based on Ella's recollections."

Rachel crossed her arms. "And the other three Oracles? I'm sure none of them was a beautiful young priestess whom you praised for her . . . what was it? . . . 'scintillating conversation'?"

"Ah . . ." I wasn't sure why, but it felt like my acne was turning into live insects and crawling across my face. "Well, according to my extensive research—"

"Some books he flipped through last night," Meg clarified.

"Ahem! There was an Oracle at Erythaea, and another at the Cave of Trophonius."

"Goodness," Chiron said. "I'd forgotten about those two."

I shrugged. I remembered almost nothing about them either. They had been some of my less successful prophetic franchises.

"And the fifth," I said, "was the Grove of Dodona."

"A grove," Meg said. "Like trees."

"Yes, Meg, like trees. Groves are typically composed of trees, rather than, say, Fudgsicles. Dodona was a stand of sacred oaks planted by the Mother Goddess in the first days of the world. They were ancient even when the Olympians were born."

"The Mother Goddess?" Rachel shivered in her patina jacket. "Please tell me you don't mean Gaea."

"No, thankfully. I mean Rhea, Queen of the Titans, the mother of the first generation of Olympian gods. Her sacred trees could actually speak. Sometimes they issued prophecies."

"The voices in the woods," Meg guessed.

"Exactly. I believe the Grove of Dodona has regrown itself here in the woods at camp. In my dreams, I saw a crowned woman imploring me to find her Oracle. I believe it was Rhea, though I still don't understand why she was wearing a peace symbol or using the term *dig it*."

"A peace symbol?" Chiron asked.

"A large brass one," I confirmed.

Rachel drummed her fingers on the couch's armrest. "If Rhea is a Titan, isn't she evil?"

"Not all Titans were bad," I said. "Rhea was a gentle soul. She sided with the gods in their first great war. I think she wants us to succeed. She doesn't want her grove in the hands of our enemies."

Chiron's tail twitched. "My friend, Rhea has not been seen for millennia. Her grove was burned in the ancient times. Emperor Theodosius ordered the last oak cut down in—"

"I know." I got a stabbing pain right between my eyes, as I always did when someone mentioned Theodosius. I now recalled that the bully had closed all the ancient temples across the empire, basically evicting us Olympian gods. I used to have an archery target with his face on it. "Nevertheless, many things from the old days have survived or regenerated.

The Labyrinth has rebuilt itself. Why couldn't a grove of sacred trees spring up again right here in this valley?"

Meg pushed herself deeper into the cushions. "This is all weird." Leave it to the young McCaffrey to summarize our conversation so effectively. "So if the tree voices are sacred and stuff, why are they making people get lost?"

"For once, you ask a good question." I hoped such praise wouldn't go to Meg's head. "In the old days, the priests of Dodona would take care of the trees, pruning them, watering them, and channeling their voices by hanging wind chimes in their branches."

"How would that help?" Meg asked.

"I don't know. I'm not a tree priest. But with proper care, these trees could divine the future."

Rachel smoothed her skirt. "And without proper care?"

"The voices were unfocused," I said. "A wild choir of disharmony." I paused, quite pleased with that line. I was hoping someone might write it down for posterity, but no one did. "Untended, the grove could most definitely drive mortals to madness."

Chiron furrowed his brow. "So our missing campers are wandering in the trees, perhaps already insane from the voices."

"Or they're dead," Meg added.

"No." I could not abide that thought. "No, they are still alive. The Beast is using them, trying to bait me."

"How can you be sure?" Rachel asked. "And why? If Python already controls Delphi, why are these other Oracles so important?"

I gazed at the wall formerly graced by my picture. Alas,

no answers magically appeared in the whitewashed space. "I'm not sure. I believe our enemies want to cut us off from every possible source of prophecy. Without a way to see and direct our fates, we will wither and die—gods and mortals alike, anyone who opposes the Triumvirate."

Meg turned upside down on the sofa and kicked off her red shoes. "They're strangling our taproots." She wriggled her toes to demonstrate.

I looked back at Rachel, hoping she would excuse my street urchin overlord's bad manners. "As for why the Grove of Dodona is so important, Python mentioned that it was the one Oracle he could not control. I don't understand exactly why—perhaps because Dodona is the only Oracle that has no connection with me. Its power comes from Rhea. So if the grove is working, and it is free of Python's influence, and it is here at Camp Half-Blood—"

"It could provide us with prophecies." Chiron's eyes gleamed. "It could give us a chance against our enemies."

I gave Rachel an apologetic smile. "Of course, we'd rather have our beloved Oracle of Delphi working again. And we will, eventually. But for now, the Grove of Dodona could be our best hope."

Meg's hair swept the floor. Her face was now the color of one of my sacred cattle. "Aren't prophecies all twisted and mysterious and murky, and people die trying to escape them?"

"Meg," I said, "you can't trust those reviews on RateMyOracle.com. The hotness factor for the Sibyl of Cumae, for instance, is *completely* off. I remember *that* quite clearly."

Rachel put her chin on her fist. "Really? Do tell."

"Uh, what I meant to say: the Grove of Dodona is a benevolent force. It has helped heroes before. The masthead of the original *Argo*, for instance, was carved from a branch of the sacred trees. It could speak to the Argonauts and give them guidance."

"Mm." Chiron nodded. "And that's why our mysterious Beast wants the grove burned."

"Apparently," I said. "And that's why we have to save it."

Meg rolled backward off the couch. Her legs knocked over the three-legged coffee table, spilling our Arizona tea and crackers. "Oops."

I ground my mortal teeth, which would not last a year if I kept hanging around Meg. Rachel and Chiron wisely ignored my young friend's display of Megness.

"Apollo . . ." The old centaur watched a waterfall of tea trickling from the edge of the table. "If you are right about Dodona, how do we proceed? We are already shorthanded. If we send search teams into the woods, we have no guarantee they'll come back."

Meg brushed the hair out of her eyes. "We'll go. Just Apollo and me."

My tongue attempted to hide in the depths of my throat. "We—we will?"

"You said you gotta do a bunch of trials or whatever to prove you're worthy, right? This'll be the first one."

Part of me knew she was right, but the remnants of my godly self rebelled at the idea. I never did my own dirty work. I would rather have picked a nice group of heroes and sent them to their deaths—or, you know, glorious success.

Yet Rhea had been clear in my dream: finding the Oracle was my job. And thanks to the cruelty of Zeus, where I went, Meg went. For all I knew, Zeus was aware of the Beast and his plans, and he had sent me here specifically to deal with the situation . . . a thought that did not make me any more likely to get him a nice tie for Father's Day.

I also remembered the other part of my dream: the Beast in his mauve suit, encouraging me to find the Oracle so he could burn it down. There was still too much I didn't understand, but I had to act. Austin and Kayla were depending on me.

Rachel put her hand on my knee, which made me flinch. Surprisingly, she did not inflict any pain. Her gaze was more earnest than angry. "Apollo, you have to try. If we can get a glimpse of the future . . . well, it may be the only way to get things back to normal." She looked longingly at the blank walls of her cave. "I'd like to have a future again."

Chiron shifted his forelegs. "What do you need from us, old friend? How can we help?"

I glanced at Meg. Sadly, I could tell that we were in agreement. We were stuck with each other. We couldn't risk anyone else.

"Meg is right," I said. "We have to do this ourselves. We should leave immediately, but—"

"We've been up all night," Meg said. "We need some sleep."

Wonderful, I thought. Now Meg is finishing my sentences.

This time I could not argue with her logic. Despite my fervor to rush into the woods and save my children, I had to proceed cautiously. I could not mess up this rescue. And I was increasingly certain that the Beast would keep his captives alive for now. He needed them to lure me into his trap.

Chiron rose on his front hooves. "This evening, then. Rest and prepare, my heroes. I fear you will need all your strength and wits for what comes next."

22

Armed to the eyeballs:
A combat ukulele
Magic Brazil scarf

SUN GODS ARE NOT GOOD at sleeping during the day, but somehow I managed a fitful nap.

When I woke in the late afternoon, I found the camp in a state of agitation.

Kayla and Austin's disappearance had been the tipping point. The other campers were now so rattled, no one could maintain a normal schedule. I suppose a single demigod disappearing every few weeks felt like a normal casualty rate. But a pair of demigods disappearing in the middle of a camp-sanctioned activity—that meant no one was safe.

Word must have spread of our conference in the cave. The Victor twins had stuffed wads of cotton in their ears to foil the oracular voices. Julia and Alice had climbed to the top of the lava wall and were using binoculars to scan the woods, no doubt hoping to spot the Grove of Dodona, but I doubted they could see the trees for the forest.

Everywhere I went, people were unhappy to see me. Damien and Chiara sat together at the canoe dock, glowering in my direction. Sherman Yang waved me away when

I tried to talk with him. He was busy decorating the Ares cabin with frag grenades and brightly decorated claymores. If it had been Saturnalia, he definitely would have won the prize for most violent holiday decorations.

Even the Athena Parthenos stared down at me accusingly from the top of the hill as if to say, *This is all your fault.*

She was right. If I hadn't let Python take over Delphi, if I'd paid more attention to the other ancient Oracles, if I hadn't lost my divinity—

Stop it, Apollo, I scolded myself. *You're beautiful and everyone loves you.*

But it was becoming increasingly difficult to believe that. My father, Zeus, did not love me. The demigods at Camp Half-Blood did not love me. Python and the Beast and his comrades at Triumvirate Holdings did not love me. It was almost enough to make me question my self-worth.

No, no. That was crazy talk.

Chiron and Rachel were nowhere to be seen. Nyssa Barrera informed me that they were hoping against hope to use the camp's sole Internet connection, in Chiron's office, to access more information about Triumvirate Holdings. Harley was with them for tech support. They were presently on hold with Comcast customer service and might not emerge for hours, if indeed they survived the ordeal at all.

I found Meg at the armory, browsing for battle supplies. She had strapped a leather cuirass over her green dress and greaves over orange leggings, so she looked like a kindergartener reluctantly stuffed into combat gear by her parents.

"Perhaps a shield?" I suggested.

"Nuh-uh." She showed me her rings. "I always use two

swords. Plus I need a free hand for slapping when you act stupid."

I had the uncomfortable sense she was serious.

From the weapon rack, she pulled out a long bow and offered it to me.

I recoiled. "No."

"It's your best weapon. You're Apollo."

I swallowed back the tang of mortal bile. "I swore an oath. I'm not the god of archery or music anymore. I won't use a bow or a musical instrument until I can use them *properly*."

"Stupid oath." She didn't slap me, but she looked like she wanted to. "What will you do, just stand around and cheer while I fight?"

That had indeed been my plan, but now I felt silly admitting it. I scanned the weapon display and grabbed a sword. Even without drawing it, I could tell it would be too heavy and awkward for me to use, but I strapped the scabbard around my waist.

"There," I said. "Happy?"

Meg did not appear happy. Nevertheless, she returned the bow to its place.

"Fine," she said. "But you'd better have my back."

I had never understood that expression. It made me think of the KICK ME signs Artemis used to tape to my toga during festival days. Still, I nodded. "Your back shall be had."

We reached the edge of the woods and found a small going-away party waiting for us: Will and Nico, Paolo Montes, Malcolm Pace, and Billie Ng, all with grim faces.

"Be careful," Will told me. "And here."

Before I could object, he placed a ukulele in my hands.

I tried to give it back. "I can't. I made an oath—"

"Yeah, I know. That was stupid of you. But it's a combat ukulele. You can fight with it if you need to."

I looked more closely at the instrument. It was made from Celestial bronze—thin sheets of metal acid-etched to resemble the grain of blond oak wood. The instrument weighed next to nothing, yet I imagined it was almost indestructible.

"The work of Hephaestus?" I asked.

Will shook his head. "The work of Harley. He wanted you to have it. Just sling it over your back. For me and Harley. It'll make us both feel better."

I decided I was obliged to honor the request, though my possession of a ukulele had rarely made anyone feel better. Don't ask me why. When I was a god, I used to do an absolutely blistering ukulele version of "Satisfaction."

Nico handed me some ambrosia wrapped in a napkin.

"I can't eat this," I reminded him.

"It's not for you." He glanced at Meg, his eyes full of misgiving. I remembered that the son of Hades had his own ways of sensing the future—futures that involved the possibility of death. I shivered and tucked the ambrosia into my coat pocket. As aggravating as Meg could be, I was deeply unsettled by the idea that she might come to harm. I decided that I could not allow that to happen.

Malcolm was showing Meg a parchment map, pointing out various places in the woods that we should avoid. Paolo—looking completely healed from his leg surgery—stood next to him, carefully and earnestly providing Portuguese commentary that no one could understand.

When they were finished with the map, Billie Ng approached Meg.

Billie was a wisp of a girl. She compensated for her diminutive stature with the fashion sense of a K-Pop idol. Her winter coat was the color of aluminum foil. Her bobbed hair was aquamarine and her makeup gold. I completely approved. In fact, I thought I could rock that look myself if I could just get my acne under control.

Billie gave Meg a flashlight and a small packet of flower seeds.

"Just in case," Billie said.

Meg seemed quite overwhelmed. She gave Billie a fierce hug.

I didn't understand the purpose of the seeds, but it was comforting to know that in a dire emergency I could hit people with my ukulele while Meg planted geraniums.

Malcolm Pace gave me his parchment map. "When in doubt, veer to the right. That usually works in the woods, though I don't know why."

Paolo offered me a green-and-gold scarf—a bandana version of the Brazilian flag. He said something that, of course, I could not understand.

Nico smirked. "That's Paolo's good-luck bandana. I think he wants you to wear it. He believes it will make you invincible."

I found this dubious, since Paolo was prone to serious injury, but as a god, I had learned never to turn down offerings. "Thank you."

Paolo gripped my shoulders and kissed my cheeks. I may have blushed. He was quite handsome when he wasn't bleeding out from dismemberment.

I rested my hand on Will's shoulder. "Don't worry. We'll be back by dawn."

His mouth trembled ever so slightly. "How can you be sure?"

"I'm the sun god," I said, trying to muster more confidence than I felt. "I *always* return at dawn."

Of course it rained. Why would it not?

Up in Mount Olympus, Zeus must have been having a good laugh at my expense. Camp Half-Blood was supposed to be protected from severe weather, but no doubt my father had told Aeolus to pull out all the stops on his winds. My jilted ex-girlfriends among the air nymphs were probably enjoying their moment of payback.

The rain was just on the edge of sleet—liquid enough to soak my clothes, icy enough to slam against my exposed face like glass shards.

We stumbled along, lurching from tree to tree to find any shelter we could. Patches of old snow crunched under my feet. My ukulele got heavier as its sound hole filled with rain. Meg's flashlight beam cut across the storm like a cone of yellow static.

I led the way, not because I had any destination in mind, but because I was angry. I was tired of being cold and soaked. I was tired of being picked on. Mortals often talk about the whole world being against them, but that is ridiculous. Mortals aren't that important. In my case, the whole world really *was* against me. I refused to surrender to such abuse. I would do something about it! I just wasn't quite sure what.

From time to time we heard monsters in the distance— the roar of a drakon, the harmonized howl of a two-headed wolf—but nothing showed itself. On a night like this, any self-respecting monster would've remained in its lair, warm and cozy.

After what seemed like hours, Meg stifled a scream. I heroically leaped to her side, my hand on my sword. (I would have drawn it, but it was really heavy and got stuck in the scabbard.) At Meg's feet, wedged in the mud, was a glistening black shell the size of a boulder. It was cracked down the middle, the edges splattered with a foul gooey substance.

"I almost stepped on that." Meg covered her mouth as if she might be sick.

I inched closer. The shell was the crushed carapace of a giant insect. Nearby, camouflaged among the tree roots, lay one of the beast's dismembered legs.

"It's a *myrmeke*," I said. "Or it was."

Behind her rain-splattered glasses, Meg's eyes were impossible to read. "A *murr-murr-key?*"

"A giant ant. There must be a colony somewhere in the woods."

Meg gagged. "I hate bugs."

That made sense for a daughter of the agriculture goddess, but to me the dead ant didn't seem any grosser than the piles of garbage in which we often swam.

"Well, don't worry," I said. "This one is dead. Whatever killed it must've had powerful jaws to crack that shell."

"Not comforting. Are—are these things dangerous?"

I laughed. "Oh, yes. They range in size from as small as dogs to larger than grizzly bears. One time I watched a colony of myrmekes attack a Greek army in India. It was hilarious. They spit acid that can melt through bronze armor and—"

"Apollo."

My smile faded. I reminded myself I was no longer a spectator. These ants could kill us. Easily. And Meg was scared.

"Right," I said. "Well, the rain should keep the myrmekes in their tunnels. Just don't make yourself an attractive target. They like bright, shiny things."

"Like flashlights?"

"Um . . ."

Meg handed me the flashlight. "Lead on, Apollo."

I thought that was unfair, but we forged ahead.

After another hour or so (surely the woods weren't this big), the rain tapered off, leaving the ground steaming.

The air got warmer. The humidity approached bath-house levels. Thick white vapor curled off the tree branches.

"What's going on?" Meg wiped her face. "Feels like a tropical rain forest now."

I had no answer. Then, up ahead, I heard a massive flushing sound—like water being forced through pipes . . . or fissures.

I couldn't help but smile. "A geyser."

"A geyser," Meg repeated. "Like Old Faithful?"

"This is excellent news. Perhaps we can get directions. Our lost demigods might have even found sanctuary there!"

"With the geysers," Meg said.

"No, my ridiculous girl," I said. "With the geyser *gods*. Assuming they're in a good mood, this could be great."

"And if they're in a bad mood?"

"Then we'll cheer them up before they can boil us. Follow me!"

23

Scale of one to ten
How would you rate your demise?
Thanks for your input

WAS I RECKLESS to rush toward such volatile nature gods?

Please. Second-guessing myself is not in my nature. It's a trait I've never needed.

True, my memories about the *palikoi* were a little hazy. As I recalled, the geyser gods in ancient Sicily used to give refuge to runaway slaves, so they must be kindly spirits. Perhaps they would also give refuge to lost demigods, or at least notice when five of them wandered through their territory, muttering incoherently. Besides, I was Apollo! The palikoi would be honored to meet a major Olympian such as myself! The fact that geysers often blew their tops, spewing columns of scalding hot water hundreds of feet in the air, wasn't going to stop me from making some new fans . . . I mean *friends*.

The clearing opened before us like an oven door. A wall of heat billowed through the trees and washed over my face. I could feel my pores opening to drink in the moisture, which would hopefully help my spotty complexion.

The scene before us had no business being in a Long

Island winter. Glistening vines wreathed the tree branches. Tropical flowers bloomed from the forest floor. A red parrot sat on a banana tree heavy with green bunches.

In the midst of the glade stood two geysers—twin holes in the ground, ringed with a figure eight of gray mud pots. The craters bubbled and hissed, but they were not spewing at the moment. I decided to take that as a good omen.

Meg's boots squished in the mud. "Is it safe?"

"Definitely not," I said. "We'll need an offering. Perhaps your packet of seeds?"

Meg punched my arm. "Those are magic. For life-and-death emergencies. What about your ukulele? You're not going to play it anyway."

"A man of honor *never* surrenders his ukulele." I perked up. "But wait. You've given me an idea. I will offer the geyser gods a poem! I can still do that. It doesn't count as music."

Meg frowned. "Uh, I don't know if—"

"Don't be envious, Meg. I will make up a poem for you later. This will surely please the geyser gods!" I walked forward, spread my arms, and began to improvise:

> "Oh, geyser, my geyser,
> Let us spew then, you and I,
> Upon this midnight dreary, while we ponder
> Whose woods are these?
> For we have not gone gentle into this good night,
> But have wandered lonely as clouds.
> We seek to know for whom the bell tolls,
> So I hope, springs eternal,
> That the time has come to talk of many things!"

I don't wish to brag, but I thought it was rather good, even if I did recycle a few bits from my earlier works. Unlike my music and archery, my godly skills with poetry seemed to be completely intact.

I glanced at Meg, hoping to see shining admiration on her face. It was high time the girl started to appreciate me. Instead, her mouth hung open, aghast.

"What?" I demanded. "Did you fail poetry appreciation in school? That was first-rate stuff!"

Meg pointed toward the geysers. I realized she was not looking at me at all.

"Well," said a raspy voice, "you got my attention."

One of the palikoi hovered over his geyser. His lower half was nothing but steam. From the waist up, he was perhaps twice the size of a human, with muscular arms the color of caldera mud, chalk-white eyes, and hair like cappuccino foam, as if he had shampooed vigorously and left it sudsy. His massive chest was stuffed into a baby-blue polo shirt with a logo of trees embroidered on the chest pocket.

"O Great Palikos!" I said. "We beseech you—"

"What was that?" the spirit interrupted. "That stuff you were saying?"

"Poetry!" I said. "For you!"

He tapped his mud-gray chin. "No. That wasn't poetry."

I couldn't believe it. Did *no one* appreciate the beauty of language anymore? "My good spirit," I said. "Poetry doesn't have to rhyme, you know."

"I'm not talking about rhyming. I'm talking about getting your message across. We do a lot of market research, and that would *not* fly for our campaign. Now, the Oscar

Meyer Weiner song—*that* is poetry. The ad is fifty years old and people are still singing it. Do you think you could give us some poetry like that?"

I glanced at Meg to be sure I was not imagining this conversation.

"Listen here," I told the geyser god, "I've been the lord of poetry for four thousand years. I ought to know good poetry—"

The palikos waved his hands. "Let's start over. I'll run through our spiel, and maybe you can advise me. Hi, I'm Pete. Welcome to the Woods at Camp Half-Blood! Would you be willing to take a short customer satisfaction survey after this encounter? Your feedback is important."

"Um—"

"Great. Thanks."

Pete fished around in his vaporous region where his pockets would be. He produced a glossy brochure and began to read. "The Woods are your one-stop destination for . . . Hmm, it says *fun*. I thought we changed that to *exhilaration*. See, you've got to choose your words with care. If Paulie were here . . ." Pete sighed. "Well, he's better with the showmanship. Anyway, welcome to the Woods at Camp Half-Blood!"

"You already said that," I noted.

"Oh, right." Pete produced a red pen and began to edit.

"Hey." Meg shouldered past me. She had been speechless with awe for about twelve seconds, which must've been a new record. "Mr. Steamy Mud, have you seen any lost demigods?"

"Mr. Steamy Mud!" Pete slapped his brochure. "*That* is

effective branding! And great point about lost demigods. We can't have our guests wandering around aimlessly. We should be handing out maps at the entrance to the woods. So many wonderful things to see in here, and no one even knows about them. I'll talk to Paulie when he gets back."

Meg took off her fogged-up glasses. "Who's Paulie?"

Pete gestured at the second geyser. "My partner. Maybe we could add a map to this brochure if—"

"So *have* you seen any lost demigods?" I asked.

"What?" Pete tried to mark his brochure, but the steam had made it so soggy, his red pen went right through the paper. "Oh, no. Not recently. But we should have better signage. For instance, did you even know these geysers were here?"

"No," I admitted.

"Well, there you go! Double geysers—the only ones on Long Island!—and no one even knows about us. No out-reach. No word-of-mouth. This is why we convinced the board of directors to hire us!"

Meg and I looked at each other. I could tell that for once we were on the same wavelength: utter confusion.

"Sorry," I said. "Are you telling me the forest has a board of directors?"

"Well, of course," Pete said. "The dryads, the other nature spirits, the sentient monsters . . . I mean, *somebody* has to think about property values and services and public relations. It wasn't easy getting the board to hire us for marketing, either. If we mess up this job . . . oh, man."

Meg squished her shoes in the mud. "Can we go? I don't understand what this guy's talking about."

"And that's the problem!" Pete moaned. "How do we write clear ad copy that conveys the right image of the Woods? For instance, palikoi like Paulie and me used to be famous! Major tourist destinations! People would come to us to make binding oaths. Runaway slaves would seek us out for shelter. We'd get sacrifices, offerings, prayers . . . It was great. Now, nothing."

I heaved a sigh. "I know how you feel."

"Guys," Meg said, "we're looking for missing demigods."

"Right," I agreed. "O, Great . . . Pete, do you have any idea where our lost friends might have gone? Perhaps you know of some secret locations within the woods?"

Pete's chalk-white eyes brightened. "Did you know the children of Hephaestus have a hidden workshop to the north called Bunker Nine?"

"I did, actually," I said.

"Oh." A puff of steam escaped Pete's left nostril. "Well, did you know the Labyrinth has rebuilt itself? There is an entrance right here in the woods—"

"We know," Meg said.

Pete looked crestfallen.

"But perhaps," I said, "that's because your marketing campaign is working."

"Do you think so?" Pete's foamy hair began to swirl. "Yes. Yes, that may be true! Did you happen to see our spotlights, too? Those were my idea."

"Spotlights?" Meg asked.

Twin beams of red light blasted from the geysers and swept across the sky. Lit from beneath, Pete looked like the world's scariest teller of ghost stories.

"Unfortunately, they attracted the wrong kind of attention." Pete sighed. "Paulie doesn't let me use them often. He suggested advertising on a blimp instead, or perhaps a giant inflatable King Kong—"

"That's cool," Meg interrupted. "But can you tell us anything about a secret grove with whispering trees?"

I had to admit, Meg was good at getting us back on topic. As a poet, I did not cultivate directness. But as an archer, I could appreciate the value of a straight shot.

"Oh." Pete floated lower in his cloud of steam, the spotlight turning him the color of cherry soda. "I'm not supposed to talk about the grove."

My once-godly ears tingled. I resisted the urge to scream, *AHA!* "Why can't you talk about the grove, Pete?"

The spirit fiddled with his soggy brochure. "Paulie said it would scare away tourists. 'Talk about the dragons,' he told me. 'Talk about the wolves and serpents and ancient killing machines. But don't mention the grove.'"

"Ancient killing machines?" Meg asked.

"Yeah," Pete said halfheartedly. "We're marketing them as fun family entertainment. But the grove . . . Paulie said that was our worst problem. The neighborhood isn't even *zoned* for an Oracle. Paulie went there to see if maybe we could relocate it, but—"

"He didn't come back," I guessed.

Pete nodded miserably. "How am I supposed to run the marketing campaign all by myself? Sure, I can use robo-calls for the phone surveys, but a lot of networking has to be done face-to-face, and Paulie was always better with that stuff." Pete's voice broke into a sad hiss. "I miss him."

"Maybe we could find him," Meg suggested, "and bring him back."

Pete shook his head. "Paulie made me promise not to follow him and not to tell anybody else where the grove is. He's pretty good at resisting those weird voices, but you guys wouldn't stand a chance."

I was tempted to agree. Finding ancient killing machines sounded much more reasonable. Then I pictured Kayla and Austin wandering through the ancient grove, slowly going mad. They needed me, which meant I needed their location.

"Sorry, Pete." I gave him my most critical stare—the one I used to crush aspiring singers during Broadway auditions. "I'm just not buying it."

Mud bubbled around Pete's caldera. "Wh-what do you mean?"

"I don't think this grove exists," I said. "And if it does, I don't think you know its location."

Pete's geyser rumbled. Steam swirled in his spotlight beam. "I—I *do* know! Of course it exists!"

"Oh, really? Then why aren't there billboards about it all over the place? And a dedicated Web site? Why haven't I seen a groveofdodona hashtag on social media?"

Pete glowered. "I suggested all that! Paulie shot me down!"

"So do some outreach!" I demanded. "Sell us on your product! Show us where this grove is!"

"I can't. The only entrance . . ." He glanced over my shoulder and his face went slack. "Ah, spew." His spotlights shut off.

I turned. Meg made a squelching sound even louder than her shoes in the mud.

It took a moment for my vision to adjust, but at the edge of the clearing stood three black ants the size of Sherman tanks.

"Pete," I said, trying to remain calm, "when you said your spotlights attracted the wrong kind of attention—"

"I meant the myrmekes," he said. "I hope this won't affect your online review of the Woods at Camp Half-Blood."

24

Breaking my promise
Spectacularly failing
I blame Neil Diamond

MYRMEKES SHOULD BE high on your list of monsters not to fight.

They attack in groups. They spit acid. Their pincers can snap through Celestial bronze.

Also, they are ugly.

The three soldier ants advanced, their ten-foot-long antennae waving and bobbing in a mesmerizing way, trying to distract me from the true danger of their mandibles.

Their beaked heads reminded me of chickens—chickens with dark flat eyes and black armored faces. Each of their six legs would have made a fine construction winch. Their oversize abdomens throbbed and pulsed like noses sniffing for food.

I silently cursed Zeus for inventing ants. The way I heard it, he got upset with some greedy man who was always stealing from his neighbors' crops, so Zeus turned him into the first ant—a species that does nothing but scavenge, steal, and breed. Ares liked to joke that if Zeus wanted such a species, he could've just left humans the way they were. I used to laugh. Now that I am one of you, I no longer find it funny.

The ants stepped toward us, their antennae twitching. I imagined their train of thought was something like *Shiny? Tasty? Defenseless?*

"No sudden movements," I told Meg, who did not seem inclined to move at all. In fact, she looked petrified.

"Oh, Pete?" I called. "How do you deal with myrmekes invading your territory?"

"By hiding," he said, and disappeared into the geyser.

"Not helpful," I grumbled.

"Can we dive in?" Meg asked.

"Only if you fancy boiling to death in a pit of scalding water."

The tank bugs clacked their mandibles and edged closer.

"I have an idea." I unslung my ukulele.

"I thought you swore not to play," Meg said.

"I did. But if I throw this shiny object to one side, the ants might—"

I was about to say *the ants might follow it and leave us alone*.

I neglected to consider that, in my hands, the ukulele made me look shinier and tastier. Before I could throw the instrument, the soldier ants surged toward us. I stumbled back, only remembering the geyser behind me when my shoulder blades began to blister, filling the air with Apollo-scented steam.

"Hey, bugs!" Meg's scimitars flashed in her hands, making her the new shiniest thing in the clearing.

Can we take a moment to appreciate that Meg did this

on purpose? Terrified of insects, she could have fled and left me to be devoured. Instead, she chose to risk her life by distracting three tank-size ants. Throwing garbage at street thugs was one thing. But this . . . this was an entirely new level of foolishness. If I lived, I might have to nominate Meg McCaffrey for Best Sacrifice at the next Demi Awards.

Two of the ants charged at Meg. The third stayed on me, though he turned his head long enough for me to sprint to one side.

Meg ran between her opponents, her golden blades severing a leg from each. Their mandibles snapped at empty air. The soldier bugs wobbled on their five remaining legs, tried to turn, and bonked heads.

Meanwhile, the third ant charged me. In a panic, I threw my combat ukulele. It bounced off the ant's forehead with a dissonant *twang*.

I tugged my sword free of its scabbard. I've always hated swords. Such inelegant weapons, and they require you to be in close combat. How unwise, when you can shoot your enemies with an arrow from across the world!

The ant spat acid, and I tried to swat away the goop.

Perhaps that wasn't the brightest idea. I often got sword fighting and tennis confused. At least some of the acid splattered the ant's eyes, which bought me a few seconds. I valiantly retreated, raising my sword only to find that the blade had been eaten away, leaving me nothing but a steaming hilt.

"Oh, Meg?" I called helplessly.

She was otherwise occupied. Her swords whirled in golden arcs of destruction, lopping off leg segments, slicing antennae. I had never seen a dimachaerus fight with such skill, and I had seen all the best gladiators in combat. Unfortunately, her blades only sparked off the ants' thick main carapaces. Glancing blows and dismemberment did not faze them at all. As good as Meg was, the ants had more legs, more weight, more ferocity, and slightly more acid-spitting ability.

My own opponent snapped at me. I managed to avoid its mandibles, but its armored face bashed the side of my head. I staggered and fell. One ear canal seemed to fill with molten iron.

My vision clouded. Across the clearing, the other ants flanked Meg, using their acid to herd her toward the woods. She dove behind a tree and came up with only one of her blades. She tried to stab the closest ant but was driven back by acid cross fire. Her leggings were smoking, peppered with holes. Her face was tight with pain.

"Peaches," I muttered to myself. "Where is that stupid diaper demon when we need him?"

The karpos did not appear. Perhaps the presence of the geyser gods or some other force in the woods kept him away. Perhaps the board of directors had a rule against pets.

The third ant loomed over me, its mandibles foaming with green saliva. Its breath smelled worse than Hephaestus's work shirts.

My next decision I could blame on my head injury. I could tell you I wasn't thinking clearly, but that isn't true. I was desperate. I was terrified. I wanted to help Meg. Mostly I wanted to save myself. I saw no other option, so I dove for my ukulele.

I know. I promised on the River Styx not to play music until I was a god once more. But even such a dire oath can seem unimportant when a giant ant is about to melt your face off.

I grabbed the instrument, rolled onto my back, and belted out "Sweet Caroline."

Even without my oath, I would only have done something like that in the most extreme emergency. When I sing that song, the chances of mutually assured destruction are too great. But I saw no other choice. I gave it my utmost effort, channeling all the saccharine schmaltz I could muster from the 1970s.

The giant ant shook its head. Its antennae quivered. I got to my feet as the monster crawled drunkenly toward me. I put my back to the geyser and launched into the chorus.

The *Dah! Dah! Dah!* did the trick. Blinded by disgust and rage, the ant charged. I rolled aside as the monster's momentum carried it forward, straight into the muddy cauldron.

Believe me, the only thing that smells *worse* than Hephaestus's work shirts is a myrmeke boiling in its own shell.

Somewhere behind me, Meg screamed. I turned in time to see her second sword fly from her hand. She collapsed as one of the myrmekes caught her in its mandibles.

"NO!" I shrieked.

The ant did not snap her in half. It simply held her—limp and unconscious.

"Meg!" I yelled again. I strummed the ukulele desperately. "Sweet Caroline!"

But my voice was gone. Defeating one ant had taken all my energy. (I don't think I have ever written a sadder sentence than that.) I tried to run to Meg's aid, but I stumbled and fell. The world turned pale yellow. I hunched on all fours and vomited.

I have a concussion, I thought, but I had no idea what to do about it. It seemed like ages since I had been a god of healing.

I may have lain in the mud for minutes or hours while my brain slowly gyrated inside my skull. By the time I managed to stand, the two ants were gone.

There was no sign of Meg McCaffrey.

25

I'm on a roll now
Boiling, burning, throwing up
Lions? Hey, why not?

I STUMBLED THROUGH the glade, shouting Meg's name. I knew it was pointless, but yelling felt good. I looked for signs of broken branches or trampled ground. Surely two tank-size ants would leave a trail I could follow. But I was not Artemis; I did not have my sister's skill with tracking. I had no idea which direction they'd taken my friend.

I retrieved Meg's swords from the mud. Instantly, they changed into gold rings—so small, so easily lost, like a mortal life. I may have cried. I tried to break my ridiculous combat ukulele, but the Celestial bronze instrument defied my attempts. Finally, I yanked off the A string, threaded it through Meg's rings, and tied them around my neck.

"Meg, I will find you," I muttered.

Her abduction was my fault. I was sure of this. By playing music and saving myself, I had broken my oath on the River Styx. Instead of punishing me directly, Zeus or the Fates or all the gods together had visited their wrath upon Meg McCaffrey.

How could I have been so foolish? Whenever I angered

the other gods, those closest to me were struck down. I'd lost Daphne because of one careless comment to Eros. I'd lost the beautiful Hyacinthus because of a quarrel with Zephyros. Now my broken oath would cost Meg her life.

No, I told myself. *I won't allow it.*

I was so nauseous, I could barely walk. Someone seemed to be inflating a balloon inside my brain. Yet I managed to stumble to the rim of Pete's geyser.

"Pete!" I shouted. "Show yourself, you cowardly telemarketer!"

Water shot skyward with a sound like the blast of an organ's lowest pipe. In the swirling steam, the palikos appeared, his mud-gray face hardening with anger.

"You call me a TELEMARKETER?" he demanded. "We run a full-service PR firm!"

I doubled over and vomited in his crater, which I thought an appropriate response.

"Stop that!" Pete complained.

"I need to find Meg." I wiped my mouth with a shaky hand. "What would the myrmekes do with her?"

"I don't know!"

"Tell me or I will *not* complete your customer service survey."

Pete gasped. "That's terrible! Your feedback is important!" He floated down to my side. "Oh, dear . . . your head doesn't look good. You've got a big gash on your scalp, and there's blood. That must be why you're not thinking clearly."

"I don't care!" I yelled, which only made the pounding in my head worse. "Where is the myrmekes' nest?"

Pete wrung his steamy hands. "Well, that's what we were talking about earlier. That's where Paulie went. The nest is the only entrance."

"To what?"

"To the Grove of Dodona."

My stomach solidified into a pack of ice, which was unfair, because I needed one for my head. "The ant nest . . . is the way to the grove?"

"Look, you need medical attention. I *told* Paulie we should have a first-aid station for visitors." He fished around in his nonexistent pockets. "Let me just mark the location of the Apollo cabin—"

"If you pull out a brochure," I warned, "I will make you eat it. Now, explain how the nest leads to the grove."

Pete's face turned yellow, or perhaps that was just my vision getting worse. "Paulie didn't tell me everything. There's this thicket of woods that's grown so dense, nobody can get in. I mean, even from above, the branches are like . . ." He laced his muddy fingers, then caused them to liquefy and melt into one another, which made his point quite well.

"Anyway"—he pulled his hands apart—"the grove is in there. It could have been slumbering for centuries. Nobody on the board of directors even knew about it. Then, all of a sudden, the trees started whispering. Paulie figured those darned ants must have burrowed into the grove from underneath, and that's what woke it up."

I tried to make sense of that. It was difficult with a swollen brain. "Which way is the nest?"

"North of here," Pete said. "Half a mile. But, man, you are in no shape—"

"I must! Meg needs me!"

Pete grabbed my arm. His grip was like a warm wet tourniquet. "She's got time. If they carried her off in one piece, that means she's not dead yet."

"She will be soon enough!"

"Nah. Before Paulie . . . before he disappeared, he went into that nest a few times looking for the tunnel to the grove. He told me those myrmekes like to goop up their victims and let them, um, ripen until they're soft enough for the hatchlings to eat."

I made an un-godlike squeak. If there had been anything left in my stomach, I would have lost it. "How long does she have?"

"Twenty-four hours, give or take. Then she'll start to . . . um, soften."

It was difficult to imagine Meg McCaffrey softening under any circumstances, but I pictured her alone and scared, encased in insect goop, tucked in some larder of carcasses in the ants' nest. For a girl who hated bugs— Oh, Demeter had been right to hate me and keep her children away from me. I was a terrible god!

"Go get some help," Pete urged. "The Apollo cabin can heal that head wound. You're not doing your friend any favors by charging after her and getting yourself killed."

"Why do you care what happens to us?"

The geyser god looked offended. "Visitor satisfaction is always our top priority! Besides, if you find Paulie while you're in there . . ."

I tried to stay angry at the palikos, but the loneliness and worry on his face mirrored my own feelings. "Did Paulie explain how to navigate the ants' nest?"

Pete shook his head. "Like I said, he didn't want me to follow him. The myrmekes are dangerous enough. And if those other guys are still wandering around—"

"Other guys?"

Pete frowned. "Didn't I mention that? Yeah. Paulie saw three humans, heavily armed. They were looking for the grove too."

My left leg started thumping nervously, as if it missed its three-legged race partner. "How did Paulie know what they were looking for?"

"He heard them talking in Latin."

"*Latin?* Were they campers?"

Pete spread his hands. "I—I don't think so. Paulie described them like they were adults. He said one of them was the leader. The other two addressed him as *imperator*."

The entire planet seemed to tilt. "Imperator."

"Yeah, you know, like in Rome—"

"Yes, I know." Suddenly, too many things made sense. Pieces of the puzzle flew together, forming one huge picture that smacked me in the face. The Beast . . . Triumvirate Holdings . . . adult demigods completely off the radar.

It was all I could do to avoid pitching forward into the geyser. Meg needed me more than ever. But I would have to do this right. I would have to be careful—even more careful than when I gave the fiery horses of the sun their yearly vaccinations.

"Pete," I said, "do you still oversee sacred oaths?"

"Well, yes, but—"

"Then hear my solemn oath!"

"Uh, the thing is, you've got this aura around you like you just *broke* a sacred oath, maybe one you swore on the River Styx? And if you break *another* oath with me—"

"I swear that I will save Meg McCaffrey. I will use every means at my disposal to bring her safely from the ants' lair, and this oath supersedes any previous oath I have made. This I swear upon your sacred and extremely hot waters!"

Pete winced. "Well, okay. It's done now. But keep in mind that if you don't keep that oath, if Meg dies, even if it's not your fault . . . you'll face the consequences."

"I am already cursed for breaking my earlier oath! What does it matter?"

"Yeah, but see, those River Styx oaths can take *years* to destroy you. They're like cancer. My oaths . . ." Pete shrugged. "If you break it, there's nothing I can do to stop your punishment. Wherever you are, a geyser will instantly blast through the ground at your feet and boil you alive."

"Ah . . ." I tried to stop my knees from knocking. "Yes, of course I knew that. I stand by my oath."

"You've got no choice now."

"Right. I think I'll—I'll go get healed."

I staggered off.

"Camp is the other direction," Pete said.

I changed course.

"Remember to complete our survey online!" Pete called after me. "Just curious, on a scale of one to ten, how would you rate your overall satisfaction with the Woods at Camp Half-Blood?"

I didn't reply. As I stumbled into the darkness, I was too busy contemplating, on a scale of one to ten, the pain I might have to endure in the near future.

I didn't have the strength to make it back to camp. The farther I walked, the clearer that became. My joints were pudding. I felt like a marionette, and as much as I'd enjoyed controlling mortals from above in the past, I did not relish being on the other end of the strings.

My defenses were at level zero. The smallest hellhound or dragon could have easily made a meal of the great Apollo. If an irritated badger had taken issue with me, I would have been doomed.

I leaned against a tree to catch my breath. The tree seemed to push me away, whispering in a voice I remembered so well: *Keep moving, Apollo. You can't rest here.*

"I loved you," I muttered.

Part of me knew I was delirious—imagining things only because of my concussion—but I swore I could see the face of my beloved Daphne rising from each tree trunk I passed, her features floating under the bark like a mirage of wood— her slightly crooked nose, her offset green eyes, those lips I had never kissed but never stopped dreaming of.

You loved every pretty girl, she scolded. *And every pretty boy, for that matter.*

"Not like you," I cried. "You were my first true love. Oh, Daphne!"

Wear my crown, she said. *And repent.*

I remembered chasing her—her lilac scent on the breeze, her lithe form flitting through the dappled light of the forest.

I pursued her for what seemed like years. Perhaps it was.

For centuries afterward, I blamed Eros.

In a moment of recklessness, I had ridiculed Eros's archery skills. Out of spite, he struck me with a golden arrow. He bent all my love toward the beautiful Daphne, but that was not the worst of it. He also struck Daphne's heart with a lead arrow, leeching all possible affection she might have had for me.

What people do not understand: Eros's arrows can't summon emotion from nothing. They can only cultivate potential that is already there. Daphne and I could have been a perfect pair. She was my true love. She could have loved me back. Yet thanks to Eros, my love-o-meter was cranked to one hundred percent, while Daphne's feelings turned to pure hate (which is, of course, only the flip side of love). Nothing is more tragic than loving someone to the depths of your soul and knowing they cannot and will not ever love you back.

The stories say I chased her on a whim, that she was just another pretty dress. The stories are wrong. When she begged Gaea to turn her into a laurel tree in order to escape me, part of my heart hardened into bark as well. I invented the laurel wreath to commemorate my failure—to punish myself for the fate of my greatest love. Every time some hero wins the laurels, I am reminded of the girl I can never win.

After Daphne, I swore I would never marry. Sometimes I claimed that was because I couldn't decide between the Nine Muses. A convenient story. The Nine Muses were my constant companions, all of them beautiful in their own way. But they never possessed my heart like Daphne did.

Only one other person ever affected me so deeply—the perfect Hyacinthus—and he, too, was taken from me.

All these thoughts rambled through my bruised brain. I staggered from tree to tree, leaning against them, grabbing their lowest branches like handrails.

You cannot die here, Daphne whispered. *You have work to do. You made an oath.*

Yes, my oath. Meg needed me. I had to . . .

I fell face forward in the icy mulch.

How long I lay there, I'm not sure.

A warm snout breathed in my ear. A rough tongue lapped my face. I thought I was dead and Cerberus had found me at the gates of the Underworld.

Then the beast pushed me over onto my back. Dark tree branches laced the sky. I was still in the forest. The golden visage of a lion appeared above me, his amber eyes beautiful and deadly. He licked my face, perhaps trying to decide if I would make a good supper.

"*Ptfh.*" I spat mane fur out of my mouth.

"Wake up," said a woman's voice, somewhere to my right. It wasn't Daphne, but it was vaguely familiar.

I managed to raise my head. Nearby, a second lion sat at the feet of a woman with tinted glasses and a silver-and-gold tiara in her braided hair. Her batik dress swirled with images of fern fronds. Her arms and hands were covered in henna tattoos. She looked different than she had in my dream, but I recognized her.

"Rhea," I croaked.

She inclined her head. "Peace, Apollo. I don't want to bum you out, but we need to talk."

26

Imperators here?
Gag me with a peace symbol
Not groovy, Mama

MY HEAD WOUND MUST have tasted like Wagyu beef.

The lion kept licking the side of my face, making my hair stickier and wetter. Strangely, this seemed to clear my thoughts. Perhaps lion saliva had curative properties. I guess I should have known that, being a god of healing, but you'll have to excuse me if I haven't done trial-and-error experiments with the drool of every single animal.

With difficulty, I sat up and faced the Titan queen.

Rhea leaned against the side of a VW safari van painted with swirling black frond designs like those on her dress. I seemed to recall that the black fern was one of Rhea's symbols, but I couldn't remember why. Among the gods, Rhea had always been something of a mystery. Even Zeus, who knew her best, did not often speak of her.

Her turret crown circled her brow like a glittering railroad track. When she looked down at me, her tinted glasses changed from orange to purple. A macramé belt cinched her waist, and on a chain around her neck hung her brass peace symbol.

She smiled. "Glad you're awake. I was worried, man."

I really wished people would stop calling me *man*. "Why are you . . . Where have you been all these centuries?"

"Upstate." She scratched her lion's ears. "After Woodstock, I stuck around, started a pottery studio."

"You . . . what?"

She tilted her head. "Was that last week or last millennium? I've lost track."

"I—I believe you're describing the 1960s. That was last century."

"Oh, bummer." Rhea sighed. "I get mixed up after so many years."

"I sympathize."

"After I left Kronos . . . well, that man was so square, you could cut yourself on his corners, you know what I mean? He was the ultimate 1950s dad—wanted us to be Ozzie and Harriet or Lucy and Ricky or something."

"He—he swallowed his children alive."

"Yeah." Rhea brushed her hair from her face. "That was some bad karma. Anyway, I left him. Back then divorce wasn't cool. You just didn't do it. But me? I burned my *apodesmos* and got liberated. I raised Zeus in a commune with a bunch of naiads and *kouretes*. Lots of wheat germ and nectar. The kid grew up with a strong Aquarian vibe."

I was fairly sure Rhea was misremembering her centuries, but I thought it would be impolite to keep pointing that out.

"You remind me of Iris," I said. "She went organic vegan several decades ago."

Rhea made a face—just a ripple of disapproval before

regaining her karmic balance. "Iris is a good soul. I dig her. But you know, these younger goddesses, they weren't around to fight the revolution. They don't get what it was like when your old man was eating your children and you couldn't get a real job and the Titan chauvinists just wanted you to stay home and cook and clean and have more Olympian babies. And speaking of Iris . . ."

Rhea touched her forehead. "Wait, were we speaking of Iris? Or did I just have a flashback?"

"I honestly don't know."

"Oh, I remember now. She's a messenger of the gods, right? Along with Hermes and that other groovy liberated chick . . . Joan of Arc?"

"Er, I'm not sure about that last one."

"Well, anyway, the communication lines are down, man. Nothing works. Rainbow messages, flying scrolls, Hermes Express . . . it's all going haywire."

"We know this. But we don't know why."

"It's them. They're doing it."

"Who?"

She glanced to either side. "The Man, man. Big Brother. The suits. The imperators."

I had been hoping she would say something else: giants, Titans, ancient killing machines, aliens. I would've rather tangled with Tartarus or Ouranos or Primordial Chaos itself. I had hoped Pete the geyser misunderstood what his brother told him about the imperator in the ants' nest.

Now that I had confirmation, I wanted to steal Rhea's safari van and drive to some commune far, far upstate.

"Triumvirate Holdings," I said.

"Yeah," Rhea agreed. "That's their new military-industrial complex. It's bumming me out in a big way."

The lion stopped licking my face, probably because my blood had turned bitter. "How is this possible? How have they come back?"

"They never went away," Rhea said. "They did it to themselves, you know. Wanted to make themselves gods. That never works out well. Ever since the old days they've been hiding out, influencing history from behind the curtains. They're stuck in a kind of twilight life. They can't die; they can't really live."

"But how could we not *know* about this?" I demanded. "We are gods!"

Rhea's laugh reminded me of a piglet with asthma. "Apollo, Grandson, beautiful child . . . Has being a god ever stopped someone from being stupid?"

She had a point. Not about me personally, of course, but the stories I could tell you about the *other* Olympians . . .

"The emperors of Rome." I tried to come to terms with the idea. "They can't *all* be immortal."

"No," Rhea said. "Just the worst of them, the most notorious. They live in human memory, man. That's what keeps them alive. Same as us, really. They're tied to the course of Western civilization, even though that whole concept is imperialist Eurocentric propaganda, man. Like my guru would tell you—"

"Rhea"—I put my hands against my throbbing temples—"can we stick to one problem at a time?"

"Yeah, okay. I didn't mean to blow your mind."

"But how can they affect our lines of communication? How can they be so powerful?"

"They've had centuries, Apollo. *Centuries*. All that time, plotting and making war, building up their capitalist empire, waiting for this moment when you are mortal, when the Oracles are vulnerable for a hostile takeover. It's just evil. They have no chill whatsoever."

"I thought that was a more modern term."

"Evil?"

"No. *Chill*. Never mind. The Beast . . . he is the leader?"

"Afraid so. He's as twisted as the others, but he's the smartest and the most stable—in a sociopathic homicidal way. You know who he is—who he was, right?"

Unfortunately, I did. I remembered where I had seen his smirking ugly face. I could hear his nasal voice echoing through the arena, ordering the execution of hundreds while the crowds cheered. I wanted to ask Rhea who his two compatriots were in the Triumvirate, but I decided I could not bear the information at present. None of the options were good, and knowing their names might bring me more despair than I could handle.

"It's true, then," I said. "The other Oracles still exist. The emperors hold them all?"

"They're working on it. Python has Delphi—that's the biggest problem. But you won't have the strength to take him head-on. You've got to pry their fingers off the minor Oracles first, loosen their power. To do that, you need a new source of prophecy for this camp—an Oracle that is older and independent."

"Dodona," I said. "Your whispering grove."

"Right on," Rhea said. "I thought the grove was gone forever. But then—I don't know how—the oak trees regrew themselves in the heart of these woods. You have to find the grove and protect it."

"I'm working on that." I touched the sticky wound on the side of my face. "But my friend Meg—"

"Yeah. You had some setbacks. But there are always setbacks, Apollo. When Lizzy Stanton and I hosted the first women's rights convention in Woodstock—"

"I think you mean Seneca Falls?"

Rhea frowned. "Wasn't that in the '60s?"

"The '40s," I said. "The 1840s, if memory serves."

"So . . . Jimi Hendrix wasn't there?"

"Doubtful."

Rhea fiddled with her peace symbol. "Then who set that guitar on fire? Ah, never mind. The point is, you have to persevere. Sometimes change takes centuries."

"Except that I'm mortal now," I said. "I don't *have* centuries."

"But you have willpower," Rhea said. "You have mortal drive and urgency. Those are things the gods often lack."

At her side, her lion roared.

"I've gotta split," Rhea said. "If the imperators track me down—bad scene, man. I've been off the grid too long. I'm not going to get sucked into that patriarchal institutional oppression again. Just find Dodona. That's your first trial."

"And if the Beast finds the grove first?"

"Oh, he's already found the gates, but he'll never get through them without you and the girl."

"I—I don't understand."

"That's cool. Just breathe. Find your center. Enlightenment has to come from *within*."

It was very much like a line I would've given *my* worshippers. I was tempted to choke Rhea with her macramé belt, but I doubted I would have the strength. Also, she had two lions. "But what do I do? How do I save Meg?"

"First, get healed. Rest up. Then . . . well, how you save Meg is up to you. The journey is greater than the destination, you know?"

She held out her hand. Draped on her fingers was a set of wind chimes—a collection of hollow brass tubes and medallions engraved with ancient Greek and Cretan symbols. "Hang these in the largest ancient oak. That will help you focus the voices of the Oracle. If you get a prophecy, groovy. It'll only be the beginning, but without Dodona, nothing else will be possible. The emperors will suffocate our future and divide up the world. Only when you have defeated Python can you reclaim your rightful place on Olympus. My kid, Zeus . . . he's got this whole 'tough love' disciplinarian hang-up, you dig? Taking back Delphi is the only way you're going to get on his good side."

"I—I was afraid you would say that."

"There's one other thing," she warned. "The Beast is planning some kind of attack on your camp. I don't know what it is, but it's going to be big. Like, even worse than napalm. You have to warn your friends."

The nearest lion nudged me. I wrapped my arms around his neck and allowed him to pull me to my feet. I managed to remain standing, but only because my legs locked up in complete fright. For the first time, I understood the trials that awaited me. I knew the enemies I must face. I would need more than wind chimes and enlightenment. I'd need a miracle. And as a god, I can tell you that those are never distributed lightly.

"Good luck, Apollo." The Titan queen placed the wind chimes in my hands. "I've got to check my kiln before my pots crack. Keep on trucking, and save those trees!"

The woods dissolved. I found myself standing in the central green at Camp Half-Blood, face-to-face with Chiara Benvenuti, who jumped back in alarm. "Apollo?"

I smiled. "Hey, girl." My eyes rolled up in my head and, for the second time that week, I charmingly passed out in front of her.

27

I apologize
For pretty much everything
Wow, I'm a good guy

"WAKE," SAID A VOICE.

I opened my eyes and saw a ghost—his face just as precious to me as Daphne's. I knew his copper skin, his kind smile, the dark curls of his hair, and those eyes as purple as senatorial robes.

"Hyacinthus," I sobbed. "I'm so sorry . . ."

He turned his face toward the sunlight, revealing the ugly dent above his left ear where the discus had struck him. My own wounded face throbbed in sympathy.

"Seek the caverns," he said. "Near the springs of blue. Oh, Apollo . . . your sanity will be taken away, but do not . . ."

His image faded and began to retreat. I rose from my sickbed. I rushed after him and grabbed his shoulders. "Do not *what*? Please don't leave me again!"

My vision cleared. I found myself by the window in Cabin Seven, holding a ceramic pot of purple and red hyacinths. Nearby, looking very concerned, Will and Nico stood as if ready to catch me.

"He's talking to the flowers," Nico noted. "Is that normal?"

"Apollo," Will said, "you had a concussion. I healed you, but—"

"These hyacinths," I demanded. "Have they always been here?"

Will frowned. "Honestly, I don't know where they came from, but . . ." He took the flowerpot from my hands and set it back on the windowsill. "Let's worry about you, okay?"

Usually that would've been excellent advice, but now I could only stare at the hyacinths and wonder if they were some sort of message. How cruel to see them—the flowers that I had created to honor my fallen love, with their plumes stained red like his blood or hued violet like his eyes. They bloomed so cheerfully in the window, reminding me of the joy I had lost.

Nico rested his hand on Will's shoulder. "Apollo, we were worried. Will was especially."

Seeing them together, supporting each other, made my heart feel even heavier. During my delirium, both of my great loves had visited me. Now, once again, I was devastatingly alone.

Still, I had a task to complete. A friend needed my help.

"Meg is in trouble," I said. "How long was I unconscious?"

Will and Nico glanced at each other.

"It's about noon now," Will said. "You showed up on the green around six this morning. When Meg didn't return with you, we wanted to search the woods for her, but Chiron wouldn't let us."

"Chiron was absolutely correct," I said. "I won't allow any others to put themselves at risk. But I must hurry. Meg has until tonight at the latest."

"Then what happens?" Nico asked.

I couldn't say it. I couldn't even *think* about it without losing my nerve. I looked down. Aside from Paolo's Brazilian-flag bandana and my ukulele-string necklace, I was wearing only my boxer shorts. My offensive flabbiness was on display for everyone to see, but I no longer cared about that. (Well, not much, anyway.) "I have to get dressed."

I staggered back to my cot. I fumbled through my meager supplies and found Percy Jackson's Led Zeppelin T-shirt. I tugged it on. It seemed more appropriate than ever.

Will hovered nearby. "Look, Apollo, I don't think you're back to a hundred percent."

"I'll be fine." I pulled on my jeans. "I have to save Meg."

"Let us help you," Nico said. "Tell us where she is and I can shadow-travel—"

"No!" I snapped. "No, you have to stay here and protect the camp."

Will's expression reminded me very much of his mother, Naomi—that look of trepidation she got just before she went onstage. "Protect the camp from what?"

"I—I'm not sure. You must tell Chiron the emperors have returned. Or rather, they never went away. They've been plotting, building their resources for centuries."

Nico's eyes glinted warily. "When you say emperors—"

"I mean the Roman ones."

Will stepped back. "You're saying the emperors of ancient Rome are alive? *How?* The Doors of Death?"

"No." I could barely speak through the taste of bile. "The emperors made themselves gods. They had their own temples and altars. They encouraged the people to worship them."

"But that was just propaganda," Nico said. "They weren't really divine."

I laughed mirthlessly. "Gods are sustained by worship, son of Hades. They continue to exist because of the collective memories of a culture. It's true for the Olympians; it's also true for the emperors. Somehow, the most powerful of them have survived. All these centuries, they have clung to half-life, hiding, waiting to reclaim their power."

Will shook his head. "That's impossible. How—?"

"I don't know!" I tried to steady my breathing. "Tell Rachel the men behind Triumvirate Holdings are former emperors of Rome. They've been plotting against us all this time, and we gods have been blind. *Blind.*"

I pulled on my coat. The ambrosia Nico had given me yesterday was still in the left pocket. In the right pocket, Rhea's wind chimes clanked, though I had no idea how they'd gotten there.

"The Beast is planning some sort of attack on the camp," I said. "I don't know what, and I don't know when, but tell Chiron you must be prepared. I have to go."

"Wait!" Will said as I reached the door. "Who is the Beast? Which emperor are we dealing with?"

"The worst of my descendants." My fingers dug into the doorframe. "The Christians called him the Beast because he burned them alive. Our enemy is Emperor Nero."

They must have been too stunned to follow me.

I ran toward the armory. Several campers gave me strange looks. Some called after me, offering help, but I ignored them. I could only think about Meg alone in the myrmekes' lair, and the visions I'd had of Daphne, Rhea, and Hyacinthus—all of them urging me onward, telling me to do the impossible in this inadequate mortal form.

When I reached the armory, I scanned the rack of bows. My hand trembling, I picked out the weapon Meg had tried to give me the day before. It was carved from mountain laurel wood. The bitter irony appealed to me.

I had sworn not to use a bow until I was a god again. But I had also sworn not to play music, and I had already broken that part of the oath in the most egregious, Neil-Diamondy way possible.

The curse of the River Styx could kill me in its slow cancerous way, or Zeus could strike me down. But my oath to save Meg McCaffrey had to come first.

I turned my face to the sky. "If you want to punish me, Father, be my guest, but have the courage to hurt *me* directly, not my mortal companion. BE A MAN!"

To my surprise, the skies remained silent. Lightning did not vaporize me. Perhaps Zeus was too taken aback to react, but I knew he would never overlook such an insult.

To Tartarus with him. I had work to do.

I grabbed a quiver and stuffed it with all the extra arrows I could find. Then I ran for the woods, Meg's two rings jangling on my makeshift necklace. Too late, I realized I had forgotten my combat ukulele, but I had no time to turn back. My singing voice would have to be enough.

I'm not sure how I found the nest.

Perhaps the forest simply allowed me to reach it, knowing that I was marching to my death. I've found that when one is searching for danger, it's never hard to find.

Soon I was crouched behind a fallen tree, studying the myrmekes' lair in the clearing ahead. To call the place an anthill would be like calling Versailles Palace a single-family home. Earthen ramparts rose almost to the tops of the surrounding trees—a hundred feet at least. The circumference could have accommodated a Roman hippodrome. A steady stream of soldiers and drones swarmed in and out of the mound. Some carried fallen trees. One, inexplicably, was dragging a 1967 Chevy Impala.

How many ants would I be facing? I had no idea. After you reach the number *impossible*, there's no point in counting.

I nocked an arrow and stepped into the clearing.

When the nearest myrmeke spotted me, he dropped his Chevy. He watched me approach, his antennae bobbing. I ignored him and strolled past, heading for the nearest tunnel entrance. That confused him even more.

Several other ants gathered to watch.

I've learned that if you act like you are supposed to be somewhere, most people (or ants) will not confront you. Normally, acting confident isn't a problem for me. Gods are allowed to be anywhere. It was a bit tougher for Lester Papadopoulos, dork teen extraordinaire, but I made it all the way to the nest without being challenged.

I plunged inside and began to sing.

This time I needed no ukulele. I needed no muse for

my inspiration. I remembered Daphne's face in the trees. I remembered Hyacinthus turning away, his death wound glistening on his scalp. My voice filled with anguish. I sang of heartbreak. Rather than collapsing under my own despair, I projected it outward.

The tunnels amplified my voice, carrying it through the nest, making the entire hill my musical instrument.

Each time I passed an ant, it curled its legs and touched its forehead to the floor, its antennae quivering from the vibrations of my voice.

Had I been a god, the song would have been stronger, but this was enough. I was impressed by how much sorrow a human voice could convey.

I wandered deeper into the hill. I had no idea where I was going until I spotted a geranium blooming from the tunnel floor.

My song faltered.

Meg. She must have regained consciousness. She had dropped one of her emergency seeds to leave me a trail. The geranium's purple flowers all faced a smaller tunnel leading off to the left.

"Clever girl," I said, choosing that tunnel.

A clattering sound alerted me to the approaching myrmeke.

I turned and raised my bow. Freed from the enchantment of my voice, the insect charged, its mouth foaming with acid. I drew and fired. The arrow embedded itself up to the fletching in the ant's forehead.

The creature dropped, its back legs twitching in death throes. I tried to retrieve my arrow, but the shaft snapped in my hand, the broken end covered in steaming corrosive goo. So much for reusing ammunition.

I called, "MEG!"

The only answer was the clattering of more giant ants moving in my direction. I began to sing again. Now, though, I had higher hopes of finding Meg, which made it difficult to summon the proper amount of melancholy. The ants I encountered were no longer catatonic. They moved slowly and unsteadily, but they still attacked. I was forced to shoot one after another.

I passed a cave filled with glittering treasure, but I was not interested in shiny things at the moment. I kept moving.

At the next intersection, another geranium sprouted from the floor, all its flowers facing right. I turned that direction, calling Meg's name again, then returning to my song.

As my spirits lifted, my song became less effective and the ants more aggressive. After a dozen kills, my quiver was growing dangerously light.

I had to reach deeper into my feelings of despair. I had to get the blues, good and proper.

For the first time in four thousand years, I sang of my own faults.

I poured out my guilt about Daphne's death. My boastfulness, envy, and desire had caused her destruction. When she ran from me, I should have let her go. Instead, I chased her relentlessly. I wanted her, and I intended to have her. Because of that, I had left Daphne no choice. To escape me, she sacrificed her life and turned into a tree, leaving my heart scarred forever. . . . But it was *my* fault. I apologized in song. I begged Daphne's forgiveness.

I sang of Hyacinthus, the most handsome of men. The West Wind Zephyros had also loved him, but I refused to share even a moment of Hyacinthus's time. In my jealousy, I threatened Zephyros. I dared him, *dared* him to interfere.

I sang of the day Hyacinthus and I played discus in the fields, and how the West Wind blew my disc off course—right into the side of Hyacinthus's head.

To keep Hyacinthus in the sunlight where he belonged, I created hyacinth flowers from his blood. I held Zephyros accountable, but my own petty greed had caused Hyacinthus's death. I poured out my sorrow. I took all the blame.

I sang of my failures, my eternal heartbreak and loneliness. I was the worst of the gods, the most guilt-ridden and unfocused. I couldn't commit myself to one lover. I couldn't even choose what to be the god of. I kept shifting from one skill to another—distracted and dissatisfied.

My golden life was a sham. My coolness was pretense. My heart was a lump of petrified wood.

All around me, myrmekes collapsed. The nest itself trembled with grief.

I found a third geranium, then a fourth.

Finally, pausing between verses, I heard a small voice up ahead: the sound of a girl crying.

"Meg!" I gave up on my song and ran.

She lay in the middle of a cavernous food larder, just as I had imagined. Around her were stacked the carcasses of animals—cows, deer, horses—all sheathed in hardened goop and slowly decaying. The smell hit my nasal passages like an avalanche.

Meg was also enveloped, but she was fighting back with the power of geraniums. Patches of leaves sprouted from the thinnest parts of her cocoon. A frilly collar of flowers kept the goo away from her face. She had even managed to free one of her arms, thanks to an explosion of pink geraniums at her left armpit.

Her eyes were puffy from crying. I assumed she was frightened, possibly in pain, but when I knelt next to her, her first words were, "I'm so sorry."

I brushed a tear from the tip of her nose. "Why, dear Meg? You did nothing wrong. I failed *you*."

A sob caught in her throat. "You don't understand. That song you were singing. Oh, gods . . . Apollo, if I'd known—"

"Hush, now." My throat was so raw I could barely talk. The song had almost destroyed my voice. "You're just reacting to the grief in the music. Let's get you free."

I was considering how to do that when Meg's eyes widened. She made a whimpering sound.

The hairs on the nape of my neck came to attention. "There are ants behind me, aren't there?" I asked.

Meg nodded.

I turned as four of them entered the cavern. I reached for my quiver. I had one arrow left.

28

Parenting advice:

Mamas, don't let your larvae

Grow up to be ants

MEG THRASHED IN HER GOO CASE. "Get me out of here!"

"I don't have a blade!" My fingers crept to the ukulele string around my neck. "Actually I have *your* blades, I mean your rings—"

"You don't need to cut me out. When the ant dumped me here, I dropped the packet of seeds. It should be close."

She was right. I spotted the crumpled pouch near her feet.

I inched toward it, keeping one eye on the ants. They stood together at the entrance as if hesitant to come closer. Perhaps the trail of dead ants leading to this room had given them pause.

"Nice ants," I said. "Excellent calm ants."

I crouched and scooped up the packet. A quick glance inside told me half a dozen seeds remained. "Now what, Meg?"

"Throw them on the goo," Meg said.

I gestured to the geraniums bursting from her neck and armpit. "How many seeds did that?"

"One."

"Then this many will choke you to death. I've turned too many people I cared about into flowers, Meg. I won't—"

"JUST DO IT!"

The ants did not like her tone. They advanced, snapping their mandibles. I shook the geranium seeds over Meg's cocoon, then nocked my arrow. Killing one ant would do no good if the other three tore us apart, so I chose a different target. I shot the roof of the cavern, just above the ants' heads.

It was a desperate idea, but I'd had success bringing down buildings with arrows before. In 464 BCE, I caused an earthquake that wiped out most of Sparta by hitting a fault line at the right angle. (I never liked the Spartans much.)

This time, I had less luck. The arrow embedded itself in the packed earth with a dull *thunk*. The ants took another step forward, acid dripping from their mouths. Behind me, Meg struggled to free herself from her cocoon, which was now covered in a shag carpet of purple flowers.

She needed more time.

Out of ideas, I tugged my Brazilian-flag handkerchief from my neck and waved it like a maniac, trying to channel my inner Paolo.

"BACK, FOUL ANTS!" I yelled. *"BRASIL!"*

The ants wavered—perhaps because of the bright colors, or my voice, or my sudden insane confidence. While they hesitated, cracks spread across the roof from my arrow's impact site, and then thousands of tons of earth collapsed on top of the myrmekes.

When the dust cleared, half the room was gone, along with the ants.

I looked at my handkerchief. "I'll be Styxed. It *does* have magic power. I can never tell Paolo about this or he'll be insufferable."

"Over here!" Meg yelled.

I turned. Another myrmeke was crawling over a pile of carcasses—apparently from a second exit I had failed to notice behind the disgusting food stores.

Before I could think what to do, Meg roared and burst from her cage, spraying geraniums in every direction. She shouted, "My rings!"

I yanked them from my neck and tossed them through the air. As soon as Meg caught them, two golden scimitars flashed into her hands.

The myrmeke barely had time to think *Uh-oh* before Meg charged. She sliced off his armored head. His body collapsed in a steaming heap.

Meg turned to me. Her face was a tempest of guilt, misery, and bitterness. I was afraid she might use her swords on me.

"Apollo, I . . ." Her voice broke.

I supposed she was still suffering from the effects of my song. She was shaken to her core. I made a mental note never again to sing so honestly when a mortal might be listening.

"It's all right, Meg," I said. "I should be apologizing to you. I got you into this mess."

Meg shook her head. "You don't understand. I—"

An enraged shriek echoed through the chamber, shaking the compromised ceiling and raining clods of dirt on our heads. The tone of the scream reminded me of Hera whenever she stormed through the hallways of Olympus, yelling at me for leaving the godly toilet seat up.

"That's the queen ant," I guessed. "We need to leave."

Meg pointed her sword toward the room's only remaining exit. "But the sound came from there. We'll be walking in her direction."

"Exactly. So perhaps we should hold off on making amends with each other, eh? We might still get each other killed."

We found the queen ant.

Hooray.

All corridors must have led to the queen. They radiated from her chamber like spikes on a morning star. Her Majesty was three times the size of her largest soldiers—a towering mass of black chitin and barbed appendages, with diaphanous oval wings folded against her back. Her eyes were glassy swimming pools of onyx. Her abdomen was a pulsing translucent sac filled with glowing eggs. The sight of it made me regret ever inventing gel capsule medications.

Her swollen abdomen might slow her down in a fight, but she was so large, she could intercept us before we reached the nearest exit. Those mandibles would snap us in half like dried twigs.

"Meg," I said, "how do you feel about dual-wielding scimitars against this lady?"

Meg looked appalled. "She's a mother giving birth."

"Yes . . . and she's an insect, which you hate. And her children were ripening you up for dinner."

Meg frowned. "Still . . . I don't feel right about it."

The queen hissed—a dry spraying noise. I imagined she would have already hosed us down with acid if she weren't worried about the long-term effects of corrosives on her larvae. Queen ants can't be too careful these days.

"You have another idea?" I asked Meg. "Preferably one that does not involve dying?"

She pointed to a tunnel directly behind the queen's clutch of eggs. "We need to go that way. It leads to the grove."

"How can you be sure?"

Meg tilted her head. "Trees. It's like . . . I can hear them growing."

That reminded me of something the Muses once told me—how they could actually hear the ink drying on new pages of poetry. I suppose it made sense that a daughter of Demeter could hear the growth of plants. Also, it didn't surprise me that the tunnel we needed was the most dangerous one to reach.

"Sing," Meg told me. "Sing like you did before."

"I—I can't. My voice is almost gone."

Besides, I thought, I don't want to risk losing you again.

I had freed Meg, so perhaps I'd fulfilled my oath to Pete the geyser god. Still, by singing and practicing archery, I had broken my oath upon the River Styx not once but twice. More singing would only make me *more* of a scofflaw.

Whatever cosmic punishments awaited me, I did not want them to fall on Meg.

Her Majesty snapped at us—a warning shot, telling us to back off. A few feet closer and my head would have rolled in the dirt.

I burst into song—or rather, I did the best I could with the raspy voice that remained. I began to rap. I started with the rhythm *boom chicka chicka*. I busted out some footwork the Nine Muses and I had been working on just before the war with Gaea.

The queen arched her back. I don't think she had expected to be rapped to today.

I gave Meg a look that clearly meant *Help me out!*

She shook her head. Give the girl two swords and she was a maniac. Ask her to lay down a simple beat and she suddenly got stage fright.

Fine, I thought. I'll do it by myself.

I launched into "Dance" by Nas, which I have to say was one of the most moving odes to mothers that I ever inspired an artist to write. (You're welcome, Nas.) I took some liberties with the lyrics. I may have changed *angel* to *brood mother* and *woman* to *insect*. But the sentiment remained. I serenaded the pregnant queen, channeling my love for my own dear mother, Leto. When I sang that I could only wish to marry a woman (or insect) so fine someday, my heartbreak was real. I would never have such a partner. It was not in my destiny.

The queen's antennae quivered. Her head seesawed back and forth. Eggs kept extruding from her abdomen, which made it difficult for me to concentrate, but I persevered.

When I was done, I dropped to one knee and held up my arms in tribute, waiting for the queen's verdict. Either she would kill me or she would not. I was spent. I had poured everything into that song and could not rap another line.

Next to me, Meg stood very still, gripping her swords.

Her Majesty shuddered. She threw back her head and wailed—a sound more brokenhearted than angry.

She leaned down and gently nudged my chest, pushing me in the direction of the tunnel we needed.

"Thank you," I croaked. "I—I'm sorry about the ants I killed."

The queen purred and clicked, extruding a few more eggs as if to say, *Don't worry; I can always make more.*

I stroked the queen ant's forehead. "May I call you Mama?"

Her mouth frothed in a pleased sort of way.

"Apollo," Meg urged, "let's go before she changes her mind."

I was not sure Mama *would* change her mind. I got the feeling she had accepted my fealty and adopted us into her brood. But Meg was right; we needed to hurry. Mama watched as we edged around her clutch of eggs.

We plunged into the tunnel and saw the glow of daylight above us.

29

Nightmares of torches
And a man in purple clothes
But that's not the worst

I HAD NEVER BEEN SO HAPPY to see a killing field.

We emerged into a glade littered with bones. Most were from forest animals. A few appeared human. I guessed we had found the myrmekes' dumping site, and they apparently didn't get regular garbage pickup.

The clearing was hemmed with trees so thick and tangled that traveling through them would've been impossible. Over our heads, the branches wove together in a leafy dome that let in sunlight but not much else. Anyone flying above the forest would never have realized this open space existed under the canopy.

At the far end of the glade stood a row of objects like football tackle dummies—six white cocoons staked on tall wooden poles, flanking a pair of enormous oaks. Each tree was at least eighty feet tall. They had grown so close together that their massive trunks appeared to have fused. I had the distinct impression I was looking at a set of living doors.

"It's a gateway," I said. "To the Grove of Dodona."

Meg's blades retracted, once again becoming gold rings on her middle fingers. "Aren't we *in* the grove?"

"No . . ." I stared across the clearing at the white cocoon Popsicles. They were too far away to make out clearly, but something about them seemed familiar in an evil, unwelcome sort of way. I wanted to get closer. I also wanted to keep my distance.

"I think this is more of an antechamber," I said. "The grove itself is behind those trees."

Meg gazed warily across the field. "I don't hear any voices."

It was true. The forest was absolutely quiet. The trees seemed to be holding their breath.

"The grove knows we are here," I guessed. "It's waiting to see what we'll do."

"We'd better do something, then." Meg didn't sound any more excited than I was, but she marched forward, bones crunching under her feet.

I wished I had more than a bow, an empty quiver, and a hoarse voice to defend myself with, but I followed, trying not to trip over rib cages and deer antlers. About halfway across the glade, Meg let out a sharp exhale.

She was staring at the posts on either side of the tree gates.

At first I couldn't process what I was seeing. Each stake was about the height of a crucifix—the kind Romans used to set up along the roadside to advertise the fates of criminals. (Personally, I find modern billboards much more tasteful.) The upper half of each post was wrapped in thick lumpy wads of white cloth, and sticking out from the top of each cocoon was something that looked like a human head.

My stomach somersaulted. They *were* human heads. Arrayed in front of us were the missing demigods, all tightly bound. I watched, petrified, until I discerned the slightest expansions and contractions in the wrappings around their chests. They were still breathing. Unconscious, not dead. Thank the gods.

On the left were three teenagers I didn't know, though I assumed they must be Cecil, Ellis, and Miranda. On the right side was an emaciated man with gray skin and white hair—no doubt the geyser god Paulie. Next to him hung my children . . . Austin and Kayla.

I shook so violently, the bones around my feet clattered. I recognized the smell coming from the prisoners' wrappings—sulfur, oil, powdered lime, and liquid Greek fire, the most dangerous substance ever created. Rage and disgust fought in my throat, vying for the right to make me throw up.

"Oh, monstrous," I said. "We need to free them immediately."

"Wh-what's wrong with them?" Meg stammered.

I dared not put it into words. I had seen this form of execution once before, at the hands of the Beast, and I never wished to see it again.

I ran to Austin's stake. With all my strength I tried to push it over, but it wouldn't budge. The base was sunk too deep in the earth. I tore at the cloth bindings but only managed to coat my hands in sulfurous resin. The wadding was stickier and harder than myrmekes' goo.

"Meg, your swords!" I wasn't sure they would do any good either, but I could think of nothing else to try.

Then from above us came a familiar snarl.

The branches rustled. Peaches the karpos dropped from the canopy, landing with a somersault at Meg's feet. He looked like he'd been through quite an ordeal to get here. His arms were sliced up and dripping peach nectar. His legs were dotted with bruises. His diaper sagged dangerously.

"Thank the gods!" I said. That was not my usual reaction when I saw the grain spirit, but his teeth and claws might be just the things to free the demigods. "Meg, hurry! Order your friend to—"

"Apollo." Her voice was heavy. She pointed to the tunnel from which we'd come.

Emerging from the ants' nest were two of the largest humans I had ever seen. Each was seven feet tall and perhaps three hundred pounds of pure muscle stuffed into horsehide armor. Their blond hair glinted like silver floss. Jeweled rings glittered in their beards. Each man carried an oval shield and a spear, though I doubted they needed weapons to kill. They looked like they could crack open cannonballs with their bare hands.

I recognized them from their tattoos and the circular designs on their shields. Such warriors weren't easy to forget.

"*Germani.*" Instinctively, I moved in front of Meg. The elite imperial bodyguards had been cold-blooded death reapers in ancient Rome. I doubted they'd gotten any sweeter over the centuries.

The two men glared at me. They had serpent tattoos curling around their necks, just like the ruffians who had jumped me in New York. The Germani parted, and their master climbed from the tunnel.

Nero hadn't changed much in one thousand nine hundred and some-odd years. He appeared to be no more than thirty, but it was a *hard* thirty, his face haggard and his belly distended from too much partying. His mouth was fixed in a permanent sneer. His curly hair extended into a wraparound neck beard. His chin was so weak, I was tempted to create a GoFundMe campaign to buy him a better jaw.

He tried to compensate for his ugliness with an expensive Italian suit of purple wool, his gray shirt open to display gold chains. His shoes were hand-tooled leather, not the sort of thing to wear while stomping around in an ant pile. Then again, Nero had always had expensive, impractical tastes. That was perhaps the only thing I admired about him.

"Emperor Nero," I said. "The Beast."

He curled his lip. "Nero will do. It's good to see you, my honored ancestor. I'm sorry I've been so lax about my offerings during the past few millennia, but"—he shrugged—"I haven't needed you. I've done rather well on my own."

My fists clenched. I wanted to strike down this pot-bellied emperor with a bolt of white-hot power, except that I had no bolts of white-hot power. I had no arrows. I had no singing voice left. Against Nero and his seven-foot-tall bodyguards, I had a Brazilian handkerchief, a packet of ambrosia, and some brass wind chimes.

"It's me you want," I said. "Cut these demigods down from their stakes. Let them leave with Meg. They've done nothing to you."

Nero chuckled. "I'll be happy to let them go once we've

come to an agreement. As for Meg . . ." He smiled at her. "How are you, my dear?"

Meg said nothing. Her face was as hard and gray as a geyser god's. At her feet, Peaches snarled and rustled his leafy wings.

One of Nero's guards said something in his ear.

The Emperor nodded. "Soon."

He turned his attention back to me. "But where are my manners? Allow me to introduce my right hand, Vincius, and my left hand, Garius."

The bodyguards pointed across to each other.

"Ah, sorry," Nero corrected. "My right hand, Garius, and my left hand, Vincius. Those are the Romanized versions of their Batavi names, which I can't pronounce. Usually I just call them Vince and Gary. Say hello, boys."

Vince and Gary glowered at me.

"They have serpent tattoos," I noted, "like those street thugs you sent to attack me."

Nero shrugged. "I have many servants. Cade and Mikey are quite low on the pay scale. Their only job was to rattle you a bit, welcome you to my city."

"*Your* city." I found it just like Nero to go claiming major metropolitan areas that clearly belonged to me. "And these two gentlemen . . . they are actually Germani from the ancient times? How?"

Nero made a snide little barking sound in the back of his nose. I'd forgotten how much I hated his laugh.

"Lord Apollo, please," he said. "Even before Gaea commandeered the Doors of Death, souls escaped from Erebos all the time. It was quite easy for a god-emperor such as myself to call back my followers."

"A god-emperor?" I growled. "You mean a delusional ex-emperor."

Nero arched his eyebrows. "What made *you* a god, Apollo . . . back when you were one? Wasn't it the power of your name, your sway over those who believed in you? I am no different." He glanced to his left. "Vince, fall on your spear, please."

Without hesitation, Vince planted the butt of his spear against the ground. He braced the point under his rib cage.

"Stop," Nero said. "I changed my mind."

Vince betrayed no relief. In fact, his eyes tightened with faint disappointment. He brought his spear back to his side.

Nero grinned at me. "You see? I hold the power of life and death over my worshippers, like any proper god should."

I felt like I'd swallowed some gel capsule larvae. "The Germani were always crazy, much like you."

Nero put his hand to his chest. "I'm hurt! My barbarian friends are loyal subjects of the Julian dynasty! And, of course, we are all descended from you, Lord Apollo."

I didn't need the reminder. I'd been so proud of my son, the original Octavian, later Caesar Augustus. After his death, his descendants became increasingly arrogant and unstable (which I blamed on their mortal DNA; they certainly didn't get those qualities from me). Nero had been the last of the Julian line. I had not wept when he died. Now here he was, as grotesque and chinless as ever.

Meg stood at my shoulder. "Wh-what do you want, Nero?"

Considering she was facing the man who killed her father, she sounded remarkably calm. I was grateful for her strength. It gave me hope to have a skilled dimachaerus and a ravenous peach baby at my side. Still, I did not like our odds against two Germani.

Nero's eyes gleamed. "Straight to the point. I've always admired that about you, Meg. Really, it's simple. You and Apollo will open the gates of Dodona for me. Then these six"—he gestured to the staked prisoners—"will be released."

I shook my head. "You'll destroy the grove. Then you'll kill us."

The emperor made that horrible bark again. "Not unless you force me to. I'm a reasonable god-emperor, Apollo! I'd much rather have the Grove of Dodona under my control if it can be managed, but I certainly can't allow *you* to use it. You had your chance at being the guardian of the Oracles. You failed miserably. Now it's my responsibility. Mine . . . and my partners'."

"The two other emperors," I said. "Who are they?"

Nero shrugged. "Good Romans—men who, like me, have the willpower to do what is needed."

"Triumvirates have never worked. They always lead to civil war."

He smiled as if that idea did not bother him. "The three of us have come to an agreement. We have divided up the new empire . . . by which I mean North America. Once we have the Oracles, we'll expand and do what Romans have always done best—conquer the world."

I could only stare at him. "You truly learned nothing from your previous reign."

"Oh, but I did! I've had centuries to reflect, plan, and prepare. Do you have any idea how annoying it is to be a god-emperor, unable to die but unable to fully live? There was a period of about three hundred years during the Middle Ages when my name was almost forgotten. I was little more than a mirage! Thank goodness for the Renaissance, when our Classical greatness was remembered. And then came the Internet. Oh, gods, I *love* the Internet! It is impossible for me to fade completely now. I am immortal on Wikipedia!"

I winced. I was now fully convinced of Nero's insanity. Wikipedia was always getting stuff wrong about me.

He rolled his hand. "Yes, yes. You think I am crazy. I could explain my plans and prove otherwise, but I have a lot on my plate today. I need you and Meg to open those gates. They've resisted my best efforts, but together you two can do it. Apollo, you have an affinity with Oracles. Meg has a way with trees. Get to it. Please and thank you."

"We would rather die," I said. "Wouldn't we, Meg?"

No response.

I glanced over. A silvery streak glistened on Meg's cheek. At first I thought one of her rhinestones had melted. Then I realized she was crying.

"Meg?"

Nero clasped his hands as if in prayer. "Oh, my. It seems we've had a slight miscommunication. You see, Apollo, Meg brought you here, just as I asked her to. Well done, my sweet."

Meg wiped her face. "I—I didn't mean . . ."

My heart compressed to the size of a pebble. "Meg, no. I can't believe—"

I reached for her. Peaches snarled and inserted himself between us. I realized the karpos was not here to protect us from Nero. He was defending Meg from *me*.

"Meg?" I said. "This man killed your father! He's a murderer!"

She stared at the ground. When she spoke, her voice was even more tortured than mine was when I sang in the anthill. "The *Beast* killed my father. This is Nero. He's—he's my stepfather."

I could not fully grasp this before Nero spread his arms.

"That's right, my darling," he said. "And you've done a wonderful job. Come to Papa."

30

I school McCaffrey
Yo, girl, your stepdad is wack
Why won't she listen?

I HAD BEEN BETRAYED BEFORE.

The memories came flooding back to me in a painful tide. Once, my former girlfriend Cyrene took up with Ares just to get back at me. Another time, Artemis shot me in the groin because I was flirting with her Hunters. In 1928, Alexander Fleming failed to give me credit for inspiring his discovery of penicillin. I mean, *ouch*. That stung.

But I couldn't remember *ever* being so wrong about someone as I had been about Meg. Well . . . at least not since Irving Berlin. *"Alexander's Ragtime Band"?* I remember telling him. *You'll never make it big with a corny song like that!*

"Meg, we are friends." My voice sounded petulant even to myself. "How could you do this to me?"

Meg looked down at her red sneakers—the primary-colored shoes of a traitor. "I tried to tell you, to warn you."

"She has a good heart." Nero smiled. "But, Apollo, you and Meg have been friends for just a few days—and only because I *asked* Meg to befriend you. I have been Meg's stepfather, protector, and caretaker for years. She is a member of the Imperial Household."

I stared at my beloved Dumpster waif. Yes, somehow over the past week she had become beloved to me. I could not imagine her as Imperial *anything*—definitely not as a part of Nero's entourage.

"I risked my life for you," I said in amazement. "And that actually *means* something, because I can die!"

Nero clapped politely. "We're all impressed, Apollo. Now, if you'd open the gates. They've defied me for too long."

I tried to glare at Meg, but my heart wasn't in it. I felt too hurt and vulnerable. We gods do not like feeling vulnerable. Besides, Meg wasn't even looking at me.

In a daze, I turned to the oak tree gates. I saw now that their fused trunks were marred from Nero's previous efforts—chain-saw scars, burn marks, bites from ax blades, even some bullet holes. All these had barely chipped the outer bark. The most damaged area was an inch-deep impression in the shape of a human hand, where the wood had bubbled and peeled away. I glanced at the unconscious face of Paulie the geyser god, strung up and bound with the five demigods.

"Nero, what have you done?"

"Oh, a number of things! We found a way into this antechamber weeks ago. The Labyrinth has a convenient opening in the myrmekes' nest. But getting through these gates—"

"You forced the palikos to help you?" I had to restrain myself from throwing my wind chimes at the emperor. "You used a nature spirit to destroy nature? Meg, how can you tolerate this?"

Peaches growled. For once I had the feeling that the grain spirit might be in agreement with me. Meg's expression was as closed up as the gates. She stared intently at the bones littering the field.

"Come now," Nero said. "Meg knows there are good nature spirits, and bad ones. This geyser god was annoying. He kept asking us to fill out surveys. Besides, he shouldn't have ventured so far from his source of power. He was quite easy to capture. His steam, as you can see, didn't do us much good anyway."

"And the five demigods?" I demanded. "Did you 'use' them, too?"

"Of course. I didn't plan on luring them here, but every time we attacked the gates, the grove started wailing. I suppose it was calling for help, and the demigods couldn't resist. The first to wander in was this one." He pointed to Cecil Markowitz. "The last two were your own children— Austin and Kayla, yes? They showed up after we forced Paulie to steam-broil the trees. I guess the grove was quite nervous about that attempt. We got two demigods for the price of one!"

I lost control. I let out a guttural howl and charged the emperor, intending to wring his hairy excuse for a neck. The Germani would have killed me before I ever got that far, but I was saved the indignity. I tripped over a human pelvis and belly-surfed through the bones.

"Apollo!" Meg ran toward me.

I rolled over and kicked at her like a fussy child. "I don't need *your* help! Don't you understand who your protector is? He's a monster! He's the emperor who—"

"Don't say it," Nero warned. "If you say 'who fiddled while Rome burned,' I will have Vince and Gary flay you for a set of hide armor. You know as well as I do, Apollo, we didn't *have* fiddles back then. And I did *not* start the Great Fire of Rome."

I struggled to my feet. "But you profited from it."

Facing Nero, I remembered all the tawdry details of his rule—the extravagance and cruelty that had made him so embarrassing to me, his forefather. Nero was that relative you never wanted to invite to Lupercalia dinner.

"Meg," I said, "your stepfather watched as seventy percent of Rome was destroyed. Tens of thousands died."

"I was thirty miles away in Antium!" Nero snarled. "I rushed back to the city and personally led the fire brigades!"

"Only when the fire threatened your palace."

Nero rolled his eyes. "I can't help it if I arrived just in time to save the most important building!"

Meg cupped her hands over her ears. "Stop arguing. Please."

I didn't stop. Talking seemed better than my other options, like helping Nero or dying.

"After the Great Fire," I told her, "instead of rebuilding the houses on Palatine Hill, Nero leveled the neighborhood and built a new palace—the Domus Aurea."

Nero got a dreamy look on his face. "Ah, yes . . . the House of Gold. It was beautiful, Meg! I had my own lake, three hundred rooms, frescoes of gold, mosaics done in pearls and diamonds—I could finally live like a human being!"

"You had the nerve to put a hundred-foot-tall bronze statue in your front lawn!" I said. "A statue of yourself as

Sol-Apollo, the sun god. In other words, you claimed to be *me*."

"Indeed," Nero agreed. "Even after I died, that statue lived on. I understand it became famous as the Colossus of Nero! They moved it to the gladiators' amphitheater and everyone began calling the theater after the statue—*the Colosseum*." Nero puffed up his chest. "Yes . . . the statue was the perfect choice."

His tone sounded even more sinister than usual.

"What are you talking about?" I demanded.

"Hmm? Oh, nothing." He checked his watch . . . a mauve-and-gold Rolex. "The point is, I had style! The people loved me!"

I shook my head. "They turned against you. The people of Rome were sure you'd started the Great Fire, so you scapegoated the Christians."

I was aware that this arguing was pointless. If Meg had hidden her true identity all this time, I doubted I could change her mind now. But perhaps I could stall long enough for the cavalry to arrive. If only I *had* a cavalry.

Nero waved dismissively. "But the Christians were terrorists, you see. Perhaps they didn't start the fire, but they were causing all sorts of other trouble. I recognized that before anyone else!"

"He fed them to the lions," I told Meg. "He burned them as human torches, the way he will burn these six."

Meg's face turned green. She gazed at the unconscious prisoners on the stakes. "Nero, you wouldn't—"

"They will be released," Nero promised, "as long as Apollo cooperates."

"Meg, you can't trust him," I said. "The last time he did this, he strung up Christians all over his backyard and burned them to illuminate his garden party. I was there. I remember the screaming."

Meg clutched her stomach.

"My dear, don't believe his stories!" Nero said. "That was just propaganda invented by my enemies."

Meg studied the face of Paulie the geyser god. "Nero . . . you didn't say anything about making them into torches."

"They won't burn," he said, straining to soften his voice. "It won't come to that. The Beast will not have to act."

"You see, Meg?" I wagged a finger at the emperor. "It's never a good sign when someone starts referring to himself in the third person. Zeus used to scold me about that constantly!"

Vince and Gary stepped forward, their knuckles whitening on their spears.

"I would be careful," Nero warned. "My Germani are sensitive about insults to the Imperial person. Now, as much as I love talking about myself, we're on a schedule." He checked his watch again. "You'll open the gates. Then Meg will see if she can use the trees to interpret the future. If so, wonderful! If not . . . well, we'll burn that bridge when we come to it."

"Meg," I said, "he's a madman."

At her feet, Peaches hissed protectively.

Meg's chin quivered. "Nero cared about me, Apollo. He gave me a home. He taught me to fight."

"You said he killed your father!"

"No!" She shook her head adamantly, a look of panic in her eyes. "No, that's not what I said. The *Beast* killed him."

"But—"

Nero snorted. "Oh, Apollo . . . you understand so little. Meg's father was weak. She doesn't even remember him. He couldn't protect her. *I* raised her. I kept her alive."

My heart sank even further. I did not understand everything Meg had been through, or what she was feeling now, but I knew Nero. I saw how easily he could have twisted a scared child's understanding of the world—a little girl all alone, yearning for safety and acceptance after her father's murder, even if that acceptance came from her father's killer. "Meg . . . I am so sorry."

Another tear traced her cheek.

"She doesn't NEED sympathy." Nero's voice turned as hard as bronze. "Now, my dear, if you would be so kind, open the gates. If Apollo objects, remind him that he is bound to follow your orders."

Meg swallowed. "Apollo, don't make it harder. Please . . . help me open the gates."

I shook my head. "Not by choice."

"Then I—I command you. Help me. Now."

31

Listen to the trees
The trees know what is up, yo
They know all the things

MEG'S RESOLVE may have been wavering, but Peaches's was not.

When I hesitated to follow Meg's orders, the grain spirit bared his fangs and hissed, "Peaches," as if that was a new torture technique.

"Fine," I told Meg, my voice turning bitter. The truth was, I had no choice. I could feel Meg's command sinking into my muscles, compelling me to obey.

I faced the fused oaks and put my hands against their trunks. I felt no oracular power within. I heard no voices— just heavy stubborn silence. The only message the trees seemed to be sending was: GO AWAY.

"If we do this," I told Meg, "Nero will destroy the grove."

"He won't."

"He has to. He can't control Dodona. Its power is too ancient. He can't let anyone else use it."

Meg placed her hands against the trees, just below mine. "Concentrate. Open them. Please. You don't want to anger the Beast."

She said this in a low voice—again speaking as if the

Beast was someone I had not yet met . . . a boogeyman lurking under the bed, not a man in a purple suit standing a few feet away.

I could not refuse Meg's orders, but perhaps I should have protested more vigorously. Meg might have backed down if I called her bluff. But then Nero or Peaches or the Germani would have just killed me. I will confess to you: I was afraid of dying. Courageously, nobly, handsomely afraid, true. But afraid nonetheless.

I closed my eyes. I sensed the trees' implacable resistance, their mistrust of outsiders. I knew that if I forced open these gates, the grove would be destroyed. Yet I reached out with all my willpower and sought the voice of prophecy, drawing it to me.

I thought of Rhea, Queen of the Titans, who had first planted this grove. Despite being a child of Gaea and Ouranos, despite being married to the cannibal king Kronos, Rhea had managed to cultivate wisdom and kindness. She had given birth to a new, better breed of immortals. (If I do say so myself.) She represented the best of the ancient times.

True, she had withdrawn from the world and started a pottery studio in Woodstock, but she still cared about Dodona. She had sent me here to open the grove, to share its power. She was not the kind of goddess who believed in closed gates or NO TRESPASSING signs. I began to hum softly "This Land Is Your Land."

The bark grew warm under my fingertips. The tree roots trembled.

I glanced at Meg. She was deep in concentration, leaning against the trunks as if trying to push them over.

Everything about her was familiar: her ratty pageboy hair, her glittering cat-eye glasses, her runny nose and chewed cuticles and faint scent of apple pie.

But she was someone I didn't know at all: stepdaughter to the immortal crazy Nero. A member of the Imperial Household. What did that even *mean*? I pictured the Brady Bunch in purple togas, lined up on the family staircase with Nero at the bottom in Alice's maid uniform. Having a vivid imagination is a terrible curse.

Unfortunately for the grove, Meg was also the daughter of Demeter. The trees responded to her power. The twin oaks rumbled. Their trunks began to move.

I wanted to stop, but I was caught up in the momentum. The grove seemed to be drawing on my power now. My hands stuck to the trees. The gates opened wider, forcibly spreading my arms. For a terrifying moment, I thought the trees might keep moving and rip me limb from limb. Then they stopped. The roots settled. The bark cooled and released me.

I stumbled back, exhausted. Meg remained, transfixed, in the newly opened gateway.

On the other side were . . . well, more trees. Despite the winter cold, the young oaks rose tall and green, growing in concentric circles around a slightly larger specimen in the center. Littering the ground were acorns glowing with a faint amber light. Around the grove stood a protective wall of trees even more formidable than the ones in the antechamber. Above, another tightly woven dome of branches guarded the place from aerial intruders.

Before I could warn her, Meg stepped across the

threshold. The voices exploded. Imagine forty nail guns fir-
ing into your brain from all directions at once. The words
were babble, but they tore at my sanity, demanding my
attention. I covered my ears. The noise just got louder and
more persistent.

Peaches clawed frantically at the dirt, trying to bury
his head. Vince and Gary writhed on the ground. Even the
unconscious demigods thrashed and moaned on their stakes.

Nero reeled, his hand raised as if to block an intense
light. "Meg, control the voices! Do it now!"

Meg didn't appear hurt by the noise, but she looked
bewildered. "They're saying something . . ." She swept her
hands through the air, pulling at invisible threads to untan-
gle the pandemonium. "They're agitated. I can't— Wait . . ."

Suddenly the voices shut off, as if they'd made their
point.

Meg turned toward Nero, her eyes wide. "It's true. The
trees told me you mean to burn them."

The Germani groaned, half-conscious on the ground.
Nero recovered more quickly. He raised a finger, admonishing, guiding. "Listen to me, Meg. I'd hoped the grove could
be useful, but obviously it is fractured and confused. You
can't believe what it says. It's the mouthpiece of a senile
Titan queen. The grove must be razed. It's the only way,
Meg. You understand that, don't you?"

He kicked Gary over onto his back and rifled through
the bodyguard's pouches. Then Nero stood, triumphantly
holding a box of matches.

"After the fire, we'll rebuild," he said. "It will be
glorious!"

Meg stared at him as if noticing his horrendous neck beard for the first time. "Wh-what are you talking about?"

"He's going to burn and level Long Island," I said. "Then he'll make it his private domain, just like he did with Rome."

Nero laughed in exasperation. "Long Island is a mess anyway! No one will miss it. My new imperial complex will extend from Manhattan to Montauk—the greatest palace ever built! We'll have private rivers and lakes, one hundred miles of beachfront property, gardens big enough for their own zip codes. I'll build each member of my household a private skyscraper. Oh, Meg, imagine the parties we will have in our new Domus Aurea!"

The truth was a heavy thing. Meg's knees buckled under its weight.

"You can't." Her voice shook. "The woods— I'm the daughter of Demeter."

"You're *my* daughter," Nero corrected. "And I care for you deeply. Which is why you need to move aside. Quickly."

He set a match to the striking surface of the box. "As soon as I light these stakes, our human torches will send a wave of fire straight through that gateway. Nothing will be able to stop it. The entire forest will burn."

"Please!" Meg cried.

"Come along, dearest." Nero's frown hardened. "Apollo is of no use to us anymore. You don't want to wake the Beast, do you?"

He lit his match and stepped toward the nearest stake, where my son Austin was bound.

32

It takes a Village
People to protect your mind
"Y.M.C.A." Yeah

OH, THIS PART IS DIFFICULT TO TELL.

I am a natural storyteller. I have an infallible instinct for drama. I want to relate what *should* have happened: how I leaped forward shouting, "Nooooo!" and spun like an acrobat, knocking aside the lit match, then twisted in a series of blazing-fast Shaolin moves, cracking Nero's head and taking out his bodyguards before they could recover.

Ah, yes. That would have been perfect.

Alas, the truth constrains me.

Curse you, truth!

In fact, I spluttered something like, "Nuh-uh, dundoot!" I may have waved my Brazilian handkerchief with the hope that its magic would destroy my enemies.

The real hero was Peaches. The karpos must have sensed Meg's true feelings, or perhaps he just didn't like the idea of burning forests. He hurtled through the air, screaming his war cry (you guessed it), "Peaches!" He landed on Nero's arm, chomped the lit match from the emperor's hand, then landed a few feet away, wiping his tongue and crying, "Hat!

Hat!" (Which I assumed meant *hot* in the dialect of deciduous fruit.)

The scene might have been funny except that the Germani were now back on their feet, five demigods and a geyser spirit were still tied to highly flammable posts, and Nero still had a box of matches.

The emperor stared at his empty hand. "Meg . . . ?" His voice was as cold as an icicle. "What is the meaning of this?"

"P-Peaches, come here!" Meg's voice had turned brittle with fear.

The karpos bounded to her side. He hissed at me, Nero, and the Germani.

Meg took a shaky breath, clearly gathering her nerve. "Nero . . . Peaches is right. You—you can't burn these people alive."

Nero sighed. He looked at his bodyguards for moral support, but the Germani still appeared woozy. They were hitting the sides of their heads as if trying to clear water from their ears.

"Meg," said the emperor, "I am trying so hard to keep the Beast at bay. Why won't you help me? I know you are a good girl. I wouldn't have allowed you to roam around Manhattan so much on your own, playing the street waif, if I didn't know you could take care of yourself. But softness toward your enemies is not a virtue. You are my stepdaughter. Any of these demigods would kill you without hesitation given the chance."

"Meg, that's not true!" I said. "You've seen what Camp Half-Blood is like."

She studied me uneasily. "Even . . . even if it was true . . ." She turned to Nero. "You told me never to lower myself to my enemies' level."

"No, indeed." Nero's tone had frayed like a weathered rope. "We are better. We are stronger. We will build a glorious new world. But these nonsense-spewing trees stand in our way, Meg. Like any invasive weeds, they must be burned. And the only way to do that is with a true conflagration—flames stoked by blood. Let us do this together, and not involve the Beast, shall we?"

Finally, in my mind, something clicked. I remembered how my father used to punish me centuries ago, when I was a young god learning the ways of Olympus. Zeus used to say, *Don't get on the wrong side of my lightning bolts, boy.*

As if the lightning bolt had a mind of its own—as if Zeus had nothing to do with the punishments he meted out upon me.

Don't blame me, his tone implied. *It's the lightning bolt that seared every molecule in your body.* Many years later, when I killed the Cyclopes who made Zeus's lightning, it was no rash decision. I'd always *hated* those lightning bolts. It was easier than hating my father.

Nero took the same tone when he referred to himself as the Beast. He spoke of his anger and cruelty as if they were forces outside his control. If he flew into a rage . . . well, then he would hold *Meg* responsible.

The realization sickened me. Meg had been trained to regard her kindly stepfather Nero and the terrifying Beast as two separate people. I understood now why she preferred to spend her time in the alleys of New York. I understood why she had such quick mood changes, going from cartwheels to full shutdown in a matter of seconds. She never knew what might unleash the Beast.

She fixed her eyes on me. Her lips quivered. I could tell she wanted a way out—some eloquent argument that would mollify her stepfather and allow her to follow her conscience. But I was no longer a silver-tongued god. I could not outtalk an orator like Nero. And I would not play the Beast's blame game.

Instead, I took a page from Meg's book, which was always short and to the point.

"He's evil," I said. "You're good. You must make your own choice."

I could tell that this was not the news Meg wanted. Her mouth tightened. She drew back her shoulder blades as if preparing for a measles shot—something painful but necessary. She placed her hand on the karpos's curly scalp. "Peaches," she said in a small but firm voice, "get the matchbox."

The karpos sprang into action. Nero barely had time to blink before Peaches ripped the box from his hand and jumped back to Meg's side.

The Germani readied their spears. Nero raised his hand for restraint. He gave Meg a look that might have been heartbreak—if he had possessed a heart.

"I see you weren't ready for this assignment, my dear," he said. "It's my fault. Vince, Gary, detain Meg but don't hurt her. When we get home . . ." He shrugged, his expression full of regret. "As for Apollo and the little fruit demon, they will have to burn."

"No," Meg croaked. Then, at full volume, she shouted, "NO!" And the Grove of Dodona shouted with her.

The blast was so powerful, it knocked Nero and his guards off their feet. Peaches screamed and beat his head against the dirt.

This time, however, I was more prepared. As the trees' ear-splitting chorus reached its crescendo, I anchored my mind with the catchiest tune I could imagine. I hummed "Y.M.C.A.," which I used to perform with the Village People in my construction worker costume until the Indian chief and I got in a fight over— Never mind. That's not important.

"Meg!" I pulled the brass wind chimes from my pocket and tossed them to her. "Put these on the center tree! Y.M.C.A. Focus the grove's energy! Y.M.C.A."

I wasn't sure she could hear me. She raised the chimes and watched as they swayed and clanked, turning the noise from the trees into snatches of coherent speech: *Happiness approaches. The fall of the sun; the final verse. Would you like to hear our specials today?*

Meg's face went slack with surprise. She turned toward the grove and sprinted through the gateway. Peaches crawled after her, shaking his head.

I wanted to follow, but I couldn't leave Nero and his guards alone with six hostages. Still humming "Y.M.C.A.," I marched toward them.

The trees screamed louder than ever, but Nero rose to his knees. He pulled something from his coat pocket—a vial of liquid—and splashed it on the ground in front of him. I doubted that was a good thing, but I had more immediate concerns. Vince and Gary were getting up. Vince thrust his spear in my direction.

I was angry enough to be reckless. I grabbed the point of his weapon and yanked the spear up, smacking Vince under his chin. He fell, stunned, and I grabbed fistfuls of his hide armor.

He was easily twice my size. I didn't care. I lifted him off his feet. My arms sizzled with power. I felt invincibly strong—the way a god *should* feel. I had no idea why my strength had returned, but I decided this was not the moment to question my good luck. I spun Vince like a discus, tossing him skyward with such force that he punched a Germanus-shaped hole in the tree canopy and sailed out of sight.

Kudos to the Imperial Guard for having stupid amounts of courage. Despite my show of force, Gary charged me. With one hand, I snapped his spear. With the other, I punched a fist straight through his shield and hit his chest with enough might to fell a rhinoceros.

He collapsed in a heap.

I faced Nero. I could already feel my strength ebbing. My muscles were returning to their pathetic mortal flabbiness. I just hoped I'd have enough time to rip off Nero's head and stuff it down his mauve suit.

The emperor snarled. "You're a fool, Apollo. You *always* focus on the wrong thing." He glanced at his Rolex. "My wrecking crew will be here any minute. Once Camp Half-Blood is destroyed, I'll make it my new front lawn! Meanwhile, you'll be here . . . putting out fires."

From his vest pocket, he produced a silver cigarette lighter. Typical of Nero to keep several forms of fire-making close at hand. I looked at the glistening streaks of oil he had splashed on the ground. . . . Greek fire, of course.

"Don't," I said.

Nero grinned. "Good-bye, Apollo. Only eleven more Olympians to go."

He dropped the lighter.

I did not have the pleasure of tearing Nero's head off.

Could I have stopped him from fleeing? Possibly. But the flames were roaring between us, burning grass and bones, tree roots, and the earth itself. The blaze was too strong to stamp out, if Greek fire even *could* be stamped out, and it was rolling hungrily toward the six bound hostages.

I let Nero go. Somehow he hauled Gary to his feet and lugged the punch-drunk Germanus toward the ants' nest. Meanwhile, I ran to the stakes.

The closest was Austin's. I wrapped my arms around the base and pulled, completely disregarding proper heavy-lifting techniques. My muscles strained. My vision swam with the effort. I managed to raise the stake enough to topple it backward. Austin stirred and groaned.

I dragged him, cocoon and all, to the other side of the clearing, as far from the fire as possible. I would have brought him into the Grove of Dodona, but I had a feeling I wouldn't be doing him any favors by putting him in a dead-end clearing full of insane voices, in the direct path of approaching flames.

I ran back to the stakes. I repeated the process—uprooting Kayla, then Paulie the geyser god, then the others. By the time I pulled Miranda Gardiner to safety, the fire was a raging red tidal wave, only inches from the gates of the grove.

My divine strength was gone. Meg and Peaches were nowhere to be seen. I had bought a few minutes for the hostages, but the fire would eventually consume us all. I fell to my knees and sobbed.

"Help." I scanned the dark trees, tangled and foreboding. I did not expect any help. I was not even used to *asking* for help. I was Apollo. Mortals called to *me*! (Yes, occasionally I might have ordered demigods to run trivial errands for me, like starting wars or retrieving magic items from monsters' lairs, but those requests didn't count.)

"I can't do this alone." I imagined Daphne's face floating beneath the trunk of one tree, then another. Soon the woods would burn. I couldn't save them any more than I could save Meg or the lost demigods or myself. "I'm so sorry. Please . . . forgive me."

My head must have been spinning from smoke inhalation. I began to hallucinate. The shimmering forms of dryads emerged from their trees—a legion of Daphnes in green gossamer dresses. Their expressions were melancholy, as if they knew they were going to their deaths, yet they circled the fire. They raised their arms, and the earth erupted at their feet. A torrent of mud churned over the flames. The dryads drew the fire's heat into their bodies. Their skin charred black. Their faces hardened and cracked.

As soon as the last flames were snuffed out, the dryads crumbled to ash. I wished I could crumble with them. I wanted to cry, but the fire had seared all the moisture from my tear ducts. I had not asked for so many sacrifices. I had not expected it! I felt hollow, guilty, and ashamed.

Then it occurred to me how many times I *had* asked for sacrifices, how many heroes I had sent to their deaths. Had they been any less noble and courageous than these dryads? Yet I had felt no remorse when I sent them off on deadly tasks. I had used them and discarded them, laid waste to their lives to build my own glory. I was no less of a monster than Nero.

Wind blew through the clearing—an unseasonably warm gust that swirled up the ashes and carried them through the forest canopy into the sky. Only after the breeze calmed did I realize it must have been the West Wind, my old rival, offering me consolation. He had swept up the remains and taken them off to their next beautiful reincarnation. After all these centuries, Zephyros had accepted my apology.

I discovered I had some tears left after all.

Behind me, someone groaned. "Where am I?"

Austin was awake.

I crawled to his side, now weeping with relief, and kissed his face. "My beautiful son!"

He blinked at me in confusion. His cornrows were sprinkled with ashes like frost on a field. I suppose it took a moment for him to process why he was being fawned over by a grungy, half-deranged boy with acne.

"Ah, right . . . Apollo." He tried to move. "What the—?

Why am I wrapped in smelly bandages? Could you free me, maybe?"

I laughed hysterically, which I doubt helped Austin's peace of mind. I clawed at his bindings but made no progress. Then I remembered Gary's snapped spear. I retrieved the point and spent several minutes sawing Austin free.

Once pulled from the stake, he stumbled around, trying to shake the circulation back into his limbs. He took in the scene—the smoldering forest, the other prisoners. The Grove of Dodona had stopped its wild chorus of screaming. (When had that happened?) A radiant amber light now glowed from the gateway.

"What's going on?" Austin asked. "Also, where is my saxophone?"

Sensible questions. I wished I had sensible answers. All I knew was that Meg McCaffrey was still wandering in the grove, and I did not like the fact that the trees had gone silent.

I stared at my weak mortal arms. I wondered why I'd experienced a sudden surge of divine strength when facing the Germani. Had my emotions triggered it? Was it the first sign of my godly vigor returning for good? Or perhaps Zeus was just messing with me again—giving me a taste of my old power before yanking it away once more. *Remember this, kid? WELL, YOU CAN'T HAVE IT!*

I wished I could summon that strength again, but I would have to make do.

I handed Austin the broken spear. "Free the others. I'll be back."

Austin stared at me incredulously. "You're going in *there*? Is it safe?"

"I doubt it," I said.

Then I ran toward the Oracle.

33

Parting is sorrow
Nothing about it is sweet
Don't step on my face

THE TREES WERE using their inside voices.

As I stepped through the gateway, I realized they were still talking in conversational tones, babbling nonsensically like sleepwalkers at a cocktail party.

I scanned the grove. No sign of Meg. I called her name. The trees responded by raising their voices, driving me cross-eyed with dizziness.

I steadied myself on the nearest oak.

"Watch it, man," the tree said.

I lurched forward, the trees trading bits of verse as if playing a game of rhymes:

> *Caves of blue.*
> *Strike the hue.*
> *Westward, burning.*
> *Pages turning.*
> *Indiana.*
> *Ripe banana.*
> *Happiness approaches.*
> *Serpents and roaches.*

None of it made sense, but each line carried the weight of prophecy. I felt as if dozens of important statements, each vital to my survival, were being blended together, loaded in a shotgun, and fired at my face.

(Oh, that's a rather good image. I'll have to use it in a haiku.)

"Meg!" I called again.

Still no reply. The grove did not seem so large. How could she not hear me? How could I not see her?

I slogged along, humming a perfect A 440 hertz tone to keep myself focused. When I reached the second ring of trees, the oaks became more conversational.

"Hey, buddy, got a quarter?" one asked.

Another tried to tell me a joke about a penguin and a nun walking into a Shake Shack.

A third oak was giving its neighbor an infomercial sales pitch about a food processor. "And you won't believe what it does with pasta!"

"Wow!" said the other tree. "It makes pasta, too?"

"Fresh linguine in minutes!" the sales oak enthused.

I did not understand why an oak tree would want linguine, but I kept moving. I was afraid that if I listened too long, I would order the food processor for three easy installments of $39.99, and my sanity would be lost forever.

Finally, I reached the center of the grove. On the far side of the largest oak tree, Meg stood with her back to the trunk, her eyes closed tight. The wind chimes were still in her hand, but they hung forgotten at her side. The brass cylinders clanked, muted against her dress.

At her feet, Peaches rocked back and forth, giggling. "Apples? Peaches! Mangoes? Peaches!"

"Meg." I touched her shoulder.

She flinched. She focused on me as if I were a clever optical illusion. Her eyes simmered with fear. "It's too much," she said. "Too much."

The voices had her in their grip. It was bad enough for me to endure—like a hundred radio stations playing at once, forcibly splitting my brain into different channels. But I was used to prophecies. Meg, on the other hand, was a daughter of Demeter. The trees liked her. They were all trying to share with her, to get her attention at the same time. Soon they would permanently fracture her mind.

"The wind chimes," I said. "Hang them in the tree!"

I pointed to the lowest branch, well above our heads. Alone, neither of us could reach it, but if I gave Meg a boost . . .

Meg backed away, shaking her head. The voices of Dodona were so chaotic I wasn't sure she had heard me. If she had, she either didn't understand or didn't trust me.

I had to tamp down my feelings of betrayal. Meg was Nero's stepdaughter. She had been sent to lure me here, and our whole friendship was a lie. She had no right to mistrust *me*.

But I could not stay bitter. If I blamed her for the way Nero had twisted her emotions, I was no better than the Beast. Also, just because she had lied about being my friend did not mean I wasn't hers. She was in danger. I was not going to leave her to the madness of the grove's penguin jokes.

I crouched and laced my fingers to make a foothold. "Please."

To my left, Peaches rolled onto his back and wailed, "Linguine? Peaches!"

Meg grimaced. I could see from her eyes that she was deciding to cooperate with me—not because she trusted me, but because Peaches was suffering.

Just when I thought my feelings could not be hurt any worse. It was one thing to be betrayed. It was another thing to be considered less important than a diapered fruit spirit.

Nevertheless, I remained steady as Meg placed her left foot in my hands. With all my remaining strength, I hoisted her up. She stepped onto my shoulders, then planted one red sneaker on top of my head. I made a mental note to put a safety label on my scalp: WARNING, TOP STEP IS NOT FOR STANDING.

With my back against the oak, I could feel the voices of the grove coursing up its trunk and drumming through its bark. The central tree seemed to be one giant antenna for crazy talk.

My knees were about to buckle. Meg's treads were grinding into my forehead. The A 440 I had been humming rapidly deflated to a G sharp.

Finally, Meg tied the wind chimes to the branch. She jumped down as my legs collapsed, and we both ended up sprawled in the dirt.

The brass chimes swayed and clanged, picking notes out of the wind and making chords from the dissonance.

The grove hushed, as if the trees were listening and thinking, *Oooh, pretty.*

Then the ground trembled. The central oak shook with such energy, it rained acorns.

Meg got to her feet. She approached the tree and touched its trunk.

"Speak," she commanded.

A single voice boomed forth from the wind chimes, like a cheerleader screaming through a megaphone:

> *There once was a god named Apollo*
> *Who plunged in a cave blue and hollow*
> *Upon a three-seater*
> *The bronze fire-eater*
> *Was forced death and madness to swallow*

The wind chimes stilled. The grove settled into tranquility, as if satisfied with the death sentence it had given me.

Oh, the horror!

A sonnet I could have handled. A quatrain would have been cause for celebration. But only the deadliest prophecies are couched in the form of a limerick.

I stared at the wind chimes, hoping they would speak again and correct themselves. *Oops, our mistake! That prophecy was for a different Apollo!*

But my luck was not that good. I had been handed an edict worse than a thousand advertisements for pasta makers.

Peaches rose. He shook his head and hissed at the oak tree, which expressed my own sentiments perfectly. He hugged Meg's calf as if she were the only thing keeping him from falling off the world. The scene was almost sweet, except for the karpos's fangs and glowing eyes.

Meg regarded me warily. The lenses of her glasses were spiderwebbed with cracks.

"That prophecy," she said. "Did you understand it?"

I swallowed a mouthful of soot. "Perhaps. Some of it. We'll need to talk to Rachel—"

"There's no more *we*." Meg's tone was as acrid as the volcanic gas of Delphi. "Do what you need to do. That's my final order."

This hit me like a spear shaft to the chin, despite the fact that she had lied to me and betrayed me.

"Meg, you can't." I couldn't keep the shakiness out of my voice. "You claimed my service. Until my trials are over—"

"I release you."

"No!" I could not stand the idea of being abandoned. Not again. Not by this ragamuffin Dumpster queen whom I'd learned to care about so much. "You can't *possibly* believe in Nero now. You heard him explain his plans. He means to level this entire island! You saw what he tried to do to his hostages."

"He—he wouldn't have let them burn. He promised. He held back. You saw it. That wasn't the Beast."

My rib cage felt like an over-tightened harp. "Meg . . . Nero *is* the Beast. He killed your father."

"No! Nero is my stepfather. My dad . . . my dad unleashed the Beast. He made it angry."

"Meg—"

"Stop!" She covered her ears. "You don't know him. Nero is good to me. I can talk to him. I can make it okay."

Her denial was so complete, so irrational, I realized there was no way I could argue with her. She reminded me painfully of myself when I fell to earth—how I had refused to accept my new reality. Without Meg's help, I would've gotten myself killed. Now our roles were reversed.

I edged toward her, but Peaches's snarl stopped me in my tracks.

Meg backed away. "We're done."

"We can't be," I said. "We're bound, whether you like it or not."

It occurred to me that she'd said the exact same thing to me only a few days before.

She gave me one last look through her cracked lenses. I would have given anything for her to blow a raspberry. I wanted to walk the streets of Manhattan with her doing cartwheels in the intersections. I missed hobbling with her through the Labyrinth, our legs tied together. I would've settled for a good garbage fight in an alley. Instead, she turned and fled, with Peaches at her heels. It seemed to me that they dissolved into the trees, just the way Daphne had done long ago.

Above my head, a breeze made the wind chimes jingle. This time, no voices came from the trees. I didn't know how long Dodona would remain silent, but I didn't want to be here if the oaks decided to start telling jokes again.

I turned and saw something strange at my feet: an arrow with an oak shaft and green fletching.

There shouldn't have been an arrow. I hadn't brought any into the grove. But in my dazed state, I didn't question this. I did what any archer would do: I retrieved it, and returned it to my quiver.

34

Uber's got nothing
Lyft is weak. And taxis? Nah
My ride is da mom

AUSTIN HAD FREED THE OTHER PRISONERS.

They looked like they had been dipped in a vat of glue and cotton swabs, but otherwise they seemed remarkably undamaged. Ellis Wakefield staggered around with his fists clenched, looking for something to punch. Cecil Markowitz, son of Hermes, sat on the ground trying to clean his sneakers with a deer's thighbone. Austin—resourceful boy!—had produced a canteen of water and was washing the Greek fire off of Kayla's face. Miranda Gardiner, the head counselor of Demeter, knelt by the place where the dryads had sacrificed themselves. She wept silently.

Paulie the palikos floated toward me. Like his partner, Pete, his lower half was all steam. From the waist up he looked like a slimmer, more abused version of his geyser buddy. His mud skin was cracked like a parched riverbed. His face was withered, as if every bit of moisture had been squeezed out of him. Looking at the damage Nero had done to him, I added a few more items to a mental list I was preparing: *Ways to Torture an Emperor in the Fields of Punishment.*

"You saved me," Paulie said with amazement. "Bring it in!"

He threw his arms around me. His power was so diminished that his body heat did not kill me, but it did open up my sinuses quite well.

"You should get home," I said. "Pete is worried, and you need to regain your strength."

"Ah, man . . ." Paulie wiped a steaming tear from his face. "Yeah, I'm gone. But anything you ever need—a free steam cleaning, some PR work, a mud scrub, you name it."

As he dissolved into mist, I called after him. "And Paulie? I'd give the Woods at Camp Half-Blood a ten for customer satisfaction."

Paulie beamed with gratitude. He tried to hug me again, but he was already ninety percent steam. All I got was a humid waft of mud-scented air. Then he was gone.

The five demigods gathered around me.

Miranda looked past me at the Grove of Dodona. Her eyes were still puffy from crying, but she had beautiful irises the color of new foliage. "So, the voices I heard from that grove . . . It's really an Oracle? Those trees can give us prophecies?"

I shivered, thinking of the oak trees' limerick. "Perhaps."

"Can I see—?"

"No," I said. "Not until we understand the place better."

I had already lost one daughter of Demeter today. I didn't intend to lose another.

"I don't get it," Ellis grumbled. "You're Apollo? Like, *the* Apollo."

"I'm afraid so. It's a long story."

"Oh, gods . . ." Kayla scanned the clearing. "I thought I heard Meg's voice earlier. Did I dream that? Was she with you? Is she okay?"

The others looked at me for an explanation. Their expressions were so fragile and tentative, I decided I couldn't break down in front of them.

"She's . . . alive," I managed. "She had to leave."

"*What?*" Kayla asked. "Why?"

"Nero," I said. "She . . . she went after Nero."

"Hold up." Austin raised his fingers like goalposts. "When you say Nero . . ."

I did my best to explain how the mad emperor had captured them. They deserved to know. As I recounted the story, Nero's words kept replaying in my mind: *My wrecking crew will be here any minute. Once Camp Half-Blood is destroyed, I'll make it my new front lawn!*

I wanted to think this was just bluster. Nero had always loved threats and grandiose statements. Unlike me, he was a terrible poet. He used flowery language like . . . well, like every sentence was a pungent bouquet of metaphors. (Oh, that's another good one. Jotting that down.)

Why had he kept checking his watch? And what wrecking crew could he have been talking about? I had a flashback to my dream of the sun bus careening toward a giant bronze face.

I felt like I was free-falling again. Nero's plan became horribly clear. After dividing the few demigods defending the camp, he had meant to burn this grove. But that was only part of his attack. . . .

"Oh, gods," I said. "The Colossus."

The five demigods shifted uneasily.

"What Colossus?" Kayla asked. "You mean the Colossus of Rhodes?"

"No," I said. "The Colossus Neronis."

Cecil scratched his head. "The Colossus Neurotic?"

Ellis Wakefield snorted. "*You're* a Colossus Neurotic, Markowitz. Apollo's talking about the big replica of Nero that stood outside the amphitheater in Rome, right?"

"I'm afraid so," I said. "While we're standing here, Nero is going to try to destroy Camp Half-Blood. And the Colossus will be his wrecking crew."

Miranda flinched. "You mean a giant statue is about to stomp on *camp*? I thought the Colossus was destroyed centuries ago."

Ellis frowned. "Supposedly, so was the Athena Parthenos. Now it's sitting on top of Half-Blood Hill."

The others' expressions turned grim. When a child of Ares makes a valid point, you know the situation is serious.

"Speaking of Athena . . ." Austin picked some incendiary fluff off his shoulder. "Won't the statue protect us? I mean, that's what she's there for, right?"

"She will try," I guessed. "But you must understand, the Athena Parthenos draws her power from her followers. The more demigods under her care, the more formidable her magic. And right now—"

"The camp is practically empty," Miranda finished.

"Not only that," I said, "but the Athena Parthenos is roughly forty feet tall. If memory serves, Nero's Colossus was more than twice that."

Ellis grunted. "So they're not in the same weight class. It's an uneven match."

Cecil Markowitz stood a little straighter. "Guys . . . did you feel that?"

I thought he might be playing one of his Hermes pranks. Then the ground shook again, ever so slightly. From somewhere in the distance came a rumbling sound like a battleship scraping over a sandbar.

"Please tell me that was thunder," Kayla said.

Ellis cocked his head, listening. "It's a war machine. A big automaton wading ashore about half a klick from here. We need to get to camp right now."

No one argued with Ellis's assessment. I supposed he could distinguish between the sounds of war machines the same way I could pick out an off-tune violin in a Rachmaninoff symphony.

To their credit, the demigods rose to the challenge. Despite the fact that they'd been recently bound, doused in flammable substances, and staked like human tiki torches, they closed ranks and faced me with determination in their eyes.

"How do we get out of here?" Austin asked. "The myrmekes' lair?"

I felt suddenly suffocated, partly because I had five people looking at me as if I knew what to do. I didn't. In fact, if you want to know a secret, we gods usually don't. When confronted for answers, we usually say something Rhea-like: *You will have to find out for yourself!* Or *True wisdom must be earned!* But I didn't think that would fly in this situation.

Also, I had no desire to plunge back into the ants' nest.

Even if we made it through alive, it would take much too long. Then we would have to run perhaps half the length of the forest.

I stared at the Vince-shaped hole in the canopy. "I don't suppose any of you can fly?"

They shook their heads.

"I can cook," Cecil offered.

Ellis smacked him on the shoulder.

I looked back at the myrmekes' tunnel. The solution came to me like a voice whispering in my ear: *You know someone who can fly, stupid.*

It was a risky idea. Then again, rushing off to fight a giant automaton was also not the safest plan of action.

"I think there's a way," I said. "But I'll need your help."

Austin balled his fists. "Anything you need. We're ready to fight."

"Actually . . . I don't need you to fight. I need you to lay down a beat."

My next important discovery: Children of Hermes cannot rap. At all.

Bless his conniving little heart, Cecil Markowitz tried his best, but he kept throwing off my rhythm section with his spastic clapping and terrible air mic noises. After a few trial runs, I demoted him to dancer. His job would be to shimmy back and forth and wave his hands, which he did with the enthusiasm of a tent-revival preacher.

The others managed to keep up. They still looked like half-plucked, highly combustible chickens, but they bopped with the proper amount of soul.

I launched into "Dear Mama," my throat reinforced with water and cough drops from Kayla's belt pack. (Ingenious girl! Who brings cough drops on a three-legged death race?)

I sang directly into the mouth of the myrmekes' tunnel, trusting the acoustics to carry my message. We did not have to wait long. The earth began to rumble beneath our feet. I kept singing. I had warned my comrades not to stop laying down the righteous beat until the song was over.

Still, I almost lost it when the ground exploded. I had been watching the tunnel, but Mama did not use tunnels. She exited wherever she wanted—in this case, straight out of the earth twenty yards away, spraying dirt, grass, and small boulders in all directions. She scuttled forward, mandibles clacking, wings buzzing, dark Teflon eyes focused on me. Her abdomen was no longer swollen, so I assumed she had finished depositing her most recent batch of killer-ant larvae. I hoped this meant she would be in a good mood, not a hungry mood.

Behind her, two winged soldiers clambered out of the earth. I had not been expecting bonus ants. (Really, *bonus ants* is not a term most people would like to hear.) They flanked the queen, their antennae quivering.

I finished my ode, then dropped to one knee, spreading my arms as I had before.

"Mama," I said, "we need a ride."

My logic was this: Mothers were used to giving rides. With thousands upon thousands of offspring, I assumed the queen ant would be the ultimate soccer mom. And indeed, Mama grabbed me with her mandibles and tossed me over her head.

Despite what the demigods may tell you, I did not flail, scream, or land in a way that damaged my sensitive parts. I landed heroically, straddling the queen's neck, which was no larger than the back of an average warhorse. I shouted to my comrades, "Join me! It's perfectly safe!"

For some reason, they hesitated. The ants did not. The queen tossed Kayla just behind me. The soldier ants followed Mama's lead—snapping up two demigods each and throwing them aboard.

The three myrmekes revved their wings with a noise like radiator fan blades. Kayla grabbed my waist.

"Is this *really* safe?" she yelled.

"Perfectly!" I hoped I was right. "Perhaps even safer than the sun chariot!"

"Didn't the sun chariot almost destroy the world once?"

"Well, twice," I said. "Three times, if you count the day I let Thalia Grace drive, but—"

"Forget I asked!"

Mama launched herself into the sky. The canopy of twisted branches blocked our path, but Mama didn't pay any more attention to them than she had to the ton of solid earth she'd plowed through.

I yelled, "Duck!"

We flattened ourselves against Mama's armored head as she smashed through the trees, leaving a thousand wooden splinters embedded in my back. It felt so good to fly again, I didn't care. We soared above the woods and banked to the east.

For two or three seconds, I was exhilarated.

Then I heard the screaming from Camp Half-Blood.

35

Buck-naked statue
A Neurotic Colossus
Where art thy undies?

EVEN MY SUPERNATURAL POWERS of description fail me.

Imagine seeing yourself as a hundred-foot-tall bronze statue—a replica of your own magnificence, gleaming in the late afternoon light.

Now imagine that this ridiculously handsome statue is wading out of Long Island Sound onto the North Shore. In his hand is a ship's rudder—a blade the size of a stealth bomber, fixed to a fifty-foot-long pole—and Mr. Gorgeous is raising said rudder to smash the crud out of Camp Half-Blood.

This was the sight that greeted us as we flew in from the woods.

"How is that thing *alive?*" Kayla demanded. "What did Nero do—order it online?"

"The Triumvirate has vast resources," I told her. "They've had centuries to prepare. Once they reconstructed the statue, all they had to do was fill it with some animating magic—usually the harnessed life forces of wind or water spirits. I'm not sure. That's really more of Hephaestus's specialty."

"So how do we kill it?"

"I'm . . . I'm working on that."

All across the valley, campers screamed and ran for their weapons. Nico and Will were floundering in the lake, apparently having been capsized in the middle of a canoe ride. Chiron galloped through the dunes, harrying the Colossus with his arrows. Even by my standards, Chiron was a very fine archer. He targeted the statue's joints and seams, yet his shots did not seem to bother the automaton at all. Already dozens of missiles stuck from the Colossus's armpits and neck like unruly hair.

"More quivers!" Chiron shouted. "Quickly!"

Rachel Dare stumbled from the armory carrying half a dozen, and she ran to resupply him.

The Colossus brought down his rudder to smash the dining pavilion, but his blade bounced off the camp's magical barrier, sparking as if it had hit solid metal. Mr. Gorgeous took another step inland, but the barrier resisted him, pushing him back with the force of a wind tunnel.

On Half-Blood Hill, a silver aura surrounded the Athena Parthenos. I wasn't sure the demigods could see it, but every so often a beam of ultraviolet light shot from Athena's helmet like a search lamp, hitting the Colossus's chest and pushing back the invader. Next to her, in the tall pine tree, the Golden Fleece blazed with fiery energy. The dragon Peleus hissed and paced around the trunk, ready to defend his turf.

These were powerful forces, but I did not need godly sight to tell me that they would soon fail. The camp's defensive barriers were designed to turn away the occasional stray monster, to confuse mortals and prevent them from detecting the valley, and to provide a first line of defense against invading forces. A criminally beautiful hundred-foot-tall Celestial bronze giant was another thing entirely. Soon the Colossus would break through and destroy everything in its path.

"Apollo!" Kayla nudged me in the ribs. "What do we do?"

I stirred, again with the unpleasant realization that I was expected to have answers. My first instinct was to order a seasoned demigod to take charge. Wasn't it the weekend yet? Where was Percy Jackson? Or those Roman praetors Frank Zhang and Reyna Ramírez-Arellano? Yes, they would have done nicely.

My second instinct was to turn to Meg McCaffrey. How quickly I had grown used to her annoying yet strangely endearing presence! Alas, she was gone. Her absence felt like a Colossus stomping upon my heart. (This was an easy metaphor to summon, since the Colossus was presently stomping on a great many things.)

Flanking us on either side, the soldier ants flew in formation, awaiting the queen's orders. The demigods watched me anxiously, random bits of bandage fluff swirling from their bodies as we sped through the air.

I leaned forward and spoke to Mama in a soothing tone. "I know I cannot ask you to risk your life for us."

Mama hummed as if to say, *You're darn right!*

"Just give us one pass around that statue's head?" I asked. "Enough to distract it. Then set us down on the beach?"

She clicked her mandibles doubtfully.

"You're the best mama in the whole world," I added, "and you look lovely today."

That line always worked with Leto. It did the trick with Mama Ant, too. She twitched her antennae, perhaps sending a high-frequency signal to her soldiers, and all three ants banked hard to the right.

Below us, more campers joined the battle. Sherman Yang had harnessed two pegasi to a chariot and was now circling the statue's legs, while Julia and Alice threw electric javelins at the Colossus's knees. The missiles stuck in his joints, discharging tendrils of blue lightning, but the statue barely seemed to notice. Meanwhile, at his feet, Connor Stoll and Harley used twin flamethrowers to give the Colossus a molten pedicure, while the Nike twins manned a catapult, lobbing boulders at the Colossus's Celestial bronze crotch.

Malcolm Pace, a true child of Athena, was coordinating the attacks from a hastily organized command post on the green. He and Nyssa had spread war maps across a card table and were shouting targeting coordinates, while Chiara, Damien, Paolo, and Billie rushed to set up ballistae around the communal hearth.

Malcolm looked like the perfect battlefield commander, except for the fact that he'd forgotten his pants. His red briefs made quite a statement with his sword and leather cuirass.

Mama dove toward the Colossus, leaving my stomach at a higher altitude.

I had a moment to appreciate the statue's regal features, its metal brow rimmed with a spiky crown meant to represent the beams of the sun. The Colossus was supposed to be Nero as the sun god, but the emperor had wisely made the face resemble mine more closely than his. Only the line of its nose and its ghastly neck beard suggested Nero's trademark ugliness.

Also . . . did I mention that the hundred-foot statue was entirely nude? Well, of course it was. Gods are almost always depicted as nude, because we are flawless beings. Why would you cover up perfection? Still, it was a little disconcerting to see my buck-naked self stomping around, slamming a ship's rudder at Camp Half-Blood.

As we approached the Colossus, I bellowed loudly, "IMPOSTOR! I AM THE REAL APOLLO! YOU'RE UGLY!"

Oh, dear reader, it was hard to yell such words at my own handsome visage, but I did. Such was my courage.

The Colossus did not like being insulted. As Mama and her soldiers veered away, the statue swung its rudder upward.

Have you ever collided with a bomber? I had a sudden flashback to Dresden in 1945, when the planes were so thick in the air, I literally could not find a safe lane to drive in. The axle on the sun chariot was out of alignment for *weeks* after that.

I realized the ants were not fast enough fliers to escape the rudder's reach. I saw catastrophe approaching in slow motion. At the last possible moment, I yelled, "Dive!"

We plunged straight down. The rudder only clipped the ants' wings—but it was enough to send us spiraling toward the beach.

I was grateful for soft sand.

I ate quite a bit of it when we crash-landed.

By sheer luck, none of us died, though Kayla and Austin had to pull me to my feet.

"Are you okay?" Austin asked.

"Fine," I said. "We must hurry."

The Colossus stared down at us, perhaps trying to discern whether we were dying in agony yet or needed some additional pain. I had wanted to get his attention, and I had succeeded. Huzzah.

I glanced at Mama and her soldiers, who were shaking the sand off their carapaces. "Thank you. Now save yourselves. Fly!"

They did not need to be told twice. I suppose ants have a natural fear of large humanoids looming over them, about to squash them with a heavy foot. Mama and her guards buzzed into the sky.

Miranda looked after them. "I never thought I'd say this about bugs, but I'm going to miss those guys."

"Hey!" called Nico di Angelo. He and Will scrambled over the dunes, still dripping from their swim in the canoe lake.

"What's the plan?" Will seemed calm, but I knew him well enough by now to tell that inside he was as charged as a bare electrical wire.

BOOM.

The statue strode toward us. One more step, and it would be on top of us.

"Isn't there a control valve on its ankle?" Ellis asked. "If we can open it—"

"No," I said. "You're thinking of Talos. This is not Talos."

Nico brushed his dark wet hair from his forehead. "Then what?"

I had a lovely view of the Colossus's nose. Its nostrils were sealed with bronze . . . I supposed because Nero hadn't wanted his detractors trying to shoot arrows into his imperial noggin.

I yelped.

Kayla grabbed my arm. "Apollo, what's wrong?"

Arrows into the Colossus's head. Oh, gods, I had an idea that would never, ever work. However, it seemed better than our other option, which was to be crushed under a two-ton bronze foot.

"Will, Kayla, Austin," I said, "come with me."

"And Nico," said Nico. "I have a doctor's note."

"Fine!" I said. "Ellis, Cecil, Miranda—do whatever you can to keep the Colossus's attention."

The shadow of an enormous foot darkened the sand.

"Now!" I yelled. "Scatter!"

36

I love me some plague
When it's on the right arrow
Ka-bam! You dead, bro?

SCATTERING WAS THE EASY PART. They did that very well.

Miranda, Cecil, and Ellis ran in different directions, screaming insults at the Colossus and waving their arms. This bought the rest of us a few seconds as we sprinted for the dunes, but I suspected the Colossus would soon enough come after me. I was, after all, the most important and attractive target.

I pointed toward Sherman Yang's chariot, which was still circling the statue's legs in a vain attempt to electrocute its kneecaps. "We need to commandeer that chariot!"

"How?" Kayla asked.

I was about to admit I had no idea when Nico di Angelo grabbed Will's hand and stepped into my shadow. Both boys evaporated. I had forgotten about the power of shadow-traveling—the way children of the Underworld could step into one shadow and appear from another, sometimes hundreds of miles away. Hades used to love sneaking up on me that way and yelling, "HI!" just as I shot an arrow of death.

He found it amusing if I missed my target and accidentally wiped out the wrong city.

Austin shuddered. "I hate it when Nico disappears like that. What's our plan?"

"You two are my backup," I said. "If I miss, if I die . . . it will be up to you."

"Whoa, whoa," Kayla said. "What do you mean *if you miss?*"

I drew my last arrow—the one I'd found in the grove. "I'm going to shoot that gorgeous gargantuan in the ear."

Austin and Kayla exchanged looks, perhaps wondering if I'd finally cracked under the strain of being mortal.

"A plague arrow," I explained. "I'm going to enchant an arrow with sickness, then shoot it into the statue's ear. Its head is hollow. The ears are the only openings. The arrow should release enough disease to kill the Colossus's animating power . . . or at least to disable it."

"How do you know it will work?" Kayla asked.

"I don't, but—"

Our conversation was ruined by a sudden heavy downpour of Colossus foot. We darted inland, barely avoiding being flattened.

Behind us, Miranda shouted, "Hey, ugly!"

I knew she wasn't talking to me, but I glanced back anyway. She raised her arms, causing ropes of sea grass to spring from the dunes and wrap around the statue's ankles. The Colossus broke through them easily, but they annoyed him enough to be a distraction. Watching Miranda face the statue made me heartsick for Meg all over again.

Meanwhile, Ellis and Cecil stood on either side of the Colossus, throwing rocks at his shins. From the camp, a volley of flaming ballista projectiles exploded against Mr. Gorgeous's naked backside, which made me clench in sympathy.

"You were saying?" Austin asked.

"Right." I twirled the arrow between my fingers. "I know what you're thinking. I don't have godly powers. It's doubtful I'll be able to cook up the Black Death or the Spanish Flu. But still, if I can make the shot from close range, straight into its head, I might be able to do some damage."

"And . . . if you fail?" Kayla asked. I noticed her quiver was also empty.

"I won't have the strength to try twice. You'll have to make another pass. Find an arrow, try to summon some sickness, make the shot while Austin holds the chariot steady."

I realized this was an impossible request, but they accepted it with grim silence. I wasn't sure whether to feel grateful or guilty. Back when I was a god, I would've taken it for granted that mortals had faith in me. Now . . . I was asking my children to risk their lives again, and I was not at all sure my plan would work.

I caught a flash of movement in the sky. This time, instead of a Colossus foot, it was Sherman Yang's chariot, minus Sherman Yang. Will brought the pegasi in for a landing, then dragged out a half-conscious Nico di Angelo.

"Where are the others?" Kayla asked. "Sherman and the Hermes girls?"

Will rolled his eyes. "Nico convinced them to disembark."

As if on cue, I heard Sherman screaming from somewhere far in the distance, "I'll get you, di Angelo!"

"You guys go," Will told me. "The chariot is only designed for three, and after that shadow-travel, Nico is going to pass out any second."

"No, I'm not," Nico complained, then passed out.

Will caught him in a fireman's carry and took him away. "Good luck! I'm going to get the Lord of Darkness here some Gatorade!"

Austin hopped in first and took the reins. As soon as Kayla and I were aboard, we shot skyward, the pegasi swerving and banking around the Colossus with expert skill. I began to feel a glimmer of hope. We might be able to outmaneuver this giant hunk of good-looking bronze.

"Now," I said, "if I can just enchant this arrow with a nice plague."

The arrow shuddered from its fletching to its point.

THOU SHALT NOT, it told me.

I try to avoid weapons that talk. I find them rude and distracting. Once, Artemis had a bow that could cuss like a Phoenician sailor. Another time, in a Stockholm tavern, I met this god who was smoking hot, except his talking sword just would *not* shut up.

But I digress.

I asked the obvious question. "Did you just speak to me?"

The arrow quivered. (Oh, dear. That was a horrible pun. My apologies.) *YEA, VERILY. PRITHEE, SHOOTING IS NOT MY PURPOSE.*

His voice was definitely male, sonorous and grave, like a bad Shakespearean actor's.

"But you're an arrow," I said. "Shooting you is the whole point." (Ah, I really must watch those puns.)

"Guys, hang on!" Austin shouted.

The chariot plunged to avoid the Colossus's swinging rudder. Without Austin's warning, I would have been left in midair still arguing with my projectile.

"So you're made from Dodona oak," I guessed. "Is that why you talk?"

FORSOOTH, said the arrow.

"Apollo!" Kayla said. "I'm not sure why you're talking to that arrow, but—"

From our right came a reverberating *WHANG!* like a snapped power line hitting a metal roof. In a flash of silver light, the camp's magical barriers collapsed. The Colossus lurched forward and brought his foot down on the dining pavilion, smashing it to rubble like so many children's blocks.

"But that just happened," Kayla said with a sigh.

The Colossus raised his rudder in triumph. He marched inland, ignoring the campers who were running around his feet. Valentina Diaz launched a ballista missile into his groin. (Again, I had to wince in sympathy.) Harley and Connor Stoll kept blowtorching his feet, to no effect. Nyssa, Malcolm, and Chiron hastily ran a trip line of steel cable across the statue's path, but they would never have time to anchor it properly.

I turned to Kayla. "You can't hear this arrow talking?"

Judging from her wide eyes, I guessed the answer was, *No, and does hallucinating run in the family?*

"Never mind." I looked at the arrow. "What would you suggest, O Wise Missile of Dodona? My quiver is empty."

The arrow's point dipped toward the statue's left arm. *LO, THE ARMPIT DOTH HOLD THE ARROWS THOU NEEDEST!*

Kayla yelled, "Colossus is heading for the cabins!"

"Armpit!" I told Austin. "Flieth—er, fly for the armpit!"

That wasn't an order one heard much in combat, but Austin spurred the pegasi into a steep ascent. We buzzed the forest of arrows sticking out of the Colossus's arm seam, but I completely overestimated my mortal hand-eye coordination. I lunged for the shafts and came up empty.

Kayla was more agile. She snagged a fistful but screamed when she yanked them free.

I pulled her to safety. Her hand was bleeding badly, cut from the high-speed grab.

"I'm fine!" Kayla yelped. Her fingers were clenched, splattering drops of red all over the chariot's floor. "Take the arrows."

I did. I tugged the Brazilian-flag bandana from around my neck and gave it to her. "Bind your hand," I ordered. "There's some ambrosia in my coat pocket."

"Don't worry about me." Kayla's face was as green as her hair. "Make the shot! Hurry!"

I inspected the arrows. My heart sank. Only one of the missiles was unbroken, and its shaft was warped. It would be almost impossible to shoot.

I looked again at the talking arrow.

THOU SHALT NOT THINKEST ABOUT IT, he intoned. *ENCHANT THOU THE WARPED ARROW!*

I tried. I opened my mouth, but the proper words of enchantment were gone from my mind. As I feared, Lester Papadopoulos simply did not possess the power. "I can't!"

I SHALT ASSIST, promised the Arrow of Dodona. *STARTEST THOU: "PLAGUEY, PLAGUEY, PLAGUEY."*

"The enchantment does *not* start *plaguey, plaguey, plaguey!*"

"Who are you talking to?" Austin demanded.

"My arrow! I—I need more time."

"We don't *have* more time!" Kayla pointed with her wrapped bloody hand.

The Colossus was only a few steps away from the central green. I wasn't sure the demigods even realized how much danger they were in. The Colossus could do much more than just flatten buildings. If he destroyed the central hearth, the sacred shrine of Hestia, he would extinguish the very soul of the camp. The valley would be cursed and uninhabitable for generations. Camp Half-Blood would cease to exist.

I realized I had failed. My plan would take much too long, if I could even *remember* how to make a plague arrow. This was my punishment for breaking an oath on the River Styx.

Then, from somewhere above us, a voice yelled, "Hey, Bronze Butt!"

Over the Colossus's head, a cloud of darkness formed like a cartoon dialogue bubble. Out of the shadows dropped a furry black monster dog—a hellhound—and astride his back was a young man with a glowing bronze sword.

The weekend was here. Percy Jackson had arrived.

37

Hey, look! It's Percy

Least he could do was help out

Taught him everything

I WAS TOO SURPRISED TO SPEAK. Otherwise I would have warned Percy what was about to happen.

Hellhounds are not fond of heights. When startled, they respond in a predictable way. The moment Percy's faithful pet landed on top of the moving Colossus, she yelped and proceeded to wee-wee on said Colossus's head. The statue froze and looked up, no doubt wondering what was trickling down his imperial sideburns.

Percy leaped heroically from his mount and slipped in hellhound pee. He nearly slid off the statue's brow. "What the—Mrs. O'Leary, jeez!"

The hellhound bayed in apology. Austin flew our chariot to within shouting distance. "Percy!"

The son of Poseidon frowned across at us. "All right, who unleashed the giant bronze guy? Apollo, did you do this?"

"I am offended!" I cried. "I am only indirectly responsible for this! Also, I have a plan to fix it."

"Oh, yeah?" Percy glanced back at the destroyed dining pavilion. "How's that going?"

With my usual levelheadedness, I stayed focused on the greater good. "If you could please just keep this Colossus from stomping the camp's hearth, that would be helpful. I need a few more minutes to enchant this arrow."

I held up the talking arrow by mistake, then held up the bent arrow.

Percy sighed. "Of course you do."

Mrs. O'Leary barked in alarm. The Colossus was raising his hand to swat the trespassing tinkler.

Percy grabbed one of the crown's sunray spikes. He sliced it off at the base, then jabbed it into the Colossus's forehead. I doubted the Colossus could feel pain, but it staggered, apparently surprised to suddenly have grown a unicorn horn.

Percy sliced off another one. "Hey, ugly!" he called down. "You don't need all these pointy things, do you? I'm going to take one to the beach. Mrs. O'Leary, fetch!"

Percy tossed the spike like a javelin.

The hellhound barked excitedly. She leaped off the Colossus's head, vaporized into shadow, and reappeared on the ground, bounding after her new bronze stick.

Percy raised his eyebrows at me. "Well? Start enchanting!"

He jumped from the statue's head to its shoulder. Then he leaped to the shaft of the rudder and slid down it like a fire pole all the way to the ground. If I had been at my usual level of godly athletic skill, I could've done something like that in my sleep, of course, but I had to admit Percy Jackson was moderately impressive.

"Hey, Bronze Butt!" he yelled again. "Come get me!"

The Colossus obliged, slowly turning and following Percy toward the beach.

I began to chant, invoking my old powers as the god of plagues. This time, the words came to me. I didn't know why. Perhaps Percy's arrival had given me new faith. Perhaps I simply didn't think about it too much. I've found that thinking often interferes with doing. It's one of those lessons that gods learn early in their careers.

I felt an itchy sensation of sickness curling from my fingers and into the projectile. I spoke of my own awesomeness and the various horrible diseases I had visited upon wicked populations in the past, because . . . well, I'm awesome. I could feel the magic taking hold, despite the Arrow of Dodona whispering to me like an annoying Elizabethan stagehand, SAYEST THOU: "PLAGUEY, PLAGUEY, PLAGUEY!"

Below, more demigods joined the parade to the beach. They ran ahead of the Colossus, jeering at him, throwing things, and calling him Bronze Butt. They made jokes about his new horn. They laughed at the hellhound pee trickling down his face. Normally I have zero tolerance for bullying, especially when the victim looks like me, but since the Colossus was ten stories tall and destroying their camp, I suppose the campers' rudeness was understandable.

I finished chanting. Odious green mist now wreathed the arrow. It smelled faintly of fast-food deep fryers—a good sign that it carried some sort of horrible malady.

"I'm ready!" I told Austin. "Get me next to its ear!"

"You got it!" Austin turned to say something else, and a wisp of green fog passed under his nose. His eyes watered. His nose swelled and began to run. He scrunched up his face and sneezed so hard he collapsed. He lay on the floor of the chariot, groaning and twitching.

"My boy!" I wanted to grab his shoulders and check on him, but since I had an arrow in each hand, that was inadvisable.

FIE! TOO STRONG IS THY PLAGUE. The Dodona arrow hummed with annoyance. *THY CHANTING SUCKETH.*

"Oh, no, no, no," I said. "Kayla, be careful. Don't breathe—"

"ACHOO!" Kayla crumpled next to her brother.

"What have I done?" I wailed.

METHINKS THOU HAST BLOWN IT, said the Dodona arrow, my source of infinite wisdom. *MOREO'ER, HIE! TAKEST THOU THE REINS.*

"Why?"

You would think a god who drove a chariot on a daily basis would not need to ask such a question. In my defense, I was distraught about my children lying half-conscious at my feet. I didn't consider that no one was driving. Without anyone at the reins, the pegasi panicked. To avoid running into the huge bronze Colossus directly in their path, they dove toward the earth.

Somehow, I managed to react appropriately. (Three cheers for reacting appropriately!) I thrust both arrows into my quiver, grabbed the reins, and was able to level our descent just enough to prevent a crash landing. We bounced off a dune and swerved to a stop in front of Chiron and a group of demigods. Our entrance might have looked dramatic if the centrifugal force hadn't thrown Kayla, Austin, and me from the chariot.

Did I mention I was grateful for soft sand?

The pegasi took off, dragging the battered chariot into the sky and leaving us stranded.

Chiron galloped to our side, a cluster of demigods in his wake. Percy Jackson ran toward us from the surf while Mrs. O'Leary kept the Colossus occupied with a game of keep-away. I doubt that would hold the statue's interest very long, once he realized there was a group of targets right behind him, just perfect for stomping.

"The plague arrow is ready!" I announced. "We need to shoot it into the Colossus's ear!"

My audience did not seem to take this as good news. Then I realized my chariot was gone. My bow was still in the chariot. And Kayla and Austin were quite obviously infected with whatever disease I had conjured up.

"Are they contagious?" Cecil asked.

"No!" I said. "Well . . . probably not. It's the fumes from the arrow—"

Everyone backed away from me.

"Cecil," Chiron said, "you and Harley take Kayla and Austin to the Apollo cabin for healing."

"But they *are* the Apollo cabin," Harley complained. "Besides, my flamethrower—"

"You can play with your flamethrower later," Chiron

promised. "Run along. There's a good boy. The rest of you, do what you can to keep the Colossus at the water's edge. Percy and I will assist Apollo."

Chiron said the word *assist* as if it meant *slap upside the head with extreme prejudice.*

Once the crowd had dispersed, Chiron gave me his bow. "Make the shot."

I stared at the massive composite recursive, which probably had a draw weight of a hundred pounds. "This is meant for the strength of a centaur, not a teen mortal!"

"You created the arrow," he said. "Only you can shoot it without succumbing to the disease. Only you can hit such a target."

"From *here*? It's impossible! Where is that flying boy, Jason Grace?"

Percy wiped the sweat and sand from his neck. "We're fresh out of flying boys. And all the pegasi have stampeded."

"Perhaps if we got some harpies and some kite string . . ." I said.

"Apollo," Chiron said, "you must do this. You are the lord of archery and illness."

"I'm not lord of anything!" I wailed. "I'm a stupid ugly mortal teenager! I'm *nobody*!"

The self-pity just came pouring out. I thought for sure the earth would split in two when I called myself a *nobody*. The cosmos would stop turning. Percy and Chiron would rush to reassure me.

None of that happened. Percy and Chiron just stared at me grimly.

Percy put his hand on my shoulder. "You're Apollo. We

need you. You can do this. Besides, if you don't, I will personally throw you off the top of the Empire State Building."

This was exactly the pep talk I needed—just the sort of thing Zeus used to say to me before my soccer matches. I squared my shoulders. "Right."

"We'll try to draw him into the water," Percy said. "I've got the advantage there. Good luck."

Percy accepted Chiron's hand and leaped onto the centaur's back. Together they galloped into the surf, Percy waving his sword and calling out various bronze-butt-themed insults to the Colossus.

I ran down the beach until I had a line of sight on the statue's left ear.

Looking up at that regal profile, I did not see Nero. I saw myself—a monument to my own conceit. Nero's pride was no more than a reflection of mine. I was the bigger fool. I was exactly the sort of person who would construct a hundred-foot-tall naked statue of myself in my front yard.

I pulled the plague arrow from my quiver and nocked it in the bowstring.

The demigods were getting very good at scattering. They continued to harry the Colossus from both sides while Percy and Chiron galloped through the tide, Mrs. O'Leary romping at their heels with her new bronze stick.

"Yo, ugly!" Percy shouted. "Over here!"

The Colossus's next step displaced several tons of salt water and made a crater large enough to swallow a pickup truck.

The Arrow of Dodona rattled in my quiver. *RELEASE THY BREATH*, he advised. *DROPETH THY SHOULDER.*

"I *have* shot a bow before," I grumbled.

MINDETH THY RIGHT ELBOW, the arrow said.

"Shut up."

AND TELLEST NOT THINE ARROW TO SHUT UP.

I drew the bow. My muscles burned as if boiling water was being poured over my shoulders. The plague arrow did not make me pass out, but its fumes were disorienting. The warp of the shaft made my calculations impossible. The wind was against me. The arc of the shot would be much too high.

Yet I aimed, exhaled, and released the bowstring.

The arrow twirled as it rocketed upward, losing force and drifting too far to the right. My heart sank. Surely the curse of the River Styx would deny me any chance at success.

Just as the projectile reached its apex and was about to fall back to earth, a gust of wind caught it . . . perhaps Zephyros looking kindly on my pitiful attempt. The arrow sailed into the Colossus's ear canal and rattled in his head with a *clink, clink, clink* like a pachinko machine.

The Colossus halted. He stared at the horizon as if confused. He looked at the sky, then arched his back and lurched forward, making a sound like a tornado ripping off the roof of a warehouse. Because his face had no other open orifices, the pressure of his sneeze forced geysers of motor oil out his ears, spraying the dunes with environmentally unfriendly sludge.

Sherman, Julia, and Alice stumbled over to me, covered head to toe with sand and oil.

"I appreciate you freeing Miranda and Ellis," Sherman snarled, "but I'm going to kill you later for taking my chariot. What did you do to that Colossus? What kind of plague makes you sneeze?"

"I'm afraid I—I summoned a rather benign illness. I believe I have given the Colossus a case of hay fever."

You know that horrible pause when you're waiting for someone to sneeze? The statue arched his back again, and everyone on the beach cringed in anticipation. The Colossus inhaled several cubic acres of air through his ear canals, preparing for his next blast.

I imagined the nightmare scenarios: The Colossus would ear-sneeze Percy Jackson into Connecticut, never to be seen again. The Colossus would clear his head and then stomp all of us flat. Hay fever could make a person cranky. I knew this because I *invented* hay fever. Still, I had never intended it to be a killing affliction. I certainly never anticipated facing the wrath of a towering metal automaton with extreme seasonal allergies. I cursed my shortsightedness! I cursed my mortality!

What I had *not* considered was the damage our demigods had already done to the Colossus's metal joints—in particular, his neck.

The Colossus rocked forward with a mighty *CHOOOOO!* I flinched and almost missed the moment of truth when the statue's head achieved first-stage separation from his body. It hurtled over Long Island Sound, the face spinning in and out of view. It hit the water with a mighty WHOOSH and bobbed for a moment. Then the air *blooped* out of its neck hole and the gorgeous regal visage of yours truly sank beneath the waves.

The statue's decapitated body tilted and swayed. If it had fallen backward, it might have crushed even more of the camp. Instead, it toppled forward. Percy yelped a curse that would have made any Phoenician sailor proud. Chiron and he raced sideways to avoid being crushed while Mrs. O'Leary wisely dissolved into shadows. The Colossus hit the water, sending forty-foot tidal waves to port and starboard. I had never before seen a centaur hang hooves on a tubular crest, but Chiron acquitted himself well.

The roar of the statue's fall finally stopped echoing off the hills.

Next to me, Alice Miyazawa whistled. "Well, that de-escalated quickly."

Sherman Yang asked in a voice of childlike wonder: "What the Hades just happened?"

"I believe," I said, "the Colossus sneezed his head off."

38

After the sneezing
Healing peeps, parsing limericks
Worst God Award? Me

THE PLAGUE SPREAD.

That was the price of our victory: a massive outbreak of hay fever. By nightfall, most of the campers were dizzy, groggy, and heavily congested, though I was pleased that none of them sneezed their heads off, because we were running low on bandages and duct tape.

Will Solace and I spent the evening caring for the wounded. Will took the lead, which was fine with me; I was exhausted. Mostly I splinted arms, distributed cold medicine and tissues, and tried to keep Harley from stealing the infirmary's entire supply of smiley-face stickers, which he plastered all over his flamethrower. I was grateful for the distraction, since it kept me from thinking too much about the day's painful events.

Sherman Yang graciously agreed not to kill Nico for tossing him out of his chariot, or me for damaging it, though I had the feeling the son of Ares was keeping his options open for later.

Chiron provided healing poultices for the most extreme cases of hay fever. This included Chiara Benvenuti, whose good luck had, for once, abandoned her. Strangely enough, Damien White got sick right after he learned that Chiara was sick. The two had cots next to each other in the infirmary, which I found a little suspicious, even though they kept sniping at each other whenever they knew they were being watched.

Percy Jackson spent several hours recruiting whales and hippocampi to help him haul away the Colossus. He decided it would be easiest to tow it underwater to Poseidon's palace, where it could be repurposed as garden statuary. I was not sure how I felt about that. I imagined Poseidon would replace the statue's gorgeous face with his own weathered, bearded mien. Still, I wanted the Colossus gone, and I doubted it would have fit in the camp's recycling bins.

Thanks to Will's healing and a hot dinner, the demigods I had rescued from the woods quickly got back to full strength. (Paolo claimed it was because he waved a Brazilian-flag bandana over them, and I was not about to argue.)

As for the camp itself, the damage might have been much worse. The canoe dock could be rebuilt. The Colossus's footstep craters could be repurposed as convenient foxholes or koi ponds.

The dining pavilion was a total loss, but Nyssa and Harley were confident that Annabeth Chase could redesign the place next time she was here. With luck, it would be rebuilt in time for the summer.

The only other major damage was to the Demeter cabin. I had not realized it during the battle, but the Colossus had managed to step on it before turning around for the beach.

In retrospect, its path of destruction appeared almost purposeful, as if the automaton had waded ashore, stomped Cabin Four, and headed back out to sea.

Given what had happened with Meg McCaffrey, I had a hard time not seeing this as a bad omen. Miranda Gardiner and Billie Ng were given temporary bunks in the Hermes cabin, but for a long time that night they sat stunned among the smashed ruins as daisies popped up all around them from the cold winter ground.

Despite my exhaustion, I slept fitfully. I did not mind Kayla and Austin's constant sneezing, or Will's gentle snoring. I did not even mind the hyacinths blooming on the windowsill, filling the room with their melancholy perfume. But I could not stop thinking of the dryads raising their arms to the flames in the woods, and about Nero, and Meg. The Arrow of Dodona stayed silent, hanging in my quiver on the wall, but I suspected it would have more annoying Shakespearean advice soon. I did not relish what it might telleth me about my future.

At sunrise, I rose quietly, took my bow and quiver and combat ukulele, and hiked to the summit of Half-Blood Hill. The guardian dragon, Peleus, did not recognize me. When I came too close to the Golden Fleece, he hissed, so I had to sit some distance away at the foot of the Athena Parthenos.

I didn't mind not being recognized. At the moment, I did not *want* to be Apollo. All the destruction I saw below me . . . it was my fault. I had been blind and complacent. I had allowed the emperors of Rome, including one of my own descendants, to rise to power in the shadows. I had let my once-great network of Oracles collapse until even Delphi was lost. I had almost caused the death of Camp Half-Blood itself.

And Meg McCaffrey . . . Oh, Meg, where were you?

Do what you need to do, she had told me. *That's my final order.*

Her order had been vague enough to allow me to pursue her. After all, we were bound together now. What I *needed to do* was to find her. I wondered if Meg had phrased her order that way on purpose, or if that was just wishful thinking on my part.

I gazed up at the serene alabaster face of Athena. In real life, she didn't look so pale and aloof—well, not most of the time, anyway. I pondered why the sculptor, Phidias, had chosen to make her look so unapproachable, and whether Athena approved. We gods often debated how much humans could change our very nature simply by the way they pictured us or imagined us. During the eighteenth century, for instance, I could not escape the white powdered wig, no matter how hard I tried. Among immortals, our reliance on humans was an uncomfortable subject.

Perhaps I deserved my present form. After my carelessness and foolishness, perhaps humanity *should* see me as nothing but Lester Papadopoulos.

I heaved a sigh. "Athena, what would you do in my place? Something wise and practical, I suppose."

Athena offered no response. She stared calmly at the horizon, taking the long view, as always.

I didn't need the wisdom goddess to tell me what I must do. I should leave Camp Half-Blood immediately, before the campers woke. They had taken me in to protect me, and I had nearly gotten them all killed. I couldn't bear to endanger them any longer.

But, oh, how I wanted to stay with Will, Kayla, Austin— my mortal children. I wanted to help Harley put smiley faces on his flamethrower. I wanted to flirt with Chiara and steal her away from Damien . . . or perhaps steal Damien away from Chiara, I wasn't sure yet. I wanted to improve my music and archery through that strange activity known as *practice*. I wanted to have a home.

Leave, I told myself. *Hurry.*

Because I was a coward, I waited too long. Below me, the cabin lights flickered on. Campers emerged from their doorways. Sherman Yang began his morning stretches. Harley jogged around the green, holding his Leo Valdez beacon high with the hope it would finally work.

At last, a pair of familiar figures spotted me. They approached from different directions—the Big House and Cabin Three—hiking up the hill to see me: Rachel Dare and Percy Jackson.

"I know what you're thinking," Rachel said. "Don't do it."

I feigned surprise. "Can you read my mind, Miss Dare?"

"I don't need to. I know you, Lord Apollo."

A week ago, the idea would have made me laugh. A mortal could not *know* me. I had lived for four millennia. Merely looking upon my true form would have vaporized any human. Now, though, Rachel's words seemed perfectly reasonable. With Lester Papadopoulos, what you saw was what you got. There really wasn't much to know.

"Don't call me *Lord*," I sighed. "I am just a mortal teen. I do not belong at this camp."

Percy sat next to me. He squinted at the sunrise, the sea breeze tousling his hair. "Yeah, I used to think I didn't belong here either."

"It's not the same," I said. "You humans change and grow and mature. Gods do not."

Percy faced me. "You sure about that? You seem pretty different."

I think he meant that as a compliment, but I didn't find his words reassuring. If I was becoming more fully human, that was hardly a cause for celebration. True, I had mustered a few godly powers at important moments—a burst of divine strength against the Germani, a hay fever arrow against the Colossus—but I could not rely on those abilities. I didn't even understand how I had summoned them. The fact that I had limits, and that I couldn't be sure where those limits *were* . . . Well, that made me feel much more like Lester Papadopoulos than Apollo.

"The other Oracles must be found and secured," I said. "I cannot do that unless I leave Camp Half-Blood. And I cannot risk anyone else's life."

Rachel sat on my other side. "You sound certain. Did you get a prophecy from the grove?"

I shuddered. "I fear so."

Rachel cupped her hands on her knees. "Kayla said you

were talking to an arrow yesterday. I'm guessing it's wood from Dodona?"

"Wait," Percy said. "You found a talking arrow that gave you a prophecy?"

"Don't be silly," I said. "The arrow talks, but I got the prophecy from the grove itself. The Arrow of Dodona just gives random advice. He's quite annoying."

The arrow buzzed in my quiver.

"At any rate," I continued, "I must leave the camp. The Triumvirate means to possess all the ancient Oracles. I have to stop them. Once I have defeated the former emperors . . . only then will I be able to face my old enemy Python and free the Oracle of Delphi. After that . . . if I survive . . . perhaps Zeus will restore me to Olympus."

Rachel tugged at a strand of her hair. "You know it's too dangerous to do all that alone, right?"

"Listen to her," Percy urged. "Chiron told me about Nero and this weird holding company of his."

"I appreciate the offer of assistance, but—"

"Whoa." Percy held up his hands. "Just to be clear, I'm not offering to go with you. I still have to finish my senior year, pass my DSTOMP and my SAT, and avoid getting killed by my girlfriend. But I'm sure we can get you some other helpers."

"I'll go," Rachel said.

I shook my head. "My enemies would *love* to capture someone as dear to me as the priestess of Delphi. Besides, I need you and Miranda Gardiner to stay here and study the Grove of Dodona. For now, it is our only source of prophecy. And since our communication problems have not gone away, learning to use the grove's power is all the more critical."

Rachel tried to hide it, but I could see her disappointment in the lines around her mouth. "What about Meg?" she asked. "You'll try to find her, won't you?"

She might as well have plunged the Arrow of Dodona into my chest. I gazed at the woods—that hazy green expanse that had swallowed young McCaffrey. For a brief moment, I felt like Nero. I wanted to burn the whole place down.

"I will try," I said, "but Meg doesn't want to be found. She's under the influence of her stepfather."

Percy traced his finger across the Athena Parthenos's big toe. "I've lost too many people to bad influence: Ethan Nakamura, Luke Castellan . . . We almost lost Nico, too. . . ." He shook his head. "No. No more. You can't give up on Meg. You guys are bound together. Besides, she's one of the good guys."

"I've known many of the good guys," I said. "Most of them got turned into beasts, or statues, or—or trees. . . ." My voice broke.

Rachel put her hand over mine. "Things can turn out differently, Apollo. That's the nice thing about being human. We only have one life, but we can choose what kind of story it's going to be."

That seemed hopelessly optimistic. I had spent too many centuries watching the same patterns of behavior be repeated over and over, all by humans who thought they were being terribly clever and doing something that had never been done before. They thought they were crafting their own stories, but they were only tracing over the same old narratives, generation after generation.

Still . . . perhaps human persistence was an asset. They never seemed to give up hope. Every so often they *did* manage to surprise me. I never anticipated Alexander the Great, Robin Hood, or Billie Holiday. For that matter, I never anticipated Percy Jackson and Rachel Elizabeth Dare.

"I—I hope you're right," I said.

She patted my hand. "Tell me the prophecy you heard in the grove."

I took a shaky breath. I didn't want to speak the words. I was afraid they might wake the grove and drown us in a cacophony of prophecies, bad jokes, and infomercials. But I recited the lines:

> *"There once was a god named Apollo*
> *Who plunged in a cave blue and hollow*
> *Upon a three-seater*
> *The bronze fire-eater*
> *Was forced death and madness to swallow."*

Rachel covered her mouth. "A limerick?"

"I know!" I wailed. "I'm doomed!"

"Wait." Percy's eyes glittered. "Those lines . . . Do they mean what I think?"

"Well," I said, "I believe the blue cave refers to the Oracle of Trophonius. It was a . . . a very dangerous ancient Oracle."

"No," Percy said. "The *other* lines. *Three-seater, bronze fire-eater*, yadda yadda."

"Oh. I have no clue about those."

"Harley's beacon." Percy laughed, though I could not understand why he was so pleased. "He said you gave it a tuning adjustment? I guess that did the trick."

Rachel squinted at him. "Percy, what are you . . ." Her expression went slack. "Oh. *Oh.*"

"Were there any other lines?" Percy urged. "Like, except for the limerick?"

"Several," I admitted. "Just bits and pieces I didn't understand. *The fall of the sun; the final verse.* Um, *Indiana, banana. Happiness approaches.* Something about *pages burning.*"

Percy slapped his knee. "There you go. *Happiness approaches.* Happy is a name—well, the English version, anyway." He stood and scanned the horizon. His eyes fixed on something in the distance. A grin spread across his face. "Yep. Apollo, your escort is on the way."

I followed his gaze. Spiraling down from the clouds was a large winged creature that glinted of Celestial bronze. On its back were two human-size figures.

Their descent was silent, but in my mind a joyous fanfare of Valdezinator music proclaimed the good news.

Leo had returned.

39

Want to hit Leo?
That is understandable
Hunk Muffin earned it

THE DEMIGODS HAD TO TAKE NUMBERS.

Nico commandeered a dispenser from the snack bar and carried it around, yelling, "The line starts to the left! Orderly queue, guys!"

"Is this really necessary?" Leo asked.

"Yes," said Miranda Gardiner, who had drawn the first number. She punched Leo in the arm.

"Ow," said Leo.

"You're a jerk, and we all hate you," said Miranda. Then she hugged him and kissed his cheek. "If you ever disappear like that again, we'll line up to *kill you*."

"Okay, okay!"

Miranda had to move on, because the line was getting pretty long behind her. Percy and I sat at the picnic table with Leo and his companion—none other than the immortal sorceress Calypso. Even though Leo was the one getting punched by everyone in camp, I was reasonably sure he was the *least* uncomfortable one at the table.

When they first saw each other, Percy and Calypso had hugged awkwardly. I hadn't witnessed such a tense greeting since Patroclus met Achilles's war prize, Briseis. (Long story. Juicy gossip. Ask me later.) Calypso had never liked me, so she pointedly ignored me, but I kept waiting for her to yell "BOO!" and turn me into a tree frog. The suspense was killing me.

Percy hugged Leo and didn't even punch him. Still, the son of Poseidon looked disgruntled.

"I can't believe it," he said. "Six months—"

"I told you," Leo said. "We tried sending more holographic scrolls. We tried Iris messages, dream visions, phone calls. Nothing worked.— Ow! Hey, Alice, how you doing?— Anyway, we ran into one crisis after another."

Calypso nodded. "Albania was particularly difficult."

From down the line, Nico di Angelo yelled, "Please do not mention Albania! Okay, who's next, folks? One line."

Damien White punched Leo's arm and walked away grinning. I wasn't sure Damien even knew Leo. He simply couldn't turn down a chance to punch someone.

Leo rubbed his bicep. "Hey, no fair. That guy's getting back in the line. So, like I was saying, if Festus hadn't picked up on that homing beacon yesterday, we'd still be flying around, looking for a way out of the Sea of Monsters."

"Oh, I hate that place," Percy said. "There's this big Cyclops, Polyphemus—"

"I know, right?" Leo agreed. "What is up with that guy's *breath?*"

"Boys," Calypso said, "perhaps we should focus on the present?"

She did not look at me, but I got the impression she meant *this silly former god and his problems*.

"Yeah," Percy said. "So the communication issues . . . Rachel Dare thinks it's got something to do with this company, Triumvirate."

Rachel herself had gone to the Big House to fetch Chiron, but Percy did a reasonable job summarizing what she had found out about the emperors and their evil corporation. Of course, we didn't know very much. By the time six more people had punched Leo in the arm, Percy had brought Leo and Calypso up to speed.

Leo rubbed his new bruises. "Man, why does it not surprise me that modern corporations are run by zombie Roman emperors?"

"They are not zombies," I said. "And I'm not sure they run *all* corporations—"

Leo waved away my explanation. "But they're trying to take over the Oracles."

"Yes," I agreed.

"And that's bad."

"Very."

"So you need our help.— Ow! Hey, Sherman. Where'd you get the new scar, dude?"

While Sherman told Leo the story of Crotchkicker McCaffrey and the Demon Peach Baby, I glanced at Calypso.

She looked very different from what I remembered. Her hair was still long and caramel brown. Her almond-shaped eyes were still dark and intelligent. But now, instead of a *chiton* she wore modern jeans, a white blouse, and a shocking-pink ski jacket. She looked younger—about my mortal age. I wondered if she had been punished with mortality for leaving her enchanted island. If so, it didn't seem fair that she had retained her otherworldly beauty. She had neither flab nor acne.

As I watched, she stretched two fingers toward the opposite end of the picnic table, where a pitcher of lemonade sweated in the sunlight. I had seen her do this sort of thing before, willing her invisible aerial servants to whisk objects into her hands. This time, nothing happened.

A look of disappointment crossed her face. Then she realized I was watching. Her cheeks colored.

"Since leaving Ogygia, I have no powers," she admitted. "I am fully mortal. I keep hoping, but—"

"You want a drink?" Percy asked.

"I got it." Leo beat him to the pitcher.

I had not expected to feel sympathy for Calypso. We'd had harsh words in the past. A few millennia ago, I had opposed her petition for early release from Ogygia because of some . . . ah, drama between us. (Long story. Juicy gossip. Please *do not* ask me later.)

Still, as a fallen god, I understood how disconcerting it was to be without one's powers.

On the other hand, I was relieved. This meant she could not turn me into a tree frog or order her aerial servants to toss me off the Athena Parthenos.

"Here you go." Leo handed her a glass of lemonade. His expression seemed darker and more anxious, as if . . . Ah, of course. Leo had rescued Calypso from her prison island. In doing so, Calypso had lost her powers. Leo felt responsible.

Calypso smiled, though her eyes were still touched by melancholy. "Thank you, babe."

"*Babe?*" Percy asked.

Leo's expression brightened. "Yeah. She won't call me Hunk Muffin, though. I dunno why.— Ow!"

It was Harley's turn. The little boy punched Leo, then threw his arms around him and broke down sobbing.

"Hey, brother." Leo ruffled his hair and had the good sense to look ashamed. "You brought me home with that beacon of yours, H-Meister. You're a hero! You know I never would've left you hanging like that on purpose, don't you?"

Harley wailed and sniffled and nodded. Then punched Leo again and ran away. Leo looked like he was about to get sick. Harley was quite strong.

"At any rate," Calypso said, "these problems with the Roman emperors—how can we help?"

I raised my eyebrows. "You *will* help me, then? Despite . . . ah, well, I always knew you were kindhearted and forgiving, Calypso. I meant to visit you at Ogygia more often—"

"Spare me." Calypso sipped her lemonade. "I'll help you if *Leo* decides to help you, and he seems to have some affection for you. Why, I can't imagine."

I let go of the breath I had been holding for . . . oh, an hour. "I'm grateful. Leo Valdez, you have always been a gentleman and a genius. After all, you created the Valdezinator."

Leo grinned. "I did, didn't I? I suppose that was pretty awesome. So where is this next Oracle you— Ow!"

Nyssa had made it to the front of the line. She slapped Leo, then berated him in rapid Spanish.

"Yeah, okay, okay." Leo rubbed his face. "Dang, *hermana*, I love you, too!"

He turned his attention back to me. "So this next Oracle, you said it was where?"

Percy tapped the picnic table. "Chiron and I were talking about this. He figures this triumvirate thingie . . . they probably divided America into three parts, with one emperor in charge of each. We know Nero is holed up in New York, so we're guessing this next Oracle is in the second dude's territory, maybe in the middle third of the U.S."

"Oh, the middle third of the U.S.!" Leo spread his arms. "Piece of torta, then. We'll just search the entire middle of the country!"

"Still with the sarcasm," Percy noted.

"Hey, man, I've sailed with the most sarcastic scalawags on the high seas."

The two gave each other a high five, though I did not quite understand why. I thought about a snippet of prophecy I'd heard in the grove: something about Indiana. It might be a place to start. . . .

The last person to come through the line was Chiron himself, pushed in his wheelchair by Rachel Dare. The old centaur gave Leo a warm, fatherly smile. "My boy, I am so pleased to have you back. And you freed Calypso, I see. Well done, and welcome, both of you!" Chiron spread his arms for a hug.

"Uh, thanks, Chiron." Leo leaned forward.

From underneath Chiron's lap blanket, his equine foreleg shot out and implanted a hoof in Leo's gut. Then, just as quickly, the leg disappeared. "Mr. Valdez," Chiron said in the same kindly tone, "if you ever pull a stunt like that again—"

"I got it, I got it!" Leo rubbed his stomach. "Dang, for a teacher, you got a heck of a high kick."

Rachel grinned and wheeled Chiron away. Calypso and Percy helped Leo to his feet.

"Yo, Nico," Leo called, "please tell me that's it for the physical abuse."

"For now." Nico smiled. "We're still trying to get in touch with the West Coast. You'll have a few dozen people out there who will definitely want to hit you."

Leo winced. "Yeah, that's something to look forward to. Well, I guess I'd better keep my strength up. Where do you guys eat lunch now that the Colossus stepped on the dining pavilion?"

Percy left that night just before dinner.

I expected a moving one-on-one farewell, during which he would ask my advice about test taking, being a hero, and living life in general. After he lent me his help in defeating the Colossus, it would have been the least I could do.

Instead, he seemed more interested in saying good-bye to Leo and Calypso. I wasn't part of their conversation, but the three of them seemed to reach some sort of mutual understanding. Percy and Leo embraced. Calypso even pecked Percy on the cheek. Then the son of Poseidon waded into Long Island Sound with his extremely large dog and they both disappeared underwater. Did Mrs. O'Leary swim? Did she travel through the shadows of whales? I did not know.

Like lunch, dinner was a casual affair. As darkness fell, we ate on picnic blankets around the hearth, which blazed with Hestia's warmth and kept away the winter chill. Festus the dragon sniffed around the perimeter of the cabins, occasionally blowing fire into the sky for no apparent reason.

"He got a little dinged up in Corsica," Leo explained. "Sometimes he spews randomly like that."

"He hasn't blowtorched anyone important yet," Calypso added, her eyebrow arched. "We'll see how he likes you."

Festus's red jewel eyes gleamed in the darkness. After driving the sun chariot for so long, I wasn't nervous about riding a metal dragon, but when I thought about what we'd be riding *toward*, geraniums bloomed in my stomach.

"I had planned to go alone," I told them. "The prophecy from Dodona speaks of the bronze fire-eater, but . . . it feels wrong for me to ask you to risk your lives. You have been through so much just to get here."

Calypso tilted her head. "Perhaps you *have* changed. That does not sound like the Apollo I remember. You definitely are not as handsome."

"I am still *quite* handsome," I protested. "I just need to clear up this acne."

She smirked. "So you haven't completely lost your big head."

"I beg your pardon?"

"Guys," Leo interrupted, "if we're going to travel together, let's try to keep it friendly." He pressed an ice pack to his bruised bicep. "Besides, we were planning to head west anyway. I got to find my peeps Jason and Piper and Frank and Hazel and . . . well, pretty much everybody at Camp Jupiter, I guess. It'll be fun."

"*Fun?*" I asked. "The Oracle of Trophonius will supposedly swallow me in death and madness. Even if I survive that, my other trials will no doubt be long, harrowing, and quite possibly fatal."

"Exactly," Leo said. "Fun. I don't know about calling the whole quest thing *Apollo's trials*, though. I think we should call it *Leo Valdez's Victory Lap World Tour*."

Calypso laughed and laced her fingers in Leo's. She may not have been immortal anymore, but she still had a grace and easiness about her that I could not fathom. Perhaps she missed her powers, but she seemed genuinely happy to be with Valdez—to be young and mortal, even if it meant she could die at any moment.

Unlike me, she had *chosen* to become mortal. She knew that leaving Ogygia was a risk, but she had done it willingly. I didn't know how she'd found the courage.

"Hey, man," Leo told me. "Don't look so glum. We'll find her."

I stirred. "What?"

"Your friend Meg. We'll find her. Don't worry."

A bubble of darkness burst inside me. For once, I hadn't been thinking of Meg. I'd been thinking about myself, and that made me feel guilty. Perhaps Calypso was right to question whether or not I'd changed.

I gazed at the silent forest. I remembered Meg dragging me to safety when I was cold and soaked and delirious. I remembered how fearlessly she fought the myrmekes, and how she'd ordered Peaches to extinguish the match when Nero wanted to burn his hostages, despite her fear of unleashing the Beast. I had to make her realize how evil Nero was. I had to find her. But how?

"Meg knows the prophecy," I said. "If she tells Nero, he will know our plans as well."

Calypso took a bite of her apple. "I missed the whole Roman Empire. How bad can one emperor be?"

"Bad," I assured her. "And he is allied with two others. We don't know which ones, but it's safe to assume they are equally cutthroat. They've had centuries to amass fortunes, acquire property, build armies . . . Who knows what they are capable of?"

"Eh," Leo said. "We took down Gaea in, like, forty seconds. This'll be easy squeezy."

I seemed to recall that the *lead-up* to the fight with Gaea had involved months of suffering and near misses with death. Leo, in fact, *had* died. I also wanted to remind him that the Triumvirate might well have orchestrated all our previous troubles with the Titans and giants, which would make them more powerful than anything Leo had ever faced.

I decided that mentioning these things might affect group morale.

"We'll succeed," Calypso said. "We must. So we will. I have been trapped on an island for thousands of years. I don't know how long this mortal life will be, but I intend to live fully and without fear."

"That's my *mamacita*," Leo said.

"What have I told you about calling me *mamacita*?"

Leo grinned sheepishly. "In the morning we'll start getting our supplies together. As soon as Festus gets a tune-up and an oil change, we'll be good to go."

I considered what supplies I would take with me. I had

depressingly little: some borrowed clothes, a bow, a ukulele, and an overly theatrical arrow.

But the real difficulty would be saying good-bye to Will, Austin, and Kayla. They had helped me so much, and they embraced me as family more than I had ever embraced *them*. Tears stung my eyes. Before I could start sobbing, Will Solace stepped into the light of the hearth. "Hey, everybody! We've started a bonfire in the amphitheater! Sing-along time. Come on!"

Groans were mixed in with the cheers, but most everyone got to their feet and ambled toward the bonfire now blazing in the distance, where Nico di Angelo stood silhouetted in the flames, preparing rows of marshmallows on what looked like femur bones.

"Aw, man." Leo winced. "I'm terrible at sing-alongs. I always clap and do the 'Old MacDonald' sounds at the wrong time. Can we skip this?"

"Oh, no." I rose to my feet, suddenly feeling better. Perhaps tomorrow I would weep and think about good-byes. Perhaps the day after that we would be flying toward our deaths. But tonight, I intended to enjoy my time with my family. What had Calypso said? *Live fully and without fear.* If she could do it, then so could the brilliant, fabulous Apollo. "Singing is good for the spirits. You should never miss an opportunity to sing."

Calypso smiled. "I can't believe I'm saying this, but for once I agree with Apollo. Come on, Leo. I'll teach you to harmonize."

Together, the three of us walked toward the sounds of laughter, music, and a warm, crackling fire.

GUIDE TO APOLLO-SPEAK

Achilles   the best fighter of the Greeks who besieged Troy in the Trojan War; extraordinarily strong, courageous, and loyal, he had only one weak spot: his heel

Admetus   the king of Pherae in Thessaly; Zeus punished Apollo by sending him to work for Admetus as a shepherd

Aeolus   the Greek god of the winds

Agamemnon   king of Mycenae; the leader of the Greeks in the Trojan War; courageous, but also arrogant and overly proud

agora   Greek for *gathering place*; a central outdoor spot for athletic, artistic, spiritual, and political life in ancient Greek city-states

Ajax   Greek hero with great strength and courage; fought in the Trojan War; used a large shield in battle

ambrosia   food of the gods; has healing powers

amphitheater   an oval or circular open-air space used for performances or sporting events, with spectator seating built in a semicircle around the stage

Aphrodite   the Greek goddess of love and beauty

apodesmos   a band of material that women in ancient Greece wore around the chest, particularly while participating in sports

Apollo   the Greek god of the sun, prophecy, music, and healing; the son of Zeus and Leto, and the twin of Artemis

Ares   the Greek god of war; the son of Zeus and Hera, and half brother to Athena

Argo   the ship used by a band of heroes who accompanied Jason on his quest to find the Golden Fleece

Argonauts   a band of heroes who sailed with Jason on the *Argo*, in search of the Golden Fleece

Artemis   the Greek goddess of the hunt and the moon; the daughter of Zeus and Leto, and the twin of Apollo

Asclepius   the god of medicine; son of Apollo; his temple was the healing center of ancient Greece

Athena   the Greek goddess of wisdom

Athena Parthenos   a giant statue of Athena; the most famous Greek statue of all time

ballista (ballistae, pl.)   a Roman missile siege weapon that launched a large projectile at a distant target

Batavi   an ancient tribe that lived in modern-day Germany; also an infantry unit in the Roman army with Germanic origins

Briseis   a princess captured by Achilles during the Trojan War, causing a feud between Achilles and Agamemnon that resulted in Achilles refusing to fight alongside the Greeks

Bunker Nine a hidden workshop Leo Valdez discovered at Camp Half-Blood, filled with tools and weapons; it is at least two hundred years old and was used during the Demigod Civil War

Caesar Augustus the founder and first emperor of the Roman Empire; adopted son and heir of Julius Caesar (*see also* Octavian)

Calliope the muse of epic poetry; mother of several sons, including Orpheus

Calypso the goddess nymph of the mythical island of Ogygia; a daughter of the Titan Atlas; she detained the hero Odysseus for many years

Camp Half-Blood the training ground for Greek demigods, located in Long Island, New York

Camp Jupiter the training ground for Roman demigods, located between the Oakland Hills and the Berkeley Hills, in California

Cassandra the daughter of King Priam and Queen Hecuba; had the gift of prophecy, but was cursed by Apollo so that her predictions were never believed, including her warning about the Trojan Horse

catapult a military machine used to hurl objects

Cave of Trophonius a deep chasm home to the Oracle Trophonius; its extremely narrow entrance required a visitor to lie flat on his back before being sucked into the cave; called "The Cave of Nightmares" due to the terrifying accounts of its visitors

Celestial bronze a rare metal deadly to monsters

centaur a race of creatures that is half-human, half-horse

Ceres   the Roman god of agriculture; Greek form: Demeter

Chiron   a centaur; the camp activities director at Camp Half-Blood

chiton   a Greek garment; a sleeveless piece of linen or wool secured at the shoulders by brooches and at the waist by a belt

Chrysothemis   a daughter of Demeter who won Apollo's love during a music contest

Circe   a Greek goddess of magic

Cloacina   goddess of the Roman sewer system

Clytemnestra   the daughter of the king and queen of Sparta; married and later murdered Agamemnon

Colosseum   an elliptical amphitheater in the center of Rome, Italy, capable of seating fifty thousand spectators; used for gladiatorial contests and public spectacles such as mock sea battles, animal hunts, executions, re-enactments of famous battles, and dramas

Colossus Neronis (Colossus of Nero)   a gigantic bronze statue of Emperor Nero; was later transformed into the sun god with the addition of a sunray crown

Cretan   of the island of Crete

Crommyon   a village in ancient Greece where a giant wild sow wreaked havoc before it was killed by Theseus

cuirass   leather or metal armor consisting of a breastplate and backplate worn by Greek and Roman soldiers; often highly ornamented and designed to mimic muscles

Cyclops (Cyclopes, pl.)   a member of a primordial race of giants, each with a single eye in the middle of his or her forehead

Cyrene   a fierce huntress with whom Apollo fell in love after he saw her wrestle a lion; Apollo later transformed her into a nymph in order to extend her life

Daedalus   a skilled craftsman who created the Labyrinth on Crete in which the Minotaur (part man, part bull) was kept

Daphne   a beautiful naiad who attracted Apollo's attention; she was transformed into a laurel tree in order to escape him

Demeter   the Greek goddess of agriculture; a daughter of the Titans Rhea and Kronos; Roman form: Ceres

dimachaerus   a Roman gladiator trained to fight with two swords at once

Dionysus   the Greek god of wine and revelry; the son of Zeus; activities director at Camp Half-Blood

Domus Aurea   Emperor Nero's extravagant villa in the heart of ancient Rome, built after the Great Fire of Rome

Doors of Death   the doorway to the House of Hades, located in Tartarus; doors have two sides—one in the mortal world, and one in the Underworld

drakon   a gigantic yellow-and-green serpentlike monster, with frills around its neck, reptilian eyes, and huge talons; it spits poison

dryads   tree nymphs

Erebos   a place of darkness between earth and Hades

Eros   the Greek god of love

Erythaea   an island where the Cumaean Sibyl, a love interest of Apollo, originally lived before he convinced her to leave it by promising her a long life

Fields of Punishment the section of the Underworld where people who were evil during their lives are sent to face eternal punishment for their crimes after death

Gaea the Greek earth goddess; mother of Titans, giants, Cyclopes, and other monsters

Germani (Germanus, sing.) tribal people who settled to the west of the Rhine river

Golden Fleece this hide from a gold-haired winged ram was a symbol of authority and kingship; it was guarded by a dragon and fire-breathing bulls; Jason was tasked with obtaining it, resulting in an epic quest

Gorgons three monstrous sisters (Stheno, Euryale, and Medusa) who have hair of living, venomous snakes; Medusa's eyes can turn the beholder to stone

Great Fire of Rome a devastating fire that took place in 64 CE, lasting for six days; rumors indicated that Nero started the fire to clear space for the building of his villa, Domus Aurea, but he blamed the Christian community for the disaster

greaves shin armor

Greek fire an incendiary weapon used in naval battles because it can continue burning in water

Grove of Dodona the site of the oldest Greek Oracle, second only to the Delphi; the rustling of trees in the grove provided answers to priests and priestesses who journeyed to the site

Hades the Greek god of death and riches; ruler of the Underworld

harpy a winged female creature that snatches things

Hebe   the Greek goddess of youth; daughter of Zeus and Hera

Hecate   goddess of magic and crossroads

Hephaestus   the Greek god of fire and crafts and of blacksmiths; the son of Zeus and Hera, and married to Aphrodite

Hera   the Greek goddess of marriage; Zeus's wife and sister

Hermes   Greek god of travelers; guide to spirits of the dead; god of communication

Herodotus   a Greek historian known as the "Father of History"

Hestia   Greek goddess of the hearth

hippocampi (**hippocampus**, sing.)   half-horse, half-fish creatures

hippodrome   an oval stadium for horse and chariot races in ancient Greece

Hittites   a group of people who lived in modern Turkey and Syria; often in conflict with Egyptians; known for their use of chariots as assault weapons

House of Hades   a place in the Underworld where Hades, the Greek god of death, and his wife, Persephone, rule over the souls of the departed

Hunters of Artemis   a group of maidens loyal to Artemis and gifted with hunting skills and eternal youth as long as they reject men for life

Hyacinthus   a Greek hero and Apollo's lover, who died while trying to impress Apollo with his discus skills

Hypnos   the Greek god of sleep

ichor   the golden fluid that is the blood of gods and immortals

imperator   a term for *commander* in the Roman Empire

Imperial gold   a rare metal deadly to monsters, consecrated at the Pantheon; its existence was a closely guarded secret of the emperors

Iris   the Greek goddess of the rainbow, and a messenger of the gods

Julian dynasty   the time period measured from the battle of Actium (31 BCE) to the death of Nero (68 CE)

karpoi (*karpos*, sing.)   grain spirits

kouretes   armored dancers who guarded the infant Zeus from his father, Kronos

Kronos   the youngest of the twelve Titans; the son of Ouranos and Gaea; the father of Zeus; he killed his father at his mother's bidding; Titan lord of fate, harvest, justice, and time; Roman form: Saturn

Labyrinth   an underground maze originally built on the island of Crete by the craftsman Daedalus to hold the Minotaur

Laomedon   a Trojan king whom Poseidon and Apollo were sent to serve after they offended Zeus

Lepidus   a Roman patrician and military commander who was in a triumvirate with Octavian and Marc Antony

Leto   mother of Artemis and Apollo with Zeus; goddess of motherhood

Lupercalia   a pastoral festival, observed on February 13 through 15, to avert evil spirits and purify the city, releasing health and fertility

Lydia   a province in ancient Rome; the double ax origi-
nated there, along with the use of coins and retail shops

Marc Antony   a Roman politician and general; part of the
triumvirate, with Lepidus and Octavian, who together
tracked down and defeated Caesar's killers; had an
enduring affair with Cleopatra

Marsyas   a satyr who lost to Apollo after challenging him
in a musical contest, which led to Marsyas being flayed
alive

Medea   a follower of Hecate and one of the great sorcer-
esses of the ancient world

Midas   a king with the power to transform anything he
touched to gold; he selected Marsyas as the winner
in the musical contest between Apollo and Marsyas,
resulting in Apollo giving Midas the ears of a donkey

Minos   king of Crete; son of Zeus; every year he made King
Aegus pick seven boys and seven girls to be sent to the
Labyrinth, where they would be eaten by the Minotaur;
after his death he became a judge in the Underworld

Minotaur   the half-man, half-bull son of King Minos of
Crete; the Minotaur was kept in the Labyrinth, where he
killed people who were sent in; he was finally defeated
by Theseus

Mithridates   king of Pontus and Armenia Minor in north-
ern Anatolia (now Turkey) from about 120 to 63 BCE;
one of the Roman Republic's most formidable and
successful enemies, who engaged three of the prom-
inent generals from the late Roman Republic in the
Mithridatic Wars

Mount Olympus   home of the Twelve Olympians

myrmeke   a giant antlike creature that poisons and paralyzes its prey before eating it; known for protecting various metals, particularly gold

Nemesis   the Greek goddess of revenge

Nero   Roman emperor from 54 to 68 CE; the last in the Julian dynasty

New Rome   a community near Camp Jupiter where demigods can live together in peace, without interference from mortals or monsters

Nike   the Greek goddess of strength, speed, and victory

Nine Muses   Greek goddesses of literature, science, and the arts, who have inspired artists and writers for centuries

Niobe   daughter of Tantalus and Dione; suffered the loss of her six sons and six daughters, who were killed by Apollo and Artemis as a punishment for her pride

nosoi (*nosos*, sing.)   spirits of plague and disease

nymph   a female nature deity who animates nature

Octavian   the founder and first emperor of the Roman Empire; adopted son and heir of Julius Caesar (*see also* Caesar Augustus)

Odysseus   legendary Greek king of Ithaca and the hero of Homer's epic poem *The Odyssey*

Ogygia   the island home—and prison—of the nymph Calypso

omphalus   stones used to mark the center—or navel—of the world

Oracle of Delphi   a speaker of the prophecies of Apollo

Oracle of Trophonius a Greek who was transformed into an Oracle after his death; located at the Cave of Trophonius; known for terrifying those who seek him

Ouranos the Greek personification of the sky; father of the Titans

palikoi (*palikos*, sing.) twin sons of Zeus and Thaleia; the gods of geysers and thermal springs

Pan the Greek god of the wild; the son of Hermes

Pandora the first human woman created by the gods; endowed with a unique gift from each; released evil into the world by opening a jar

Parthenon a temple dedicated to the goddess Athena located at the Athenian Acropolis in Greece

Patroclus son of Menoetius; he shared a deep friendship with Achilles after being raised alongside him; he was killed while fighting in the Trojan War

pegasus (**pegasi**, pl.) a winged divine horse; sired by Poseidon, in his role as horse-god

Peleus father of Achilles; his wedding to the sea-nymph Thetis was well attended by the gods, and a disagreement between them at the event eventually lead to the Trojan War; the guardian dragon at Camp Half-Blood is named after him

Persephone the Greek queen of the Underworld; wife of Hades; daughter of Zeus and Demeter

phalanx (**phalanxes**, pl.) a compact body of heavily armed troops

Phidias a famous ancient Greek sculptor who created the Athena Parthenos and many others

Polyphemus the gigantic one-eyed son of Poseidon and Thoosa; one of the Cyclopes

Poseidon the Greek god of the sea; son of the Titans Kronos and Rhea, and brother of Zeus and Hades

praetor an elected Roman magistrate and commander of the army

Primordial Chaos the first thing ever to exist; a void from which the first gods were produced

Prometheus the Titan who created humans and gifted them with fire stolen from Mount Olympus

Pythia the name given to every Oracle of Delphi

Python a monstrous serpent that Gaea appointed to guard the Oracle at Delphi

Rhea Silvia the queen of the Titans, mother of Zeus

Riptide the name of Percy Jackson's sword; *Anaklusmos* in Greek

River Styx the river that forms the boundary between earth and the Underworld

Saturnalia an ancient Roman festival celebrating Saturn (Kronos)

satyr a Greek forest god, part goat and part man

shadow-travel a form of transportation that allows creatures of the Underworld and children of Hades to use shadows to leap to any desired place on earth or in the Underworld, although it makes the user extremely fatigued

Sibyl a prophetess

Sibylline Books a collection of prophecies in rhyme written in Greek; Tarquinius Superbus, a king of Rome, bought them from a prophetess and consulted them in times of great danger

siccae   a short curved sword used for battle in ancient Rome

Sparta   a city-state in ancient Greece with military dominance

Stygian iron   a magical metal, forged in the River Styx, capable of absorbing the very essence of monsters and injuring mortals, gods, Titans, and giants; has a significant effect on ghosts and creatures from the Underworld

Talos   a giant mechanical man made of bronze and used on Crete to guard its shoreline from invaders

Tantalus   According to legend, this king was such a good friend of the gods that he was allowed to dine at their table—until he spilled their secrets on earth; he was sent to the Underworld, where his curse was to be stuck in a pool of water under a fruit tree, but never be able to drink or eat

Tartarus   husband of Gaea; spirit of the abyss; father of the giants; a region of the Underworld

Theodosius   the last to rule over the united Roman Empire; known for closing all ancient temples across the empire

Thracian   of Thrace, a region centered on the modern borders of Bulgaria, Greece, and Turkey

Titan War   the epic ten-year battle between the Titans and the Olympians that resulted in the Olympians taking the throne

Titans   a race of powerful Greek deities, descendants of Gaea and Ouranos, that ruled during the Golden Age and were overthrown by a race of younger gods, the Olympians

trireme   a Greek warship, having three tiers of oars on each side

triumvirate   a political alliance formed by three parties

Trojan War   According to legend, the Trojan War was waged against the city of Troy by the Achaeans (Greeks) after Paris of Troy took Helen from her husband, Menelaus, king of Sparta

Troy   a Roman city situated in modern-day Turkey; site of the Trojan War

Tyche   the Greek goddess of good fortune; daughter of Hermes and Aphrodite

Typhon   the most terrifying Greek monster; father of many famous monsters, including Cerberus, the vicious multi-headed dog tasked with guarding the entrance to the Underworld

Underworld   the kingdom of the dead, where souls go for eternity; ruled by Hades

Zephyros   the Greek god of the West Wind

Zeus   the Greek god of the sky and the king of the gods

Can't get enough of Apollo? Read the first chapter of
Book Two in the Trials of Apollo series,
THE DARK PROPHECY

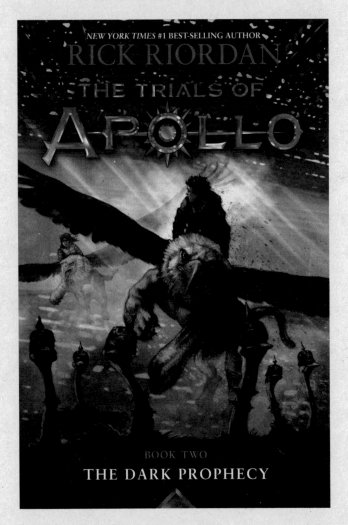

1

Lester (Apollo)
Still human; thanks for asking
Gods, I hate my life

WHEN OUR DRAGON declared war on Indiana, I knew it was going to be a bad day.

We'd been traveling west for six weeks, and Festus had never shown such hostility toward a state. New Jersey he ignored. Pennsylvania he seemed to enjoy, despite our battle with the Cyclopes of Pittsburgh. Ohio he tolerated, even after our encounter with Potina, the Roman goddess of childhood drinks, who pursued us in the form of a giant red pitcher emblazoned with a smiley face.

Yet for some reason, Festus decided he did not like Indiana. He landed on the cupola of the Indiana Statehouse, flapped his metallic wings, and blew a cone of fire that incinerated the state flag right off the flagpole.

"Whoa, buddy!" Leo Valdez pulled the dragon's reins. "We've talked about this. No blowtorching public monuments!"

Behind him on the dragon's spine, Calypso gripped Festus's scales for balance. "Could we *please* get to the ground? *Gently* this time?"

For a formerly immortal sorceress who once controlled air spirits, Calypso was not a fan of flying. Cold wind blew her chestnut hair into my face, making me blink and spit.

That's right, dear reader.

I, the most important passenger, the youth who had once been the glorious god Apollo, was forced to sit in the back of the dragon. Oh, the indignities I had suffered since Zeus stripped me of my divine powers! It wasn't enough that I was now a sixteen-year-old mortal with the ghastly alias Lester Papadopoulos. It wasn't enough that I had to toil upon the earth doing (ugh) heroic quests until I could find a way back into my father's good graces, or that I had a case of acne which simply *would not* respond to over-the-counter zit medicine. Despite my New York State junior driver's license, Leo Valdez didn't trust me to operate his aerial bronze steed!

Festus's claws scrabbled for a hold on the green copper dome, which was much too small for a dragon his size. I had a flashback to the time I installed a life-size statue of the muse Calliope on my sun chariot and the extra weight of the hood ornament made me nosedive into China and create the Gobi Desert.

Leo glanced back, his face streaked with soot. "Apollo, you sense anything?"

"Why is it *my* job to sense things? Just because I used to be a god of prophecy—"

"You're the one who's been having visions," Calypso reminded me. "You said your friend Meg would be here."

Just hearing Meg's name gave me a twinge of pain. "That doesn't mean I can pinpoint her location with my mind! Zeus has revoked my access to GPS!"

"GPS?" Calypso asked.

"Godly positioning systems."

"That's not a real thing!"

"Guys, cool it." Leo patted the dragon's neck. "Apollo, just try, will you? Does this look like the city you dreamed about or not?"

I scanned the horizon.

Indiana was flat country—highways crisscrossing scrubby

brown plains, shadows of winter clouds floating above urban sprawl. Around us rose a meager cluster of downtown high-rises—stacks of stone and glass like layered wedges of black and white licorice. (Not the yummy kind of licorice, either; the nasty variety that sits for eons in your stepmother's candy bowl on the coffee table. And, no, Hera, why would I be talking about you?)

After falling to earth in New York City, I found Indianapolis desolate and uninspiring, as if one proper New York neighborhood—Midtown, perhaps—had been stretched out to encompass the entire area of Manhattan, then relieved of two-thirds of its population and vigorously power-washed.

I could think of no reason why an evil triumvirate of ancient Roman emperors would take interest in such a location. Nor could I imagine why Meg McCaffrey would be sent here to capture me. Yet my visions had been clear. I had seen this skyline. I had heard my old enemy Nero give orders to Meg: *Go west. Capture Apollo before he can find the next Oracle. If you cannot bring him to me alive, kill him.*

The truly sad thing about this? Meg was one of my better friends. She also happened to be my demigod master, thanks to Zeus's twisted sense of humor. As long as I remained mortal, Meg could order me to do anything, even kill myself. . . . No. Better not to think of such possibilities.

I shifted in my metal seat. After so many weeks of travel, I was tired and saddle sore. I wanted to find a safe place to rest. *This* was not such a city. Something about the landscape below made me as restless as Festus.

Alas, I was sure this was where we were meant to be. Despite the danger, if I had a chance of seeing Meg McCaffrey again, of prying her away from her villainous stepfather's grasp, I had to try.

"This is the spot," I said. "Before this dome collapses under us, I suggest we get to the ground."

Calypso grumbled in ancient Minoan, "I already *said* that."

"Well, excuse me, sorceress!" I replied in the same language. "Perhaps if *you* had helpful visions, I'd listen to you more often!"

Calypso called me a few names that reminded me how colorful the Minoan language had been before it went extinct.

"Hey, you two," Leo said. "No ancient dialects. Spanish or English, please. Or Machine."

Festus creaked in agreement.

"It's okay, boy," Leo said. "I'm sure they didn't mean to exclude us. Now let's fly down to street level, huh?"

Festus's ruby eyes glowed. His metal teeth spun like drill bits. I imagined him thinking, *Illinois is sounding pretty good right about now.*

But he flapped his wings and leaped from the dome. We hurtled downward, landing in front of the statehouse with enough force to crack the sidewalk. My eyeballs jiggled like water balloons.

Festus whipped his head from side to side, steam curling from his nostrils.

I saw no immediate threats. Cars drove leisurely down West Washington Street. Pedestrians strolled by: a middle-aged woman in a flowery dress, a heavyset policeman carrying a paper coffee cup labeled CAFÉ PATACHOU, a clean-cut man in a blue seersucker suit.

The man in blue waved politely as he passed. "Morning."

"'Sup, dude," Leo called.

Calypso tilted her head. "Why was he so friendly? Does he not *see* that we're sitting atop a fifty-ton metal dragon?"

Leo grinned. "It's the Mist, babe—messes with mortal eyes. Makes monsters look like stray dogs. Makes swords look like umbrellas. Makes me look even more handsome than usual!"

Calypso jabbed her thumbs into Leo's kidneys.

"Ow!" he complained.

"I know what the Mist is, *Leonidas*—"

"Hey, I told you never to call me that."

"—but the Mist must be very strong here if it can hide a monster of Festus's size at such close range. Apollo, don't you find that a little odd?"

I studied the passing pedestrians.

True, I had seen places where the Mist was particularly heavy. At Troy, the sky above the battlefield had been so thick with gods you couldn't turn your chariot without running into another deity, yet the Trojans and Greeks saw only hints of our presence. At Three Mile Island in 1979, the mortals somehow failed to realize that their partial nuclear meltdown was caused by an epic chainsaw fight between Ares and Hephaestus. (As I recall, Hephaestus had insulted Ares's bell-bottom jeans.)

Still, I did not think heavy Mist was the problem here. Something about these locals bothered me. Their faces were too placid. Their dazed smiles reminded me of ancient Athenians just before the Dionysus Festival—everyone in a good mood, distracted, thinking about the drunken riots and debauchery to come.

"We should get out of the public eye," I suggested. "Perhaps—"

Festus stumbled, shaking like a wet dog. From inside his chest came a noise like a loose bicycle chain.

"Aw, not again," Leo said. "Everybody off!"

Calypso and I quickly dismounted.

Leo ran in front of Festus and held out his arms in a classic dragon-wrangler's stance. "Hey, buddy, it's fine! I'm just going to switch you off for a while, okay? A little downtime to—"

Festus projectile-vomited a column of flames that engulfed

Leo. Fortunately, Valdez was fireproof. His clothes were not. From what Leo had told me, he could generally prevent his outfits from burning up simply by concentrating. If he were caught by surprise, however, it didn't always work.

When the flames dissipated, Leo stood before us wearing nothing but his asbestos boxer shorts, his magical tool belt, and a pair of smoking, partially melted sneakers.

"Dang it!" he complained. "Festus, it's cold out here!"

The dragon stumbled. Leo lunged and flipped the lever behind the dragon's left foreleg. Festus began to collapse. His wings, limbs, neck, and tail contracted into his body, his bronze plates overlapping and folding inward. In a matter of seconds, our robotic friend had been reduced to a large bronze suitcase.

That should have been physically impossible, of course, but like any decent god, demigod, or engineer, Leo Valdez refused to be stopped by the laws of physics.

He scowled at his new piece of luggage. "Man . . . I *thought* I fixed his gyro-capacitor. Guess we're stuck here until I can find a machine shop."

Calypso grimaced. Her pink ski jacket glistened with condensation from our flight through the clouds. "And if we find such a shop, how long will it take to repair Festus?"

Leo shrugged. "Twelve hours? Fifteen?" He pushed a button on the side of the suitcase. A handle popped up. "Also, if we see a men's clothing store, that might be good."

I imagined walking into a T.J. Maxx, Leo in boxer shorts and melted sneakers, rolling a bronze suitcase behind him. I did not relish the idea.

Then, from the direction of the sidewalk, a voice called, "Hello!"

The woman in the flowery dress had returned. At least she *looked* like the same woman. Either that or lots of ladies in Indianapolis wore purple-and-yellow honeysuckle-pattern dresses and had 1950s bouffant hairstyles.

She smiled vacantly. "Beautiful morning!"

It was in fact a miserable morning—cold and cloudy with a smell of impending snow—but I felt it would be rude to ignore her completely.

I gave her a little parade wave—the sort of gesture I used to give my worshippers when they came to grovel at my altar. To me, the message was clear enough: *I see you, puny mortal; now run along. The gods are talking.*

The woman did not take the hint. She strolled forward and planted herself in front of us. She wasn't particularly large, but something about her proportions seemed off. Her shoulders were too wide for her head. Her chest and belly protruded in a lumpy mass, as if she'd stuffed a sack of mangos down the front of her dress. With her spindly arms and legs, she reminded me of some sort of giant beetle. If she ever tipped over, I doubted she could easily get back up.

"Oh, my!" She gripped her purse with both hands. "Aren't you children *cute*!"

Her lipstick and eye shadow were both a violent shade of purple. I wondered if she was getting enough oxygen to her brain.

"Madam," I said, "we are not children." I could have added that I was over four thousand years old, and Calypso was even older, but I decided not to get into that. "Now, if you'll excuse us, we have a suitcase to repair and my friend is in dire need of a pair of pants."

I tried to step around her. She blocked my path.

"You can't go yet, dear! We haven't welcomed you to Indiana!" From her purse, she drew a smartphone. The screen glowed as if a call were already in progress.

"It's him, all right," she said into the phone. "Everybody, come on over. Apollo is here!"

My lungs shriveled in my chest.

In the old days, I would have expected to be recognized as soon as I arrived in a town. *Of course* the locals would rush to welcome me. They would sing and dance and throw flowers. They would immediately begin constructing a new temple.

But as Lester Papadopoulos, I did not warrant such treatment. I looked nothing like my former glorious self. The idea that the Indianans might recognize me despite my tangled hair, acne, and flab was both insulting and terrifying. What if they erected a statue of me in my present form—a giant golden Lester in the center of their city? The other gods would never let me hear the end of it!

"Madam," I said, "I'm afraid you have mistaken me—"

"Don't be modest!" The woman tossed her phone and purse aside. She grabbed my forearm with the strength of a weight-lifter. "Our master will be delighted to have you in custody. And please call me Nanette."

Calypso charged. Either she wished to defend me (unlikely), or she was not a fan of the name Nanette. She punched the woman in the face.

This by itself did not surprise me. Having lost her immortal powers, Calypso was in the process of trying to master other skills. So far, she'd failed at swords, polearms, shurikens, whips, and improvisational comedy. (I sympathized with her frustration.) Today, she'd decided to try fisticuffs.

What surprised me was the loud CRACK her fist made against Nanette's face—the sound of finger bones breaking.

"Ow!" Calypso stumbled away, clutching her hand.

Nanette's head slid backward. She released me to try to grab her own face, but it was too late. Her head toppled off her shoulders. It clanged against the pavement and rolled sideways, the eyes still blinking, the purple lips twitching. Its base was smooth stainless steel. Attached to it were ragged strips of duct tape stuck with hair and bobby pins.

"Holy Hephaestus!" Leo ran to Calypso's side. "Lady, you broke my girlfriend's hand with your face. What *are* you, an automaton?"

"No, dear," said decapitated Nanette. Her muffled voice didn't come from the stainless-steel head on the sidewalk. It emanated from somewhere inside her dress. Just above her collar, where her neck used to be, an outcropping of fine blond hair was tangled with bobby pins. "And I must say, hitting me wasn't very polite."

Belatedly, I realized the metal head had been a disguise. Just as satyrs covered their hooves with human shoes, this creature passed for mortal by pretending to have a human face. Its voice came from its gut area, which meant . . .

My knees trembled.

"A *blemmyae*," I said.

Nanette chuckled. Her bulging midsection writhed under the honeysuckle cloth. She ripped open her blouse—something a polite Midwesterner would never think of doing—and revealed her true face.

Where a woman's brassiere would have been, two enormous bulging eyes blinked at me. From her sternum protruded a large shiny nose. Across her abdomen curled a hideous mouth—glistening orange lips, teeth like a spread of blank white playing cards.

"Yes, dear," the face said. "And I'm arresting you in the name of the Triumvirate!"

Up and down Washington Street, pleasant-looking pedestrians turned and began marching in our direction.

Need even more Apollo? Read this bonus short story by Rick Riordan:

"PERCY JACKSON AND THE SINGER OF APOLLO"

I KNOW WHAT YOU'RE GOING TO ASK.

Percy Jackson, why are you hanging from a Times Square billboard without your pants on, about to fall to your death?

Good question. You can blame Apollo, god of music, archery, and poetry—also the god of making me do stupid quests.

This particular disaster started when I brought my friend Grover some aluminum cans for his birthday.

Perhaps I should mention . . . I'm a demigod. My dad, Poseidon, is the lord of the sea, which sounds cool, I guess, but mostly it means my life is filled with monster attacks and annoying Greek gods who tend to pop up on the subway or in the middle of math class or when I'm taking a shower. (Long story. Don't ask.)

I figured maybe I'd get a day off from the craziness for Grover's birthday, but of course I was wrong.

Grover and his girlfriend, Juniper, were spending the day in Prospect Park in Brooklyn, doing naturey stuff like dancing with the local tree nymphs and serenading the squirrels. Grover's a satyr. That's his idea of fun.

Juniper seemed to be having an especially good time. While Grover and I sat on the bench together, she frolicked across Long Meadow with the other nature spirits, her chlorophyll-tinted eyes glinting in the sunlight. Since she is a dryad, Juniper's life source is tied to a juniper bush back on Long Island, but Grover explained that she can take short trips away from home as long as she keeps a handful of fresh juniper berries in her pockets. I didn't want to ask what would happen if the berries got accidentally smashed.

Anyway, we hung out for a while, talking and enjoying the nice weather. I gave Grover his aluminum cans, which may sound like a lame gift, but that's his favorite snack.

He happily munched on the cans while the nymphs started discussing what party games we should play. Grover pulled a blindfold out of his pocket and suggested Pin the Tail on the Human, which made me kind of nervous since I was the only human.

Then, without warning, the sunlight brightened. The air turned uncomfortably hot. Twenty feet away, the grass hissed and a cloud of steam whooshed up like somebody had opened a big pressing machine at a Laundromat. The steam cleared, and standing in front of us was the god Apollo.

Gods can look like anything they want, but Apollo always seemed to go for that I-just-auditioned-for-a-boy-band look. Today he was rocking pencil-thin jeans, a white muscle shirt, and gilded Ray-Ban sunglasses. His wavy blond hair glistened with product. When he smiled the dryads squealed and giggled.

"Oh, no . . ." Grover murmured. "This can't be good."

"Percy Jackson!" Apollo beamed at me. "And, um, your goat friend—"

"His name is Grover," I said. "And we're kind of off duty, Lord Apollo. It's Grover's birthday."

"Happy birthday!" Apollo said. "I'm so glad you're taking the day off. That means you two have time to help me with a small problem!"

Naturally, the problem wasn't small.

Apollo led Grover and me away from the party so we could talk in private. Juniper didn't want to let Grover go, but she couldn't argue with a god. Grover promised to come back safely. I hoped it was a promise he'd be able to keep.

When we got to the edge of the woods, Apollo faced us. "Allow me to introduce the Chryseae Celedones."

The god snapped his fingers. More steam erupted from the ground, and three golden women appeared in front of us. When I say golden, I mean they were literally gold. Their metallic skin glittered. Their sleeveless gowns were made from enough gilded fabric to finance a bailout. Their golden hair was braided and piled on top of their heads in a sort of classical beehive hairdo. They were uniformly beautiful, and uniformly terrifying.

I'd seen living statues—automatons—many times before. Beautiful or not, they almost always tried to kill me.

"Uh . . ." I took a step back. "What did you say these were? Krissy Kelly something?"

"Chryseae Celedones," Apollo said. "Golden singers. They're my backup band!"

I glanced at Grover, wondering if this was some kind of joke.

Grover wasn't laughing. His mouth hung open in amazement, as if the golden ladies were the largest, tastiest aluminum cans he'd ever seen. "I—I didn't think they were real!"

Apollo smiled. "Well, it's been a few centuries since I brought them out. If they perform too often, you know, their novelty wears off. They used to live at my temple in Delphi. Man, they could rock that place. Now I only use them for special occasions."

Grover got teary-eyed. "You brought them out for my birthday?"

Apollo laughed. "No, fool! I've got a concert tonight on Mount Olympus. Everyone is going to be there! The Nine Muses are opening, and I'm performing a mix of old favorites and new material. I mean, it's not like I need the Celedones. My solo career has been great. But people will expect to hear some of my classic hits with the girls: 'Daphne on my Mind,' 'Stairway to Olympus,' 'Sweet Home Atlantis.' It's going to be awesome!"

I tried not to look nauseous. I'd heard Apollo's poetry before, and if his music was even half as bad, this concert was going to blow harder than Aeolus the wind god.

"Great," I said halfheartedly. "So what's the problem?"

Apollo's smile faded. "Listen."

He turned to his golden singers and raised his hands like a conductor. On cue, they sang in harmony: "Laaaa!"

It was only one chord, but it filled me with bliss. I suddenly couldn't remember where I was or what I was doing. If the golden singers had decided to tear me to pieces at that moment, I wouldn't have resisted, as long as they kept singing. Nothing mattered to me, except that sound.

Then the golden girls went silent. The feeling passed. Their faces returned to beautiful, impassive metal.

"That . . ." I swallowed. "That was amazing."

"Amazing?" Apollo wrinkled his nose. "There are only three of them! Their harmonies sound empty. I can't perform without the full quartet."

Grover was weeping with joy. "They're so beautiful. They're perfect!"

I was kind of glad Juniper wasn't within earshot, since she's the jealous type.

Apollo crossed his tan arms. "They're not perfect, Mr. Satyr. I need all four or the concert will be ruined. Unfortunately, my fourth Celedon went rogue this morning. I can't find her anywhere."

I looked at the three golden automatons, staring at Apollo, quietly waiting for orders. "Uh . . . how does a backup singer go rogue?"

Apollo made another conductor wave, and the singers sighed in three-part harmony. The sound was so mournful my heart sank into my gut. At that moment, I felt sure I'd never be happy again. Then, just as quickly, the feeling dissipated.

"They're out of warranty," the god explained. "Hephaestus made them for me back in the old days, and they worked fine . . . until the day after their two-thousand-year warranty expired. Then, naturally, WHAM! The fourth one goes haywire and runs off to the big city." He gestured in the general direction of Manhattan. "Of course I tried to complain to Hephaestus, but he's all, *Well, did you have my Protection Plus package?* And I'm like, *I didn't want your stupid extended warranty!* And he acts as if it's my fault the Celedon broke, and says if I'd bought the Plus package, I could've had a dedicated service hotline, but—"

"Whoa, whoa, whoa," I interrupted. I really didn't want to get in the middle of a god-versus-god argument. I'd been there too many times. "So if you know that your Celedon is in the city, why can't you just look for her yourself?"

"I don't have time! I have to practice. I have to write a set list and do a sound check! Besides, this is what heroes are for."

"Running the gods' errands," I muttered.

"Exactly." Apollo spread his hands. "I assume the missing Celedon is roaming the Theater District, looking for a suitable place to audition. Celedones have the usual starlet dreams— being discovered, headlining a Broadway musical, that sort of thing. Most of the time I can keep their ambitions under control. I mean, I can't have them upstaging me, can I? But I'm sure without me around she thinks she's the next Katy Perry. You two need to get her before she causes any problems. And hurry! The concert is tonight, and Manhattan is a large island."

Grover tugged his goatee. "So . . . you want us to find her, while you do sound checks?"

"Think of it as a favor," Apollo said. "Not just for me, but for all those mortals in Manhattan."

"Oh." Grover's voice got very small. "Oh, no . . ."

"What?" I demanded. "What *oh, no?*"

Years ago, Grover created a magic empathy link between us (another long story) and we could sense each other's emotions. It wasn't exactly mind reading, but I could tell he was terrified.

"Percy," he said, "if that Celedon starts singing in public, in the middle of afternoon rush hour—"

"She'll cause no end of havoc," Apollo said. "She might sing a love song, or a lullaby, or a patriotic war tune, and whatever the mortals hear . . ."

I shuddered. One sigh from the golden girls had plunged me into despair, even with Apollo controlling their power. I imagined a rogue Celedon busting into song in a crowded city—putting people to sleep, or making them fall in love, or urging them to fight.

"She has to be stopped," I agreed. "But why us?"

"I like you!" Apollo grinned. "You've faced the Sirens before. This isn't too different. Just put some wax in your ears. Besides, your friend Grover here is a satyr. He has natural resistance to magical music. Plus he can play the lyre."

"What lyre?" I asked.

Apollo snapped his fingers. Suddenly Grover was holding the weirdest musical instrument I'd ever seen. The base was a hollowed-out tortoise shell, which made me feel really bad for the tortoise. Two polished wooden arms stuck out one side like bull's horns, with a bar across the top and seven strings stretching from the bar to the base of the shell. It looked like a combination harp, banjo, and dead turtle.

"Oh!" Grover almost dropped the lyre. "I couldn't! This is your—"

"Yes," Apollo agreed cheerfully. "That's my own personal lyre. Of course if you damage it, I'll incinerate you, but I'm sure you'll be careful! You can play the lyre, can't you?"

"Um . . ." Grover plucked a few notes that sounded like a funeral dirge.

"Keep practicing," Apollo said. "You'll need the lyre's magic to capture the Celedon. Have Percy distract her while you play."

"Distract her," I repeated.

This quest was sounding worse and worse. I didn't see how a tortoiseshell harp could defeat a golden automaton, but Apollo clapped me on the shoulder like everything was settled.

"Excellent!" he said. "I'll meet you at the Empire State Building at sunset. Bring me the Celedon. One way or another I'll persuade Hephaestus to fix her. Just don't be late! I can't keep my audience waiting. And remember, not a scratch on that lyre."

Then the sun god and his golden backup singers disappeared in a cloud of steam.

"Happy birthday to me," Grover whimpered, and plucked a sour note on the harp.

We caught the subway to Times Square. We figured that would be a good place to start looking. It was in the middle of the Theater District and full of weird street performers and about a billion tourists, so it was the natural place for a golden diva to get some attention for herself.

Grover hadn't bothered disguising himself. His white T-shirt read WHAT WOULD PAN DO? The tips of his horns stuck out from his curly hair. Usually he wore jeans over his shaggy legs and specially fitted shoes over his hooves, but today from the waist down he was au naturel goat.

I doubted it would matter. Most mortals can't see through the Mist, which hides the true appearance of monsters. Even without Grover's normal disguise, people would have to look really closely to notice he was a satyr, and even then they probably wouldn't bat an eye. This was New York, after all.

As we pushed through the crowd, I kept searching for the glint of gold, hoping to spot the rogue Celedon, but the square was packed as usual. A guy wearing only his underwear and a guitar was having his picture taken with some tourists. Cops hung out on the street corners, looking bored. At Broadway and West Forty-Ninth, the intersection was blocked and a crew of roadies was setting up some sort of stage. Preachers, ticket scalpers, and hawkers shouted over each other, trying to get attention. Music blasted from dozens of loudspeakers, but I didn't hear any magical singing.

Grover had given me a ball of warm wax to stuff in my ears whenever necessary. He said he always kept some handy, like chewing gum, which didn't make me anxious to use it.

He bumped into a pretzel vendor's cart and lurched back, hugging Apollo's lyre protectively.

"You know how to use that thing?" I asked. "I mean, what kind of magic does it do?"

Grover's eyes widened. "You don't know? Apollo built the walls of Troy just by playing this harp. With the right song, it can create almost anything!"

"Like a cage for the Celedon?" I asked.

"Uh . . . yeah!"

He didn't sound too confident, and I wasn't sure I wanted him playing Guitar Hero with a godly tortoise banjo. Sure, Grover could do some magic with his reed pipes. On a good day, he could make plants grow and tangle his enemies. On a bad day, he could only remember Justin Bieber songs, which didn't do anything except give me a headache.

I tried to think of a plan. I wished my girlfriend, Annabeth, was here. She was more of the planning type. Unfortunately, she was off in San Francisco visiting her dad.

Grover grabbed my arm. "There."

I followed his gaze. Across the square, at the outdoor stage, workers scurried around, installing lights on the scaffolding, setting up microphone stands, and plugging in giant speakers. Probably they were prepping for a Broadway musical preview or something.

Then I saw her—a golden lady making her way toward the platform. She climbed over the police barricades that cordoned off the intersection, squeezed between workers who completely ignored her, and headed for the steps, stage right. She glanced at the crowd in Times Square and smiled, as if imagining their wild applause. Then she headed for the center microphone.

"Oh, gods!" Grover yelped. "If that sound system is on . . ."

I stuffed wax in my ears as we ran for the stage.

Fighting automatons is bad enough. Fighting one in a crowd of mortals is a recipe for disaster. I didn't want to worry about the mortals' safety and mine and figure out how to capture the Celedon. I needed a way to evacuate Times Square without causing a stampede.

As we wove through the crowd, I grabbed the nearest cop by the shoulder.

"Hey!" I told him. "Presidential motorcade coming! You guys better clear the streets!"

I pointed down Seventh Avenue. Of course there was no motorcade, but I did my best to imagine one.

See, some demigods can actually control the Mist. They can make people see what they want them to see. I wasn't very good at it, but it was worth a shot. Presidential visits are common enough, with the United Nations in town and all, so I figured the cop might buy it.

Apparently he did. He glanced toward my imaginary line of limos, made a disgusted face, and said something into his two-way radio. With the wax in my ears, I couldn't hear what, but all the other cops in the square started herding the crowd toward the side streets.

Unfortunately, the Celedon had reached center stage.

We were still fifty feet away when she grabbed the mike and tapped it. BOOM, BOOM, BOOM echoed through the streets.

"Grover," I yelled, "you'd better start playing that lyre."

If he responded, I didn't hear it. I sprinted to the stage. The workers were too busy arguing with the cops to try stopping me. I bounded up the steps, pulled my pen from my pocket and uncapped it. My sword, Riptide, sprang into existence, though I wasn't sure it would help me. Apollo wouldn't be happy with me if I decapitated his backup singer.

I was twenty feet from the Celedon when a lot of things happened at once.

The golden singer belted out a note so powerful I could hear it through the wax plugs. Her voice was heartbreakingly sad, filled with longing. Even muffled through the wax, it made me want to break down and cry—which is what several thousand people around Times Square did. Cars stopped. Police and tourists fell to their knees, weeping, hugging each other in consolation.

Then I became aware of a different sound—Grover, frantically strumming his lyre. I couldn't exactly hear it, but I could feel the tremor of magic rippling through the air, shaking the stage under my feet. Thanks to the empathy link, I caught flashes of Grover's thoughts. He was singing about walls, trying to summon a box around the Celedon.

The good news: it sort of worked. A brick wall erupted from the stage between me and the Celedon, knocking over the mic stand and interrupting her song. The bad news: by the time I figured out what was going on, I couldn't stop my momentum. I ran straight into the wall, which wasn't mortared, so I promptly collapsed on top of the Celedon along with about a thousand bricks.

My eyes watered. My nose felt broken. Before I could regain my bearings, the Celedon struggled out of the pile of bricks and pushed me off. She raised her arms in triumph as if the whole thing had been a planned stunt.

She sang, "Ta-daaaaah!"

She was no longer amplified, but her voice carried. The mortals stopped sobbing and rose to their feet, clapping and cheering for the Celedon.

"Grover!" I yelled, not sure if he could hear me. "Play something else!"

I picked up my sword and struggled to my feet. I tackled the golden lady, but it was like tackling a lamppost. She ignored me and launched into song.

As I wrestled her, trying to pull her off balance, the temperature on stage began to rise. The Celedon's lyrics were in ancient Greek, but I caught a few of the words: Apollo, sunlight, golden fire. It was some kind of ode to the god. Her metal skin grew hot. I smelled something burning and realized it was my shirt.

I stumbled away from her, my clothes smoldering. The wax had melted out of my ears so I could hear her song clearly. All around Times Square, people started dropping from the heat.

Over at the barricades, Grover played wildly on the lyre, but he was too anxious to focus. Random bricks fell from the sky. One of the monitor speakers on stage morphed into a chicken. A plate of enchiladas appeared at the Celedon's feet.

"Not helpful!" I shouted through the pain of the rising heat. "Sing about cages! Or gags!"

The air felt like a blast furnace. If the Celedon kept this up, Midtown would burst into flames. I couldn't afford to play nice anymore. As the Celedon started her next verse, I lunged at her with my sword.

She lurched away with surprising speed. The tip of my blade missed her face by an inch. I'd managed to stop her singing, and she was not happy about it. She glared at me with outrage, then focused on my blade. Fear flickered across her metallic face. Most magical beings knew enough to respect Celestial bronze, since it could vaporize them on contact.

"Surrender and I won't hurt you," I said. "We just want to take you back to Apollo."

She spread her arms. I was afraid she was going to sing again, but instead the Celedon changed form. Her arms grew into golden feathery wings. Her face elongated, growing a beak. Her body shrank until I was staring at a plump metal bird about the size of a quail. Before I could react, the Celedon launched herself into the air and flew straight for the top of the nearest building.

Grover stumbled onto the stage next to me. All across Times Square, the mortals who had collapsed from the heat were starting to recover. The pavement still steamed. Police started shouting orders, making a serious effort now to clear the area. Nobody paid us any attention.

I watched the golden bird spiral up until she disappeared over the highest billboard on the Times Tower. You've probably seen the building in pictures: the tall skinny one that's stacked with glowing advertisements and Jumbotron screens.

To be completely honest, I didn't feel so great. I had molten wax oozing out of my ears. I'd been charbroiled medium rare.

My face felt like it had just been rammed into a brick wall . . . because it had. I had the coppery taste of blood in my mouth, and I was really starting to hate music. And quails.

I turned to Grover. "Did you know she could morph into a bird?"

"Uh, yeah. . . . But I kind of forgot."

"Great." I nudged the enchilada plate at my feet. "Could you try to summon something more helpful next time?"

"Sorry," he murmured. "I get hungry when I get nervous. So what do we do now?"

I started up at the top of the Times Tower. "The golden girl wins round one. Time for round two."

You're probably wondering why I didn't put more wax in my ears. For one thing, I didn't have any. For another thing, wax melting out of my ears hurts. And maybe part of me was thinking: Hey, I'm a demigod. This time I'm prepared. I can face the music, literally.

Grover assured me he had the lyre figured out. No more enchiladas or bricks falling from the sky. I just had to find the Celedon, catch her by surprise, and distract her by . . . well, I hadn't figured out that part yet.

We took the elevator to the top floor and found stairs to the roof. I wished I could fly, but that wasn't one of my powers, and my pegasus friend Blackjack hadn't been answering my calls for help lately. (He gets a little distracted in the springtime when he's searching the skies for cute lady pegasi.)

Once we made it to the roof, the Celedon was easy to find. She was in human form, standing at the edge of the building with her arms spread, serenading Times Square with her own rendition of "New York, New York."

I really hate that song. I don't know anybody who's actually from New York who doesn't hate that song, but hearing her sing it made me hate it a whole lot more.

Anyway, she had her back to us, so we had an advantage. I was tempted to sneak up behind her and push her off, but she was so strong I hadn't been able to budge her before. Besides, she'd probably just turn into a bird and . . . Hmm. A bird.

An idea formed in my mind. Yes, I do get ideas sometimes.

"Grover," I said, "can you use the lyre to summon a birdcage? Like a really strong one, made from Celestial bronze?"

He pursed his lips. "I suppose, but birds shouldn't be caged, Percy. They should be free! They should fly and—" He looked at the Celedon. "Oh, you mean—"

"Yeah."

"I'll try."

"Good," I said. "Just wait for my cue. Do you still have that blindfold from Pin the Tail on the Human?"

He handed me the strip of cloth. I shrank my sword to ballpoint-pen form and slipped it in the pocket of my jeans. I'd need both hands free for this. I crept up on the Celedon, who was now belting out the final chorus.

Even though she was facing the other way, her music filled me with the urge to dance (which, believe me, you never want to see). I forced myself to keep going, but fighting her magic was like pushing my way through a row of heavy drapes.

My plan was simple: gag the Celedon. She would turn back into a bird and try to escape. I would grab her and shove her into a birdcage. What could go wrong?

On the last line of "New York, New York," I jumped on her back, locking my legs around her waist and yanking the blindfold across her mouth like a horse's bridle.

Her grand finale was cut short with a "New Yor—urff!"

"Grover, now!" I yelled.

The Celedon stumbled forward. I had a dizzying view of the chaos below in Times Square—cops trying to clear the crowd, lines of tourists doing impromptu high-kick routines like the Radio City Rockettes. The electronic billboards down the side of the Times Tower looked like a very steep, psychedelic waterslide, with nothing but hard pavement at the bottom.

The Celedon staggered backward, flailing and mumbling through the gag.

Grover desperately strummed his lyre. The strings sent powerful magic vibrations through the air, but Grover's voice quivered with uncertainty.

"Um, birds!" he warbled. "La, la, la! Birds in cages! Very strong cages! Birds!"

He wasn't going to win any Grammys with those lyrics, and I was losing my grip. The Celedon was strong. I'd ridden a Minotaur before, and the golden lady was at least that hard to hold on to.

The Celedon spun around, trying to throw me. She clamped her hands around my forearms and squeezed. Pain shot up to my shoulders.

I yelled, "Grover, hurry!" But with my teeth clenched, the words came out more like, "Grr—huh."

"Birds in cages!" Grover strummed another chord. "La, la, la, cages!"

Amazingly, a birdcage shimmered into being at the edge of the roof. I was too busy getting tossed around to have a good look, but Grover seemed to have done a good job. The cage was just large enough for a parrot, or a fat quail, and the bars glowed faintly . . . Celestial bronze.

Now if I could just get the Celedon into bird form. Unfortunately, she wasn't cooperating. She spun hard, breaking my grip and shoving me over the side of the building.

I tried not to panic. Sadly, this wasn't the first time I'd been thrown off a skyscraper.

I'd like to tell you that I did some cool acrobatic move, grabbed the edge of a billboard, and vaulted back up to the roof in a perfect triple flip.

Nope. As I bounced off the first Jumbotron screen, a metal strut somehow snagged my belt and stopped me from falling. It also gave me the ultimate wedgie of all time. Then, as if that wasn't bad enough, my momentum spun me upside down and I peeled right out of my pants.

I plummeted headfirst toward Times Square, grabbing wildly for anything to slow me down. Luckily, the top of the next billboard had a rung across it, maybe for extremely brave maintenance workers to latch their harnesses onto.

I managed to catch it and flipped right side up. My arms were nearly yanked out of their sockets, but somehow I kept my grip. And that's how I ended up hanging from a billboard over Times Square without my pants.

To answer your next question: Boxers. Plain blue boxers. No smiley faces. No hearts.

Laugh all you want. They're more comfortable than briefs.

The Celedon smiled at me from the top of the roof, about twenty feet above. Just below her, my jeans hung from the metal strut, blowing in the wind like they were waving me good-bye. I couldn't see Grover. His music had stopped.

My grip weakened. The pavement was maybe seven hundred feet down, which would make for a very long scream as I fell to my death. The glowing screen of the Jumbotron was slowly cooking my stomach.

As I was dangling there, the Celedon began a special serenade just for me. She sang about letting go, laying down my troubles, resting by the banks of a river. I don't remember the exact lyrics, but you get the idea.

It was all I could do to hold on. I didn't want to drop, but the Celedon's music washed over me, dismantling my resolve. I imagined that I would float down safely. I would land on the banks of a lazy river, where I could have a nice relaxing picnic with my girlfriend.

Annabeth.

I remembered the time I'd saved Annabeth from the Sirens in the Sea of Monsters. I'd held her while she cried and struggled, trying to swim to her death because she thought she would reach some beautiful promised land.

Now I imagined she was holding me back. I could hear what she'd say: *It's a trick, Seaweed Brain! You've got to trick her back or you'll die. And if you die, I'll never forgive you!*

That broke the Celedon's spell. Annabeth's anger was way scarier than most monsters, but don't tell her I said that.

I looked up at my jeans, dangling uselessly above. My sword was in pen form in one of the pockets, where it did me no good. Grover had started to sing about birds again, but it wasn't helping. Apparently the Celedon only turned into bird form when she was startled.

Wait. . . .

Out of desperation, I formed Stupid Plan Version 2.0.

"Hey!" I called up. "You really are amazing, Miss Celedon! Before I die, can I have your autograph?"

The Celedon halted midsong. She looked surprised, then smiled with pleasure.

"Grover!" I called. "Come over here!"

The lyre music stopped. Grover's head poked over the side. "Oh, Percy . . . I—I'm sorry—"

"It's okay!" I faked a smile, using our empathy link to tell him how I really felt. I couldn't send complete thoughts, but I tried to get the general point across: He needed to be ready. He needed to be quick. I hoped he was a good catch.

"Do you have a pen and paper?" I asked him. "I want to get this lady's autograph before I die."

Grover blinked. "Uh . . . jeez. No. But isn't there a pen in the pocket of your jeans?"

Best. Satyr. Ever. He totally got the plan.

"You're right!" I gazed up at the Celedon imploringly. "Please? Last request? Could you just fish the pen out of my jeans and sign them? Then I can die happy."

Golden statues can't blush, but the Celedon looked extremely flattered. She reached down, retrieved my jeans, and pulled out the pen.

I caught my breath. I'd never seen Riptide in the hands of a monster before. If this went wrong, if she realized it was a trick, she could kill Grover. Celestial bronze blades work just fine on satyrs.

She examined the pen like she'd never used one before.

"You have to take the cap off," I said helpfully. My fingers were beginning to slip.

She laid the jeans on the ledge, next to the birdcage. She uncapped the pen and Riptide sprang to life.

If I hadn't been about to die, it would've been the funniest thing I'd ever seen. You know those gag cans of candy with the coiled-up toy snake inside?

It was like watching somebody open one of those, except replace the toy snake with a three-foot-long blade.

The Celestial sword shot to full length and the Celedon thrust it away, leaping backward with a not-very-musical shriek. She turned into a bird, but Grover was ready. He dropped Apollo's lyre and caught the fat golden quail in both hands.

Grover stuffed her in the cage and slammed the door shut. The Celedon went crazy, squawking and flapping, but she didn't have room to turn back to human form, and in bird form—thank the gods—she didn't seem to have any magic in her voice.

"Good job!" I called up to Grover.

He looked sick. "I think I scratched Apollo's lyre. And I just caged a bird. This is the worst birthday ever."

"By the way," I reminded him, "I'm about to fall to my death here."

"Ah!" Grover snatched up the lyre and played a quick tune. Now that he wasn't in danger and the monster was caged, he seemed to have no problem using the harp's magic. Typical. He summoned a rope and threw it down to me. Somehow he managed to pull me to the top, where I collapsed.

Below us, Times Square was still in complete chaos. Tourists wandered around in a daze. The cops were breaking up the last of the high-kick dance routines. A few cars were on fire, and the outdoor stage had been reduced to a pile of kindling, bricks, and broken sound equipment.

Across the Hudson River, the sun was going down. All I wanted to do was lie there on the roof and enjoy the feeling of not being dead. But our job wasn't done yet.

"We've got to get the Celedon back to Apollo," I said.

"Yeah," Grover agreed. "But, uh . . . maybe put your pants on first?"

Apollo was waiting for us in the lobby of the Empire State Building. His three golden singers paced nervously behind him.

When he saw us, he brightened—literally. A glowing aura appeared around his head.

"Excellent!" He took the birdcage. "I'll get Hephaestus to fix her up, and this time I'm not taking any excuses about expired warranties. My show starts in half an hour!"

"You're welcome," I said.

Apollo accepted the lyre from Grover. The god's expression turned dangerously stormy. "You scratched it."

Grover whimpered. "Lord Apollo—"

"It was the only way to catch the Celedon," I interceded. "Besides, it'll buff out. Get Hephaestus to do it. He owes you, right?"

For a second, I thought Apollo might blast us both to ashes, but finally he just grunted. "I suppose you're right. Well, good job, you two! As your reward, you're invited to watch me perform on Mount Olympus!"

Grover and I glanced at each other. Insulting a god was dangerous, but the last thing I wanted to do was hear more music.

"We aren't worthy," I lied. "We'd love to, really, but you know, we'd probably explode or something if we heard your godly music at full volume."

Apollo nodded thoughtfully. "You're right. It might distract from my performance if you exploded. How considerate of you." He grinned. "Well, I'm off, then. Happy birthday, Percy!"

"It's Grover's birthday," I corrected, but Apollo and his singers had already disappeared in a flash of golden light.

"So much for a day off," I said, turning back to Grover.

"Back to Prospect Park?" he suggested. "Juniper must be worried to death."

"Yeah," I agreed. "And I'm really hungry."

Grover nodded enthusiastically. "If we leave now, we can pick up Juniper and reach Camp Half-Blood in time for the sing-along. They have s'mores!"

I winced. "No sing-along, please. But I'll go for the s'mores."

"Deal!" Grover said.

I clapped him on the shoulder. "Come on, G-man. Your birthday might turn out okay after all."

FROM *NEW YORK TIMES* BEST-SELLING AUTHOR

RICK RIORDAN

ALSO AVAILABLE

PERCY JACKSON
AND THE OLYMPIANS

Follow @ReadRiordan

FROM *NEW YORK TIMES* BEST-SELLING AUTHOR

RICK RIORDAN

CELEBRATING 10 HEROIC YEARS
WITH A FRESH NEW LOOK!

Follow @ReadRiordan

FROM *NEW YORK TIMES* BEST-SELLING AUTHOR

RICK RIORDAN

EXPLORE THE WORLDS OF NORSE MYTHOLOGY

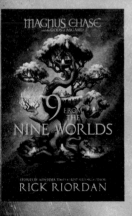

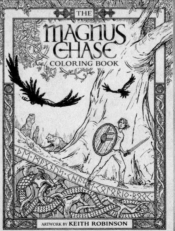

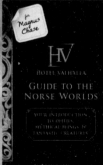

AVAILABLE NOW WHEREVER BOOKS ARE

DISNEY•HYPERION

FOLLOW @READRIORDAN